HAUNTED LILY

Also by Sidney Fox

Enchanted Shadows—
The Story of a Ghost

HAUNTED LILY

The Nightmare Ball

Book One of the Ghost Memoirs

Sidney Fox

Author of *Enchanted Shadows—The Story of a Ghost*

iUniverse, Inc.

New York Bloomington Shanghai

HAUNTED LILY
The Nightmare Ball

iUniverse books may be ordered through booksellers or by contacting:

iUniverse
1663 Liberty Drive
Bloomington, IN 47403
www.iuniverse.com
1-800-Authors (1-800-288-4677)

Cover Art—"Skull and Corset Bones"—Kerry Kate, October Effigies

ISBN: 978-0-595-48597-0 (pbk)
ISBN: 978-0-595-48767-7 (cloth)
ISBN: 978-0-595-60690-0 (ebk)

Printed in the United States of America

To my wonderful husband, Douglas
& beautiful son, Logan—

I love you more!

"The boundaries which divide life
from death are at best shadowy and vague.
Who shall say where one ends and where the other begins."
Edgar Allen Poe

"Unless we attempt the absurd, we cannot achieve the impossible."
Albert Einstein

"While I'm still warm."
Marilyn Monroe

DEATH OF A PARTY

"Southern trees bear strange fruit. Blood on the leaves and blood at the root," the girl sang along to the eerie, Billie Holiday, classic. The music emanated loudly from the sleek silver convertible, maneuvering along the winding roadways and across scenic bridges, stretching over the sun-sparkling Savannah waterways. The drive itself took much longer then she anticipated. The sun was just starting to set when the car turned onto a desolate road, literally in the middle of nowhere.

A small cloud of dirt flew up, as the car came to a halt in front of a stately iron gate. Attached to the gate was a long abandoned, crumbling, gatehouse with a rather ominous warning sign—NO TRESPASSING! VIOLATERS WILL BE PROSECUTED!

Without a thought, the girl grabbed a purple velvet bag from the backseat, and proceeded to walk up to the gateway. Standing on her tiptoes, she grabbed onto the tarnished gate, elevating herself just enough to catch a glimpse of the spiraling turrets looming just above the tops of the trees. Looking over the many locks and chains that adorned the long black bars, she grimaced; she would not be getting in that way.

At the top of the stone arch she noticed a word engraved in gothic letters, SANCTUARY. Such a simple word that someone had rather tactlessly spray-painted, SPOOK PALACE, over. The girl smiled; this was absolutely the right place.

Leaves crunched under her feet as she walked along the nasty tangle of barb-wire fence erected to keep the "uninvited guests" out. She noticed some cuts at the bottom of the fence made by, no doubt, the "uninvited guests". Quickly crawling through the enclosure, she began making her way up the lengthy drive, excitedly walking under a canopy of soaring moss-laden oak trees, whose witch-hand branches swayed in the cool fall breeze.

Halfway up the road, she came upon an enormous fountain, badly stained and weathered by years of neglect. Standing majestically in the middle of the fountain was an elegant marble statue of a woman wearing a long flowing gown with a good portion of her head missing. A swan with outstretched wings sat in her arms, looking as though it was about to take flight. The girl jumped up on the side of the fountain and looked down at the dirt and dead leaves littering its dried-up basin. In the back of the fountain, a rusted metal staircase led down into a graffiti-laden tunnel. Somewhere she had remembered reading about a series of underground tunnels that connected all the fountains on the property.

Four years of Latin were finally to pay off, she thought, as she curiously peered into the tunnel and saw the eerily prophetic words. *"Cursum Perficio—My journey ends."*

The girl jumped down and continued walking up the road. Along the way she noticed many more disfigured statues, left to fend for themselves against the untamed weeds slowly consuming them. After rounding a corner bank of trees, she abruptly stopped and a huge Cheshire cat grin grew across her face.

It sat in silhouette at the top of the hill; a massive structure backlit by the setting sun. It was so much bigger than she ever imagined, she squinted, trying to make out the features of the enormous formation as she approached. Her heart raced, she walked faster and faster, coming closer and closer to the imposing edifice. She had waited so many years for this very moment, trying to imagine what it would look like, what it would feel like. As a teenager, she had read every book and article she could get her hands on, analyzing every picture, every detail. She would always try to think about it right before she went to bed. Hoping if it was the last thing she thought of, just maybe, she would be lucky enough to dream about it, and often she would.

Walking onto a crumbling cobblestone courtyard … *it* finally came clearly into view. Her smile suddenly turned confused and quickly vanished from her face.

"No, no, no," she whispered, her head shook in disbelief, as many years of dreams shattered instantly before her eyes. She had heard the stories of how bad it had become and knew there would be some damage. But never in her wildest imagination could she ever believe it was this dreadful. She fell to her knees; this was not what she had expected.

Once a glorious grand dame, the enormous mansion standing before her now sat shamed, rotting ... disgraced. Raped and beaten by time, nothing more than a corpse left to decompose, having gone to seed long ago. The girl could barely make out the original four pedestal columns holding up the towering forty-foot portico above the front porch. Long dark watermarks stained the once beautiful exterior, moss spread far and wide like a malignant fungus. The extravagant lime-stone façade was barely visible through the overgrowth of kudzu vines creeping over every inch of it. The weeds were like claws of a great green monster, slowly overtaking and devouring it; clutching the house in its angry grasp, slipping its elongated fingers into the cracks and holes, invading it without permission.

Every window and door on the first floor had been completely boarded shut. The upper floors had no windows at all, leaving the interior exposed to the elements. Numerous chimneys with scrolled pediments, some looking rather close to collapse, sprouted out from the rooftop. Elaborate plaster cornices and carved finials sat along the roofline, their elegance forgotten amid the disintegrating wreckage the mansion had become. A few shredded pieces of dark red fabric blew eerily out of the shattered windows in the fourth floor tower, which had been one of the mansions crowning glories.

Closing her eyes tightly, the girl could easily picture the amazing palatial estate of her dreams, pristine and celebrated. A magnificent wonderland sitting at the top of a hill like royalty surrounded by lush flowering gardens and manicured lawns. But when she opened her eyes, reality punched a solid blow. Lowering her head in her hands, she sobbed; her wonderland had virtually vanished before she ever got to see it.

After a few minutes, she stood up, unable to look away from the remains. Her sadness now turned to anger. She could feel her jaw clench and her hands formed fists as she screamed out loud, cursing at the uninvited guests, the vandals, the vultures, who caused this destruction. Her head continually shook in disgust. After a few moments, she calmed. She wiped her tears on her sleeve, took a few deep shaky breathes and continued walking toward the dilapidated ruin. The closer she walked, the more horrific it became. How could something so amazing, so unbelievably beautiful, be left to decay as though its splendor never existed; such opulence, such grace, such a magnificent waste.

Feeling as though she was being watched, she peered up and saw numerous stone gargoyles leering down at her, suspiciously. They were eyeing her from their various perches on the roofline. Looking on helplessly, as yet another stranger was attempting to enter their dwelling without their consent. Putting a hand on what was left of the balustrade rail, she began to climb the wide stone steps onto the porch. The first step completely disintegrated under her foot. She grabbed the rail tightly and took another step, then another and another, until she was finally up on the enormous, weed-infested, front porch.

JIMI HENDRIX IS GOD had been spray-painted in red on the boards that securely covered the front door. Enormous terracotta planters, some still holding the branches of long deceased occupants, sat crumbling on the porch. The girl searched through the jungle of weeds for a way to get inside. Frustrated, she angrily ripped some of the vines, then abruptly stopped.

A harsh concentration filled her eyes, as she remembered the graffiti tunnel behind the fountain that she had passed on the way up to the mansion. Down the front steps she ran, sending chunks of loose stone flying, as she headed back down the drive.

The tunnel was dark, pitch dark and damp with a rather rotten smell. A loud dripping echoed, emanating from somewhere deep inside the chilly passage. It wasn't until that very moment she began to feel uneasy. Taking a small flashlight from her bag, she could still not see more than five feet in front of her. She scanned the dark tunnel, illuminating a giant neon marijuana leaf painted overhead with the words "FEED YOUR HEAD" scrawled under it. Layers of vicious words and drawings were plastered on every surface and the "uninvited guests", so thoughtfully, scribbled their autographs. The tunnel was obviously a party hangout; beer cans and cigarette butts plagued the muddy ground. The girl could hear, *Dorothy from Kansas,* repeat over and over in her head, "*I don't like this place, it's dark and creepy*".

It certainly did seem like the perfect place for your friendly neighborhood psychopath to spend his time. But nothing was going to stop her from getting inside the mansion; she had to see it for herself, even if she had a feeling she wouldn't like what she saw. Down the narrow passageway she walked. The deeper she ventured into the murky tunnel, the colder it became. She took a tattered black sweater from her bag and put it on, pulling the long sleeves down over her hands for warmth. A small surprised squeal, followed by a relieved giggle, escaped her lips, as two rats scurried past her feet.

The tunnel seemed to go on forever. Occasionally, she came upon several smaller tunnels that led off in different directions, but something told her to keep going straight and she would eventually find her way out of the rabbit hole. Pointing the flashlight along the wall she saw, "THE END IS NEAR!" scrawled in sinister foreboding letters. A large grinning devil head with a long cigar clenched in his teeth was painted on the wall directly in front of her.

"Not a dead end," she whispered, a slight feeling of panic shot through her body, until she realized it was not a dead end at all, just a bend in the passage. Cautiously looking around the corner, she saw a sharp bright light cutting through the inky darkness, shining down upon metal steps at the very end of the tunnel. She breathed a thankful sigh of relief, and then quickly climbed up the steps into the light.

The brilliant luminosity shining down upon the girl was sunlight pouring in through a lofty stained-glass dome towering above. The dome inadvertently created a giant kaleidoscope, which beamed different colored rays of light all around her. She held her arms out, tilted her head back and stood basking in the warmth. To her, it felt as though the house was welcoming her, she clapped her hands together in giddy delight, she did it … she finally had made it inside.

Looking around, she found herself in another massive fountain basin. This one featured a towering statue of King Poseidon, holding his three-pronged trident, standing astride a giant angry fish. She had instantly recognized the enormous area as, the Palm Court, a sunken circular room that used to house full-sized palm trees. Inspired by a throne room in an ancient Moroccan palace, the walls were carved from limestone and had been decorated with the finest imported mosaic tiles. The area was used mainly for informal meals and afternoon tea. Massive iron cathedral lanterns, which used to burn with fire, still hung down from the top of the dome. Some were missing, most likely taken by the "uninvited guests".

The girl grabbed onto one of Poseidon's powerful arms and stepped out onto tiny gleaming jewels scattered all over the ground. Upon closer inspection, she saw that they were really colored glass shards, which had fallen from the stained-glass dome and were reflecting the overhead light. The girl had remembered the pictures of the once magnificent stained glass dome. It had been captivating from every angle, now it was nothing more than a fabulous disaster.

Countless long vines of thick kudzu had invaded the area through the broken windows of the dome. This created a stunning cascade of shimmering emerald curtains, turning the room into an enormous greenhouse "garden of weeds". It was truly extraordinary. The girl felt like she was in a jungle temple of an ancient lost city. And as sad as she was to see what had happened to the dome, she couldn't help but applaud the performance that Mother Nature had staged.

Anywhere outside the circle of light beaming down on the fountain had been shaded in complete darkness, as all of the first floor windows and doors had been completely boarded up. From her bag, the girl took an orange paper from a protective plastic sleeve. The paper was an invitation and map of the mansion that had been given to guests attending one of the past Halloween parties. Having completely memorized the map, she could easily have found her way through the sprawling corridors. But in its present condition, she wasn't going to take any chances. The girl turned on her flashlight and ventured into the darkness.

She walked down a vast arched hallway that used to boast elaborate gothic tapestries and a row of Australian crystal chandeliers. The hall now sat practically barren, except for tall skeletons someone had painted dancing along the wall. She shined the flashlight up at a chandelier hanging crooked from the exposed ceiling. *Funny*, she thought. *All the crystals had been thieved, yet one light bulb still remained intact.*

A breeze whistled down the passage giving her an instant chill. She carefully climbed over the fallen plaster from the ceiling, and steered clear of the piles of dead leaves and debris, blowing and swirling around the ground like tiny tornados. The walls were covered with peeling shards of paint that scarred the walls and fluttered with the brisk gusts of air. Looking down, she noticed that the original oak floor was still discernible, but warped from the years of neglect.

She came upon a closed doorway and cautiously pushed one of the creaky doors open. Peering into a massive two-story room with a dramatic vaulted ceiling, she knew right away this had been the Gold Ballroom. The door hinge suddenly buckled and broke off, causing the heavy door to fall to the ground with a loud thunderous *crash*. Startled pigeons fluttered and cooed up on the second floor balcony, overlooking what had been the dance floor. Scanning the room with her flashlight, she was pleased to see that the patina of gilded gold leaf on the ceiling survived.

Closing her eyes, she tried to envision what the mansion must have been like. She could almost hear faded music and laughter from the past, wafting through the abandoned rooms and corridors. No expense was spared on this magnificent estate, which had hosted elaborate parties for hundreds of "invited" guests, and could have given any castle in Europe a run for its money. With its fifty-plus rooms, eighteen fireplaces, gourmet kitchen, library, billiard room, theatre, indoor-outdoor pool, boat house and dock, stable, acres of coiffed lawns, fruit and grape orchards, perfumed gardens, and underground wine cellar. It had been a sight to behold.

Now the mansion sat in silence, an abandoned kingdom slowly being devoured by time.

Continuing down the hallway, she saw a bright light coming through a large open entryway. Having seen so many incredible pictures of the grand entrance hall, her anticipation peaked. She hurried down the hallway, excitedly hopping over debris, running right into the immense open atrium. The late evening light poured into the area from the broken windows on the upper floors, illuminating what was left of this, once spectacular, entrance hall. For the first time, she could truly see the horror.

The foyer had resembled a sixteenth-century gothic cathedral, but every ounce of glitz had been stolen. It now resembled an abandoned hotel lobby where a bomb had gone off. Huge piles of plaster from the crumbling columns littered the ground, along with loads of rubbish and empty liquor bottles. The sprawling mahogany staircase, which curved up three stories, was now missing whole steps, looking more like the stairs in a distorted funhouse ruin. The custom-crafted iron railing ... disappeared. The inlaid Italian marble floor ... destroyed. The five-tier Baccarat crystal chandelier ... vanished. The dramatic etched glass front doors ... gone. The pedestals carved into the alcove walls stood empty, robbed of their treasures. The brass elevator sat idle and tarnished in its cage. A metal barrel sat in the middle of the broken marble floor, obviously used for bonfires. And, of course, the "uninvited guests" left more autographs.

There she stood, feeling insignificant amongst the ruins, trying to take in the devastating size of the wreckage, while pigeons loitered at her feet. She giggled a crazed little laugh, which echoed through the vast space. This was not what she had expected.

Looking at her watch, she knew there was no time to debate. It would be getting dark soon and she still had further to go. Shooing pigeons, she grasped her bag tightly with one hand and held onto the wall with the other, as she carefully headed up the remains of the crumbling staircase to the third floor.

A cool breeze blew through the open hallway. Only the sound of creaking wood occasionally broke the silence. The girl briefly peered into some of the rooms, every window had been broken out and just a few sparse pieces of toppled furniture remained. Coming to the end of the hall, she stopped. Looking around, she knew there had to be another set of stairs leading up to the fourth floor tower, yet there was nothing but wood paneling. From the long shadows cast on the walls, she knew the sun would be setting very soon and she became anxious. This was the one room in the mansion she wanted to, needed to ... absolutely had to see.

Frantically, she felt all over the wall for a secret button or handle, there was none. In frustration, she kicked at the wall and a small sliver of light appeared on the floor. She pushed harder against the panel. It quickly popped back at her and opened, revealing a spiral staircase that led up into the tower.

Almost blinded by the vibrant radiance shining down from the top of the stairs, she couldn't wipe the smile off her face. Each step she took was bringing her closer to her destiny, her heart was pounding. She was nervous, not really sure how she was going to react if the room was destroyed. In dreams she would always wake up before she got to see what was inside. It was the only room in the mansion that had never been photographed; she had only read about it.

Finally standing at the top of the steps, it took a few seconds for her eyes to adjust to the light flooding in through a bank of broken windows, bathing the enormous open room in golden twilight. She took a deep breath, the air smelled oddly sweet. Looking around the master bedroom suite, she was suddenly overcome with emotions she had never felt before; tears turned to streams. The spectacle on display before her overwhelmed her whole being. It was like a fevered hallucination; a vision from a mad dream. The energy in the room was fierce, so powerful she could literally feel it. The entire room was simply *alive*.

Every inch of wall space was covered, layered in years of loving graffiti, written in every size, color, and language imaginable. The girl ran her shaky hand over the bizarre mosaic of devotion; eloquent poems, beautiful drawings, Shakespearean sonnets and lyrics from songs. The whole room looked like a giant guest book at a punk-rock funeral.

"You may be gone, but you will never, ever, be forgotten! Sleep tight."

"Lily, you always held yourself with such dignity and grace." Livvy, Madrid Spain

"The world seems a much darker place without you here!" Jason & Grant, Warwick, RI

"Viel so fruh bist du gestorben! Much too early you died." B. Aachen, Germany.

"Dear Lillian, very seldom in life are we so touched by exceptional people of great love and light." Gary, UK

"Kita kitsna lang sa heaven saying namatay ka pa—See you in heaven!"

"You were beautiful and I looked up to you!" Carrie, age six

Flowers, mainly calla lilies and tiger lilies, some fresh, some older, some dead; had been placed all around the room and floor. A ratty gold couch sat in a corner with some mismatched chairs, creating a conversation area for the "uninvited guests". Walking up a wide set of steps, she explored the mahogany tower. The arched windows still held the tattered remnants of the dark burgundy drapes, which blew in the evening breeze. The room reminded her of a tower in a fairytale castle, where a princess awaited her Prince Charming.

As she looked around the room, she clapped with excitement, seeing a tremendous dragon-head fireplace, which still adorned one wall. She had read about the magnificent fireplace and was sure it would be gone. But there it stood, obviously too heavy to be stolen, yet she could see where people had chipped away at the white stone for souvenirs. Inside the dragon's mouth were hundreds of candles in different shapes and colors. They had all melted into one another over the years, creating one massive candle with numerous wicks.

Walking back down into the master suite, the girl noticed that clear plastic sheets had been hung in the glassless windows. They were shredded and yellowed, but still fairly effective protection from the outside elements. And considering how the rest of the mansion had been trashed, the master suite was rather well preserved, perhaps out of respect. Almost as if the devotees were trying to preserve the room. The hostility she had felt for the "uninvited guests" was gone.

She wandered out onto the terrace porch, which was almost completely covered with overgrown vines, blooming with sweet smelling honeysuckle flowers. Leaning against the porch balustrade, she watched the sun set behind the horizon. Two swans glided along the calm water, just beyond the vast overgrown foliage in what had been the glorious back gardens of the estate. The view was incredible, serene and peaceful. A symphony of crickets chirped in the cool night air. The girl stood quietly basking in the moment. For the first time in her life, she actually felt like she belonged somewhere. This place was the puzzle piece that had always been missing from her life.

No, it wasn't what she expected, but then again, deep down, she knew nothing ever was. The thought made her smile. No, it wasn't what she expected, it was so much *better*.

CHAPTER 1

▼

Vow

Darby was in a glorious mood, gazing out the soaring windows at the dazzling city lights, watching the sight-seeing boats, packed with tourists, leisurely cruise down the Thames. He was sitting at the absolute best table in his favorite restaurant, Skylon, wearing a sharp black Armani suit. His normally wavy, slightly untamed, shoulder-length brown hair was combed back neatly. Looking around, he saw all the hip, well-heeled, young Londoners out for a relaxing Friday evening to top off the end of a usually hectic work week.

Two pretty girls sitting up at the bar had spied him out. They were whispering and giggling, obviously chatting about him. Darby was used to getting this kind of attention from the opposite sex; he was a good looking young man, who always made the most of it. He was smart and clever, with a wonderful dry English wit. He knew how to charm those of the female persuasion.

But there was only one person whose attentions he was after, and this was going to be a very special night; everything had to be just perfect.

Rushing into the restaurant, Angela was late as usual, but always worth the wait. She shook out her dark hair, like a prize Afghan posing for best-in-show. Everyone, men and women alike, turned to look at her. She was simply stunning, a true grace, tall and thin, an exotic beauty, half Brazilian and half French, who had been a runway model in her younger years. Now she was an interior designer for the rich and powerful. Angela was Darby's angel; that's what he called her, his angel. Angela spotted Darby and waved. He watched her make her way across the crowded room with the same daft smile that appeared on his face every time she came into his presence.

He could remember the first night he met her. It was at the very same restaurant, one year ago to the very night; the night of the BAFTA awards. A documentary Darby made the previous year, chronicling the daily life of a young African boy and his family, as they struggled for survival in the wake of mass genocide in the Darfur, had won for best long-form documentary. The award was hard earned and well deserved. Darby had spent eight months truly living in hell. He existed in horrific conditions, narrowly cheating death himself, as he followed the boy from one body-ridden slum to the next.

The film was a huge success and brought much needed attention to the area, as well as making Darby a sort of pseudo-celebrity. His passion for the subject made getting the award a great honor and after winning he knew he could pretty much write his own ticket. He could finally do any project he wanted and get funding, without having to max out his credit cards, as he did in the past. Darby was the new "boy genius". His previous films were critically acclaimed, but not financially successful; all that was about to change, including his personal life.

After the award ceremony that evening, a celebration in Darby's honor was thrown by his colleagues in a private room on the second floor of the restaurant. Halfway through the party, Darby snuck out and went to sit at the bar. Propping his award up on the under-lit glass bar in from of him, he ordered a bottle of McCallum Scotch, his favorite.

"Here's to you mate, cheers!" he toasted the shiny golden, comic-tragic, statuette in his distinctive crisp English accent. Life was good. He was at the top of his game and finally reaping some of the rewards for all his hard work, both professionally and monetarily. Although he came from a wealthy family, he wanted to make it on his own terms and spent many years struggling to get to his current stature. He loved his career, but a good chunk of his new found wealth went into another of his passions; the restoration of old buildings.

Darby had rescued a dilapidated, eighteenth-century, Catholic Church known as, St. Michaels, from the wrecking ball. The ornate gothic church located in the Shepherds Bush area of London, had been a coffeehouse for years and had a perpetual coffee aroma wafting through the soaring vaulted ceilings.

Darby painstakingly restored the fabulous stained-glass windows and the monuments of wood and bronze, trying to keep as much of the church's original features as possible. He stripped years of paint off the massive arched wood doorway, restoring its natural oak. He fixed the ornate laced-wood confessionals and hand-painted pipe organ. He repaired the staircase, which was barely hanging onto the wall by two nails. The staircase, which originally led up to the lofty choir balcony, had been turned into a dramatic master suite with a catwalk overlooking the sanctuary, now the living room and gourmet kitchen.

After two long years of hard work, Darby had restored St. Michaels from a crumbling ruin, back to its former glory with a new sleek modern edge. This fabulous grand residence was his pride and joy, truly a labor of love. After so many years living out of a suitcase, he finally had a permanent home base.

Yes, Darby McGregor was right where he should be, literally, skipping out on his party to sneak a drink at the bar that evening was to change his life forever. He was already on his third scotch and feeling no pain, when he noticed a stunning young woman with curly dark hair and porcelain skin, sitting a few barstools down from him. She looked horribly bored, as she gazed down at the red wine in her glass.

"Hello," he said with a sweet smile.

"Allo," she replied in a soft French accent, looking up at Darby. There was a sudden commotion behind them. Darby turned to see a very impatient man, full of complaints, strutting across the bar as he hounded one of the restaurant hostesses.

"This is ridiculous! Do you know how long I've been waiting for a table?" the man scowled. "I had a nine o'clock reservation! Nine o'clock! Do you know what time it is now? Can you even tell time?"

"Yes sir, I'm so sorry," the hostess said, trying to be polite. "Your table is ready now."

"It's about bloody time!" he announced angrily, walking up behind the French woman, taking her firmly by the arm like she was his property.

"Our table is finally ready," he barked loud enough, so that everyone in the restaurant could hear. "We've only been waiting forty minutes!"

The man practically pulled the woman off her chair. She was obviously mortified by him. As she passed, she stumbled and fell onto Darby; her perfume was intoxicating. She looked at him with sparkling green eyes that took his breath away.

"Are you … alright?" Darby asked, quickly helping the girl to her feet. She leaned in close and *whispered* something in his ear.

"She's fine," the man rudely broke in. "You're fine, right?"

"Yes, I'm fine," she said, trying to compose herself.

The striking dark-haired beauty gave Darby a pleading look as they walked away. Darby sat back down on his stool and looked at his watch, before getting back to his drink and chatting about that nights football scores with the bartender. After five minutes, he excused himself from the conversation, took out his cell phone and dialed a number. The phone rang a few times before it was answered.

"Bonjour," answered a cheery female voice with a distinctive French accent.

"Good evening," Darby said, nonchalantly. "It's me, the rather debonair gentleman from the bar."

"Oh yes, Allo," came the voice. "How have you been?"

"I'm fine thanks, but you seem to be having a rather dreadful night. It's been a rather long time since I've seen you, five minutes to be precise. I was thinking maybe you could join me for a drink."

"She died, oh no, is so terrible," cried the voice in broken english. "I cannot believe it!"

"I know, neither can I, she was so young," Darby stated, playing along. "Right, so how about you dump that lunatic you are with and come have a drink with me?"

"I will be right there, don't worry. I will be there for you."

"Brilliant," Darby exclaimed with a grin, shutting his phone. "Brilliant."

Darby waited at the bar for the stunning girl with the dazzling green eyes. After a long while, he saw her uncouth date leave the restaurant, alone. Disappointed, he figured the girl must have ducked out without him seeing. He took one last sip of his scotch and stood up. As he laid money his on the bar, he felt a pair of soft arms wrap around him from behind.

"You are so my hero," whispered a feminine voice. "I thought he would never leave."

Darby turned to see the French beauty. She smiled and sat down on the stool next to him.

"I thought you might have left," he said, sitting back down.

"No, I have been hiding out in the powder room, waiting for that oaf to leave," she moaned. "He stayed and ate his dinner, such a troll!"

"Well, I'm very glad you're here," he mused. "Can I buy you a drink?"

"No, no, I owe you a drink," she said, beaming with appreciation. "My name is Angela."

At the time they met Darby was very content being a bachelor. He loved his freedom, but admittedly fell hard for the Parisian beauty and treated her like a queen. He had been in relationships with women before, but this was different. She was different. She had class and style. He felt Angela was the female version of himself, which was both good and bad. They had many things in common; they were both strong-willed and stubborn. The fights could be brutal, with neither side wanting to relent, but the making up, well, it was worth it. Within a month of their meeting, Darby had asked Angela to move into his bachelor pad, his beloved, St. Michaels. He had never been happier in his life, she fit right in.

That brought him to this particular evening … in the same restaurant, exactly one year to the day. Darby had been waiting for just the perfect time and tonight was the night. Angela finally arrived at the table and gave him a big hug, while showering him with apologetic kisses.

"I'm so sorry, my darling," she cooed. "I lost track of myself."

"Don't even worry about it," Darby said. "Hungry?"

Angela noticed Darby smiling like a mischievous schoolboy all through dinner.

"What are you so … grinning for? You are like, the cat who got the canary."

Darby would just shrug and smile nonchalantly. He had a surprise for her, a wonderful surprise and he could hardly contain himself.

When dinner was finished, Darby ordered Angela her favorite dessert; a hot fudge sundae with white chocolate ice cream. When it arrived at the table it had an extra special topping—a three karat, pear-shaped, diamond on a platinum band, which poked up through the whip cream. Angela didn't see the ring at first. She scooped the topping up in her spoon and continued chatting about the events of her day. As she brought the spoon up to her mouth, she stopped, noticing a panicked look on Darby's face.

"What is it?" she asked, finally looking down at the diamond ring with amazement; a tear twinkled in her eye.

"Darby?" she whispered.

"Yes?"

"Is this, what I think it is?"

"Yes."

Darby stood up and kneeled down on one leg next to Angela, taking her hand.

"I love you, my angel," he said, his voice melancholy. "With all I am, and all my heart, would you do me the honor … of being my wife?"

By now people sitting at the surrounding tables took notice of the proposal. Even the wait staff stopped to watch. Darby dipped the ring in a glass of water and wiped the whip cream off with a napkin. He then gently placed it upon her trembling finger; she stared at it in awe, as he took his hand and tilted her chin up to look at him.

"I want you to be with me always, I can't imagine my life without you."

Angela was so overwhelmed she couldn't speak.

"So what's it gonna be, love?" teased a man having dinner with his wife at a table close by. "Don't leave the lad hanging."

Everyone watching laughed and cheered for her answer, then listened intently.

"I can't imagine life without you either," Angela smiled, taking his rugged boyish face in her hands. "I would be honored to be Mrs. Darby McGregor."

"That's a yes then, love?" the man asked.

"Yes ... yes," she smiled, overjoyed.

The crowd erupted with applause and whistles, as Darby took Angela in his arms and kissed her tenderly.

"You've made me the happiest man alive," he whispered in her ear.

"I love you," she said.

"I love you ... *more*."

From that day on Angela's whole world revolved around the wedding. Every detail was planned to perfection; she was on top of the world. After searching every bridal shop in London, she finally found an exquisite, beaded-bodice, gown in a small boutique in Holland Park. She told Darby, it was the dress she had "always dreamed of". Darby had wanted to marry Angela in a quiet ceremony in the sanctuary of their home, St. Michaels. But with the ever-increasing guest list, it was decided that they would have a sunset ceremony at the country estate owned by Darby's older barrister brother, Andrew.

"Not much you can do about it really," Darby said in a matter of fact tone. He was standing at the enormous, flower covered front counter, playfully opening the mouths of some snapdragons with his fingers, making them talk. "If it's going to rain, it's going to rain."

On a bright sunny day, the couple went to a busy London florist.

"Don't be silly, rain good luck at wedding," the friendly old Korean woman, who owned the shop, informed him as she walked to the counter carrying a vase spilling over with begonias. "And you, you are very lucky man. You both, such pretty people, you make beautiful babies."

"Babies? You're getting a little ahead of us," Darby laughed, adding a sly wink.

"I don't know, they're all so lovely," Angela said, happily dancing over to Darby.

"What you like, dear?" the woman asked. "What about lilies?"

"Oh no, lilies remind me of funerals. Roses ... tons of red roses,"

"Red roses it is! Go into my refrigerator, see my beautiful roses ... they so beautiful, go look," the woman insisted. "I make you anyting you want."

Angela excitedly grabbed Darby's hand and led him into the large, glass-encased, refrigerated room. As she looked around at all the different floral arraigments, Darby suddenly grabbed her from behind with a growl and kissed her passionately on the neck.

"Darby, everyone can see us."

"Good."

She turned and kissed him, causing the windows in the refrigerator to steam up.

The morning of the wedding, Darby was awoken by soft tapping.

"Darling … darling, wake up."

He sleepily reached over to Angela's side of the bed; she wasn't there.

"Angela?" Darby yawned, raising his sleepy head from the pillow.

"I'm in the hall. I'm going to have lunch with my mother and sisters at the hotel. Then we are going to the salon to have our hair done."

Darby could only see Angela's slim silhouette, standing on the other side of the frosted glass window in the bedroom door.

"What are you doing out there?" he asked. "Come in here and give us a big kiss."

"No, no, you can't see me! It is very bad luck, Darby! We can't see each other before we say, I do."

"That's silly, superstition," he said, getting out of bed and walking to the door.

"No Darby, please don't open the door, it's important to me."

"Okay, okay."

Darby saw that Angela had placed her hand upon the frosted glass; he put his hand up to the shadow of her small hand.

"One little kiss," he pleaded. "Pleeeaasse."

"Alright, just one," she giggled, pressing her full lips up against the glass. Darby pressed his lips up to hers and they kissed through the window. He could feel the warmth of her skin through the cold glass.

"Mmmmm," she cooed. "I love you."

"I love you, more."

"Go back to sleep. We will see each other in a few hours, I'll be the one in white," she teased and walked away from the door. Darby flopped into the bed and fell back to sleep.

It was a full-blown fairytale come to life. Everyone was eagerly anticipating the ceremony on such a glorious spring evening, waiting to see the bride and groom exchange the sacred vows and kiss that would forever bond them, man and wife. Located behind Darby's older brothers regal country manor house, sat a huge white tent covering a dance floor and lavish tables set with the finest china. Bottles of Dom Perignon sat chilling in buckets of ice on each table, awaiting a toast. The wedding was set to begin at sunset.

Friends, family, and business colleagues, mingled in the lush flower gardens overlooking a heavenly tranquil lake. They laughed and sipped cocktails, while a harpist played selections of Beethoven, Mozart and The Beatles. Great iron candelabras were lit with long white tapered candles, as the groomsmen escorted the guests to their seats. Darby walked down the flower petal strewn aisle to the elaborate rose-covered arbor. He shook the Vicar's hand, then turned to his brother Andrew, his best man, and gave him a warm hug. Darby was simply beaming in his elegant black tuxedo.

At six-thirty, the sun was starting to set behind the clouds, highlighting them in a spectacular golden hue. Darby stood at the alter, nervously fiddling with the red rose attached to his lapel. He couldn't help but notice the tall candles dwindling, as the wax melted and dripped down the candelabras. It was getting very late; even by Angela's standards. Darby just kept looking up the flower draped aisle in anticipation of seeing his bride.

"Don't worry, you know how birds are," Andrew whispered to him. "She's probably just finishing her hair or something. She'll be here any minute."

"I know, I know," Darby tried to assure himself.

A low rumbling of thunder echoed in the distance, as some dark clouds gathered in the sky above. Not a minute later, Angela's sister Marie came rushing down the isle.

Thank God, Darby thought to himself, a smile appearing across his face, feeling immediate relief. Everyone turned to look at the pretty girl in the beautiful lavender bridesmaid dress, her hair done up in an upsweep of delicate tea roses. Marie stopped abruptly at the sight of Darby. Something was wrong, her face was distressed and dark mascara encased her swollen eyes. Trying desperately to keep it together, she continued reluctantly walking toward Darby shaking her head, knowing she was the one that had to tell him.

A large drop of rain hit Darby's cheek. He did not move … he did not flinch; he just watched the girl coming toward him, moving in slow motion, as more drops of rain began to fall. He saw her lips moving, she was telling him something in a frantic manner, something bad, something very bad … *accident* …

died. Faces quickly appeared in front of him. To Darby, they looked distorted, like faces in funhouse mirrors.

The sky opened up and rain began to pour down from the dark clouds above. Darby just stood there; hearing the voice of the old Korean woman from the flower shop.

"Don't be silly, rain good luck at wedding."

CHAPTER 2

▼

THREADS

Angela always loved a good thunderstorm, the bigger the bolt of lightning and crash of thunder, the better. During really intense storms they would inevitably lose power and all the lights in the old church would go out. Most people would be annoyed, but Darby and Angela loved it. They would grab a cold bottle of wine and blankets, then lay on the floor in each other's arms watching the lightshow.

Inevitably, they would end up making love in the flashes of light bursting through the arched stained-glass windows surrounding the church sanctuary. The guises of various saints peered out through the darkness, curiously watching the sinners' sin.

Darby thought back to stormy London nights, just like this one, as he lit another cigarette. The thought was so wonderful; it gave him a warm feeling for a moment … before it brought him to tears. The thought hurt. The memory caused him actual physical pain; it was just one more thing he would never be able to do with her again. He tried to shut out all thoughts, not just of Angela … everything. But no matter how hard he tried, the memories just came flooding back. Every thought was painful and he was simply too exhausted to fight them.

Grief had taken Darby McGregor away from the world for a while. He didn't know how long he had been gone, sitting alone in the dark, nursing yet another bottle of scotch. He didn't care. It didn't matter; he was numb.

Little gems of colored light flickered from small glass candle holders on the metal prayer table. The glow from the candles was the only light in the otherwise darkened loft. Whenever a candle went out, Darby would immediately jump up and relight it, almost frantically. He remembered finding the prayer table in the church cellar covered by a sheet. He cleaned it and brought it up into the living room where Angela made it the centerpiece of the altar. They weren't really religious people; the table was more for decoration. The only time they ever lit the candles were holidays, parties or when someone ... died. He remembered lighting them as soon as he came home from the ...

"NO!" Darby grunted, grabbing his head in his hands, trying to kill the memory. But he couldn't, someone did die.

The morgue was quiet. The people who worked in the morgue were quiet. The morgue, yes, he did go to the morgue, he had to. Surely it was all a mistake, someone had made a terrible mistake and he had to go and clear things up like he always did. He would make things right, it was one of his many talents. He would fix it, talk his way out of it and make everything better. He didn't remember leaving the wedding site. He didn't know how he got back to London. He didn't even remember how he got home; but he did remember the morgue. Unfortunately, it was the one thing he begged God to let him forget.

Through his haze, Darby recalled walking through the reception area. There were quite a few people sitting in the waiting room, he was struck by so many sad faces. Darby caught the eye of a little boy, who must have been about eight, sitting in a corner chair being consoled by an older woman. His delicate face was bright red, tears streamed down his puffy cheeks, as he struggled to catch his breath. The boy looked up at Darby as he walked by; their eyes locked. Complete strangers, bonding with each other in that single moment. Sharing the same hurt, the same feeling of loss and confusion, for different people and different reasons, but it was the same exact pain. Andrew was practically holding Darby up as they approached the desk. The staff knew right away who the two men in tuxedos were there to see.

"Would you follow me," instructed a nurse. The brothers followed the portly woman down a long hallway, which seemed to glow with stale fluorescent lights, their footsteps echoed sharply on the ugly linoleum floor. They came to a set of large steel doors with a sign above that read, MORGUE. They continued through the doors and down another long hallway with closed doors on either side. The whole area was cold and had a strange smell. Darby was aware people were staring at him. He heard a voice whisper, "the groom".

The nurse stopped in front of one of the doors and motioned for them to enter the dimly lit room. They watched her walk to a wall of stainless steel drawers and open one in the middle of the wall. She pulled out a metal table and turned on a small overhead light. The light shined directly down on the table, creating a spotlight on the female form lying under a pristine white sheet, displaying it, like it was a window display at Harrods.

"Come on, Darby. I'm right here with you," Andrew whispered to his little brother, taking his arm, as they started toward the table where the nurse was standing. Darby felt lightheaded listening to the nurse ramble on, *"cut out of the car"*, *"the neck"* and *"lost a large amount of blood"*. He heard her, but it was all mumbles and murmurs.

Staring down at the white sheet, all he could think about was the last words Angela spoke, *"I'll be the one in white"*. He squinted, noticing a small shock of *red* slowly appearing, soaking up through the sheet. The harder he stared at it, the larger the stain became. The nurse just continued babbling, as the red stain saturated the white sheet and drops of blood began to drip onto the floor.

"Are you ready?" asked the nurse, breaking Darby's trance. He looked up into the nurses' severe face. When he looked back down at the cloth, there was nothing more than a small red spot on the sheet. Without really waiting for an answer, the nurse pulled back the sheet and the air was suddenly sucked out of Darby's body. He felt the ground move out from under him and he slightly swayed; Andrew held him steady.

There she was, set out in horrific display before him, her arms laid flat at her sides. Darby could recognize her, but she was obviously … damaged. Her body had been washed, her beautiful dark hair was still wet and had been pulled back from her face. Her skin was pale and bluish; a scattering of dark purple bruises adorned her face and body. Her right cheek had been crushed and her head tilted to the side unnaturally, like a broken doll. Darby put his hand on her arm and closed his eyes, his head suddenly fell forward and he let out a small whimper.

"She's cold," Darby whispered, not looking up from her body. "She needs a blanket."

"Darby …" Andrew said, covering his own mouth, not knowing what to say.

"She's cold, Andrew."

"Could you get a blanket?" Andrew asked the nurse.

"She's dead," the nurse responded to the odd request.

"She's cold," Darby repeated, caressing her arm.

"Please, could you just get a blanket," Andrew repeated.

"She can't feel anything anymore, honey, she's dead," explained the nurse, trying to be comforting, but coming across condescending.

"GET … A GOD DAMN BLANKET!" Darby abruptly shouted, then quickly calmed, never looking up. "Please!"

Caught off guard, the nurse quickly ran out of the room like a scolded child. She came back a few moments later with a cotton blanket. The brothers carefully placed the blanket over the young bride's lifeless body.

"There, that's better," Darby assured her sweetly, tucking the blanket under her. "I know you don't like to be cold."

"Darby, are you okay?" Andrew asked.

He did not answer. The room was silent for a long while.

"She is in a better place now," the nurse finally stated.

"No, she is not … she is not in a better FUCKING place! There is no better place than right here! Right here, with me! Right here, with me!" Darby laid his head down on Angela's chest and he began to cry, his sobs made a swift crescendo into a low moan. "God, please tell me this isn't happening. I will do anything you ask, anything!"

Andrew motioned to the nurse and they left the room, closing the door, leaving Darby alone with his love. He sat for hours, transfixed, just looking at her. This person that he loved so much, this beautiful being that was so vibrant and full of life. Her eyes were slightly open, as was her mouth. Darby traced her full lips with his fingers. How many times had he kissed those lips in playful pecks and passionate embraces? Her bottom lip was badly cut, he patted it, somehow trying to make it better, but he knew he could not. Just a few hours earlier she was happily primping in front of a mirror. It was her wedding day, the happiest day of her life, she had no idea it was to be the last day of her life. Darby sat most of the night talking to her, but was unable to say, goodbye.

The next day, Angela's sisters helped Darby pick out a lovely green dress for the funeral. It was a vintage Pucci; Angela had bought it on a trip to Italy the previous year. Darby remembered how excited she was when she found it. She carefully hung it up in a fancy dress bag and tucked it away for a "special occasion". Looking at the dress, all Darby could think was how horrified she would have been if she knew what the "special occasion" turned out to be.

A few hours later, they all went to the florist and helped Darby decide on the floral arraignments for the funeral. The same old Korean woman, who had helped Angela and he pick out their wedding flowers, looked up and saw Darby walk through the door to her shop. By the look on his face, she didn't need to be told what happened. She just knew whatever it was, it wasn't good. Darby didn't speak, he just pointed to the flowers he wanted; all red roses.

The funeral was mostly a blur, the cemetery too. Family and friends who had flown in for the wedding, stayed to attend the funeral. The wake was held at St. Michaels, with Darby's brother Andrew and his wife Paula, attending to the guests.

"What a grand time we would all be having together, if it were a different occasion," Darby overheard a woman say, as she munched on a finger sandwich. Darby sat slumped down in a corner chair, remembering how composed Princes William and Harry were when their beloved mother, Princess Diana, was unexpectedly killed. The young men handled their grief with such class and dignity. All Darby wanted to do was toss people out of his house and get drunk. No one quite knew what to say to him and he didn't really care to hear their condolences. He just continually looked down at his hand, Angela's wedding band fit tightly on his pinky finger. No, he didn't want their condolences; he wanted to be in the Bahamas with his new bride on their honeymoon cruise; drinking too much, getting too much sun, and making love for hours.

After the funeral, Darby stayed in complete seclusion. Andrew came by every day, bringing with him food from some of Darby's favorite restaurants, trying to entice him to eat. Andrew would turn off the extremely loud music emanating from the old church and try talking to him for hours on end, trying to wake his comatose little brother out of his intense mourning. Darby would only request more cigarettes and more scotch.

When his exhausted body gave in to a few brief moments of sleep, Darby would have wonderful dreams of his beloved Angela, their life and future. But when he awoke, reality always crushed him. The waking world was more of a nightmare than he could bear. So he stayed, day after day, drunk and alone in a stupor he could not shake.

The rain steadily fell from the sky, like it had ever since it began on that fateful evening. Lying on the hardwood floor, Darby stared up at the large raindrops pounding on the stained-glass windows. He lit another cigarette and took a long drag. Then something made him pick his cell phone up off the floor, press the speaker button, and dial a number. The phone rang twice before it answered.

"Hello, this is Angela; I can't get to the telephone right now. Please leave me a message and I will call you back as soon as I can. Merci, bye-bye."

Angela's sweet voice and charming Parisian accent echoed through the rooms of the darkened loft. Darby hung up the phone, then turned it back on and hit redial.

"Hello, this is Angela; I can't get to the telephone right now. Please leave me a message and I will call you back as soon as I can. Merci, bye-bye."

He hit redial again.

"Hello, this is Angela; I can't get to the telephone right now. Please leave me a message and I will call you back as soon as I can. Merci, bye-bye."

Darby took another drag on his cigarette before hitting redial again.

"Hello, this is Angela; I can't get to the telephone right now. Please leave me a message and I will call you back as soon as I can. Merci, bye-bye."

Darby sat up and looked around the loft. It was filled with beautifully wrapped wedding presents. Large bouquets of flowers flooded the rooms. Some were starting to lay limp in their vases, while others seemed fresher. He didn't know if they were from the wedding or the funeral. He took another swig of scotch and hit redial.

"Hello, this is Angela; I can't get to the telephone right now. Please leave me a message and I will call you back as soon as I can. Merci, bye-bye."

This was all he had left of Angela; a voice on the answering system. He wanted to know exactly how it happened. Did she know the car was about to crash? Was she afraid? Did she suffer? Did she think of him in her last moments of life? Did she whisper his name with her dying breath? A sudden flash of Angela alive and laughing was quickly overwhelmed by flashes of her lying on the slab in the morgue.

Making a fist, he hit his forehead, trying to stop the horrible images of Angela from overpowering the happy ones. Over and over, everyone told him the body was just a shell. But he could not stop thinking of his beautiful young Angela lying in her coffin in the dark of her grave, buried so far under ground, the dirt and bugs, the slow erosion of her porcelain skin. He shivered, the thoughts refusing to leave. He closed his sore eyes tightly and again hit redial, this time more angrily.

"Hello, this is Angela; I can't get to the telephone right now. Please leave me a message and I will call you back as soon as I can. Merci, bye-bye."

A raw surge of anger seethed up inside him; his lips tightened, his eyes narrowed.

"Hello, this is Angela; I can't get to the telephone right now. Please leave me a message and I will call you back as soon as I can. Merci, bye-bye."

Darby tightened his body until he could no longer stand it; he finally lost it. Raising the phone, he slammed it down on the floor, over and over, smashing it to pieces, destroying it. Standing up, his intoxicated body stumbled, as he viciously threw wedding gifts to the floor, kicking and crushing them. He smashed huge flower arrangements into the walls, sending crystal vases shattering and flowers flying. He yelled, growled, and cussed incoherently at the world.

"FUCK! YOU FUCKERS! WHY? WHY? WHY?"

He began punching the wall over and over in a violent rage, unable to stop, unable to control himself. The pain felt good, deserved. He slammed his fist into the wall with every ounce of force and anger left in his body, crushing and splintering the plaster, until he had completely exhausted himself. He stumbled backwards and slid down the wall into a heap on the floor, breathing heavily.

"Why, why, why?" he moaned, leaning back, utterly drained. Then, in one sudden movement, he picked up a thick shard of broken glass lying by his foot. Gripping the glass tightly in his shaking hand, he held the sharp tip to the side of his pulsing neck. He sat for a long moment contemplating the swift relief that death could bring. But as quickly as the idea came into his mind, it just as quickly dissolved, and he threw the piece of glass, sliding on the floor down the hallway.

Calming, he realized how desperately he needed that burst of emotion to release all the pain and anger that had been boiling up inside him. Darby sat quietly reflecting on what had just happened. He could never kill himself; he loved the world too much. He loved to laugh, he loved music, and movies, and traveling. He loved wonderful food and drink. He loved seeing the sun-rise and beautiful moon-lit nights. He loved his friends and family, and most important ... he loved *life*.

Then, a strange thought popped into his head. He thought about the little boy he had seen crying in the morgue waiting room. He wondered how the little boy was doing. Was he still feeling as helpless as Darby did? Was his heart still in knots? Or had the child been able to move on with his life? It was the first time in a long time that Darby thought about anyone or anything, other than himself and his situation. It was time to move on.

Looking down at his throbbing hand, he saw it was badly cut and was pretty sure it was broken. He went to the sink and stuck his hand under cold running water, watching the blood swirl down the drain. He picked up a dish towel, filled it with ice from the freezer, and wrapped his hand. He was feeling very happy to have been drunk at this moment, knowing that the pain would have been considerably worse had he been sober.

Walking over to the telephone, he picked up the receiver on the kitchen wall, holding it between his shoulder and his ear, as he dialed. After two rings, the phone answered.

"Hello, this is Angela; I can't get to the telephone right now. Please leave me a message and I will call you back as soon as I can. Merci, bye-bye."

The phone beeped and Darby was finally able to leave a message.

"I love you so much, and I miss you! Why did you have to leave me? I want you here with me! God, I miss you so fucking much, and I will always love you. I will always love you … my angel."

The phone beeped ending the call.

"Goodbye," Darby whispered, and then hung up the phone. After a pause, he dialed another number.

"Hello," a male voice answered.

"Andy, it's me."

"Darby?"

"Can you give us a ride?

"Yeah, yeah sure … where to?"

"Hospital."

CHAPTER 3

▼

TOURNIQUET

During the passing weeks Darby was making every effort to try and to get back into life and work. One afternoon he had lunch with Angela's sisters, Marie and Jasmine, who brought him pictures of Angela taken on the day of the wedding. The first set of pictures showed Angela and her bridesmaids, as they helped her get into her wedding gown.

"Cheeky," Darby said with a sad smile, seeing the risqué pictures taken of the girls all raising their dresses and showing off their legs, while making silly sexy faces at the camera. Another set of pictures were taken of just the bride, standing alone in front of a large spouting fountain in front of a ritzy hotel. The sunlight reflecting off her veil and white dress, made her look almost luminous, creating a halo around her body; she was just dazzling. The last set of pictures was of Angela getting into the 1950 Rolls Royce limousine; the car she died in. It was hard for him to see the pictures, but he was appreciative to have just one more look at her.

After months of having a cast on his broken hand, due to his unfortunate clash with the wall, Darby was thrilled to finally have it removed and be able to play football again. He just tried his best to go on with his life, day after day, month after month, trying to stay busy and retain his sanity. He took to having chats with the life-size, wood-carved Saints, who stood in different areas of the church. He felt less alone chatting with his new friends, St. Joseph and St. Francis. Real friends would set him up on dates, but inevitably they all ended in disaster. He simply wasn't ready, and couldn't help comparing all other women to Angela.

A current big night out for Darby was meeting his mates at The Old Queen's Head Pub on Essex, to drink and watch football. Other than that, he was totally focused on his work. He grasped onto a new project he really wasn't all that excited about, but as always, he put everything he had into it. He would stay up late at night working on his computer. He felt he was most creative at night, plus it got his mind off other *things*.

Occasionally on these late nights, which were often, he would look up to the open catwalk on the second floor landing of the church, and memories of Angela would come back to him. He remembered how she used to come out onto the catwalk from the bedroom in her skimpy satin nightgown and call down to him.

"When are you coming to bed, my love?" she would coo, playfully. "I need you."

"Give me, another half hour," he would reply, barely looking up at her.

"You said that a half hour ago."

"Half hour, I promise."

"I'll be waiting for you," Angela would tease. She would then blow him a kiss and flash her bare behind at him, before scurrying back across the catwalk into the bedroom. What he would give to be able to go up to that room and see her there waiting for him in bed. He longed to feel her skin and make love to her, just one more time. Darby was haunted by his memories. All he could do was continually remind himself, that there are some things in life, which no matter how hard we want them, no matter how much money we can pay or how many prayers we say, there are some things that are unattainable. These things we simply must make peace with.

On the one-year anniversary of Angela's death, the day that should have been their first wedding anniversary, Darby's mates did their best to keep his mind occupied. They took him out to the pub and made a special toast to Angela, then played a late game of football against a rival area team. Later that evening, Darby came into the darkened church, dirty, sweaty and hot.

"Good evening, Saint Francis. How are you this fine evening?" Darby respectfully greeted the patron saint of animals, dressed in robes of an Italian Franciscan monk with a baby bird perched in his hand. Darby continued into the kitchen and tossed his keys on the counter. He grabbed a bottle of cold water from the refrigerator and ran up the stairs to take a shower.

Moonlight shined down into the bedroom from a skylight above the bed. As Darby made his way through the room, he peeled off his sweaty football attire and tossed them on a chair in the corner of the room. He then walked into the bathroom and turned on the overhead light.

"Bullocks," he cried out with surprise, as the light sharply *popped* and went out, leaving him in darkness. He sighed in annoyance, not sure how to get out of the bathroom with broken glass on the ground all around his bare feet. "Buggery, bullocky, hell!"

Before he could make his next move, he heard a soft *rustling* behind him; he froze and listened intensely. Only his eyes darted around, looking for the source of the strange noise. He heard it again, but saw nothing but shadows.

"Hello?" Darby called out politely. For a split second, he swore he saw someone or something, reflected in the bathroom mirror, moving very swiftly in the bedroom behind him. Suddenly, an extremely cold whoosh and strong breeze came quickly around him, moving from one side to the other. It felt like a long silken dress brushing up against his naked body, making every hair on his body stand straight up. Darby tried to escape the eerie presence, but as he went for the door, he felt something roughly shove him, causing him to step on slice of broken glass.

"Shit! WHO'S THERE?"

Just as he turned to look out into the bedroom, the bathroom door slammed shut, narrowly missing his face. Darby stood shaking in the dark cold bathroom, his heart beating a million miles a minute. He waited for a few minutes, gathering up his courage. Whatever it was, it was gone, but it left a strong pungent perfumed odor. His trembling hand reached out and felt for the doorknob and he slowly opened the door. Peering into the moon-lit bedroom, he saw no one was there. He stepped out into the bedroom and sat down on the chair, where he had thrown his clothes, then carefully extracted a small piece of glass from the bottom of his foot. He sat back in the chair studying the room, trying to figure out what had just happened to him.

Standing up, he grabbed a box of wooden matches from his night stand and stood in the bathroom doorway. Striking a match on the box, a small flame arose; he held the lit flame up in front of his face. It did not move, as there was no draft; the flame did not waver at all.

Then the flame suddenly went out, as if someone standing right next to him sharply blew on it. That was enough. Darby had never been a scared or nervous person, but at that point, even he had had enough. He threw on some clothes and cautiously opened the bedroom door. No one was in the landing hall or stairs, and there was no trace of anyone having been there. He quickly headed down the staircase, grabbed his shoes and keys and left the church, slamming the enormous wooden door behind him.

Blending into the crowded streets, Darby was just thankful to be around other people. He nervously smoked one cigarette after another, trying to rationalize what had just happened to him. He wasn't sure what it was that happened, but he was sure it happened, and that frightened him more than anything else.

In the hour that passed, Darby had talked himself into believing he had blown things out of proportion. He put the key in the ancient door; it creaked open. He walked back into St. Michaels, carrying a few cartons of take-out. All was peaceful and quiet.

"Good evening, St. Francis," Darby said, patting the tall saint on the cheek. "Yes, I know, I'm just being paranoid." He walked down the hallway to the kitchen, put the cartons of food on the counter and fetched a new light bulb, before heading upstairs to clean up.

In the darkened bathroom, Darby was careful not to step on any of the shattered glass that fell from the light bulb to the floor. He stood up on the toilet and reached for the dead bulb, but surprisingly, the bulb was intact. He unscrewed it and replaced it with a new one, which immediately lit up. He jumped at the sight of himself in the mirror and almost fell.

"Silly bastard," he laughed, holding onto the sink. But on the bathroom floor, there was broken glass lying in some sort of water. In the middle of the mess, Darby noticed the top of Angela's favorite bottle of Valentino perfume. The lovely scent immediately brought back thoughts of Angela. But that wasn't what he had smelled during the incident. It was stronger than that. It was a stale ugly odor that reminded him of sulfur, rotting flesh, and dead roses.

After he cleaned up the mess, he was finally able to get his shower, where he once again wracked his brain trying to find a proper explanation for what happened. He was quite sure there was an explanation; he just had no idea what it was.

Later that night, Darby went down to his workspace in the sanctuary of the old church. He sat at his desk, clicked on a small lamp, and put some headphones on to listen to a soothing Mozart symphony. Drinking a cold beer, he ate from cartons of Thai take-out with chopsticks and set to work on his computer. He scoured the internet doing some background work for his new project, looking through different sites, as he diligently took notes.

Admittedly, he was still spooked from the bathroom incident, but he managed to convince himself he was just stressed out. Still, he couldn't shake the feeling he wasn't alone. The church just felt sort of "funny". Looking around the spacious area, he kept looking over his shoulder, feeling like someone was standing behind him. Other than the life-size saints peering out of the shadows, no one was there. He took another bite of food and continued searching the web. After a few minutes, he stopped again, hearing a series of *bangs* from the cellar below.

"That's bloody well it!" Darby mumbled, as he angrily got up and went to the cellar door. He flicked on the lights and descended the stairs; nothing was out of place and nothing was amiss. As he ascended the stairs, he scolded himself, "Nothing there, now stop it you silly git."

He sat back down at his desk, put his headphones on and went back to work. He tilted his head to the side, as he ate a long Pad Thai noodle that hung precariously off his chopsticks. Out of the corner of his eye, he glimpsed a shadow rapidly darting across the wall. He sat straight up in his chair, utterly startled, then quickly took off the headphones and looked around. After a few seconds of listening, he heard a long *scraping* sound. It sounded like something heavy, a chair, a piece of furniture; something was slowly moving or being pulled. It softly scraped across the hardwood floors in the corner shadows, but he couldn't see anything moving. Then the sound abruptly ceased.

"Keep it together mate," he whispered, sure his mind was playing tricks, when his computer shut itself off. Darby stared at the dark screen perplexed, then cautiously ventured around the church, searching. For what, he was not sure. Once again, everything was in its proper place, nothing had been moved. "Maybe I just need some sleep? I'm bloody exhausted is all and I'm freaking myself out."

He took the cartons of take-out and tossed them into the rubbish bin in the kitchen, then headed upstairs, purposely leaving a few lights on.

"Good night, Saint Francis," he yawned, as he made his way through the foyer and up the staircase, pulling himself up each step with the help of the ornate iron banister. His eyes were heavy, he was tired.

Entering the bedroom, he turned the late Sky News broadcast on the television for company, took off his clothes, and tossed them on his chair. Sticking his hand into the bathroom, he flicked on the lights before actually walking into the bathroom. He was aware of the incident that took place in the bathroom earlier that evening, but decided to do his best to ignore it. After brushing his teeth, he examined his head; a few sporadic grey hairs mingled in with his dark brown hair. The past few months had taken their toll on his physical, as well as, mental health.

Darby turned off the bathroom light and crawled into bed. The weatherman was giving the forecast, "Bright sunshiny days and occasional evening thunderstorms." Using the remote, he flipped through the channels, landing on a Spanish station with scantily clad young women dancing on a beach. He watched the pretty girls gyrate and shake their ample bodies. As much as he liked watching them, he just wasn't in the mood. He flipped some more channels and landed on a movie that was just starting; an old black and white film with Gloria Swanson called, "Sunset Boulevard", a film about an aging film star trying to buy the love of a young screenwriter. It was good. He remembered seeing it years ago in film school. Darby blinked his sleepy eyes, turned out the light and finally settled into his big comfortable bed to watch the movie. In just a matter of minutes, his eyes finally surrendered and closed.

After a short slumber, Darby woke with a sudden jerk, bolting up in bed. He immediately hit the mute button, believing he had heard a sound, but everything was totally quiet. He took a drink from a bottle of water on the nightstand and went back to watching the end of the movie. Darby watched as Swanson's character, Norma Desmond, play her greatest scene. It was only a matter of seconds before he hit the mute button again and listened. It sounded as if someone was *talking* downstairs. He figured it must have been someone outside the church, possibly a drunken pub patron meandering home late.

He turned the sound back on ... then abruptly hit the mute again. He did hear something, this time he was sure of it. Now, it sounded like many *voices,* and they seemed to be having a conversation. But the voices were not coming from outside; it felt like they were all around him, discussing him. Darby sat up in bed, concentrating, trying to make sense out of the garbled incoherent words that sounded like a distant out-of-tune radio.

Then, as soon as they started, the voices abruptly stopped, leaving him sitting in the flickering electric glow emanating from the television. He sat completely still and listened. It was quiet, nothing but the sound of his own heart beating in his ears. Darby was quite sure he was losing his mind, when he heard a low muffled cry, echoing up from the cellar three floors below. Then he heard it again; it was a horrible sad cry that was swelling into more of a heartbreaking moan, becoming louder and stronger. Within a few seconds, it sounded like whomever or whatever was making that horrid moan had started to ascend the basement stairs up to the first floor.

As "Norma Desmond" descended the grand staircase to meet her fate, the unearthly moaning from the floor below, seemed to rapidly intensify and continue to ascend the stairs to the third floor of the church. Coming closer and closer to where Darby was. He hit the remote, quickly shutting off the television, leaving him in darkness. The deep sad moaning was now approaching a loud wail. The wail was that of a woman; he didn't know how he knew that, but he was sure it was *female*. The wailing continued for what seemed like an eternity. Then it seemed to quiet down to a sad sobbing cry, as it finally stopped right outside Darby's closed bedroom door.

Darby could feel how cold the room had become in just a matter of seconds. He slipped out of bed, grabbed a cricket bat from his closet, and slowly inched across the bedroom approaching the door. He had no idea what he was going to do, but felt he had to do something. The lights he had left on downstairs would have backlit the outline of any person approaching the frosted glass window in the door. He watched the door intensely, but could see no silhouette or shadow of a person through the glass. Yet he could still hear the soft crying right outside the door. The cries were inconsolably sad, gutted … heartbroken. He cautiously put his ear up to the glass; the crying suddenly stopped and a dark *hand* swiftly struck the glass and held there.

"Jesus!" Darby screamed in a whisper, as he jumped and scattered back, crouching behind the bed. After a moment, he peered over the bed at the door. The hand remained pressed up against the glass; someone or something … was there. Darby closed his eyes tightly and then quickly opened them. The hand was *still* pressed on the glass. It had not moved.

"It's not real," he whispered, shaking his head in disbelief. "It's not real, it's not real." Gathering all his courage, he stood up and walked toward the door. He held the cricket bat out in front of him, trying to feel through the darkness, then cautiously placed his shaking hand on the glass opposite the disembodied hand. The hand quickly slid all the way down the glass door and disappeared, leaving a frosty imprint on the glass.

Darby jumped away from the door and the moaning started up again. It was a horrible crescendo, a shrill of inconsolable pain. He quickly got back into the bed, holding his ears, trying to shield them from the unbearable piercing noise. He could hear it descend the stairs, moving slowly down to the first floor and back into to the cellar from where it had come. The moaning abruptly stopped and the basement door slammed shut, so hard it shook the walls. The church was once again absolutely quiet. Darby sat in bed perfectly still, he could not blink, he could not swallow; he was too freaked out to move.

The sun rose at six-thirty, flooding the bedroom in a radiant light. The morning found Darby McGregor, a grown man, Oxford University graduate, and award-winning filmmaker, who had survived mass genocide in Africa, sitting in his bed, still gripping his cricket bat like a frightened little boy, scared by the monster in his closet. He had been in the same position all night long, staring at the door, waiting for *whatever* had visited him in the night to return. Thankfully, it never did.

Darby got up, got dressed, and cautiously opened the bedroom door. He examined the glass in the door for any signs of anything strange. He saw only the faint outline of light-pink lipstick on the glass, where Angela had kissed the window the morning she died.

"Maybe you were asleep and it was just a nightmare," Andrew said, pouring tea from a small teapot. "Or maybe, it was a cat in heat that somehow got into your house."

The small sidewalk café was crowded with people having a leisurely Saturday brunch. Darby sat with his brother at a small table, leaning sleepily on his hand, as he dipped some chips into the soft yellow yolk of an over-easy egg.

"Look, I know how this all sounds crazy," Darby admitted. "But I have gone through every possible scenario in my brain. I was awake, totally awake. Whatever it was, it was there. I've tried to rationalize what I bloody well know I heard, and what I bloody well know I saw! But I swear to God, the closer it came to the door, the more I lost my sense of reality."

"Did you maybe have a drink or two before you went to bed?"

"I had a beer, one beer that I didn't even finish."

"Well, maybe …"

"I wasn't drunk, Andrew."

"I don't know what to tell you then Darby."

Darby sat back and looked at his brother, preparing him for his next statement.

"Okay yes, just know before I even say this … I do know it is going to sound a bit mad. Just bear with me here? What if … it was Angela?"

"Angela?"

"Like her spirit or something."

"Her spirit? Her ghost?" Andrew smiled. "You're kidding, right?"

"It was female, I don't exactly know how I know that for sure, but it felt distinctly female. God, I don't know, maybe I am losing it. I mean, think about how many funerals there must have been in that church over the years."

"Possibly … hundreds."

"I've never really been afraid of anything in my life."

"The gorilla."

"Yes, right, brilliant Andrew, but I don't think the imaginary gorilla at my window when I was four really counts … frightening as it was," Darby laughed. "I admit I am really at a loss here. I don't know what I should do … call a priest?"

"Darby seriously, you have to get hold of yourself. Maybe it was some kind of freak thing, but you sound a little …"

"Crazy? This *thing* was like really, truly terrifying! It was there, it did happen! I mean, it was wicked, a God forsaken shrill … and the hand. I thought I was going to die from fright. All I could think was if I even dare tell anyone about this, they are going to think I've lost it and send me off to the loony bin. They'll say the grief was so overwhelming, the poor lad just snapped. I debated even telling you. You were kind of my only hope, but I don't blame you for not believing me. You don't believe me, right?"

"I believe … that you believe."

Oh God, that's such complete tosh! Please, do me a favor, don't be so bloody nice! I know that's hard for you, but please, be a bastard! Don't be such a polite fuckin' wank! I can take it! Say what you really think or piss off!"

"Okay, alright, you really want to know what I think? I think there is always a logical explanation for everything that happens. There were no such things as ghoulies, ghosties or long leggedy beasties for the good Lord to deliver us from. Spirits or spooks, ghosts or phantoms, specters or apparitions, whatever you want to call them, it's all just a bunch of bloody, buggery, rubbish. Honestly, the closest we have ever come to seeing spooks was at the Haunted Mansion in Disney World on that summer holiday we took to the States when we were kids. It was cartoon-like and fun, nothing to be afraid of. Mum and dad brought us up believing that you are born, you live a good life, you get old, you die. You know … ashes to ashes, dust to dust. You have just gone through a very difficult time in your life. You need to respect that! It is perfectly understandable that you are a little … skittish."

"I'm not skittish!" Darby said loudly. Noticing people eyeing him, he quieted down. "I have seen and heard things that I cannot explain. Things I wouldn't even try to explain. I have asked myself over and over, did that really just happen? Did I really feel that? I'm sane, I know I'm sane and I know exactly what I saw."

"Darby, it's just a little far fetched is all. I mean a windstorm in your loo, a disembodied hand on your bedroom door? I think the ghosts are perhaps just in your head. You're creating this. You need to be in control, use your common sense. I'm sorry, I just don't buy into this sort of thing. When you die, you're dead, end of story. Here's a thought, who did the laundry?"

"Well, I did."

"Right, why?"

"Because, Angela didn't … like going down into the cellar, she said it was creepy."

"Exactly, I don't think her ghost is hanging out in your cellar."

"What if she was maybe, trying to tell me something?"

"Maybe you should go on holiday, just go sit on a beach somewhere and relax."

"Forget it," Darby said, visibly hurt.

"Darby, don't get mad. I'm sorry, really, but look at it from my point of view. You think it might be Angela, your recently deceased fiancée, trying to have a chat. I just don't think so. I know how much you miss her, but you have to just let it go, let her go. I really think you are just stressed out beyond belief and it is starting to affect you. You know, you're more than welcome to stay with the family for a bit. Paula and the kids would love it, there's plenty of room."

"Appreciate it, but no. You're right, I have to deal with this," Darby admitted, as he stood up, tossing some money on the table. "Breakfast is on me. Thanks for listening."

"Darby," Andrew said, grabbing his arm. "I love you little brother and I really hate seeing you like this. But, I really do think you've been through a lot in a short period of time and you need to appreciate that. Maybe you need to go see someone, a shrink or something. It's time to get on with your life. Sometimes ghosts are just memories you can't let go of."

"Perhaps, you're right," Darby smiled, as he ruffled up his brother's perfectly coiffed hair. "Maybe it was the gorilla. See ya, mate."

After the long rainy night, it was turning out to be a beautiful fall day in London. The enormous towering trees rustled in the cool breeze, dropping their colorful leaves. Darby sat on a bench in St. James Park and watched some children playfully chase a ball. As much as he tried to shake it, the memory of the previous night was still fresh in his mind. He was angry at himself for not opening the door and could not stop thinking about what might have happened. What would he have seen? What if it was Angela in some form? What if she needed help?

"Oh for fucks sake, Darby, stop it!" he cringed, quietly berating the thoughts consuming his mind. He was starting to doubt himself, something he had never done before. He was always full of confidence and nothing could shake that, until last night. Darby always thought Andrew was right about everything, but he did understand why he didn't believe him. "Maybe, I do need to see a shrink?"

Darby walked out to the road and flagged down a cab. He got off at Piccadilly Circus, where he spent the day wandering around. He stopped at a local record shop and bought a few CDs, then stopped for a slice of pizza and played a marathon game of *Galaga* in an arcade for a few hours. Still not ready to go home, he decided to waste more time and went to see a movie, which he paid absolutely no attention to.

The sunny afternoon had turned rather ominous, dark clouds loomed heavy in the sky above, just waiting for the right moment to open up and pour down on him. But Darby didn't care, he just kept walking through the spawning city as its lights illuminated.

Standing on a busy street corner, he noticed a blue neon sign in the window of a two-story flat that read: SPIRITUAL COUNSELOR—MADAME BETTY ANNE. Darby walked up the stoop of the old building and stared at the bright sign, contemplating.

"What the hell," he murmured, climbing the steps and knocking on the door.

"Hold on love, I'm on the way, I'm on the way," Darby heard a faint voice through the door, along with the sound of numerous locks and bolts opening, and faint meowing. When the door finally opened it revealed, Madame Betty Anne, a tiny woman with pink curlers in her bluish hair, wearing a flowered housecoat and sweet smile.

"Madame ..." Darby asked.

"... Betty Anne. Yes, yes, I know, please come in out of the gloom," she insisted in a thick cockney accent. "Aren't you a tall handsome thing? What's your name, love?"

"Darby," he said politely. "I'm sorry ... I may have made a mistake."

"No, no, you've come to the right place. It's perfect; I just made a pot of tea."

"Brilliant."

"Alright Darby, we have important things to discuss," she informed him, as she pulled him into her cluttered little flat. Everywhere Darby looked he saw cats ... cats on the counters, cats on the furniture, cats on the television, cats everywhere. Madame Betty Anne excitedly sat Darby down at a table covered with a red velvet cloth, and cats. The old woman politely shooed them with her hands. "Down babies, down Kiki."

"You have many cats."

"They are the best company in the world," she said, placing a fancy rose-etched tea cup down in front of him. "Drink this, love."

Darby sipped the hot tea, as Madame Betty Anne leaned in close.

"This is very exciting isn't it?" she beamed.

"Yes, it sure is," Darby agreed, trying to figure out how he got himself into this mess. But he felt it couldn't harm anything to see what she had to say.

"So, what can I do for ya, love?"

"You are a spiritual counselor, right? I was hoping, you could answer some questions, I have about … what can you tell me, I mean, what happens when a person dies? What do you think happens to them?"

"You mean, what happens to their soul?"

"Their souls or spirits … what happens to them? Where do you think they go? Is it possible they could get stuck here on Earth?"

"Oh, you have a ghostie?"

"I'm not sure if my mind is just playing tricks on me or …"

"I think when we die … we go to heaven, if we were good, of course. At least, that's what I hope happens. I'm not going to lie to you, love. I'm not going to tell you some big cock and bull story about something no one can know about. No one really knows what happens, do they? Because to find out what truly happens to our souls, we have to die, don't we? But to answer your question, in my opinion, I think that there are instances when death comes very fast or unexpectedly, and perhaps some people may not know they are dead and they might linger here. But I can better tell you about your future."

"I see."

"Alright, have you finished your tea, love?"

Darby smiled and drank the rest of his tea.

"Let me have it," she requested, taking the cup from him. Madame Betty Anne carefully examined the scattering of tea leaves left in the bottom of the cup.

"Mmmm! Oh, my goodness!"

"What?"

"Oh, this is wonderful! You are going to have a baby, a little girl!"

CHAPTER 4

▼

LULLABY

Darby left Madame Betty Anne's flat heavily disappointed and even more disillusioned. He listened politely, as the old woman spoke of his rather preposterous future. But it was as he had expected; she was a fraud.

Heading home, he decided to stop at the pub to get a pint and some dinner. He knew he was killing time; he just didn't want to go home. The tavern was crowded with rambunctious football revelers watching an important game on the large screen television in the front room. Normally, Darby would have joined in with the cheers and jeers of the crowd, but he had a lot on his mind, not to mention he was exhausted having had no sleep. He sat in a quieter area at the back bar and ordered his usual—bangers and mash with a pint.

Taking a swig of his beer, he eyed a small television that hung over the bar. The campy British television program "The Dark Side" was playing. Darby always thought the show about supernatural encounters was purely a waste of time. Silly people running around with cameras looking for spooks, most often just scaring themselves. But it was always good for a laugh. Darby watched a female reporter standing under a bright streetlight, speaking very dramatically into a microphone.

"People were out enjoying their weekend, basking in the warmth of the southern California sun. Children were playing, mail was being delivered, and lawns were being mowed in this picturesque American neighborhood. Suddenly, there was a thunderous explosion and the booming sound of a massive jet engine revving. Neighbors ran out of their homes and saw an enormous commercial jet on fire, flying low … way too low. They could only watch helplessly as the plane nose-dived and fell careening into some houses right across the street. Most people in the quiet suburban neighborhood thought the impact was an earthquake, that is, until they ran outside and saw the devastation. A Boeing 747 jetliner was making its approach to the Orange County airport, when the unthinkable happened. The plane suddenly burst into flames after the right wing was clipped by a passing Cessna. The crippled airplane managed to remain in the air for a few moments before faltering, breaking into pieces, and plummeting inverted into the neighborhood. All sixty-three passengers, eight crew members, the pilot of the Cessna, and twenty-two people on the ground perished in the fiery crash."

Darby watched the terrible news footage shown on the television from the day of the crash. A massive portion of the neighborhood was ablaze. Houses and cars were engulfed in flames; it was a scene of horrible panic and chaos. Local residents and rescue workers were running around trying to pull bodies out of the burning wreckage, houses and trees.

"The impact, explosion and ensuing fires, destroyed eleven homes and severely damaged many others," the reporter continued. "It has been many years since the crash. The people in the area have rebuilt some of the houses and turned the crash site into a memorial park, a place to remember the victims of this terrible disaster. The crash and its aftermath will always be remembered in this area as a true American tragedy."

The reporter continued talking to the camera, as she walked under the luminous streetlamps in a perfect middle-class neighborhood. Numerous *FOR SALE* signs dotted the front yards. She finally stopped in a park at the end of road.

"But this tragic accident is only a part of our story. This beautiful area is Gower Street Park, the crash site of Flight 108. Twelve houses in this idyllic neighborhood are currently up for sale, all on the same block. The reason, well, many people here say there has been some odd, unexplainable, activity going on. Here at, The Dark Side, we have heard that some of the victims of Flight 108 may not be at rest. Tonight, renowned psychic and bestselling author, Gaia, has been invited to the park on the twentieth anniversary of the crash. The residents, family, and friends of the victims, are all hoping Gaia can contact their loved ones."

The reporter continued talking, as she and the cameraman walked over to interview Gaia, a rotund woman in her mid-forties, wearing a colorful silk moo-moo, which looked more like a costume than clothing. The medium was sitting on a park bench, flanked by many assistants, cooling herself with a vibrant

Chinese fan. Gaia was famous and beloved, having made millions chatting with the dead in order to milk money from the living.

"Well, good evening," Gaia looked up at the approaching reporter, as though surprised by her unexpected appearance.

"Gaia, why do you think there has been so much supernatural activity in this particular Orange County neighborhood?"

"I believe, we little human beings are very emotional creatures," Gaia answered in her thick Spanish accent, her eyes wild with expression. "We have moments of madness, moments of passion, moments of fear and moments of shear joy. Love affairs can go awry, hearts can be broken and sometimes something so horrific happens, so suddenly or violently, that the spirit is ripped from its earthly host body and it doesn't know or cannot accept that they have died. Some of these spirits are inconsolable. These spirits, we have to remember, are really just people without bodies. They have intelligence and emotions, just as they did when they were alive. They may feel threatened, or feel like the living have invaded their space. In my book, "*DARK JOURNEY TO THE OTHER SIDE*", I discuss how the fragments of these spirits can exist. That is why God has placed my blessed soul on this earth, to be a guide for these confused children, God's children."

"Gaia, thank you so much for speaking to us, I think they are ready to begin."

"Thank you, my dear," the psychic softly touched the reporters cheek. After being helped to her feet, she walked into the crowd of people standing in a large circle around her. They were holding candles, praying for even the slightest sign from the crash victims. Gaia stood in the middle of the crowd, lit by many bright camera lights from the media covering the event.

Gaia closed her eyes tightly and seemed to go into a strange trance. Sweating profusely, she continually dabbed her face with a cloth, while releasing her dramatic rhetoric, speaking very theatrically. The scene was almost comical; Darby thought she was putting on quite a performance.

"Ohhh yesss, ohhh yesss, thank you sweet spirit, Asreal. My spirit guide tells me these poor confused souls are with us. My dear children, my sweet spirits, I feel you. I know you are here with me. I want to guide you to the other side. Come to me, my children, almighty God awaits your arrival."

"What a crock of shite," Darby mumbled with a disbelieving smirk.

"Ed, look at that ... over there," the reporter could be heard speaking off camera. "Turn off your light." The camera man turned off the bright light attached to the top of his camera and looked with disbelief through his lens. He did not need the light; there was an extraordinary illumination that he zeroed in on, coming from the woods, beyond the area where Gaia was holding court. The reporter and camera man quickly and quietly headed into a wooded area, where they saw an astonishing sight; a young girl surrounded by tiny glowing, *balls of light*. It looked as though large fireflies were dancing all around her. The spheres of light moved up the girls' slender body, bathing her in the most breathtaking radiance.

Darby put his beer down on the bar and watched curiously. The girl could have been no more than ten. She was simply extraordinary, strange yet beautiful in a mystical sort of way. Her full cherub face was framed by long golden hair, and her sheer sleeveless dress blew lightly in the gentle breeze, which seemed to encompass her body. She was barefoot, standing on the vibrant green grass, gracefully swaying, waving her outstretched arms in the air. The lights seemed to be responding to her, coming to her.

"Hey, Graham," Darby called to his bartender friend. "Turn this up a tick, will ya?"

The bartender came over and turned the volume on the television up.

"Who's the bird?" Graham asked.

"I have no bloody idea," Darby answered, completely enthralled with the girl. "Pretty."

"Um … hmm."

The peculiar scene playing out on the television, reminded Darby of a painting Angela always loved by the artist, Edward Hughey, called "Midsummer Eve". In the painting, a Fairy princess in a flowing dress is surrounded by small naked fairies, holding little glowing lanterns of light. Angela had hung a framed copy of the painting in the foyer hall. It was the first thing she did when she moved into the church with him. He passed the painting every day and thought it was frilly, girly. He never really paid any attention to it until he saw the painting seem to come to life on the television in front of him.

"That's a … pretty good trick," Darby mused, completely intrigued.

By now, some of the younger children from the neighborhood started to gather around the girl, giggling and dancing, trying to play with the orbs of light dancing through the air. The crowd watching Gaia slowly made their way over to where the girl stood. Gaia continued to rant louder, trying in vain to get them to stay. But even she was curious about the lightshow in the woods and reluctantly walked over.

The crowd stared with disbelief and wonder, quietly commenting with astonishment at what they were witnessing. Some people were moved to tears. Others just stood in stunned silence, watching the young girl sway to unheard music, seemingly unaware of the crowd gathered around her. A woman in the crowd prayed quietly in Spanish, clasping a white rosary, like she was watching a divine, "Act of God".

"Don't be scared," the girl whispered, as she suddenly threw her arms straight up over her head. The balls of light rapidly swirled up into the air and disappeared into the starlit sky. "Don't be scared."

The girl smiled, watching the last sphere of light disappear, leaving her standing alone in the darkness. Just then, she looked around and noticed the people and cameras surrounding her. She looked flustered, smiling nervously at the crowd staring at her, unsure if they were angry or just amused. Truth was they were simply dumbfounded. They knew they had just witnessed something of major significance, created by the enchanted girl standing before them.

"They're gone," she stated in a hushed, almost embarrassed tone. One by one, the people in the crowd came over and embraced her. They just wanted to touch her, to be near her, to be in the presence of a blessed being. Even Darby felt he just witnessed something … *profound.*

"ENGLAND FIVE, GERMANY ONE!" someone yelled, and the pub erupted in cheers and screams of celebration. The television Darby was watching was quickly switched to the end of the game, as revelers rushed over to the bar for a victory drink.

"Hey, hey, I was watching that!" Darby exclaimed.

"Sorry Darby, victory is ours," the bartender yelled over the crazed crowd. Darby jumped off the barstool and ran out the pub door. "Darby! What about your food?"

It was the moment of truth; Darby knew he had to go home.

It was almost eleven o'clock and the dark clouds had finally released a vicious thunderstorm. He thought, very seriously, about going to spend the night at a hotel. That was the plan he had set in his mind if anything were to *happen.* He turned the key in the door and peered into the loft, very happy to see all the downstairs lights were on, just as he had left them the night before. He took his jacket off and hung it in the foyer where he saw the, "Midsummer Eve" painting Angela had loved so much, hanging on the wall. He leaned in and examined it carefully, as flashes of lightning brightened the details.

It really was quite beautiful, he thought. *And the girl, it was eerie how much she looked like the young girl on the television program.* Just then, the phone rang; startling him. Darby quickly rushed up the hallway to the kitchen, cautiously looking around as he went. The phone rang once again. He picked it up from the receiver and answered it.

"Hello."

"Hey, it's me," Andrew said, on the other end of the line. "I was betting you would go spend the night in a hotel."

"Don't laugh, I still haven't ruled it out," Darby laughed, opening the refrigerator, grabbing a beer and then sitting down on the couch. He turned the television on with the remote and after flipping through a few channels, landed on an old episode of "The Young Ones."

"I just wanted to make sure you were okay. I tried calling your mobile."

"I didn't have it with me."

"Right, well, how are you?"

"I'm okay, I …" Darby suddenly stopped talking, hearing a nasty loud *crackle* on the phone line. He flinched and gritted his teeth, as a large flash of lightning brightened the room, immediately followed by a huge crash of thunder that echoed all through London. "Andy, are you still there?"

"Yeah, but … can … barely hear you," Andrews's voice cut in and out on the phone line erratically. "Sounds … quite … a storm."

"It's a monster," Darby spoke louder.

"Why don't … come stay … me, Paula … and boys … rest of … weekend."

"Thanks, but I'm okay. I'm going to take one of the pain killers I have left from breaking my hand, which ought to knock me out."

"Great idea … a … night … sleep … you good."

"Listen, I saw something amazing at the pub tonight."

"Yeah, I … England five … Germany one. Did you … last goal, bloody brilliant!"

"Not the game, it was this girl …"

"Ah, you met … girl … that's fantast …"

Another sharp *crack* on the line, and the phone quickly went dead, taking all the power in the church with it.

"Andrew! Are you there? Andrew! Buggery, bullocky, hell … *damn, damn, damn!*"

Throwing the phone onto the couch in frustration, the normally calm and cool, Darby McGregor, was feeling that now familiar tinge of fear. He was angry with himself for feeling so anxious, but he couldn't help it. Once again, he sat alone in the darkness afraid to move.

Darby, once again, debated getting a good night sleep in a comfy hotel. But if he stayed and nothing happened, he would prove to himself he was not as big a pouf as he felt. If he left, he would never forgive himself and would undeniably be a big pouf. He wanted to just find a place to run and hide, but a streetlight from the large window above the landing spied him out. He did not want to go on doubting himself, he was determined to stay and face his fears, or maybe just the nightmares in his head. Which ever it was … he needed to know, he needed to know for his own sanity.

Trees outside the large window above the catwalk blew around, creating tall shadows on the walls. Each time the thunder boomed, Darby heard some wine bottles on top of the refrigerator vibrate; softly clinking together. He grabbed a lighter off the coffee table and lit a cigarette. It was the only thing he could think to do in the darkness to calm himself. Each pull on the cigarette, lit his face in a yellow glow. He sat on the couch completely still for about an hour, looking at the front door down the hallway, between the flashes of lightening. He snuffed out one of many cigarettes and lit another, trying to stay awake, but he was very tired from the previous sleepless night and the macabre events leading up to it. The sound of the rain was hypnotizing; it amplified loudly, as it fell on the roof.

Darby pulled out a leather cord he wore around his neck. Hanging at the bottom of the cord was Angela's wedding band. He held the ring up and watched the diamonds sparkle in the flashes of lightning. But as hard as he tried to fight it, Darby's eyes felt heavy; his head was nodding and sleep was taking over his body. Hot ash fell from the end of his cigarette onto his jeans; he quickly brushed it off and snuffed the cigarette out.

Lying down on the couch, Darby covered himself up with an old chenille blanket. Looking around the wood-beamed church ceiling and the open landing above, he tried to clear his head of all thoughts. Time had passed, nothing had happened, perhaps nothing would. He tried desperately not to fall asleep, but after a few minutes, he couldn't fight it any longer and drifted off.

In the passing hours, Darby slept peacefully. The thunder had faded to a distant rumble, the rain softened to a light patter.

Very slowly, the door to the cellar opened under its own will with the slightest soft creak. Then the *crying* began once again, very faintly, echoing out from somewhere deep within the cellar; it was the same sad cries heard the previous night. A few moments passed and a *mist* emerged from the cellar, so cold and thick, it could be seen with the naked eye. The mist glided effortlessly over the furniture, floating among the piles of books, paintings, and empty pizza boxes. Finally making its way over to where Darby lay sleeping. The cold vapor encompassed his entire body. His teeth chattered slightly, his breath was visible with each exhale from his mouth, yet he remained asleep.

The storm clouds had given way to a bright beam of moonlight shining in from the window onto the second floor landing above Darby. The mist swiftly grew into a long silhouette, which wandered down the front hallway and up the stairs to the catwalk. The banister could easily be seen through the transparent figure, bathed in an unearthly bluish-green light.

As it moved along in its deliberate slow manner, the mist began to materialize into the form of a *woman* wearing a full gown with some kind of shroud and lengthy train covering her head. The soft rustling of crinoline and the sound of heavy fabric could be heard slowly dragging along the hardwood floors, as the woman stiffly glided along the landing in a peculiar daze. Her cries became louder, intensifying into a horrible howling moan, like that of a wounded animal.

Darby shot up on the couch, eyes wide, immediately seeing the glowing figure on the second floor landing above him. Once again, the strong pungent smell of sulfur, rotting flesh, and dead roses, permeated the church. He instantly knew he was not asleep. He was absolutely awake and fully aware, trying his hardest to grasp what he was seeing. Yet, he was not afraid; he was too in awe to be afraid. He drank in the unbelievable spectral presence, which brought a chill to his skin and a tear to his eyes. He watched the apparition head toward the bedroom door at the end of the catwalk above. She did not have legs coming from under her gown; she literally floated a few feet above the ground. As hard as he tried, he could not clearly make out the features of her shadowy face.

Letting out a small *gasp*, Darby quickly covered his mouth, praying she didn't hear him. But in the middle of the landing, she stopped, creating a slight shade upon where he was sitting. The ghost turned her head and looked directly down at him, causing a shiver to run through every inch of his body. She opened her mouth, trying to speak, but no sound came out. It was like she was in a silent movie; she seemed to be frantically pleading with him, trying to tell him something of great importance.

"Please, I don't understand," Darby called out to her, as he noticed a spot of red appearing on the front of her gown, quickly growing, soaking the fabric from the inside. Then the disembodied voices began their frenzied whispering again. Darby could feel them all around him, angrily reprimanding him.

"Stop it, shut up!" he screamed, putting his hands over his ears, trying to block them out.

The spirit did not seem to notice the blood, now saturating the front of her gown. She reached out her arms, gesturing for Darby to come to her. He wanted to see her, he had to see her; all his fears were gone. He got up from the couch, quickly rushed down the hallway toward the stairs and grabbed onto the banister. He had made it halfway up the steps, when he stopped dead in his tracks.

"Angela," he whispered, as he looked up at his beautiful bride. It *was* Angela. She stood at the top of the curving staircase in her wedding gown, looking down upon him. She looked so lucid and sad, her beautiful dark eyes so full of gloom. "Angela, what is it? What can I do?"

The apparition reached out to him, gesturing for him to come closer, pleading silently. The longer Darby looked at her, the braver he became. All he wanted was to take her in his arms and hold her. He moved up another few steps and could see her more clearly now. It was then he noticed something, something strange. Her eyes had *changed*, her expression had turned cold; she stared, looking right through him.

"Come with me," the words slithered from her pale lips, deep and gravely. The sound was disturbing … not of this world.

"Come with me," the voices all joined in, loudly taunting, echoing all around Darby. "Come with me, come with me, come with me …"

Unexpectedly, her eyes rolled violently back in her head, leaving just the whites glowing in the darkness. A vicious smile erupted across her face; her eyes grew wild … crazed, and then sunk deep into their sockets. Her skin began to dehydrate rapidly, until it was clinging tightly to her bones, making her look skeletal. Then her neck swayed and sharply popped, tilting to the side, unnaturally, as she rapidly decomposed and rotted right in front of him.

This was not Angela. This *thing* may have looked like Angela, but Darby knew it wasn't her. It was someone or something else, something not human.

"Who are you?" Darby demanded.

"Come with me, my darling," she said, holding out her bony emaciated hand. Darby watched small red beads of blood fall onto the floor from the grotesque drenched gown. A long, putrid-smelling, breath escaped the spirits lips in a chilling hiss.

"What … are you?"

The bride began to laugh, a frightening deep shrill. The voices all joined in laughing with it. They felt so close to his face, he could feel cold sensations on his skin, yet no one was there. Darby backed down a few steps, trying to escape them.

It was then the apparition suddenly stopped laughing. Its face contorted and it slowly rose up several feet above the steps, towering over him. Darby's whole body shook uncontrollably, as he looked up at the horrifying entity, hovering motionless in the air above him. He could see the delicate pearls and sequins sparkling eloquently on her gown, reflecting the moonlight coming in through the window landing.

Then, in one swift movement, the apparition flew down the steps straight at him; its gown blowing wildly. Darby quickly raised his arms up in front of his face, trying to shield himself. But the apparition passed directly through him, he could feel a freezing cold veil of moisture cover his body. The intense energy forced him backwards and he fell down the rest of the staircase. Darby stayed motionless on the floor, too stunned to move.

Looking up from his disoriented angle on the floor, Darby watched the ghost glide in its slow deliberate manner, down the front hall and dissolve back into the darkness of the cellar. After a moment, the cellar door slammed shut, violently shaking the church to its foundation.

Darby got up, grabbed his wallet, cell phone and keys, and then calmly walked out the front door.

CHAPTER 5

▼

WISH

Darby decided his new home would be the rather posh, Cadogan Hotel, mainly because it was situated nicely between, Knights Bridge and Sloane Square, and in walking distance of Harrods. When he checked into the hotel, he was completely exhausted. He slept for two days straight, waking only to order room service and going right back to sleep. He had not been back to his house since the incident, and had no plans to do so.

A few days later, when Darby officially woke up, he already had a firm plan set in his head and knew exactly what needed to be done. He knew he couldn't be honest and tell his friends and colleagues why he had chosen this *new* project, mainly because he didn't want to be ridiculed. But he did want some answers, more for his own self-preservation, then anything else.

Darby phoned his financier, Ian Sharpe, a high-strung New York film producer, who had been transplanted in London, and informed him he was scrapping the project he had been working on and beginning a new one. He never really gave a reason why, he just let Ian know he was setting up shop in the hotel while his house was being "worked on".

Having asked a production assistant to go to his house and pick up some of his things, Darby was very curious to see if anything "unusual" happened to the young man. But all he had to report was that all the lights were on. As requested, the boy brought him some clothes, his laptop, and the "Midsummer Eve" painting, which Darby immediately propped up on a chair, so he could easily view it.

After the young man left, Darby gazed at the painting, almost studying it. The resemblance was truly uncanny to the image of the young girl he saw dancing in the dark woods with the glowing orbs of light. The girl indeed impressed Darby. In fact, she was all he could think about. She was to be the answer to all the questions plaguing him. He was sure of it.

Her name was Lillian Dufrene and for all intents and purposes … she did not exist. But Darby was going to find her; he had no choice. He pulled every possible string he could, calling in many favors from people who owed him over the years, trying to get all the information he could on the infamous enchanted girl. And although he was admittedly frightened, at the same time, he was *fascinated*. After his experience, he knew there was so much more to the human spirit than what most people realized.

"Jules, I knew you'd come through for me!" Darby exclaimed into the phone, having received a call later that evening from an old girlfriend, who currently worked in the research department at the BBC. "What did you find?"

"Darby, it was unbelievably hard to find any information at all!"

"Well, I'll take whatever you have," Darby stated, taking notes as she spoke.

"Okay, this is what I know so far. Lily's mother, Karla, met a young man by the name of Sutton Dufrene, while he was visiting New York after completing his tour of duty in the army. Sutton was this kind-hearted, southern boy, from Savannah Georgia. For Sutton, it was love at first sight. For Karla, it was love of money; she had found her shortcut to easy street. I guess his family was rather wealthy. Sutton loved children and wanted to start a family immediately. Within a year, Karla gave birth to a boy and a girl; Tyler William Dufrene and Lillian Rose Dufrene."

"Twins?"

"Yes, twins. Apparently, when Sutton's father died, he left his mother, Lillian, a massive fortune, including land acquisitions and some stocks he bought many years before. Mr. Dufrene also took a chance on a sugary elixir called, "Coca-Cola". Needless to say, they're rich, as in filthy."

"I bet."

"One night, Sutton went out on a fishing trip with some of his buddies. They got caught in a freak storm and never returned home. It has been documented, that Karla became very depressed and slowly broke down, unable to cope with her new life of having to raise two small children alone. She was angry, feeling that it was Sutton who had wanted children, and now she was stuck with them. Sutton's mother Lillian wanted Karla and the children to come live in the family mansion with her. Lillian desperately pleaded with Karla, but she refused. You see, Karla didn't like Lillian. She was very jealous of her great wealth and freedom. Karla began drinking heavily, and as time moved on, bitter Karla made it difficult for Lillian to see her beloved grandchildren. Lillian knew her daughter-in-law was going downhill fast. So every month, she made sure her bills and mortgage were paid. Karla knew how all this extra money got into her account, but never acknowledged or thanked Lillian for her kindness."

"Nice."

"Karla started seeing a therapist a few months after Sutton disappeared. He described Mrs. Dufrene as being quite level-headed and smart. She was under the doctor's care for only two months before her arrest."

"Her arrest?"

Hold your horses, I'm getting to that. Karla told the doctor that she had been having some problems with her seven-year-old daughter, Lillian. According to Karla, the child had begun to exhibit some rather "strange behavior". Lily was very close to her father and was horribly traumatized by his death. She would sit on the porch of the family house for hours, waiting for him to come home. Mrs. Dufrene admitted her daughter's curious behavior had begun even before her father passed away. When Lily was about four, Karla and Sutton were awakened in the middle of the night to find Lily standing at the end of their bed. She told them that there were people in her room, trying to "talk to her". Sutton would take her back to her bed and stay with her until she fell back to sleep. These visits from Lily became more frequent. Night after night, Sutton would take his daughter back to her room and sit and talk with her until she fell back to sleep. Karla later admitted to being angry with her husband for not scolding the child and insisting she stop her nonsense. Karla felt it would only perpetuate Lily's ability to "tell more lies, just to get attention".

"Unbelievable."

"After the death of her father, Lily began to sleepwalk. Karla said she would find the little girl every morning asleep in different rooms of the house. She also began to have something known as "night terrors". She would wake up in the middle of the night, thrashing and screaming in her bed. Okay, now this is creepy … she told her mother that a burned clown she called, *Varton Muntz*, was living in her closet. Lily said, the clown would tell her to "do things, naughty things". Karla informed the doctor that she would not go to check her daughter, when she cried out during the night. When pressed by the doctor as to why she would not go and comfort the little girl, she stated she was, "afraid of her".

"She was afraid of her own child? That's just so bizarre."

"Oh, it gets worse, trust me. Around this same time, little Lily had become fascinated with fire. Karla recalled waking up in the middle of the night smelling gas. Through the darkness, she followed the smell and saw a blue glow coming from her kitchen. She could feel the heat as she was coming down the hallway. So she peered in and saw Lily sitting on a chair in front of the stove watching the fire perform. The little "pyromaniac" had turned all the burners on to the highest setting and was just staring, transfixed by the flames shooting up. Then small fires started mysteriously popping up around the house. Karla became more afraid that Lily would try to set the house on fire. So when her daughter went to sleep, Karla began locking the little girl's door … from the outside. On those nights, when whatever horrible nightmares came to torment Lily, Karla would just lie in bed and listen, as the child cried out and desperately tried to open her bedroom door. It was around this time, Karla admitted to crushing up her sleeping pills and stirring them into Lily's hot cocoa. Karla knew it was wrong, but said, she needed to get some sleep. She said, it was the only way to get through the night without the girl freaking out."

"She drugged her daughter so that *she* could sleep, "Mum of the Year!""

"So here's where it goes beyond madness. I don't have exact details yet, but apparently at some point, Karla finally lost it and tried to kill herself and her kids; she said, they were *damaged*. Oh yeah, get this, mum of the year was pregnant at the time. The mother was put in a nut house and so was the little girl. The boy died at the scene."

"Incredible. Do you have any idea how old Lily Dufrene may be?"

"Well, the footage from "The Dark Side" was shot sometime in the eighties. That's about all I know right now."

"Thanks so much, now I owe you one!"

"No problem, Darby. I'll get you more info as soon as I can."

"That's great. Talk to you soon."

Darby had just hung up the phone, when it suddenly *rang*. He quickly picked it up.

"Hello."

"She won't do it," Darby's film financier, Ian Sharpe, announced angrily.

"What do you mean?"

"I explained who you were and the awards you had won. I explained how you wanted to do a documentary about her."

"Did you tell her …"

"No, you don't understand, I didn't tell her anything. I couldn't even get through to talk to her. She has people who must be protecting her. I was rudely told that she was, and I quote, "not interested". I think this one may be a lost cause."

"Who did you speak to?"

"She's just a little girl, right? I assumed it was her guardian I spoke to."

"She may be a bit older than we thought."

"Well, whomever I spoke with stated, rather emphatically, she doesn't do interviews or want any publicity. She is very private, apparently. Do you know how difficult it was just to get her telephone number?"

"I have to talk to her. Give me the number and let me try."

"If you think you can do better than me hotshot, go for it!"

Darby took down the number and hung up with Ian. He was very excited to start on his new project. The only problem was … the subject didn't want anything to do with it, and that made things a bit difficult. But Darby felt if he could just talk to her, he could convince her. He sat down at a table where his laptop was set up and dialed the number.

As the phone rang, Darby hit a button on his computer. He watched the film from "The Dark Side" television program of Lily and her dancing orbs, until the phone was answered.

"Yes," a languid voice answered. Darby was unsure whether it was male or female.

"Hello, yes, I am trying to locate Lillian Dufrene, please."

"Who are *you*?" the voice asked in a condescending tone.

"Right … yes, I'm sorry. My name is Darby McGregor; I'm a documentary filmmaker from London."

"Hmmm, impressive," said the voice, totally unimpressed.

"It is really important that I speak to Ms. Dufrene."

"Yes, well, Mr. McGregor is it? Ms. Dufrene is not interested. Thank you so very much for your call. It was lovely talking to you. Have a nice day."

"Wait!" Darby cried, as the line went *dead*.

Never one to give up easily, Darby re-dialed the number. He had to speak to her and was not going to be swayed by one of her handlers. He replayed the film of Lily and the orbs again, impatiently tapping his pen on the table, as he waited through the rings.

"Yes?"

"Yes, hello, it's me again."

"You?"

"Darby McGregor, filmmaker, London. Look, I'm sorry to disturb …"

"Then why did you call back?"

"It is of great importance that I speak to Ms. Dufrene."

"It is of great importance, to whom?"

"To me."

"You? Who are *you*?"

"Really, you don't have to be such a … so rude! Might I ask, who are *you*?"

"Why?"

"No, you don't have to tell me. I know who you are. You are nothing more than one of Lillian Dufrene's … *lackeys*.

"*Lackeys*?"

"That's right, lackeys!"

"How do you know? Maybe Ms. Dufrene tells us, lackeys, to be rude. Maybe, she insists upon it in order to keep people, like yourself, away from her?"

"I don't think she's like that."

"You don't, hmmm?"

No, I don't, I think maybe Ms. Dufrene would appreciate knowing that someone such as yourself, someone who worked for her, and was representing her, was being very ill-mannered."

"Ohhhh, I see. Are you going to tell on me? Get me in trouble?"

"Not if you let me speak to her."

"So, now you are threatening me?"

"Call it what you will, I just think she may want to know."

"Okay."

"Okay?"

"I'll let her know."

"What?"

"You see, Mr. McGregor that is where I have the advantage. Have a nice day."

A sharp *click* and the phone went dead, once again.

"Shit!" Darby cussed in frustration. He paused for a moment, took a deep drag on his cigarette and dialed again.

"Yes?"

"Don't hang up, please," he pleaded. "Listen, I'm sorry, I was a total and complete bastard! It's just, I've been through hell and back and I'm not really sure how to handle what is happening around me. I feel like I'm stuck here, like I'm closely teetering on the edge of insanity and I'm not really sure at this point if I can make it back. If I don't get some answers soon, I don't know what I'm going to do. It's not like I can go back to my life; it's gone. I can't even go back to my own fucking home! Everything has changed for me. I have been wracking my brain trying to figure it all out, the whole *death* … thing. I just can't do it by myself. Its bloody well beyond anything I can comprehend and I feel so alone. I can't tell anyone or they will think I've gone off the deep end. It just seems like when someone dies … when someone that you loved so much is just, all of a sudden, taken from you … it hurts so horribly. You feel like you want to die, just to stop the pain. I'm so unbelievably lost. Look, I don't expect you to understand or even care," Darby paused, watching the beautiful little girl smiling and dancing on the computer monitor. "But if you have even a shred of compassion in your heart, you will let me speak to her. Please …"

There is only silence on the other end of the phone.

"… Please," the silence continued, then Darby asked cautiously, "Hello? Are you there?"

"Yes … I'm here."

"Pretty please, sugar on top."

Darby heard a *laugh* come from the other end of the line. The laugh was like a soft summer breeze, it warmed him. It was sincere, sweet and definitely *female*.

"Lily?

"You have to wear a costume."

"Pardon?"

"Saturday is my little Halloween … soiree. You'll have to wear a costume. It's mandatory."

"Does that mean?"

"Yes."

"Yes, you'll do it, Lily?"

"You can set everything up through Nadine."

"Okay … brilliant. Thank you, thank you, thank you."

"Remember, no costume, no admission."

"Right."

"And bring *her* ring."

"What?"

"See ya, Saturday."

It Creeps! It Crawls! It eats you alive!
You are cordially invited as an honored guest of our
Dearly departed host—Lillian Dufrene
Run! Don't Walk! Save Yourself!
The 12th Annual
NIGHTMARE BALL
Saturday, October 31st—9pm—All Hallows Eve

Dufrene Family Funeral Parlor, Crypt 10
NO ADMISSION WITHOUT COSTUME!
You do not even want to know the unthinkable tortures you will have to endure,
if you do not have a costume. And NO, your own frightening face will not do!
Spirits will be flowing, but you may bring your own, booze or blood, which ever
you prefer.
Festivities will include:
Gas Chamber Maze, good luck finding your way out in time!
Burning all witches at midnight, you know who you are!
Sacrificing of a virgin, you *really* know who you are!
And other blood curdling, skin-crawling, painstaking tortures,
that will send shivers down your spine!
Go ahead and scream! No one will hear you, the neighbors are already dead!
We are dying to eat … oops, meet you!
* Free castration with flyer

It was perhaps the fifth time Darby had read the invitation, getting more of a
kick out of it each time he read it. He flipped the pumpkin-orange invitation over
to view a map of Lily's house printed on the other side. The map also described
the activities going on in each area.

Darby couldn't wait. In just a few more hours he would finally be face to face
with the one person, he believed, may hold the answers to all his questions.
Although he was curious why Lily had all of a sudden agreed to open her very private life to a complete stranger and his film crew, he didn't question it. He didn't
want her to question it either or she may rethink her decision and tell him to
bugger off.

From the day Lily agreed to the documentary, Darby had been busy putting
together the financing, equipment and crew in record time. His best mate and
partner in crime for many years, Nigel Parsons, came onboard as cameraman. It
was with Nigel's help and dedication that Darby had won his prestigious awards.
Nigel was over the top; a striking black man, who owned his open *flamboyance*,
and took no crap from anyone regarding his sexual orientation. He was quick
witted and had no fear or reservation about *anything*.

Darby and Nigel arrived in New York City, where they waited in the airport
to be joined by a UCLA film school student named, Dustin, whom Darby
recruited to be his assistant/sound person. Dustin was obliviously singing along
with his iPod, when he stumbled off the jet way into the airport. He moved with
the ease of a cartoon character, carrying a gnarled guitar case covered with dozens

of stickers, "*Legalize Everything!*", "*My kid had sex with your honor student*" and "*Horn broken—watch for finger*".

The kid was a totally laid back, good-natured, surfer-type; his body bronzed a golden hue. He wore an oversized Mexican beer sweater over a pair of long wrinkled surf shorts and a knit Rasta cap, covering his sun-bleached blonde hair. Darby and Nigel shared a, "this ought to be interesting" glance, as Dustin spotted them and saluted.

"You must be Dustin," Darby said.

"I must be," Dustin agreed, with a charming smile. "That's what my drivers' license says, or it did when I had one."

"I'm Darby and this is Nigel," Darby said, as he and Nigel shook Dustin's hand.

"Great to meet you, I love your work, man! You so rock! I'm a total fan! I want to thank you so much for giving me this chance to work with you. It's going to look amazing on my resume, you know, and it gives me school credit. Whatever you need me to do chief, I'm there for you. I'm super psyched!"

"Well Dustin, it's good to have you on board," Darby said. "Right, well we need to get going if we are going to make our connecting flight."

They rushed down the concourse to another gate and boarded a flight bound for Savannah Georgia. Nigel sat next to Darby in first class, resting one of his long legs on the arm of the empty seat in front of his own. He was intensely scrutinizing the footage from "The Dark Side" television show on Darby's laptop. Nigel watched the film, laughing and outwardly chiding the over-the-top performance given by the Spanish psychic, Gaia. But when it came to Lily, he analyzed every move she made with extreme skepticism. He observed the young girl charming the little balls of light dancing all around her. Darby knew Nigel would be very cynical, which is what he was hoping for.

"See that there, that could be fiber optic strands dangling above her," Nigel commented.

"No, just watch," Darby said, pointing to the screen. "The camera rises over her and shows nothing but sky above."

"Bloody hell, I don't know how they did it then, Darby. I'm pretty good at figuring this kind of scam out, but I'm at a loss. I mean the Spanish bird, Gaia ... clearly a nut job, but the little girl ... I'm simply gob-smacked."

Nigel backed up the scene to watch it again. Darby smiled, feeling like he was really on to something. He wanted Nigel to question everything, to figure everything out. He wanted him to say Lily was nothing more than a good "con-woman". But so far, he couldn't. Thankfully, he couldn't. Nigel was honest, sometimes brutally so, but he was a great friend and had a wicked sense of humor that floored Darby.

"This is so awesome! I've never sat in first class before," Dustin said, excitedly leaning over the seat directly behind Darby and Nigel. He peered at the little girl dancing with the spheres of light on the computer screen. "That's the chick, huh? Those … fireflies or somethin'?"

"Too big to be fireflies," Nigel added.

"Hey chief, when you say we are going to try to get like, spirits or ghosts on film, do you mean like going into graveyards?"

"I don't really know where we will be going yet. Why?"

"Oh, just curious."

Darby and Nigel shared a glance and smile, noticing Dustin's apprehension.

"You scared?" Nigel asked him.

"Scared … me? No way! I'm totally cool with it."

"You're scared," Darby laughed.

"Come on, you'll be just fine," Nigel said, patting his cheek playfully. "We'll protect you from the spooky spooks!"

"I'm not scared, really. I'm cool. I'm good."

"Riiiiight, keep telling yourself that," Nigel chided. "And you might just believe it."

"I'm cool," Dustin kept repeating, as he sat back down in his seat. "I'm good."

"Leave him alone," Darby laughed.

"I was just teasing. Besides, you never know what we might see, right?"

"Do you believe in "spooks" Nigel? You know … things that go bump in the night?"

"Sure, I mean, I've never seen anything "supernatural" myself, but I don't believe when you die, you just *die*. It's like, what happens to your soul, your spirit, the thing that makes you, you? When you called and told me what you wanted to do, I was absolutely into it mate! All I have to say is "*bring it on*!" If it's bollocks, its bollocks, and we'll call her on it. But if it's not … I can't bloody well wait! What about you?"

"Me?"

"Yeah, ever see anything … *otherworldly*?"

"Um," Darby thought about telling Nigel what had happened to him, but was interrupted.

"Here you go, gentleman," said a pretty blonde stewardess, placing Darby's scotch, along with an assortment of fancy warm nuts, on the arm rest between his and Nigel's seats. "Your scotch, sir."

"Ah, bless you," Darby smiled, thankfully.

"And a Martini, three olives, for you," she said, placing a martini on Nigel's tray.

"Fabulous!" Nigel said, eating an olive off a toothpick. "Patsy, I think I love you!"

"And one hot fudge sundae with whipped cream and pistachios," Patsy smiled, handing Dustin a massive ice cream sundae. "Topped with a cherry."

"Sweeeet," Dustin lusted.

"If I can get anything else, please let me know?"

"Thank you, Patsy," Darby said, with a polite nod.

The stewardess gave Darby a flirty smile and headed back up the aisle.

"Now, what were you saying?" Nigel asked Darby.

"I said, I can't think of anyone I would rather take on this wild ghost chase … than you. Thanks mate."

"My pleasure, I wouldn't miss it for the world. Cheers!"

Darby and Nigel clinked glasses in private celebration. Darby, once again, took out the invitation and read it. The invitation had been sent to him by Lily, along with many legal forms from her lawyer. The lawyers for the new production company were none too happy about all the stipulations regarding Lily and her nonsensical "ghost-activities". The bottom line from Lily's camp was that the documentary could not be released unless she gave "complete approval" of the finished film. And if she didn't approve, the entire trip would have been for nothing. The lawyers thought it was ridiculous to waste time and money on such an absurd project, but Darby didn't care what anyone thought. He had his own reasons.

Every hour that passed, every mile they flew, brought Darby McGregor closer to Lillian Dufrene. Regardless of whether he actually saw anything, *paranormal*, he felt that a documentary on Lily and her bizarre life would be interesting enough. Here was this girl who had spent her entire childhood being afraid of the world around her, and was believed to enjoy fire a "little too much". A little girl, whose mother had tried to extinguish her short life, before it really began.

Darby was getting excited to meet Lily, even if the girl may be crazy. He felt you couldn't make this madness up. This might not end up being a documentary about haunted houses, but of a haunted person; a person who may not be hearing the voices of the dead, but rather the voices in her head.

CHAPTER 6

▼

EVERYTHING ZEN

Immediately upon arriving in Savannah, Darby and company rented an SUV at the airport, and then quickly drove to Acme Costumes. But being Halloween night there was not many costumes left, and they were already late for the party.

Nigel stepped out of the dressing room as a fabulous, black, "British Elvis". The bright purple, rhinestone encrusted jumpsuit, and teased pompadour wig, he pranced in front of the mirror wearing, gave him an ultra-flashy, Vegas drag club look, which would have made even "Little Richard" blush. But not Nigel … he loved it. Dustin found a caveman costume made of faux leopard fur with a fiber-glass club,which he taped his microphone onto. This regrettably left Darby with the illustrious choice of being either Raggedy Andy or a cockroach.

"I can't go in any of these," Darby grumbled, staring into the mirror, which reflected back a large hairy cockroach with long feelers.

"You look rad, really chief," Dustin said, enthusiastically.

"Nigel?" Darby looked to Nigel questioningly.

"I think we should call an exterminator," Nigel chided.

"Piss off," Darby sighed. "I have to have a costume! This is rubbish; I knew I should have brought one from London."

"Wait, I do believe I have a rather brilliant idea," Nigel announced. "Come on."

They paid the rental fee for the costumes and headed back outside to the SUV.

"Damn, my last cigarette," Darby mumbled, deciding to hold onto it for an emergency nicotine fit. He put the cigarette pack back into his jacket for safe keeping.

"Put these on," Nigel instructed, as he opened his suitcase and rummaged through his clothes. He found a well-worn black leather jacket and a white t-shirt, which he tossed to Darby.

"I have no idea where you are going with this," Darby curiously stated.

"Be right back!" Nigel said, dashing across the street to a pet shop.

"What's he doin'?" Dustin asked.

"Who knows, buying a hound dog to go with his costume," Darby scoffed. "We're going to be so late!"

Nigel begged the reluctant clerk to let him run into the store that was just about to close. After a few minutes, he emerged and ran back to the SUV with a small bag and a big smile.

"Success!" Nigel sang, triumphantly. Taking a pair of scissors from his case, he began to rip and shred Darby's jeans and t-shirt in strategic places. Then, kneeling down, he rolled Darby's jeans up, revealing his black Doc Marten boots. He then took a small lock that had been holding a film tin together off and produced a silver dog chain from the bag. He put the chain around Darby's neck and promptly locked it.

"You have a key to this, right mate?" Darby asked, pulling the collar secure.

"Yes, yes, somewhere," Nigel said, with a sly smile. "I think."

"You think?" Darby rolled his eyes. "You better!"

"Bitch, bitch, bitch! You should be thanking me for my fabulous creation," Nigel scolded him, as he took out a bottle of hair gel and squeezed a large glob into his hands. He then rubbed it through Darby's hair; pulling on it, making it spiky.

"This is basically how I looked as a teenager," Darby joked, looking in the side view mirror, completely comfortable in his new threads.

"There you go!" Nigel said, helping Darby put the leather jacket on. Then he stood back and looked at his creation. "Right, now give me a sneer and say anarchy!"

"Anarchy," Darby growled, gritting his teeth and snarling the side of his upper lip.

"Brilliant! You're Sid Vicious," Nigel smiled, proud of his handy work. "Oi, let's go!"

Savannah was exactly as Darby expected it to be; such southern beauty would have made Scarlet O'Hara proud. They drove through the heart of the historic district. It was simply lovely. It was refined elegance in the midst of lush gardens, sweeping verandas, and tranquil spouting fountains, nestled under graceful live oak trees laden with Spanish moss. There were grand old mansions adorned with Victorian architecture, which had been lovingly restored to their original opulence. The air was perfumed with the scent of magnolias and azaleas. It almost felt like stepping back in time, back into the charm of the nineteenth century.

The brilliant ginger sunset crept across the sky on Halloween night. Darby was in heaven, as a filmmaker you couldn't ask for a better backdrop. He instructed Nigel to lean out the window with a camera and film the cityscape. The porches were done up with glowing pumpkins and other fun Halloween nightmares. Children were running rampant through the streets and sidewalks, wearing their most ghoulish guises. They shouted with delight their, *trick or treats*, carrying bags packed with sweet candy treasures, as their exhausted parents tried to keep up.

By the time they drove out of town and across the island bridges that lead out to a more remote area, it was already dark. They followed a very long winding road, passing such illustrious establishments as the "Pig in the Pit Barbeque" and "Bubba's Grocery, Bait and Tackle", before finally arriving at a large stone gatehouse with an ornate iron gate.

The headlights on the SUV lit up the enormous stone arch overpass. Darby noticed a single word, *SANCTUARY*, had been carved into the stone at the top of the arch. A tremendous twenty-foot tall scarecrow, with a lighted pumpkin head, loomed down from the gate with an evil smirk and slanting wicked eyes. Its tattered garments covered mangled tree branch arms, which blew in the cool October breeze and beckoned brave souls to "Enter at your own risk!"

"This is it, 11538 Riverside Drive," Nigel confirmed.

There was a sudden unexpected *knock* on Darby's window, which caused everyone in the car to jump. They looked over to see the overly enthusiastic, perky, smiling faces of a young man and woman. They were both wearing matching white button down shirts, adorned with name tags, and white Bermuda shorts, a la 1978. The woman playfully gestured for Darby to roll the window down, which he did.

"Hello and welcome aboard! My name is Julie McCoy and I'll be your cruise director. And this is Gopher."

"Welcome folks," Gopher said, leaning down, waving enthusiastically into the car.

"They're from *The Love Boat*," Dustin whispered. "This is soooo trippy!"

"Can I get your name?" Julie requested, flipping back her shoulder-length feathered hair.

"My name is Darby McGregor. Miss Dufrene should be expecting us."

"McGregor," Julie mused, searching her five-page list of names. "McGregor … plus two. There you are. Great!"

"Okay, what you want to do is follow the road all the way up to the main house," Gopher chimed in. "Parking is tough, so wherever you can find a spot on the drive, take it. Also, we will be having a shuffleboard match on the Lido deck later. Hope to see you there!"

"Have fun!" Julie beamed. "Buh-bye!"

"Okay, thanks!" Darby said a bit bewildered. "Bye-bye."

Spanish moss blew gently in the soaring oak trees lining the narrow road. Darby drove through the gate and up the steep drive, covered with cars parked on either side of the road. The treetops were aglow from the colored spotlights shining up at the top of the hill. As they came around a corner, Darby abruptly stopped the car.

"Good Lord!" Nigel exclaimed. "I didn't know, Vlad the Impaler, had a summer place!"

The full harvest moon looked as though it was perched on the roof of the enormous, renaissance revival mansion, rising ominously among the trees; it was spectacular. The exterior was bathed in spooky colored lights. Incredibly ornate wrought iron cupolas spiraled high into the sky above the fourth story tower. For Darby, it was all too perfect. Here they were on their way to meet a woman who lives in this amazing old mansion and has been conversing with the dead since she was a small child. Even if it was not true, you had to admit, it was entertaining.

Parking the SUV in a grassy area a fair distance from the house, they got out and began to remove the film equipment. Darby stared up at the massive structure in the distance with awe. He was expecting a big old house, but this was more like a *castle*. He grabbed a camera and took some still shots of the house.

A track of scary sound effects; growls, screams, moans, and thunder, echoed through the night air. In the distance, he could hear muffled music and screams of laughter; the party was in full swing. As Elvis, Sid and the caveman, made their way up the drive carrying their equipment, three little kids ran down the drive past them, shrieking and giggling with delight.

"I told you that house would be cool, that's the Spook Palace … a *witch* lives there!" a little boy, dressed as Austin Powers, squealed to his friends; Darth Vader and SpongeBob.

Sheet ghosts, lit with unseen blue spotlights, hung in the trees and seemed to dance in the gentle wind. Dozens of grinning and scowling pumpkins were aglow in the yellow haze, peering out through the thick veil of fog, drifting eerily across the immense porch, which was decorated with life-size ghouls and goblins.

A skeleton-faced grim reaper, wearing a long hooded cloak, stood frozen on the porch holding a long curved sickle in his boney fingers. And a witch with neon green hair, sat motionless in a chair at the top of the porch steps, her wretched hands grasping a black cauldron full of candy on her lap.

"I've seen this before, when I was a kid. That witch is a real person," Dustin stated. "When you go up to get some candy from her cauldron, she'll grab your hand."

"Nah, they're just mannequins, you big pouf," Nigel mocked.

"Nigel, how about getting a wide shot of the porch," Darby instructed. "Dustin, go get some candy from "witchy-poo".

"What, no way dude!"

"Oh, I'm sorry, I thought you weren't scared?" Darby taunted.

"I'm not chief."

"So, go get some candy," Nigel pushed. "Come on, be a big brave bunny."

"Alright fine," Dustin said, handing Darby the microphone and sound machine pack. Nigel filmed Dustin, as he cautiously climbed the steps leading up to the spooky green witch. Her cold wrinkled eyes stared out at him menacingly from under her pointy black hat.

"Don't be scared, my pretty, I won't bite … *hard*!" Nigel called out in a scary voice.

"I'm cool, I'm good," Dustin mumbled, as he nervously walked up the steps of the porch, over to the witch. He leaned in close, waving his hands in front of its dead eyes. It didn't flinch. He then *poked* it several times with his finger, it still didn't move. "You're right, it's just a mannequin!"

"Get some candy," Darby called out to him.

"Don't mind if I do," Dustin confidently mused, quickly sneaking a Snickers bar from the witches' cauldron, smiling triumphantly. Suddenly, the reaper *swooped* down, undetected, from its perch and glided up behind Dustin. Just as Dustin turned to face Nigel and Darby, the witch suddenly reached out and grabbed Dustin's arm.

"What the hell!" he shrieked, immediately turning, running right into the arms of the reaper. As Dustin scrambled backwards, he fell to the ground. The Ghoul *growled* monstrously, looking down into his terrified eyes.

The Reaper then courteously reached out his boney hand and helped Dustin to his feet, as the witch opened the front door. They both bowed silently and motioned graciously for the guests to enter the house. It was obvious the reaper and witch were more hired entertainers for the party.

"That was so not cool man," Dustin murmured, skirting quickly by them.

"That was brilliant," Nigel said, as he bowed back to the grim greeters. They entered the house through a magnificent glass door, and walked into the vast marble paved entrance hall.

"Glorious," Darby said out loud. He was standing in the middle of the enormous foyer gazing at the wrought iron fixtures, Corinthian columns, eloquent stucco Fleur de Lys windows, and grand mahogany staircase. It was almost too much to take in.

The mansion was loud, vibrant, and most of all … *alive*. It was packed with tons of people, dressed in every imaginable costume, drinking and laughing. The air was sweet with the smell of warm pumpkin, given off from the intricately carved pumpkins glowing everywhere.

"She said, it was her *little* Halloween soiree, talk about underestimating," Darby laughed loudly over the noise, as he looked around the elaborately decorated residence. "We have permission to shoot the party, let's just go through the rooms and get whatever footage we can."

Nigel filmed the entire area, panning over the vast space and party guests. A caped and masked, *Phantom of the Opera*, sat at a vintage pipe organ in the grand entrance hall, playing a ghostly operatic tune. Zombies sluggishly moved through the rooms, moaning, and carrying platters full of appetizers and drinks.

Darby followed his map into the Palm Court, an impressive sunken room filled with gigantic palm trees and flowers from the gardens around the estate. The walls and arched doorways were made of exquisite limestone. In the middle of the beautiful mosaic tile floor stood an enormous marble fountain saturated in red light. An imposing statue of King Poseidon stood in the middle of the spouting fountain, spouting red liquid into the air, making an actual, *blood bath*. Nigel filmed the forty-foot high ceiling, covered with a dramatic stained-glass dome and massive black iron lanterns, which hung down into the forecourt, burning with fire.

Passing by a family of furry snow covered Yeti, they continued on into the packed Billiard Room. The rustic walls of exposed brick were partially covered with fabulous woven tapestries. Lush burgundy draperies flowed down from the long floor to ceiling windows. A vintage fifties, neon juke box, played classic rock n' roll songs, as guests enjoyed a game of pool. Nigel filmed a young woman wearing a sexy "little red riding hood" outfit, sitting on the lap of the big bad wolf; making out with him.

"So much for making it to Grandma's house, little red riding hood," Darby joked.

"More like little red riding *ho*," Nigel added, snickering.

"Driiinnnk?" a zombie moaned, offering drinks from his tray to people, as it slugged slowly through the room.

"This is better than I could have ever imagined," Darby stated. "It's overwhelming, like wandering through some sort of mad dream."

"Check this guy out!" said Dustin, seeing a man slowly, painstakingly, trying to make his way through the house, grasping onto furniture, people and walls. His suit was overly starched and stiff, his tie blown straight over his shoulder, his hair slicked straight back, looking like he is being blown by a massive unseen wind. As they continued down the hall, Medusa *hissed* into Nigel's camera.

Darby knew the next room they were entering was the Banquet Hall. He looked again at the map and noticed this room was also known as, "Miss Haversham's Room".

A crystal chandelier dimly lit the room, which was covered in many layers of spider web. A wrinkled old woman stood at the end of a long dining table, elaborately set with the finest china, wearing a tattered and yellowed wedding dress. She painstakingly cut pieces from her tremendous five-tier wedding cake, covered with spun sugar spider webs and chocolate spiders; decorated to look like it has been sitting there for years. Party guests stood in line to get a piece of the fabulous rotting cake.

"Come in, precious children. Have a piece of my cake," she sighed. "Cutting this cake is like cutting into my heart again, and again, and again."

Darby had noticed a number of dogs roaming freely amongst the crowd. One dog in particular, a petite black and white Border collie wearing miniature blinking red devil horns, seemed to be following him.

"Hello there, devil dog," Darby said, kneeling down to greet the dog. He looked at a tag on the dogs' collar. "Bozzy, is that your name?"

The dog *barked*, hearing her name.

"Very nice to meet you," Darby said.

The crew followed a conga line, passing from room to room. They danced through a smaller more intimate area, known as the Salon. The crew and the little dog followed them into the room where a roaring fire burned in the stone fire-place. A small crowd had gathered watching three, sheet ghosts, singing in high-pitched voices, rocking back and forth in unison.

"Spirits of the night won't you come out tonight.
Come out tonight, come out tonight.
Spirits of the night won't you come out tonight.
And dance by the light of the moon."

The ghosts finished their odd little dance, and then bowed to the applause and laughter of the audience, before literally gliding off to another room. Darby grinned, seeing roller-blades under their sheets.

"Did you get all that?" Darby asked Nigel.

"Are you kidding?" Nigel laughed. "It's like an acid trip."

"Hey!" A voice hollered over the party noise. "Over here!"

Darby noticed a cute, dead girl, wearing a long hot pink satin dress with a white sash across her chest that read, "PROM QUEEN". She was sitting in an oversized chair, flirting with Superman. A sparkling tiara sat atop her vibrantly dyed red hair and a rope noose was wrapped tightly around her bruised neck; the end of the rope sticking straight up into the air. A big smile overtook the dark purple lips on her pale-blue face. She hopped up and rushed over to them. "Y'all must be the film crew, right?"

"That pesky camera always gives us away," Nigel teased.

"I'm Chloe," she announced. "Lily's sister."

Darby was floored. From the time they entered the house, through all the sights and sounds, he had almost forgotten that this amazing party was not even what he came for. The real dessert, it hadn't been served yet.

"Nice to meet you, Chloe. I didn't realize Lily had a sister," Darby said, his mind flashing back to the information he received regarding Lillian Dufrene's past. He remembered her mother was pregnant when she tried to get rid of her "damaged children". He figured this pretty young girl must have been that baby.

"She does, it's me!"

"I'm Darby," he said, shaking her hand.

"It's very nice to meet you, Darby," Chloe beamed, biting her bottom lip coyly, obviously taken by his good looks.

"And this is ..."

"Prince, I love your music," Chloe announced with excitement.

"Prince, that's right!" Nigel played along, doing a very Prince-esque squeal. "Ahwooah!"

"Chloe, this is Nigel," Darby introduced.

"Nigel Parsons … charmed," Nigel shook her hand.

Dustin excitedly pushed through Darby and Nigel to get to the pretty girl.

"We haven't been formally introduced yet," Dustin stated in his most suave voice.

"And this rather dashing young man is …" Darby announced.

"I'm Dustin, very pleased to make your acquaintance," Dustin awkwardly kissed her pale blue hand, but Chloe could not take her eyes off of Darby. Dustin didn't care; he couldn't take his eyes off of Chloe. He whispered sweetly, "Will you marry me?"

"Nice to meet you all! God this is so neat," Chloe said loudly. "Lily's in wonderland, come on, I'll show you." They followed the dead prom queen through the massive house and into the state of the art gourmet kitchen, where a small army of chefs were busy primping enormous platters of food. Zombies momentarily left character, as they feverishly ran around the kitchen, grabbing the morsel-filled platters, and then slowly crept back out into the party.

"Mama Nadine!" Chloe called out to a charming older woman, wearing a "Mini Pearl" getup; a floral country dress and hat with the price tag dangling from the brim. The slender woman was perfectly orchestrating the fevered chaos surrounding her, when she turned around to see Chloe waving to her.

"How-Dee!" Nadine cheerfully yelled back in a thick southern drawl.

"What are you up to tonight, prom queen?" Nadine laughed, as she gave Chloe a hug. "Who are your friends?"

"Nadine, this is Darby, Nigel and Dustin. They're here to do the movie about Lily, isn't that cool?"

"Very nice to meet you, Nadine," Darby added. "It's a documentary, actually."

"Documentary … right," Chloe corrected herself, giving Darby a flirty smile. "Mama Nadine is the coolest! She takes care of us."

"And the house and the animals, the whole circus," Nadine stated sweetly. "So if there is anything you need … please y'all, don't hesitate to ask."

"Mama Nadine! Where do you want the dim sum?" a zombie called out.

"By the sushi!" Nadine chuckled. "I will be so happy to make it through this night. But Miss Lily, she has to have her Halloween shindig. Well, I have to say you're very brave young men to want to do this. Good luck with your movie! Y'all are gonna need it."

CHAPTER 7

▼

THERE IS A LIGHT

To Wonderland, a sign pointed to an enormous keyhole in the vast heavily-treed backyard. The film crew followed Chloe, as she excitedly stepped through the keyhole and walked down a path.

The little black devil dog continued to tag along with Darby; its tiny red horns blinking in the darkness. Colorful paper lanterns hung in the trees overhead, lit their way down a winding stone path, amid the perfumed flowers and plants in the immaculately coiffed gardens. Darby inhaled the sweet fragrance of weed wafting up the path and noticed some people standing in a circle sharing smoke in some remote bushes.

Moonlight sparkled off the water and seemed to dance with a symphony of frogs and crickets, echoing in the cool night air. Laughter could be heard up ahead, as they made their way down a steep flight of steps. A crowd of costumed guests had gathered on a large wooden dock overlooking the river that ran behind the house. They joined the crowd, who were standing around an enormous mushroom.

It was dark, except for some unseen black lights, which shined up from under the mushroom, lighting the vibrant colorful swirls and swishes painted wildly all over it. The sight reminded Darby of an old psychedelic velvet poster from the seventies.

The crowd was listening to a story being told by a girl sitting atop the mushroom, reading from an over-sized book. She was wearing a light blue dress with a white apron tied around her wait, and black satin ribbon, which lay neatly in her long blonde hair. A striped cat lounged sleepily on her lap. Darby felt all the light seemed to be focused on the girl, or was the light coming from her? It was hard to tell; she was simply luminous, shining like a vibrant supernova. He smiled knowingly, without a doubt, this girl was *Lily*.

He finally realized, the "who are you" on the phone was from "Alice in Wonderland". Lily was being the "Caterpillar". He laughed; he had not been quick enough to catch the joke. Lily was older than he had anticipated. He had watched the video so many times he thought of her as a young girl. But she was no longer the little girl from the video … she was a beautiful full-grown woman.

As they walked closer, Darby motioned for Nigel and Dustin to film Lily. Nigel moved closer and set the camera upon her, as Dustin quickly held out a microphone. Darby stood in the back of the crowd, the devil-dog plopped down beside him.

"It was all very curious I must say, more and more curious," Lily spoke, a la Alice. "A few minutes later, Joe and his date arrived. He showed the pretty girl in the pale pink dress into the front hall. She looked at all the bouquets of fresh flowers. Joe took a rose from one of the vases and handed it to her. She sniffed the silky red flower, inhaling its scent."

"They were from yesterday," Joe explained. "It was old Mrs. Clarke's funeral."

"Oh," replied the girl, remembering where she was. Joe ushered her into the front parlor and said, "You can wait for me in here."

"The girl looked around the room and saw what she was hoping she wouldn't; a *coffin*."

"It's empty," Joe said, noticing her apprehension. "There is nothing to be afraid of."

"I don't want to be late," said the girl.

We won't, I promise. I told my folks I would lock up the house while they were out of town. I just have to get a key from the basement."

"Can't I go with you?" she asked.

"The embalming room is in the basement. It's dirty and smells really bad. Just relax, have a seat, I'll be right back."

"Promise?"

"I promise," he smiled sweetly, giving her a quick peck on the cheek. She watched him disappear through the basement door and sat down on a big couch by a window. The sun was just setting. She smelled the rose again, and then smoothed her taffeta dress down with her hands. It was the most beautiful dress she had ever worn. She studied the tiny flower appliqués sewn into the waist, and then took two tickets out of her handbag."

Oakridge High School—Senior Class Dance
Crystal Moon Ball—1955
8 PM School Gymnasium—Formal Dress Required.

"She smiled at the thought of what lay ahead that night. She was very surprised that Joe even asked her to the dance. She thought he didn't even know she was alive. He was handsome, popular, and rather persuasive. Surely, she would be seen by all her friends. And wouldn't Sue Carver and the other girls be so jealous. The thought made her happy. Of course, they would dance and, hopefully, slow dance. She wondered if tonight would be the night she finally had her first *real kiss*, maybe? She put the tickets back in her bag and took out a tube of lipstick and small mirror. She applied a pink hue to her lips and rubbed them together, pleased with her refection. She looked pretty and more important, she felt pretty. The girl sat quietly for a few moments. But she couldn't help herself; from under her dark curled bangs, she peered at the shiny grey coffin looming in the corner."

"*BANG!* She heard a noise come from, what sounded like, the coffin."

"Hello?"

"Another *BANG!* The girl squeaked, jumping to her feet."

"Is someone there, Joe?" she whispered. There was no answer. She could have sworn when she first looked at the coffin the lid was closed. It was now, *open.* Curiosity got the best of her; she knew she shouldn't but … maybe just a little peek. Across the dimly lit room she crept, her heart racing. She saw a pale hand, then a face; she gasped. There *was* a body in the satin-lined box, a boy about her age. He was nice-looking, wearing a black suit and tie, lying motionless, arms folded across his chest."

"You look like you're … asleep," she said softly to the boy, looking down at his pale white pallor. "Why did someone so young have to die?"

"Suddenly, the boys eyes shot open, and he smiled up at her with a frightening grin."

"How's about a kiss?" he hissed, reaching up and *kissing* her hard on the lips. The girl in the pale pink dress screamed, backing away from the coffin in horror, as the corpse boy rose from the wooden box. "What's a matter, don't you think I'm handsome?"

"He sneered, swiftly hopping out of the coffin, walking toward her. She tried to run, but hit a chair and fell. The dead boy stood over her. "Come be with me … in my grave."

"Nooooooo!" she screamed again, pushing him off; her eyes were wide like a frightened cat. The corpse boy got up and began to walk after her, arms out-stretched, a cold stare in his dead eyes. The girl ran to the front door; it was locked, bolted shut. She looked over her shoulder and saw him slowly coming after her, sheer panic registered on her face. The girl saw the basement door and frantically ran over to it."

"JOE! HELP ME!" she cried out.

"Wait!" the corpse boy laughed, calling after her. "It's just a joke ... WAIT!"

"But it was too late. The girl hurled the basement door open and bolted through at a full run. She had fallen head first down the lengthy flight of wooden steps, to the concrete floor below. The sounds coming from the basement were horrible; a short stifled *scream,* followed by loud blunt banging thuds. Then, complete *silence.*"

"Where is she?" Joe laughed, coming out from the kitchen, seeing the horri-fied look on the corpse boys' face. "Robert, what happened?"

"I don't know."

"Where is she?" he asked, again.

"Down there ... in the basement."

"What are you talking about? What have you done?"

"Nothing, I tried to stop her, but she wouldn't listen!"

"The brothers stood at the top of the basement stairs, looking down into the darkness. Joe tried to turn the light switch on, but it didn't work. He quickly got a flashlight from the pantry and shined the light down the steps. All they could see was a heap of pink crinoline, covered in dark red blotches, lying crumpled at the bottom of the stairs. The boys just stared at the ever-expanding puddle of blood flowing from the girl's head, like a crimson halo. The girl in the pale pink dress was ... dead."

"What should we do?" Robert asked.

"I don't know, just shut up, let me think!"

"Maybe we should call somebody?"

"No, we can't. Do you know what will happen to us if anyone ever finds out about this? It was your stupid idea! I told you it wasn't a good idea."

"You are such a liar! You wanted to do this as much as I did!"

"Fine, I did, but it was just a joke. It's not our fault, it was an accident."

"We need to call someone!"

"NO! I'm starting college in the fall. Look, nobody knew I was taking her to the dance. I told her not to tell so it would be a big surprise. We have no choice; we need to get *rid of her.*"

"They truly felt it wasn't their fault the girl died. It was just a joke, just a great prank they could tell their buddies about the next day at school. In retrospect, the boys thought they were being terribly clever. They thought they had every little thing worked out; nothing could go wrong, boy ... were they wrong.

They dragged the girls' lifeless body across the basement to the embalming table, lifted it onto the stainless steel table, and turned on the bright fluorescent light above. They quickly looked away from the horrible sight of the girl; her arms and legs were obviously broken, her lips blue, teeth missing. Her body was stiffening, her glazed eyes staring out into space. Joe had turned as white as the baby powder on his brother's face. The boys cleaned the body with disinfectant. Joe took charge. He had never preformed the bloodletting process, but had assisted his father a hundred times before. With shaky hands, Joe began to cut the girls skin with a sharp scalpel. A shot of blood, hit his cheek. For a split second, he could have sworn he saw her eyes *dart* over and look at him. He froze."

"What's wrong?" Robert asked.

"Nothing ... just shut up and let me do this!"

"After draining her blood, Joe began again, making small incisions on the right side of the girls' lower neck into two arteries. He attached the tube connected to the embalming fluid pump and formaldehyde began to push into her body. The boys cleaned everything, including themselves. They changed clothes and carried the body upstairs and placed it in the grey coffin they had used to play their prank."

"The sun had risen on a new day, as they put the coffin on a gurney and wheeled it out to a hearse that was sitting in the drive. It was Joe's regular job to drive the bodies to the cemetery. He had all the proper paperwork filled out, and everyone at the cemetery knew him. He was the mortician's son; no one ever questioned him. He gave the instructions ... and a *Jane Doe* was buried. That was that ... they got away with murder."

The crowd of party guests sat in stunned silence.

"That happened here in this house?" a pirate asked.

"Indeed, this house was used as a funeral parlor during World War II and for some years afterward," Lily stated. "Joe and Robert were my father's brothers, making them my uncles. And did you know ... those naughty boys were never caught."

"Come on, that's bullshit!" the pirate stated.

"How do you know exactly what happened?" a mermaid questioned, skeptically.

"Why the girl in the pale pink dress told me, of course. If you don't believe me, go ask her yourself," Lily said, innocently blinking her eyes. "She's in the basement, still awaiting that first kiss."

The crowd either, laughed or gasped, at Lily's story; regardless if they believed it or not, they were entertained and applauded her enthusiastically. Darby jumped up on a wooden bench, filming Lily with his handheld camera from the back of the crowd, as she chatted with friends and gave hugs. A few party guests wanted to have their pictures taken with "Alice" on the mushroom, which she happily obliged.

For some reason, amid all the activity around her, Lily casually turned her head and looked right at Darby. This surprised him. Out of the large crowd of people surrounding her, she looked right at him, nodded and smiled sweetly. It was as if she was saying, "Hello, I know you are here", without ever having said a word. He smiled back and gave a slight wave … he couldn't wait to get into her head.

"Darby, come meet Lily," Chloe said, pulling him over to the base of the mushroom. "Lily, this is …"

"The infamous, Darby McGregor," Lily announced formally, reaching down to shake his hand. "We meet at last."

"Yes, I've heard so much about you," Darby said, firmly grasping her hand.

"Oh Lord, please don't let that frighten you," Lily laughed. "Well, I guess it hasn't, you're here, right?"

"Right," Darby said, looking up into Lily's large green eyes. It was at that very moment Darby felt something he hadn't felt in a while; a strong attraction to another human being. It was an extraordinary feeling to have such an instantaneous bond with a complete stranger. But for the first time, Lily really felt like a real person to him. She was no longer the ethereal child dancing in the woods, illuminated with magical lights.

"I see you've met my Bozzy," Lily said, seeing the small black dog at Darby's side.

"Yes, she's been following me for the past hour," Darby added.

"I told her to go find you … and she did."

"She sure did!" Darby admitted, amazed. Nigel loudly cleared his throat, getting Darby's attention. "Oh right, let me introduce you to the crew. This is Elvis!"

"I knew you weren't dead," Lily smiled at Nigel, as she slid down off the mushroom and gently placed the cat on the ground.

"Otherwise known as, Nigel," Darby continued. "Cameraman extraordinaire."

"Nigel ... Elvis, very nice to meet you," Lily nodded.

"Thank you ... thank you very much," Nigel sneered, doing his best Elvis impersonation.

"You throw a tremendous party, Miss Dufrene!" Nigel complimented her.

"Please, call me Lily."

"And this is Dustin," Darby added. "He'll be handling sound."

"Hi. Hey, that story about the girl in the pink dress, is that true?" Dustin asked Lily.

"You seem like a brave guy, Dustin," Lily teased. "Why don't you go find out?"

Nigel raised his eyebrows to Darby.

"I'm cool, I'm good," Dustin assured, shaking Lily's hand. "I'll take your word for it."

"Y'all don't have any drinks?" Lily noticed. "Chloe, our guests do not have drinks."

"Well we must do something about that! Come on!" Chloe exclaimed, grabbing Lily's arm, motioning for the others to follow. "We must get drinks!"

Darby followed behind Lily, filming her scurrying up the winding stone footpath, illuminated by dim-colored lanterns hanging in the trees. Wearing her blue *Alice* dress and black Patten leather shoes, it really felt to Darby like he was following Alice through wonderland. Lily was so extraordinary to him, so confident and outgoing ... he simply couldn't take his eyes off her. She was like no other female, no other *human being*, he had ever met. He wanted to know everything about her.

A fine fog drifted across the old decaying graveyard, where a few boney skeletons appeared to be clawing up from the depths of their graves; the back lawn behind the mansion had also been decorated, as realistically as any cemetery.

Lily held court amongst the crumbling mausoleums and gravestones, sitting beneath enormous oak trees, lit with eerie green lights.

"Zombie, come to me, bring me your poisons!" Lily spoke dramatically, enticing a zombie carrying a tray of shot glasses to come over. She handed small shot glasses out to a group of party-goers, and then raised her glass high.

"Nastrovya!" she toasted.

"Nastrovya!" they toasted back.

"Prost!" Lily called out.

"Prost!" the crowd called back and everyone drank.

"You're not drunk yet, Darby McGregor," Lily teased. "I don't understand, I thought you English liked to drink."

"We do actually," Darby admitted.

"Then let me get you a *real* drink. Excuse me, Zombie," Lily called out to a passing zombie, who obeyed and slugged over carrying a tray of frozen shot glasses, filled with 100-proof Rumple Mintz liqueur. She took a drink from the tray and passed it to Darby, before snagging one for herself. Darby took one swallow; his face cringed from the icy burn.

"Good Lord, that is strong! How can something this cold, burn so much? What is this?"

"The nectar of the Gods," Lily laughed, clinking her glass against his. Just as they finished the potent drinks, Lily grabbed two more and again handed Darby one. "Compai!"

"Compai," Darby quivered, as he quickly swallowed the liquid.

"Last one," Lily said, handing him another. "I promise."

"You're mad!" Darby laughed.

"Funny," Lily stated, without missing a beat. "I've heard that before. Mazel Tov!"

Lily smiled, tilting the bottom of his glass with her finger, forcing him to finish the drink.

"Lillian Dufrene, are you trying to get me drunk?"

"Why good sir," Lily responded in a deep southern drawl and cheeky smile. "I would never think to do such a thing."

"Lily, we should head back to the hotel," Darby said, feeling the alcohol beginning to kick in. "Before one of us, I mean, none of us, can drive."

"Nope, y'all are going to stay put. I had Nadine set it all up."

"Lily, that's very nice, but …"

"But nothin', the whole third floor is empty, and I have a special room all picked out especially for you. I thought it would help you with your film."

"Really?"

"I generally don't take *no* for an answer."

Darby wouldn't have said no to Lily if his life depended on it. If she had told him to go jump into a pit of fire, he most likely would have. He was enthralled, like a young boy with a schoolyard crush; he hung on her every word and every movement. Something about her emanated "goodness". It was just something he felt when looking into her eyes. She seemed blessed with the ability to make everyone around her feel welcome.

Lily reminded Darby of a little girl trapped in a grown woman's body. Like a female version of Peter Pan, she might have just refused to grow up or never had the chance to be a child and was making up for lost time. Whatever the case, he was just pleased to be in her presence.

"Stay here, we would love it!" Nigel excitedly jumped up and down, like a little kid.

"Um … but," Dustin said, not pleased, not wanting to stay in the house where the girl in the pale pink dress died.

"Besides, this is the busiest time of the year for us," Lily smiled sweetly. "And I mean, I am your subject. I would think you should stay as close to me as possible."

The high proof liquor flowing through Darby's veins made him feel almost giddy. He couldn't wipe the silly smile off his face, if he even knew there was a silly smile on his face. Darby wondered, in his tipsy state, if Lily was flirting with him. She sure seemed to be. He was trying to act cool, but everything was becoming blurred. It was the first time in many months he actually enjoyed a drink and was not using it to numb himself.

"So you filmed the party, yes?" Lily asked.

"We got some incredible footage," Nigel informed her.

"Okay then, you are now officially off the clock. Y'all are my guests … its fun time!"

"But …" Darby started to speak.

"No buts," Lily instructed, grabbing more shots from a zombie's tray. "More drinks!"

"I think…." Darby laughed, losing his thought, thoroughly enjoying his buzz. "Oh what the hell, one more couldn't hurt, I suppose."

"Good for you!" Lily egged him on. "We'll have such fun!"

"Hey, guess what I am?" A loud voice called over the crowd. Everyone turned to see a ruggedly handsome guy with shoulder-length brown hair, walking out into the yard from the back of the house. He was wearing a black velvet vest and weathered leather pants with a large gold belt buckle, reminiscent of Jim Morrison. He held up a bottle of Jack Daniels in one hand and a bottle of Jose Cuervo in the other. "An ALCOHOLIC!"

"DAVE!" a few partygoers called out to him.

"Dave! How's it hangin'?" a guy in a ninja costume yelled.

"Low and to the left, my brother, low and to the left," Dave shamelessly laughed, as he sauntered through the crowd. Obviously very well liked, he shook hands and hugged friends. A giggling red-head, wearing a grass skirt and bikini top, barely covering her ample breasts, hung intoxicated on his arm.

"Dave, Dave!" Chloe called out to him. "Come here!"

Dave saw Chloe waving to him through the crowd and headed over.

"Hey, what's up?" Dave grinned; taking a puff on a cigar perched between his fingers.

"How are you?" Chloe asked.

"I got my two best friends here, Jack and Jose, and we are here to cause a little havoc!" Dave proclaimed, giving Chloe a hug and kiss on the cheek. "How ya doin', hot dead prom queen?"

Dave then turned his attention to Lily.

"Lillian."

"David."

"Fabulous party, as always," he said graciously, before checking out her costume. "And yes, there is a wonderland in Alice!"

"Nice," Lily quipped.

Dave gave Darby a *look*, then nodded to him. Darby nodded back, the silent "guy nod" of respect. He could feel the strong tension between them and they had just met. There was something about this guy Darby instantly took a dislike to.

"Y'all doin' a little … porn later?" Dave asked, eyeing Nigel's camera.

"This is the film crew," Lily explained. "The ones doing the documentary, remember?"

"I thought you were kidding," Dave admitted, taking a swig of tequila.

"No, actually, we'll be following you around for the next few weeks," Darby stated.

"Well, lucky us," Dave quietly snarled. He then looked over at Nigel. "Just so you know, RuPaul, I photograph better from the right side."

Dave leaned over and respectfully hugged and kissed Lily on the cheek.

"Behave David," Lily whispered to him.

"They'll never make it, Lillian," Dave whispered back.

"Let me worry about them, David."

"Oh, I never worry Lillian, you know that."

"I see you finally made it with Melissa, the inflatable sex doll. Good for you!"

"Am I sensing a little catty jealousy?"

"Not quite."

Lily broke their quick embrace and secret discussion.

"If you all will excuse me, I have a little … grass to cut," Dave stated, reaching under the hula-girls short green skirt, grabbing her bottom.

"Davey stop!" the hula-girl giggled, her bosoms bouncing.

As Dave walked away, he glanced at Lily, and then gave Darby one more sharp look. Darby held his ground, watching Dave disappear into the crowd of party-goers.

"Sorry, he's a bit of a … well, he can be a bit of an ass," Lily turned to Darby and smiled. "There is no excuse for him really, especially when he's been drinking. All I can say is he really is a good guy; he always has my back and always will."

"Seems like a lovely chap," Darby said sarcastically.

"Excellent!" Lily excitedly clapped her hands, hearing the opening guitar chords to a song begin. "The band is starting, come on!"

With that, Alice from Wonderland, grabbed Sid from London's arm, and pulled him into the massive house, through the crazed rooms and hallways, until they arrived in the Ballroom.

Darby stopped at the door, looking around the incredible room and balcony. Crystal chandeliers flickered dimly, reflecting off the shining gilded gold leaf ceiling. A full bar was manned by a crew of devils and demons with black feather wings. The night's specialty, vodka martinis with a few drops of grenadine blood.

The vampire band, Ana Black, played the gothic anthem, "Bela Lugosis' Dead" to a packed crowd of costumed friends and fiends. The light show around the stage was hypnotic.

Darby watched Lily run into the crowd and dance to the intense driving rhythm. In his drunken state, everyone else seemed to just *disappear*. It was as if they were completely alone in the massive ballroom. As she danced, Lily appeared to change before his eyes. Soft glowing orbs circled around her, enveloping her in their golden light, as they had when she was a young girl. Her Alice costume changed into a long billowy dress, which flowed and fluttered with each move she made. Darby gazed at her, mesmerized. She didn't seem from this world. She was like an otherworldly being to him; untouchable, unattainable, unreal. But there she was … a real flesh and blood woman.

Lily turned to look at Darby, catching his gaze. He quickly snapped out of his daydream and smiled at her. He simply couldn't help himself, since the day he first saw her he had become a bit obsessed. Lily danced over to Darby, leaned in close and whispered in his ear.

"I'm glad you came here. I really want you to see that I'm ..." Lily was stopped mid-sentence, as the song ended and a bright spotlight focused on her.

"Let's all raise our goblets," the fanged singer toasted, holding his glass high. "To our ghostess, Miss Lillian Dufrene!"

The crowd applauded. Lily curtsied graciously and then was escorted up onto the stage.

"Happy Halloween, everyone," Lily beamed. "Thank you all for coming!"

The band broke into a rousing version of the *Rocky Horror* classic, "Time Warp". Darby watched Lily sing and dance on the stage to the cheers of the crowd, truly enjoying herself and enjoying the happiness on her guests' faces. She reminded him of a modern-day Holly Golightly.

Looking around the ballroom at the crowd of costumed revelers, Darby laughed, seeing real people and fictitious characters, from different worlds and different eras, all mingling together, if only for a night. It was all so wonderfully surreal. He watched Nigel jump up on the stage to dance with Lily and others. Dustin was sitting on a large sofa, deep in discussion with Albert Einstein, Buddha, and Madonna, during her "Blonde Ambition" era.

Darby thought he would start to come out of his alcohol-induced haze, but instead he felt like the liquor and jet-lag were finally catching up to him. He was dizzy, light-headed. He hadn't had that feeling in a while, but he knew that feeling well ... he was officially drunk.

Making his way out of the ballroom, Darby ventured down a vast arched hallway adorned with elaborate gothic tapestries, hanging under a row of crystal chandeliers, glowing with flickering light. Darby felt the entire house seem to tilt, he held onto the walls for support. The sad melody, "Nearer my God to Thee", was being played in the middle of the hallway by a doomed and shivering, *string quartet*. Their faces blue and frozen, wearing tuxedos under bulky white life vests that read: RMS TITANIC.

"Would you gentlemen know where I might find ... a restroom?" Darby asked.

"Excuse me sir, but you really should be getting to a lifeboat," the violin player responded in a thick Irish accent, never missing a note. "It's not safe."

"Right, thank you," Darby said, continuing down the hall. Remembering the map of the house stashed in his pocket, he pulled it out and located one of the bathrooms on the first floor. "Thank God."

Something made Darby look up through his drunken haze. He saw the outline of a *ghostly bride* in a long shimmering gown, dancing down the hallway towards him. She was backlit, a vision in white with a long flowing veil. To

Darby, she moved *slowly*, as everything else seemed to move so fast. He felt a slight tinge of fright shoot through his body like an electric shock; his face felt hot, his hands were sweaty. He dropped the map and slowly slid down the wall, as she drew near. The bride looked down at him, reaching out, placing her hand on his shoulder. He reached up and touched her wrist; she was warm, solid, *alive*. Darby realized she was just a girl, just a girl in a costume.

"Are you alright?" the bride asked.

"I'm, fine," he stammered. The bride smiled and danced off into the ballroom with her friends. The incident brought Darby right back to reality. It was a grim reminder as to why he had made this trip.

Holding onto the bathroom sink, Darby splashed some cold water on his face, hoping to come out of his alcohol-induced stupor. He looked into the mirror and laughed at his "vicious" punk rock reflection. Then a flash of *red* caught his eye. He jumped in sudden horror, and then shook his head with a relieved grin and sigh, seeing a few mannequin heads floating in the tub. Obviously, no indulgence had been spared for this party.

Darby took off his leather jacket and wandered back out to the backyard, which by this time was much quieter, as most of the guests were in the ballroom. He laid down among the misty gravestones. The grass felt so cool and a wonderful breeze had picked up. Looking up at the moon peeking through the moss-laden trees above, he heard the soft whistle of a distant train. He closed his tired eyes.

"Taking a siesta?" Darby heard a soft voice ask. He opened his eyes and saw Lily's sister, Chloe, sitting down on the grass next to him. "Party too much for ya?"

"I think I'm, a bit pissed out of my skull," he said, trying to stand up but failing miserably and falling back onto the grass. "Maybe, I better stay down."

"I'll take you to bed," Chloe stood, offering her hand, while looking down at Darby with a mischievous grin. "Come with me."

Chloe held tightly onto Darby's arm, as they made their way through the crowded party into the kitchen. They passed a young couple dressed as, Lucy and Desi, who were peeking down through the basement door at the long wooden staircase.

"Such a long way she fell," Lucy stated. "It gives me the creeps!"

Darby and Chloe continued into the entrance hall, where they entered the brass elevator.

"So … do you have a girlfriend?" Chloe asked.

"Girlfriend? No … nope."

The elevator stopped on the third floor. Chloe led Darby down a lengthy darkened hallway lined with paintings. He stopped briefly, looking up at one of the paintings, really looking at the abstract picture and signature.

"This is a Picasso?"

"Yep."

"This is a *real* Picasso, it's signed! And that's a Norman Rockwell."

"Come on, we're almost there."

"Chloe, tell me, that Dave fellow, were he and your sister an item?"

"Yep, since high school, but it didn't work out, he couldn't handle it, said 'three was a crowd."

"Three?"

"Here we are," Chloe announced, opening the door to one of the dark rooms and led Darby in. He immediately stumbled and fell onto the bed. Chloe conveniently fell on top of him. "Oooopppsie, I slipped."

"You'll have to excuse me," Darby apologized. "I think, I may be smashed."

"Oh yeah, you are," Chloe laughed, her blue lips only inches from his. "I like your accent, very James Bond."

"Thank you."

Chloe just continued to look at him, smiling.

"And I like your hair," she said, touching his spiky locks.

"Chloe, I don't mean to be rude, but I think, perhaps, I should get some sleep," Darby said politely. "It was a long flight and …"

"I get the hint," she said.

Just then, Mama Nadine entered the room and turned on a small light on the side table, paying no attention to Chloe and Darby on the bed.

"Alright, Miss Chloe, get off him. Leave the boy alone."

"I was just leaving."

"Yes, you were," Mama Nadine added.

"Nighty-night, don't let the bed bugs bite," Chloe smiled, slowly walking to the door.

"Goodnight, Chloe," Darby said, trying to steady himself.

"*Goodbye*, Chloe," Mama Nadine pressed. Chloe disappeared through the door. "That girl is boy crazy. If it has an X chromosome, she's interested."

"We weren't …"

"Don't worry, Mr. Darby, I didn't think you were," the older woman laughed. "Miss Lily asked me to check on you, tuck you in."

"That's very nice, but I'm …"

Before he could finish his thought, Nadine pulled his shirt off over his head, like he was a little boy getting ready for bed. She then reached for the belt buckle on his jeans.

"I got it," he said, quickly taking off his pants, leaving him standing in his underwear.

"Let's get you some fresh air," Mama Nadine said, opening one of the tall windows in the room. The sheer drapes rose and fell in the cool night breeze. She then pulled down the sheets. "Into bed you go, Mr. Darby."

Darby got under the covers and Mama Nadine, in her motherly way, tightly tucked the sheets under him. She kissed her hand and touched his forehead.

"Now, you get a good night sleep. If you need anything, don't be shy, help yourself. Brunch will be served at eleven o'clock sharp in the Palm Court. Goodnight, Mr. Darby."

"Thank you, Nadine. Goodnight."

Mama Nadine turned off the light and closed the door, leaving Darby alone in the unfamiliar dark room. He could still hear the melodic eerie drone of the vampire band, faintly from downstairs. The music was swimming through his head, strange and dreamy. He closed his eyes and laid still. After a few seconds the bed began to feel like it was spinning. The alcohol that saturated his body made him feel warm, too warm to be tucked so tightly in the bed. He felt like he was in a cocoon. Wrestling with the sheets, he kicked them off and lay back down. The bed was soft and comfortable, he nestled into the cushy down mattress, totally relaxed, but his mind would not shut off.

A myriad of *visions* went through Darby's mind, as he watched the shadows from the great oak trees blowing around outside the windows, dance across the wall and ceiling. The shadows cast upon the walls formed into the sheet-ghosts, he saw earlier that night, singing in high-pitched voices, their macabre Halloween carol.

> *"Spirits of the night won't you come out tonight.*
> *Come out tonight, come out tonight.*
> *Spirits of the night won't you come out tonight.*
> *And dance by the light of the moon."*

Darby's mouth formed a silly drunken grin; while he watched the ghosts do their little dance on the wall above and then float off. A vision of Lily in her *Alice* dress, sitting atop the psychedelic mushroom, smiling at him, then graced the wall. Darby wanted nothing more than to get out of bed to join her in the party, but he could barely lift his head. He was fearful that if he fell asleep, he would awake in the morning in his own bed, and the whole night would have been just a dream. But it was no use, he couldn't fight it; his eyes slowly closed and he just gave in to the spinning bed, falling fast asleep, happily falling down the rabbit hole.

A sharp clap of thunder woke Darby from his sound sleep. He opened his eyes and saw the drapes in his room flying wildly in the brisk wind that had kicked up outside. He quickly jumped out of bed and closed the window, yet he could still hear the wind softly whistling through the windowpanes. In a gentle flash of lightning that brightened the room, he saw a singed and tattered "Snoopy" stuffed toy sitting up on a shelf. He went over to examine it, sniffing its musty smoky scent. He put the toy back up on the shelf and sat down on the bed.

A small clock on the night stand read; three-fifteen. Darby's mouth was dry; he was dying of thirst and would kill for a glass of milk. Putting on his shirt and jeans, he ventured into the hallway. The house was now quiet and dark, the party obviously over. He wished he had held onto the map of the house, but he thought he could at least find his way to the kitchen.

"I should have left myself a trail of crumbs," he mused, making his way through the darkness of the hallway that seemed to go on forever. Once he passed the Picasso, he knew he was on the right track and could already taste the cold milk in his mouth. Down the three flights of stairs and through the open entrance hall he walked, finally arriving in the dimly lit, completely cleaned, kitchen.

He spotted the massive stainless steel refrigerator. As he started toward it, he heard *footsteps* coming up the basement stairs and saw a sliver of light under the closed door. He watched as the light went out and the door opened. All he could see was a shadow—the outline of a female wearing a pouffy dress. He panicked, his mind raced. Was this girl in the pale pink dress from Lily's story? The girl who came to such a dreadful end down those stairs? It was supposed to be a true story, and after the past few weeks, not much would surprise him. Darby felt his nose tickle, and as hard as he tried, he couldn't stop himself; he let out a soft *sneeze*.

"Bless you," the shadow whispered. Suddenly the lights in the kitchen turned on illuminating Lily, who was standing by the light switch, still in her *Alice* costume, holding a few bottles of wine. She put the bottles on the counter and looked curiously at Darby's terrified face. "Oh, I'm sorry, did I scare you?"

"No, no. Yes, yes! You scared the tosh right out of me," he laughed, relieved. "For a second, I thought you were the girl from your story, the one that died in the basement."

"Her name was Anna."

"Anna, right."

"What are you doing up this ungodly hour?"

"I was going to get a glass of milk, trying to stop what might potentially be a rather wicked hangover."

"Wicked hangover, huh? Here, have a seat. I'll make you a secret family concoction, guaranteed to stop even the wicked of hangovers. It's called a … Nasty-Nasty! It's so you don't look nasty and feel nasty the next morning."

Darby sat on a stool at the large marble island, situated in the middle of the kitchen. He watched Lily pull the magical ingredients out of the refrigerator, put them into a blender and whip them all together. She poured the unusual mixture into two tall glasses, handing one to Darby and drinking the other one herself. Darby took a swallow; it was surprisingly sweet.

"That's actually pretty good, thank you," he said with surprise, licking his lips. "I overdid it last night. I think my drinking days are numbered."

"Always do sober what you say you're going to do drunk. That will teach you to keep your mouth shut," Lily smiled. "Ernest Hemingway. That's one of my all-time favorite quotes."

"I always liked, 'Life is what happens to you, while you're busy making other plans.'

"Ah, John Lennon, a classic," Lily said. "How about, "I knew when we met … an adventure was to begin."

"Hmmm, don't think I know that one."

"Winnie the Pooh."

"A-ha ha! You know I can't top, Winnie the Pooh!" Darby laughed out loud. "Lily, I really want to thank you for agreeing to let me into …"

"The demented fairytale that is my life."

"Yes," Darby grinned. "Actually, I'm really looking forward to seeing what you see."

"I think you may have already seen what I see, Darby. I think that may be why you're here. Well, I need to at least attempt to get some sleep. Tomorrow is always a busy day for us. Actually, from this point on we are usually on the road. We have a bus. I hate to go anywhere in a plane; it reminds me of a flying coffin. I'm a big scaredy cat when it comes to flying, but I'll do it if I must."

"I know … I did my homework on you."

"Really?" she mused, adding. "I did my homework on you, too."

"Touché," Darby said with a raised eyebrow, caught off guard. "Can I ask you a question? Is that a true story? Did a girl really fall down those stairs to her death?"

There is a pause between them, then Lily gave him a sly smile.

"Goodnight, Darby."

"Goodnight, Lily."

As Lily turned to leave the kitchen, she stopped and opened the basement door, slightly.

"Goodnight, Anna," Lily whispered into the darkness, then closed the basement door and walked off into the night.

"Clever," Darby said amused, shaking his head. "Clever."

CHAPTER 8

▼

FIXING A HOLE

"Mr. Darby!" a voice with a distinct southern accent, boomed through the room. Darby shot straight up in bed, half-asleep. He shielded his eyes from the rays of brilliant sunlight bursting through the window like a spotlight.

"Hello," he grunted, looking for the source of the voice.

"Are you awake, Mr. Darby?"

He recognized the voice; it was Mama Nadine's, and she was speaking through an intercom on the wall by the bed.

"I think so," he spoke aloud.

"Well, good morning, Mr. Darby, this is your wake up call! Your bags have been placed outside your door. It's almost eleven; brunch is being served in the Palm Court."

"Thank you, I'll be right down," he answered politely. Darby sat on the small single bed and realized he didn't have a headache; in fact, he felt amazing. It was the first truly good night's sleep he had had in months. Lily's magic "Nasty-Nasty" hangover potion must have done the trick. Darby opened the door to the room and brought his luggage in from the hall. There were two other doors in the room. The first door turned out to be a closet, the other, a full bathroom. He quickly jumped into the shower, happy to get the stiff "punker" gel out of his hair.

After his much-needed shower, Darby dressed and took a closer look around at the room. It was the first time he really got to see where he was. The small room seemed out of place with the rest of the modernized ritzy house. It looked like a room belonging to a little girl, a room that had been frozen in time. Lavender wallpaper, featuring budding flowers, lined the walls. A bookcase held an audience of stuffed toys. Darby also noticed a framed picture of two children—a little boy and a little girl, hugging each other in a huge pile of leaves, big smiles on their faces. He assumed they must be Lily and her twin brother Tyler, when they were about five.

There was a soft scratching on his door. Darby opened it cautiously. Sitting in the hallway was Lily's dog, Bozzy. She wagged her tail excitedly and barked seeing him.

"Okay, okay ... I'm coming."

Darby smelled the wonderful aromas of breakfast greet him as he walked into the sunken solarium filled with towering palm trees. The stained-glass windows in the enormous atrium flooded the room with warm light, while its grand King Poseidon fountain still spouted red water. Nigel, Dustin and Chloe were already sitting at a table filled with platters of breakfast foods.

"Good morning, Darby," Chloe said, jumping up and giving him a big hug.

"Chloe wow, your hair really is that red! It's lovely," Darby exclaimed with a grin, as he touched her shockingly bright hair. "Thank you for helping me crash last night. I owe ya."

"I'll remember that," Chloe chirped. "Take a seat, have some breakfast."

Darby took a seat between Chloe and Nigel.

"This food is incredible," Nigel beamed. "Try the cinnamon buns, to die for."

"I trust you had a good night?" Darby asked Nigel.

"Fucking-fantastic, I had the best time. What a party, eh? You missed the burning of the witch, it was hysterical."

"I'm afraid I was a tad ... wasted," Darby mused. He then looked over at Dustin, who looked exhausted, as he picked at his stack of pancakes. "How did you sleep, Dustin?"

"Any visits from dead girls in pale pink taffeta?" Nigel added with a snicker.

"Yeah, ha ha, very funny," Dustin stated, unamused. "I didn't sleep at all."

"Where's Lily?" Darby inquired.

"Lily's a true insomniac. She's kind of like a bat, up most of the night and asleep most of the day," Chloe informed him.

"Well, good morning, Mr. Darby," Mama Nadine said with a grin, as she walked down the steps into the room, offering him a warm biscuit. "How did you sleep?"

"You know, I slept great. Better than I have in quite some time."

"Nobody has slept in Miss Lily's childhood bedroom for years," Mama Nadine stated. "I was surprised when she suggested you sleep in there. It's been closed off for some time."

"I slept just fine. I did get up at about three for a drink. It was funny, I just knew I was to have a terrible hangover today, but Lily was up and she made me this concoction called a ..."

"Nasty-Nasty, sickeningly sweet, but will kill any hangover," Dave stated, as he casually sauntered barefoot, down the steps into the room, wearing a pair of old faded jeans and an unbuttoned motorcycle shirt. "Good morning campers! Are you ready for your first day of fun activities?"

"Activities?" Dustin questioned, shoveling a cinnamon bun into his mouth.

"That's right, Spicoli. We already received an email full of fun photos that look to be authentic. We need to be on the road soon, so when y'all are done filling your faces, meet me in the stable."

Dave kissed Chloe's head, grabbed a few strips of bacon, belched, and walked off.

"All charm, that young man," Nigel scoffed. "All charm."

Just a short stroll from the main house stood the original horse stable. Darby, Nigel and Dustin could hear the loud melodic guitar chords of *Led Zeppelin's*, "Kashmir" as they came to the end of the winding cobblestone path. Darby and Nigel looked on, as Dustin knocked on the enormous barn door. There was no answer, so he knocked again, this time harder.

"It's open!" Dave shouted from inside. They entered the massive wooden structure, which had been converted and modernized into the ultimate bachelor domicile.

"Snap!" Dustin exclaimed, looking around the extravagant domain. "If you gave a sixteen year-old boy a million dollars and told him he could do his room any way he wanted, this would be it."

"Dave?" Darby called out, but Dave was nowhere to be seen. "Hello!"

They were greeted by a life-sized, Darth Vader, which stood menacingly just inside the front double doors, holding a lit red light saber. The exposed wood-beamed ceiling arched over the cavernous space. A loft bedroom, where hay had once been stored, overlooked the space at one end. The creature from the movie "Alien" clung dormant, looming down from the rafters at the other end. Vintage pinball machines, and other classic videogame machines stood in a far corner. An enormous *Dracula* poster, took up the area above the fully stocked bar. Different colored vintage guitars, hung on the opposite wall above a bank of black amplifiers. A massive television was set up in front of a long black leather sofa.

"Just wait by the computer; I'll be right down," Dave called out to them from the loft. A custom-made black granite desk held the "state of the art" computer equipment and monitors available. An enormous shelf, containing hundreds of DVDs, took up the wall above the desk.

Darby looked up at the loft, watching the pretty hula-girl from the party, come down the stairs looking a bit disheveled, still wearing her costume. Dave followed close behind, walking the girl to the front door. He whispered something in her ear that made her smile and gave her a passionate kiss before she left. He then, walked back across the room, picked up a remote control that operated the entire electrical system, and lowered the music.

"Alright, let's see what we have here," Dave said, sitting down at the computer desk in front of the wide computer screen. Darby, Nigel and Dustin stood behind him, watching the photos pull up on the screen.

"Where are these pictures from?" Darby asked.

"There was a Halloween party in a frat house at the University of Georgia last night. Apparently, a girl was attacked in the attic. She's in the hospital; her boyfriend is sitting in the Clarke County jail. Both are adamant that something attacked them, something they couldn't see. These pictures were taken by someone at the party on a digital camera."

The first picture on the screen showed a group of college kids, from the previous night, mooning and beery mugging for the camera, but there was nothing out of the norm. The next picture was bathed in a soft blue light. It showed a few kids sitting on a couch, holding up beers.

"There ya are," Dave quietly grinned, enlarging the picture. "Do you see them … there in the background?"

"Incredible," Darby said. Sure enough, he saw a, *woman* and two *small children*, standing in front of a dark window in the background of the picture. They looked very pale and out of place in their old fashioned clothes. The window and sill could be seen through their transparent bodies.

"They look so sad," Nigel said.

"They looked pissed off," Dustin added. "What is … that blue haze?"

"Usually, a light like that indicates that electromagnetic energy is present." Dave informed Dustin, as he pulled up another picture. In this picture, the college students had changed positions and expressions. Yet, the lucid people stood in exactly the same place, staring blankly out at the camera.

"Couldn't these pictures be easily faked?" Nigel asked.

"Of course," Dave stated. "Photo shop is fuckin' amazing, ain't it? We only get film or photos after they have been checked by the X. Atencio Parapsychology Society. They generally check everything out before we ever get wind of them. But even then, you're never really sure if they are real or fake. These pictures were emailed to us by a Professor friend of Lily's from UGA. I just chatted with Lily; she feels that because there were so many witnesses to the aftermath of the event, she wants to move fast, before anyone else can be hurt."

"Do you have any footage that you know is *real*?" Darby asked.

"Are you kidding?" Dave asked with annoyance. He stood up and grabbed one of the discs marked "EASON" from the shelf, popped it into the computer and hit play. "In 1962, a small Baptist church in Tallahassee Florida was completely destroyed by a sudden tornado. All the people in the church attending Sunday service were killed instantly. A sprawling farmhouse was built on the land where the little white church once stood. In 1990, Douglas and Claudia Eason, bought the house after it had had been abandoned for years. One night, soon after they completely renovated the house and moved in, Claudia Eason awoke in the middle of the night. She said she saw a young, *black girl*, wearing a light blue dress, standing at the foot of her bed smiling at her. She said she was too stunned to even think about waking her husband. After a few moments, she watched the little girl walk into one of the bedroom walls and *poof*, disappear. This happened several nights over the span of a month. We went out to the house and set up our cameras and equipment. I mounted one camera on the headboard, and this is what I got."

Darby and crew watched the screen with a great deal of curiosity. The night vision camera filmed the end of the king-size, brass bed, and wall beyond. They watched for a few minutes, but nothing happened. Then an electrical static glitch popped up on the screen and they heard a soft *laugh*; the laugh of a child. A small white *figure* materialized through the wall, and walked over to the end of the bed where Mrs. Eason was sleeping.

"It is a little girl," Nigel whispered, truly surprised to actually see something. The girl was just barely visible in the haze, wearing a frilly lace dress and white ribbons tied in her hair. She giggled and pulled on the quilt playfully, then hid below the footboard of the bed and peered up at Mrs. Eason. She then quickly lowered down again, giggling, playing a game of hide and seek. Suddenly, the girl turned and looked at the wall she had just come through, watching more *figures* materialize and come through the wall.

Darby moved closer to the screen, straining to see a dozen or so black men, women and children, walk up behind the little girl, wearing their Sunday best. They did not stop; they were simply making their way through the room, and then disappearing into another wall on the other side of the room. One of the ghost women held her hand out to the little girl, who ran over and took her hand. Together they follow the others, vanishing into the wall. Dave turned off the computer, sat back and smiled at the bewildered faces.

"I got that footage myself. It is *not* fake, it is very *real*," he announced proudly with a hint of arrogance. "About ninety-five percent of hauntings are pure, unadulterated, bullshit. But that five percent … only seeing is believing. Come on, we have to get going, it's almost eleven-forty and I still need to load the bus."

"I swear to God, it's bigger than my whole freakin' apartment, seriously dude!" Dustin exclaimed, stepping off the forty-two foot, means of transportation. The bus, also known as, "the big black beast", was more like a mobile mansion on wheels than anything else. One word was posted on the front destination sign—LOST.

Darby heard strange melodic music playing quietly on the sound system, as he eased up the steps onto the bus. Opening the curtains, he looked around at an interior that had been customized for comfort. The bus was like a ritzy hotel suite; no expense was spared, no luxury overlooked. Just beyond the driver's seat was a luxurious sitting area, made up of two long black leather couches which faced each other. A flat screen television with satellite access was mounted above the driver's area. A modest kitchenette sat just beyond the seating area with a sink, microwave, espresso machine, stove, fully stocked bar, and a refrigerator, which was across the dining booth.

Walking further down the narrow passageway, Darby came to four curtained sleeping compartments, and a bathroom containing a full size shower, sink and privy. In the very back of the bus was a large compartment with a queen-sized bed, boasting lush bed linens and big cushy pillows. A television and sound system were mounted on the mirrored wall behind the bed. Darby figured this must be Lily's private area.

Stepping down off the bus, Darby walked over to where Dave was loading his gear into a storage compartment on the side. Dustin held out a microphone, and Nigel filmed Dave, as he described his equipment.

"I love film. It captures the soul, dead or alive. It captures it and preserves it forever for others to see. Everyone will die someday, but that little piece of your soul will always live on," Dave explained, rather passionately, into Nigel's camera.

"The human eye just cannot pick up spirits or vortexes like film can. Sometimes, I use this amazing photo-reconnaissance infrared film, and I like digital cameras. I simply adore my Fuji."

"What speed film do you use?" Darby inquired.

"400, 800, I like color, but black and white just really seems to capture the moment sometimes, don't you find? Then here we have flashlights, night vision goggles, IR illuminator cameras, as well as, tons and tons of spare batteries."

"Why so many batteries?" Darby inquired.

"Spirits just love to suck the juice out of them. It feeds their energy, which helps them to manifest. Then we have white candles, waterproof matches, which are a must, walkie-talkies, and a lovely assortment of cell phones."

"What about all those ghost hunting devices and equipment?" Darby asked. "Don't you use EMF meters and handheld devices to help find apparitions and things?"

"I have all that shit, don't really use any ... don't have to," Dave admitted. "Look, there are amazing ghost hunters all over the world; some get amazing proof. You know, photos, sounds, you name it. Lucky ones can sometimes get a full body apparition, the "Holy Grail" for ghost hunters. They need those things to do their work. I don't ... I have Lily."

"She's kind of like, having all the *Ghostbusters* in one pretty package," Nigel joked.

Dave turned and looked at Darby and Nigel, and gave them an un-amused grin.

"You have absolutely no idea what you're about to delve into here, do ya?" Dave smiled knowingly at Darby and Nigel. "What are y'all thinkin' ... you'll get a few blurry orbs on film and get an Academy Award. You have no clue, none of ya do. So *no*, we do not need any of those items. Nothing, none of that shit is as important as your own eyes, your own common sense and a really good first aid kit."

"Has anyone ever been really hurt?" Darby asked.

Dave just smirked at him.

"I'll take that as a, yes."

"Most spirits are usually not Casper, and usually not very friendly. I think most people, when they die, go onto wherever it is they go. It's the ones that didn't die peacefully, the ones that are desperate for help, desperate to be heard; they're usually who we deal with. It's like they are trapped in their own personal tragedies. Lily's kind of like a magnet. Sort of a beacon of light to those who are lost or have just been left in darkness, they're drawn to her."

"How do they know she can do this?" Darby asked.

"I don't know. You'd have to ask her. They just seem to seek her out."

"Are there better places than others to see spirits?"

"As far as seeing spirits, anywhere is good really. Anywhere there is or was life at one time, which is pretty much everywhere. Cemeteries, as cliché as it sounds, are a good place. Some people think they are portals to the other side. Others think spirits are just drawn to where their bodies rest; I think it's a load of shit myself. I don't think I've ever seen an apparition in a cemetery. The best actual time to set up surveillance is between nine pm and six am. For whatever reason, photos usually come out better at night. Ghosts are just seen so much better in the dark; that way their energy doesn't have to compete with the energy of the light. Then there is dead time."

"Dead time?"

"Yeah, dead time. I don't know how accurate it is, but some people believe the half hour before midnight is a time when "good" spirits tend to materialize. And the half hour after midnight, the "bad" spirits haunt. Like I said, I don't know how accurate it is. I think it's a load of crapola myself. But I don't make the rules; I just go with the flow."

"Why do you think there are good and bad spirits?" Darby inquired. "How do you know?"

"Oh you know, trust me, you know. Spirits, ghosts, whatever you want to call 'em, are just people if you think about it. Just because they died doesn't mean they all of a sudden change personalities. If you were a good, decent, cool person in life, you will most likely be a cool spirit in death. If you were an evil, mean, son of a bitch in life, chances are you are an evil mean son of a bitch in death."

"Makes sense," Darby agreed.

"Thing is, some bad people, who knew they were bad people, don't want to cross over. They're afraid of what awaits them, afraid of some kind of judgment. And then there are demons. A demon will appear as something desirable, to make you believe it, to make you trust it, with the promise of giving you exactly what you want. It will lure you into a position of vulnerability and change into the shape of the monster it really is. Usually, by the time you see through their illusion, it's too late. Once it has your trust, you're pretty much fucked! Never play with a demon. They don't play nice. We let demonologists play with the demons."

"I see."

"A lot of hauntings are by more than one spirit. Sometimes there can be several spirits, from different decades or even different centuries, who don't even know of the others presence. You never know. There are residual hauntings; that's kind of like when something so strong or so traumatic happened that the energy of the incident is imprinted on a place. Kind of like a constant playback of the past. A house or building can absorb the energy of whatever might have happened there. Some places can take on a life of their own; hence the term "haunted house". But anywhere can be haunted, anywhere there was once life. There are intelligent hauntings, where the dead like to interact with the living; have a nice little conversation about current events, the weather, the afterworld, ya know, this and that. Most don't want to hurt you; they just want to be heard, and some will not be fuckin' ignored. Then there are the spirits that refuse to leave; they can be the most dangerous of all. That's about it, fellas!" Dave announced, shutting the side compartment. "We should have been outta here like twenty minutes ago."

"Right, I just have to grab my duffle bag," Nigel said, shutting off the camera.

"Hurry it up, queer eye," Dave grunted, having to reopen the compartment. Nigel glanced back with a dirty look, as he passed Chloe, who was walking out the front door with her bags.

"Chloe, can you light a fire under your sister's ass, please!"

"Yessss," she moaned, turning around and heading back inside, passing Nigel once again.

"Shotgun!" Nigel cried, like an excited little kid, tossing Dave his duffel bag and hopping on the bus. Darby stood alone with Dave, helping him put the last bag into the compartment.

"I'm curious," Darby said.

"About what, pray tell?"

"About your past relationship ... with Lily."

Dave slammed the compartment door and gave Darby a hard look.

"My personal life is just that ... *personal.* I intend to keep it that way. I wasn't exactly thrilled when I heard that you were going to be coming out with us. I still think this whole documentary bullshit is just a bad idea. Y'all are nothing more than a liability. What we do can be fucking dangerous, I suggest you just stay out of the way, alright?

Dave turned away from Darby and walked toward the bus door.

"Yeah, alright. Can I ask you one more thing?"

"What?" Dave sighed, turning back to Darby.

"Do you really believe ghosts exist?"

"I believe that each one of us has a spirit and I like to think that spirits are eternal. Now where it goes or what form it takes when the physical body dies, I don't know. Most people believe that if you can't see it, feel it, or annihilate it, well then, it must not be. What I can tell you for sure is that fragments of the deceased *do* exist. I've seen evidence of it, I've felt it, and at times, it has kicked my ass, so I respect it!"

"Then why do you do it?"

"Ahhhh …" a soft voice exhaled from behind them. Both Dave and Darby turned to see Lily strolling out the front door, flanked by three hyper-happy dogs. "Sorry you can't come with us guys. Be good."

"Let's just say," Dave mused, gazing at Lily. "I have my reasons."

"What a glorious day!" Lily walked over to them; her blond hair casually piled onto her head with a few tendrils cascading free. She was wearing a large black sweater, a well-worn pair of blue jeans and pink sneakers. She looked much different from her, "Alice in Wonderland", alter-ego, she looked like more like a rock star stepping onto her tour bus.

"I'm coming!" Chloe said breathlessly, bounding out the front door behind Lily. Dustin was waiting for her at the base of the bus steps.

"Your chariot, me lady," Dustin announced formally, taking her hand, helping her board the bus, then following her up the steps, much like a love sick puppy. Lily walked back down the steps, stopped and lowered her dark sunglasses to look at Dave and Darby. "What are we waiting for boys?"

"I can't help it," Dave said, acting as though he is being pulled into the bus by an invisible force. "I'm caught in her tractor beam, I'm defenseless!"

"Come on, Darby," Lily smiled. "Off we go into the wild blue yonder!"

"Good afternoon, lady and gentlemen. My name is Inga and I will be your stewardess today," Lily announced over the intercom in a sexy Swedish voice, as Dave drove the bus down the long drive away from the house. "Please keep your arms and legs inside the vehicle at all times and enjoy your … trip."

The ride up to Athens felt more like heading off to summer camp than to a ghost hunt. After a few hours, the group stopped to get some fuel and load up on junk food at a truck stop. The last hour of the ride, everyone sat on the front couches, dancing and singing to a karaoke machine built into the plasma television.

Darby was sitting alone in the booth by the kitchenette. He had received some more information from his contact at the BBC, who sent along some bizarre crayon drawings of a rather horrifying, *burned clown*, made by Lily when she was small. The other item was an early psychiatric evaluation from one of Lily's doctors, made when she was first admitted to the hospital.

Dr. Ellen Greene—Chambers Psychiatric Hospital—Savannah, Georgia.

My first impression of Lillian Dufrene, age seven-years, was that of a severely trau-matized little girl. I believe this distress has been brought on by the attempted murder/suicide on January 17th of this year, which her twin brother did not survive. Lillian had been hospitalized at the same hospital where her mother had initially been taken following the incident. They were both treated for carbon monoxide poisoning. Mrs. Dufrene was transferred to Sheret Psychiatric Hospital. Lillian was transferred to Chambers Psychiatric in Savannah, where she was placed in a "Psychiatric Intensive Care Unit for Children".

When Lillian was first brought to the hospital, she would not sleep. She told the nurses that she could see a young man with a belt wrapped around his neck, calling himself "Dax". She said, Dax had told her he was very angry. Note: A sixteen year-old boy, Dax Griffin, had committed suicide in the exact same room, hanging himself with a belt he had concealed. The suicide happened several months prior to Lillian being admitted. The child stated, she was very afraid and wanted to go home. At this time, it is unclear how much Lillian remembers regarding the incident involving her pregnant mother and twin brother. Whether real or imaginary, the child is convinced spirits are drawn to her.

CHAPTER 9

▼

EXIT MUSIC FOR A FILM

A few hours later, Darby looked out the bus window at a huge water tower that read—*Welcome to Athens*. The bus drove through the heart of the funky college town, where a mixture of free-spirited bohemians, collegiate preps and beatnik musicians, loitered around a cluster of pizzerias, record shops and bars.

The sun was just starting to set when the bus pulled down Fraternity Row, a street full of beautiful old southern houses, proudly displaying some sort of flag or plaque with the Greek letters of the fraternity or sorority that inhabited it. Nigel filmed the surroundings from his window—a fat bulldog sprawled lazily on a porch, being stroked by some chatting students. A delivery man running up to one of the houses carrying three large pizza boxes and a few pretty sorority girls, walking down the sidewalk giggling. A large red banner hanging from the balcony of a football fraternity read—"GO BULLDOGS! SIC 'EM—WOOF WOOF WOOF!"

"I wonder which house it is?" Chloe excitedly asked, eyeing some of the handsome, flat-topped boys, tossing a football on the grass in front of their fraternity. The bus continued down to the end of fraternity row and turned onto another more desolate road, where a tremendous old house sat crumbling and trashed.

The house was a pigsty, sitting out in a desolate overgrown field, littered with tattered pieces of furniture and crumpled beer cans. As with the other fraternities and sororities, this house also had a flag proudly hanging from the second floor porch, with very appropriate Greek Letters describing the frat perfectly—"D Phi U".

Dave parked the bus a short distance away from the house, and then he and Darby got off and immediately started unloading the equipment. Nigel helped Dustin place a small microphone and transmitter on Lily. From that point on, anything she said would be recorded. Lily asked to be alone for a few minutes, so Nigel and Dustin joined Darby and Dave at the side of the bus.

"*This* is a fraternity?" Chloe asked, as she hopped off the bus. "Icky."

Darby took out a digital camera and began taking pictures of the house. He could see, through its rough and unkempt façade, how beautiful it must have once been. But something about the house seemed dark to him, perhaps darker than it should be. When they finished unloading the bus, Dustin followed close behind Nigel, carrying a sound machine pack, headphones over his ears and a small boom microphone. He looked up at the house with a bit of trepidation.

"You'll be fine, just relax," Nigel smiled, putting a comforting hand on Dustin's shoulder.

"Okay, first things first, always look for the logical explanation before coming to any conclusions," Dave warned everyone, as he put on a military-style field jacket and filled the many pockets with his gadgets. "If you need to use the "chicken shit card", please do."

"Chicken shit card?" Dustin questioned.

"If things get too intense, we pull out the chicken shit card, and leave. Do not, I repeat, do not panic or freak out if something happens. That is how people get hurt! And no negative thoughts; apparitions feed on the energy of the living to manifest themselves. Negative energy is bad."

"Bad," Nigel repeated, just to annoy him.

"People, who don't believe, don't give off positive energy and rarely see anything. And it messes up my energy," Dave stated. "Don't mess up my energy, please. And if that wasn't polite enough, stay the hell out of the way! Lily, you ready?"

Lily was ready. No one had noticed that she was already out of the bus, standing under a streetlight, staring with great intensity up at the dark old house, fifty-feet in front of her. She looked *far away* … like she was caught in her own personal fog.

"Lily, are you alright?" Darby asked.

She didn't answer and didn't seem to hear. It was as though she was somewhere else and no one else existed.

"She's okay," Dave whispered. "This is what she does sometimes."

Darby quietly motioned for Nigel to begin filming her. He watched curiously, as Lily squinted and blinked her eyes, as though an unseen wind was hitting her, yet there was no wind; the night air was completely still. She took a few steps toward the house, her sights now clearly set upon the boarded window up in the third-story attic crow's nest. She suddenly jumped back and cringed, as though in pain.

She was definitely watching *something happening,* but everything was calm. She jumped and cringed, again, and again, and again. Darby watched, as tears rolled down her cheeks. Then a great surge of energy, seemed to crackle through the air all around her, or was it coming from her, he couldn't tell. Lily suddenly lost consciousness and fell to the ground just as the streetlight above exploded, shattering into thousands of tiny shards of glass all around her.

"Lily!" Dave yelled, quickly running over and helping her up. Visibly shaken, she grabbed onto him and seemed to come back from whatever trip from reality she had just taken. "What was it? What did you see?"

"Something horrible. It was night and there was so much lightening it lit up the sky every few seconds, as bright as daylight. It was pouring rain and there were shots, loud gunshots up in the attic."

Darby wasn't sure what to think. He didn't see anything come from the house and he was quite sure there was no violent thunderstorm anywhere close.

"Hello," a distinguished, grey-hair man, called out to the group.

"Hello, Professor Harkett," Lily hugged the man. "Everyone, this is Professor Harkett."

"Pleasure to meet you," Professor Harkett, smiled. "I saw that light break, are you okay?"

"Yep, just an occupational hazard," Lily joked.

"Please come up to the house. I have two of the boys who live in the fraternity up on the porch," the professor explained. "They want to tell you what happened last night. They have been sitting out there for hours; too afraid to go back in the house."

"It's quite a house," Darby said. "Do you know how old it is?"

"This was a lovely house, built back in the late eighteen-hundreds," the professor explained, as he escorted the crew to the house. "You know, it's a registered historical landmark."

"Of what, the holocaust?" Nigel whispered to Darby.

A gigantic pumpkin from the previous nights' party, sat up on the porch railing. Having sat out in the sun all day, its carved face had begun to rot and disintegrate, forming a ghoulish evil smirk. Two young men; Carter, a slender bohemian hippy-type, and Deek, a football player the size of a Mac-truck, sat on a battered couch on the porch. They both looked rather pathetic and nervous, as they retold the events of the previous night.

"She got to the party late, about eleven; she had to work until then. And yes, I will admit we both had a bit to drink, but I didn't hurt her, I swear to God! I would never hurt her!" Carter explained; his face badly bruised, his eyes blackened, a cast covered his right arm. He looked as though he was definitely on the losing end of the fight. "We hung out in my room until midnight. We smoked a bit, and as usual people began coming into my room. We just wanted to be alone, but my room always becomes the party room. The attic has a mattress and stereo up there, so that's where we went.

"Did you see anything out of the ordinary?" Lily asked.

"We were kind of oblivious to everything, ya know," Carter said. "But the more I think about it, about what happened, the more I remember. It was really dark when we were coming down the second floor hallway. I remember seeing this woman; she just kind of appeared out of the darkness. She was wearing like an old fashioned dress; like *Little House on the Prairie*, that kind of long dress. She looked funny, really pale and she was moving like she was in a hurry. I asked her if anyone was using the attic and she just blew right by us, totally ignoring my question, like she didn't even see us. I thought she was going to hit us. But she didn't. She just kind of went past us, or almost like ... through us."

"Did she say anything?" Lily asked.

"No, I don't know, it's all blurry. I thought she was just some chick in a Halloween costume. She just stared straight ahead and I watched her disappear into the darkness at the other end of the hall. I don't know why it didn't freak me out at the time, but it didn't. I was thinking of other things, I guess.

"What happened then?" Lily pressed.

"We walked up the stairs to the attic, plugged the lava light in and put some music on. Then we started to kiss and undress and got down on the mattress. Jennifer was on top of me and, ya know, we start goin' at it. Then, out of the blue, she says, "stop it, that hurts!" And I'm like, not touching her at all! I look up at her and I freaked out. Her breasts were being fondled by these invisible hands; she looked down and saw it too. It was really rough; her skin was turning really red. Then she kind of flew backwards off me, like someone had grabbed her from behind, and pulled her back. But I swear to God, no one was there! She screamed and I immediately got up and tried to run over to her and this *force*, punched me in the stomach. It felt like a freight train hit me and I flew across the room into the wall. When Jennifer got up, whatever this *thing* was immediately pushed her back down on the floor. I mean, I could see she was being held down, but there was nothing there. It had her pinned, and she was screaming my name. I tried to get up again, but it just kept hitting me, over and over again. After a few minutes, I must have just blacked out."

"Hey man, did you see what happened to his girlfriend?" Dave asked the other boy, Deek.

"I was standing out in the front yard having a beer with some of the other football players, when we heard these screams," Deek explained in his soft-spoken, polite manner. "Then Jennifer came running out the front door in her underwear. It looked like blood was coming from her nose, she was totally hysterical! She ran right out the front door and just collapsed in my arms. Somebody called the police and they came and arrested my man, Carter."

"Carter's father bonded him out of jail this afternoon. Jennifer is still in the hospital, she's in pretty rough shape. But she confirms the story," Professor Harkett added. "Unfortunately, her parents think she is just protecting him. They want to charge him with aggravated assault. I know these boys, they're good boys."

"I didn't do anything to her, I swear to God. I love her more than anything," Carter pleaded to Lily, begging her to believe him. "I felt it … there is something evil in that house."

"I believe you, Carter," Lily rubbed Carter's disheveled head, then turned and opened the door to the old house, while saying a quiet protection prayer. "In the name of God, I bind all powers and all forces that are not from God … in the air, the sky, the ground, the underground, the waters and the netherworlds. Please protect all who enter here from any evil forces. Please forbid any kind of demonic interaction or communication, in Gods name … amen."

The crew followed Lily, quietly filming her every move. The two frat boys tailed nervously behind. Looking around, she surveyed the sprawling chaotic rooms, which looked as if a cyclone touched down. She cautiously walked into the lofty, two-story, center entrance hall. Beer cans were strewn about the floors. Spray paint had ravished most of the walls. A few cheesy Halloween decorations, orange lights and yards of tacky fake spider web, were draped all over the stairs. Lily looked up at the top of the steps, her face brightened and she smiled.

"Well hello, don't be scared. We won't hurt you. Come here … come see us." Lily said sweetly, crouching down, talking to the empty staircase. Without ever looking away from the stairs, she explained what she was seeing to the others.

"There is a little boy in overalls and a little girl wearing a long dress. I think they're afraid or shy, but they're very interested in us."

Darby filmed the bizarre scene with his handheld digital camera. Lily backed away from the stairs, like she was making room for the invisible children to come down into the foyer. Darby, once again, was perplexed; there was absolutely nothing there.

"Temperature just dropped ten degrees," Dave stated, looking at his digital thermometer.

"What are your names?" Lily asked. She then listened to the *silence*, before responding. "Won't you talk to us?"

"Jesus!" Darby exclaimed out loud. He was astonished, feeling his left hand become *ice cold*, like he had just submerged his hand in ice water. A chill shuddered up his back and throughout his entire body. It was the kind of chill he couldn't just shake off.

"She must like you," Lily whispered, looking down at Darby's side. "She's holding your hand. You can feel her, can't you?"

"My hand is freezing cold!"

"What are your names?" Lily asked the air.

All of a sudden Darby's hand warmed up. Immediately, he looked up at the ceiling; there were no air-conditioning vents in the ancient house. He could find no reasonable explanation for what he just experienced. If it was some sort of trick, he thought, it was a pretty damn good one.

"They went back up the stairs," Lily stated nonchalantly, as she walked into the living room. "Let's wait in here."

Darby looked at Nigel, completely perplexed. Nigel just raised his eyebrows and shrugged, not knowing what to say. They followed Lily into the living room and continued filming her. She quickly spotted a fancy Ouija board, with carved letters and numbers, set up on a table in front of the old stone fireplace.

"Were people using this board?" Lily sharply questioned the frat boys.

"I, I don't know," Carter stammered.

"Yeah, just a few people," Deek added. "But they were just screwin' around."

"Burn it! Take it outside and burn it until it's nothing more than ashes!" Lily sternly tossed them the board. "Do it now!"

The boys threw the Ouija board into a metal trash can, sprayed kerosene on it and threw in a lit match, then watched the Ouija board burn into oblivion.

"What's with that?" Darby asked Dave.

"Ouija boards are extremely dangerous, especially when used by people who have no clue what they are doing. If you ask, through the Ouija, for a spirit to provide physical proof of its existence, well that's just what you might get. It can open a doorway or portal, allowing a possible destructive soul or evil entity to enter into our world. The only way to get rid of the board … is to burn it."

"Done!" Deek stated, as the frat boys came back into the room. Then they all waited … for what, they were not sure.

"Chloe, lights," Dave instructed.

"Got it," Chloe said, flicking off the lights. She then lit a single white candle in an empty beer bottle on a chest in front of the couch.

"Now what?" Darby asked.

"Now … we wait," Lily stated. "Sometimes that's all we do. It's a big game of sit around and wait. But no matter what happens, no matter what you see, no matter what you hear, you must always be respectful of where you are. This was somebody's house and for whatever reason, they may still be attached to it. Respect them … respect the dead."

The group sat around the room and waited for hours for something to happen. Darby sat in a chair holding his camera. Lily was sitting on a beat-up couch with Chloe's head in her lap. Something, unseen and unheard, made her look at the doorway; she took a deep nervous breath.

"Here we go," Lily quietly announced, as Darby and Nigel quickly started filming. "Hello, is there anyone here that would like to speak to us? Hello?"

Nothing happened, nothing moved, nothing stirred. The room was entirely dark except for the soft light from the glowing candle. A moment later, Darby noticed the entire room seem to brighten and take on a soft hazy glow. The candle, which had dwindled down to almost half its size, seemed to get much brighter, as the flame mysteriously grew.

"We'd like to talk to you, if that's okay? What is your name?" Lily asked, looking at the doorway, waiting a few beats, as though she was getting answers to her questions. "Hello Olivia, my name is Lily; these are some of my friends. I can hear you, Olivia. Why are you still here? Was this your house? Why do you stay in this house?"

Again, there was nothing but silence.

"Bean?" Lily asked. "What is Bean?"

Darby looked over at Deek, the huge football player; he had tears running down his face.

"What is Bean?" Lily asked again.

"Bean?" Deek repeated in a whisper.

"Olivia, it's okay! Please we want to help you," Lily pleaded, looking all around the room, obviously trying to pinpoint where the spirit was moving. "We are here to help you Olivia. Please calm down. She's just panicking, saying help, over and over."

"Help," Deek wept.

"Who are you afraid of?" Lily implored, desperately. "We want to help you!"

"Help," Deek whispered.

A door loudly *creaked* open from somewhere upstairs, then *slammed* shut with such enormous strength it rattled the windows, as well as their nerves. Everyone sat in silence, waiting, anticipating. Darby and the others looked up at the ceiling, hearing heavy footsteps on the hardwood floors above. A few moments later, the room seemed to change. There was a plunge in temperature, as a very cold breeze entered the room, bringing with it a foul smell. The candle on the table began to flicker angrily and blew out, leaving them in darkness. Only glimpses of moonlight shined in through the front windows.

"Well looky here … look what the cat dragged in," a sharp voice with a harsh Irish accent seethed in the darkness. Dave turned on a powerful flashlight. One by one, he shined the light at the scared faces around the room. When he got to Deek, he held the light on him. The mellow young man had drastically changed. He was now irate. His breathing was rapid, his face contorted with a vicious smile, his eyes wild. Someone or something had possessed him. "We have a room full of crows!"

"Leave him be!" Lily yelled, quickly rushing over. "Leave him!"

"Everyone just remain calm!" Dave said, holding out his arms, anticipating anything.

"Where's my boy at, Olivia!" Deek demanded of Lily.

"I'm not Olivia." Lily said calmly.

"Lyin' hussy!" Deek snarled at her. Lily quickly tried to back away, but it was too late. Deek grabbed her by the throat with his enormous hands and held her in his grasp.

"LET HER GO!" Dave screamed, as he jumped on Deek's back, and the large boy released Lily. She fell to the ground, coughing. The football player then concentrated on Dave, throwing him off his back with powerful ease, slamming him full force into the wall, like he was a rag doll.

"Yer' in my house, this here's my house!" Deek said, grabbing a poker from the fireplace. He stood above Dave and raised the poker over his head, preparing to take him out. "You the one trespassin' little crow!"

Darby tossed his camera down and quickly picked up a chair, sending it crashing down on Deek's back, causing his massive body to fall on top of Dave.

"Hit the lights, the lights!" Dave yelled, and Chloe quickly turned the lights on. In an instant the chaos ended. Darby watched some playing cards, which had somehow been flying around the room, slowly flutter to the ground and the candle re-lit itself.

"What just happened?" Carter asked, looking around, disoriented.

"Is everyone, okay?" Chloe asked.

"Why did you hit me, dude?" Deek asked, lying in a heap on the floor, crying like a baby, as he looked up at Darby.

"Sorry, mate," Darby said, helping him to his feet. "You were a bit out of sorts."

Darby then offered his hand to Dave, who reluctantly took it.

"Did you get all that?" Darby asked Nigel.

"No, my bloody battery died," Nigel stated, quickly replacing the battery.

"What the hell just happened, Lily?" Dave asked. "Lily?"

But Lily was, once again, walking through her own little world. Darby watched her walk out the living room door and head back into the foyer.

"Show me," she whispered, closing her eyes, she went into another self-induced trance, hearing a dreamy song, drifting, echoing through the house on a scratchy Victrola phonograph.

When she opened her eyes, she was transported back into *another time*.

Though she still stood in the same foyer; she was now alone, it was nighttime and a thunderstorm was raging outside. Looking around, she noticed the house was also different. It was clean and beautifully decorated transformed back to its original early nineteenth-century glory. There was a fire burning in the fireplace and a grandfather clock ticked by the front door.

"Make a wish!"

Lily heard a female voice, with an airy Irish brogue, from somewhere in the house. Oil lamps hanging on the walls dimly lit her way, as she walked down a long hallway through the house, following the music and the sweet smell of fresh-baked cake. At the entrance of the dining room, she peered in. The room was decorated with colorful balloons and crepe paper. Lily watched a young boy, concentrating deeply, staring at the lit candles on a cake on the table in front of him. Two younger twin children, a boy and a girl, sat around the table with him cheering him on. Lily quickly realized these were the two children, she had seen earlier in the foyer. The boy blew out the candles and grinned, hoping his wish would come true.

"What did you wish for?" Albert, the younger boy, asked excitedly.

"What did you wish for, Bean?" Emma, the little girl, repeated in a sing-song voice.

"He can't tell you Emma or his wish may not come true," a red-haired woman said, as she breezed into the room, walking right *through* Lily, from the kitchen. Lily was now a *ghost* in their world. She looked at the pretty petite woman and knew instantly … she was Olivia.

"I want a big piece mama," Emma said, clapping her hands.

"How does it feel to be eleven, string bean?" Olivia asked her son, as she cut the cake.

"Bean's old!" the little boy teased.

"Hush up, Albert!" Bean quipped. "I'm older than you!"

"Children, stop fussin'. This is Bean's night and I want to dance with the birthday boy!" Olivia said happily, turning up the phonograph, taking her son in her arms. They danced around the room and around the table, as the other children giggled, looking on with delight. Even the rain pouring outside could not dampen this festive occasion.

Over the music and thunder, no one heard the front door open. And they didn't hear the heavy wet footsteps on the hardwood floors, coming closer to the dining room. Lily jumped, when a *flash* of lightening revealed a tall wiry man with a scraggily beard. The man stood silhouetted in the dining room doorway, right next to Lily, but oblivious to her presence. He held a long package, wrapped in plain beige paper, under his arm. As he watched the festive celebration going on without him, water dripped off the front of his wide-brimmed hat.

"Whoooo-wheeee!" the man suddenly shouted, startling the children. Their faces quickly turned sullen; they knew the party was over, and it was just a matter of time before all hell broke loose. The man grabbed the stunned mother from behind, taking her roughly into his arms, forcing her to dance with him around the room. He was visibly intoxicated, his lips formed a devilish grin, as he swung and twirled her. Olivia pulled away from him and turned off the music.

"Natas, where have you been?" Olivia asked, in a hushed reserved manner.

"Out celebratin' Mrs. Flynn," he cackled, taking off his drenched hat and overcoat.

"He's been drinkin' again," Bean whispered to the other children.

"It's my boy's birthday and I got him a present!" Natas exclaimed, staggering over to Bean, offering the package. The boy looked to his mother, who nodded for him to take the gift.

"Well, come on boy! Open it!" Natas urged.

Bean un-wrapped the paper, revealing a long black gun.

"It's a shotgun, a proper shotgun, a Remington single barrel, 12-gague, shotgun!" Natas announced proudly. "Now you can do some real huntin' with your pa!"

"Natas, that's very dangerous," Olivia said quietly. "I don't think …"

"No, you don't think," Natas snapped, disregarding her words. "You like it boy?"

"Yes sir," Bean answered, intimidated.

"I knew ya would. Go on, give it a try. All ya gotta do is cock it and aim," Natas explained. He stood behind Bean, helping him hold the gun up. He cocked the gun and positioned it in the boy's arms, taking aim at some overhead balloons.

"Natas, please," Olivia tried to step in. "Not tonight!"

"Then, you slowly, pull …" Natas whispered into the terrified boys' ear, forcing him to squeeze. "… the trigger."

Natas swung the gun sharply, aiming it directly at Olivia, just as the trigger was pulled.

"Nooooooo!" Bean screamed, looking away.

"BANG!" Natas yelled out. The gun made a clicking sound, but nothing happened. Natas cackled viciously, mocking the child's panic, as he took a box of shells out of his pocket and tossed them onto the table. "Ya need these."

"That's enough!" Olivia yelled, grabbing the gun from Natas, laying it on a shelf.

"What's the matter with you woman! Hell, this is my boy's party!" Natas ranted, picking up a bottle of whiskey and flopping down into a chair, hiking his muddy boots up on the table. The twins remained hidden behind Olivia's long skirt.

"Come here boy, sit down," Natas insisted. "Have a drink with your pa."

Bean cautiously sat down at the table across from his father; fear in his eyes.

"Natas, Bean's just a boy!"

"Stop callin' him that woman. *Bean*, his name is Dean, he ain't a boy anymore! That's his problem; he needs to be a man," Natas snarled, pouring the whiskey into a glass. The gruff father smiled at his son, then slid the glass across the table to him. Bean just stared at it. "Go on, drink!"

"Natas!"

"Shut your mouth, Olivia!" Natas waited for the boy to take a drink, but the child was too afraid to even move. Natas quickly got impatient and slammed his fist onto the table, causing the glass to tremble. "I said, DRINK!"

Bean quickly downed the drink, spilling some on himself. Natas rejoiced in spirit, as his son set the empty glass down, coughing and wincing at the bitter taste of the liquid.

"That's my boy! I knew you could do it!" Natas grabbed Bean's glass and refilled it, then poured himself one more. "Here, let's have another, you and me boy!"

Natas walked over and forced the glass up to his son's mouth; he had no choice but to drink. He coughed, almost choking, as his father snickered and finished off his own drink.

"Another!"

"I can't," the boy said in a shy timid voice.

"Yes, you can! You're a man now!"

"I can't."

"Drink it!"

"Please, pa."

"Drink," Natas leaned in close to the boys' face.

"No."

"What?" Natas asked, surprised by his disobedience. "What did you say to me?"

"I said, NO!"

Natas smiled dangerously. Then, without warning, he sharply hit the glass off the table, sending it shattering into the dining room wall.

"What's the matter with this family? Why does no one have any respect for the man of the house? What you need is a good whoopin' boy! That'll teach you respect! Come here!"

Lily watched in horror, as Natas took off his belt and reached out to grab Bean. But Olivia quickly jumped between them and pushed Bean behind her.

"ENOUGH! GET OUT!" Olivia screamed. "GET OUT OF THIS HOUSE!"

"You tellin' me … to get out of my own house, woman? The house I built with my own hands for my ungrateful family," Natas growled, suddenly *slapping* her to the ground, then grabbing her by the hair and whipping her with the belt. She fought and kicked, trying to get away from him. The terrified younger children huddled in a corner.

"Let her go!"

Natas heard a loud, *click*. He turned to see Bean, pointing the shiny black shotgun just a few inches from his head. Natas released Olivia from his fierce grip; she quickly scrambled to her feet, completely disheveled.

"Well, well, well, what are you gonna do with that there gun boy? You gonna shoot me? Gonna shoot yer old man? You're forgetting … you need the," Natas stopped, seeing the *open* box of shells on the table. "Bullets. You don't have the guts, coward … mama's boy!"

Bean raised the gun and began to squeeze the trigger. He was fully intending to kill his rancid father, wanting to finally rid his mother and his siblings from the plague inhabiting their house. The boy felt the warmth of the whiskey course through his veins, making him feel a bit woozy. He squinted his left eye to get his aim perfect.

BAM! A stream of blood rushed down Natas' startled face. Bean was stunned; he had not yet pulled the trigger. He looked up from the gun, just as his father fell, face-first, to the ground revealing his mother, who was standing behind Natas, breathing heavily, grasping a heavy iron skillet in her shaky hands.

"Is he dead?" Bean asked.

"Pray God, I hope so," Olivia leaned down, noticing a trickle of blood coming from the corner of his mouth. She whispered into her husbands' ear. "I hope … that you choke!"

Lily followed the panicked mother, as she herded her children up the staircase and down the darkened hallways, instructing them to grab whatever clothing and personal items they could. Olivia then ran into her bedroom, pulled back a rug, and frantically yanked a board up from the hardwood floor. Hidden under the floorboards was a mason jar full of money.

"Breathe, keep breathing," she told herself. "Don't lose your nerve … today we escape."

"Mama, I'm scared," Emma whispered, standing at the door, looking worried.

"It's alright, we are gonna go see Nana and Poppy. Won't that be fun?" Olivia tried to reassure her little girl. "Let's hurry now, come on!"

"Go … go!" Lily quietly pleaded, knowing they could not hear her, but she couldn't help herself. She continued following the nervous mother and her children down the staircase into the foyer. Olivia grabbed the doorknob, but it wouldn't budge. She frantically tried to open the door, but it is locked and the key; vanished. Her heart sank, as she sensed a presence behind her. Slowly turning toward the living room, she saw a fiery red glow brighten the dark room.

"Now, that wasn't very nice Olivia," Natas spoke flatly, staring out the front window at the violent storm raging outside. He was sitting casually with his legs spread wide apart in his favorite leather chair; Bean's shiny new rifle lying across his lap. He pulled on his cigar, and then took a swig from his bottle of whiskey. A steady flow of blood, to which he seemed oblivious, ran down the side of his long thin face. "Where ya goin'? Party ain't over … yet."

"UPSTAIRS, RUN!" Olivia yelled to the children.

The children quickly obeyed, dropping their bags and running back up the staircase. Lily stayed behind; watching Natas casually finish his cigar, taking his time, knowing his prey was trapped. She watched him stand up, stretch and then do a demented little dance. Lily followed Natas, as he stumbled up the staircase to the second floor. Olivia had turned off all the oil lamps in the upstairs hall, making it inky dark and harder for him to find them in his inebriated state.

Lily watched Natas, through the flashes of lightening, opening each of the doors along the hallway with the barrel of the gun. When he came to the middle of the hall, he stopped in front of the door leading up to the attic stairs.

"Little crows, little crows, I've come to play with ya. It's a fun game called, shootin' crows in the attic." Natas said, as he politely knocked on the door. He then tried to turn the knob, but the door was jammed from the inside. Natas tried to kick the door in, but it had been barricaded with pieces of old furniture from the attic. Lily noticed Natas getting more and more frustrated, as he frantically *kicked* at the door and fumbled awkwardly up the steps. He was very drunk and very mad by the time he reached the attic.

"DEAN, WHERE YOU AT BOY?" Natas demanded.

"It's me you want. Leave the children alone. They're innocent."

Lily could hear Olivia speak, as she climbed up the dark steps and crouched at the attic doorway. Olivia was not trying to hide; she faced her husband, standing in front of the oval glass window in the middle of the room, the fury of the lightening outside silhouetting her body. Lily didn't see any of the children, only the back of Natas, as he confronted the brave mother.

"I know you're in here, Dean!" Natas scowled. "Stop playin' games and come out!"

"Natas, why did you leave us? Why did you let money and whiskey, take you from us?"

"You don't know what your talkin' bout!"

"You've changed. You're a different person."

"COME OUT, YOU LITTLE COWARD!"

"He's gone. He climbed out a lower window with the other children. I told them to run, I told them to run and never come back."

"That so? Okay, I'll call yer bluff Olivia," he smirked, raising the gun at her. "Boy, you got to the count of five to show yourself, or … I shoot your ma'!"

"Natas don't do this. You were such a good man once, a good father."

"Five seconds!" Natas called out. "One …"

Lily saw Bean quietly crawl up the attic stairs and sit on the step right next to her. She looked at his tear filled blue eyes; his face was red, flush with terror. He saw his father pointing the rifle at his mother. The boy was trembling with fear, his head woozy from the alcohol that saturated his small body. Lily wanted so much to wipe away his tears, but she was nothing more than a witness to the dramatic horror being played out in front of her.

"Two …"

"Please …" Olivia whispered.

"Three …"

"You're a monster!" she gasped.

"Four …"

"Wait!" the boy cried out.

"Dean … no!" Olivia screamed.

Natas saw Bean standing in the doorway. He smiled, then turned back to Olivia.

"… Five."

BOOM! The shotgun blast echoed loudly through the attic. The force of the blast blew Olivia back into the glass window, shattering it to pieces. The fury of rain and wind outside blew through the broken window with fierce rage, causing debris to fly everywhere. Bean ran to his mother and held her in his arms, as she lay gasping for breath. He watched helplessly as the life faded from her eyes.

Bean heard Natas reload the shotgun and looked up through his blurry eyes to see his father now pointing the gun at him.

"You respect me now, boy?" Natas seethed under his breath. There was no way Bean could fight anymore; he closed his eyes tightly and prepared for the impact. Natas squeezed the trigger and *CLICK*; nothing happened. Bean looked up at his father's crazed face; he was distracted, cussing at the gun, fumbling to remove the dud shell and reload a fresh one from his shirt pocket. Bean wobbled, slowly making it to his feet.

"Run …" Lily said quietly, praying the boy could somehow hear her. "Just run!"

"Now …" Natas, once again, raised the loaded gun at his son. A frightening drunken grin beamed across his twisted face. "Where were we?"

Suddenly, the grandfather clock in the foyer rang out loudly, catching Natas off guard. Bean ran straight at Natas, full force, hitting his father with every ounce of strength left in his slight body, just as Natas pulled the trigger.

A loud *shot* rang out, narrowly missing the boy, going straight through Lily and splintering the wall behind her. Bean just kept running, not once looking back. Natas continued to reload and fire at him, as he stumbled down the stairs, clumsily falling over the toppled barricade of furniture. Buck-shots ripped the walls narrowly missing him.

"COME BACK ... COWARD!" Natas screamed after him. Lily watched the drunken father stumble and fall to the dirty attic floor, right in front of where she was crouched. She could smell the sweet whiskey on his breath and the gunpowder in the air. The great loss of blood seemed to finally be catching up with Natas; he struggled to stand, only to fall back to the floor.

The angry wind blowing through the broken attic window lifted a white sheet covering a dusty armoire, revealing a mirror on the front of the old wardrobe closet. Natas looked up and saw a red-faced demon staring back at him from the mirror; it was his own bloodied face. He saw something else in the mirror, and smiled. Hidden behind a steamer trunk, cowering with fear in the mirror's reflection, were two small bodies.

"Come out little ones," Natas cooed in a soothing voice. "Papa won't hurt you."

Bean made it down to the first floor and ran into the foyer. He frantically grabbed the doorknob, before remembering it was bolted shut. Looking around for another way out, he ran into the living room and grabbed a poker from the fireplace. He then proceeded to smash out one of the narrow glass windows that ran along either side of the front door and squeezed through the window, cutting his left arm badly. Falling onto the porch, he took off running down the front steps, as fast as his little legs would carry him. He ran out into the vast fields that surrounded the house, as the torrential rain poured down on his fragile terrified face.

A *gunshot* blast rang out, loudly echoing through the stormy night air. Stopping dead in his tracks, he looked back at the dark house looming in the distance.

"No ..." Bean whispered, realizing his father must have found the precious treasures his mother tried so desperately to hide. As he started to run back to the house, one shot after another lit up the crow's nest, resonating along with the thunder.

"*NOOOOO!*" the boy screamed, as a final shot rang out.

"No," Bean whimpered, standing frozen, staring up at the house, knowing his whole family was gone. Lily had stayed in the attic and watched the deranged father dispose of his entire family, and then take his own life with a single blast to the head.

Lily walked over to the crows nest window and stood looking out through the jagged shards of broken glass, as the wind and rain harshly blew on her. She saw Bean standing out in front of the house in the pouring rain. He seemed so small, so sad, so helpless, standing in the storm, staring up at the attic.

A sudden rapid heat overtook Lily; her head began to spin and she promptly *fell* to the ground, unconscious.

"Lily! Can you hear me? Open your eyes!"

Lily opened her eyes. Dave was leaning over her with a worried expression.

"He killed his family," she whispered. "The father ... he shot them."

It had been almost an hour since Darby and the others watched Lily go into the strange trance. It was one of the most bizarre encounters Darby had ever witnessed, starting with everyone following Lily through the different rooms of the house, as she watched the "invisible" drama unfold. She seemed to have absolutely no knowledge of the cameras presence. The peculiar drama finally came to an end with Lily passing out in front of a boarded up window in the attic.

Everyone retreated to the bus. Lily sat on the couch sipping coffee, describing to Darby and the others, what she had "allegedly" witnessed. She told them about the festive birthday party and the murders that followed in the house, so many years ago. She believed the mother was still searching for her son, the only child that did *not* die.

"She's damn convincing," Nigel whispered quietly to Darby. "I mean, if what she went through was true, and she did stand witness to this twisted celebration of evil, she would have experienced the exact same emotional impact this doomed family had. I don't know how a human being could endure going through other people's traumas, over and over, without losing it.

"Well, if it isn't true and she made the whole scenario up," Darby added. "Well, I have to say, she is quite a good actress."

"They called him Bean," Lily said. "But I think his name is Dean ... Dean Flynn."

"I know a Dean Flynn, he's a mean ol' bastard and a serious-ass drunk," Carter informed them. "The guy is like ancient. He owns a bar downtown, a real dive."

"It's worth a shot! It's still relatively early, I'll see if I can locate him," Professor Harkett added. "What was the name of the bar?"

Dean Flynn was an angry man who never had a pleasant day or kind word for anyone. And he did not want to be bothered, stating emphatically that, "he most certainly was not about to go back to the house, where his entire family had been massacred." He hung up on Professor Harkett, while he was trying to explain what was happening at his childhood home.

It was getting late. The crew waited for another half hour, hoping the old man would change his mind. Then, as they began to pack up the equipment, headlights shined upon the plagued dwelling.

A rusted red pickup drove up the long drive and stopped abruptly, kicking up a cloud of dust. Lily and the others watched an old man get out of the car. Darby figured him to be in his mid-to-late eighties, but he was tall and strong as an ox. He stood between the headlights of his truck and looked up at the house with defiance. To Dean Flynn, this house was nothing more than a pit of hell, which had infested his every waking thought, not to mention his all too-frequent nightmares.

"That's him," Lily quietly informed the others. "He looks just like his father."

Lily walked over to the man, motioning for the others to stay back. Nigel filmed the meeting from a distance. Darby quickly grabbed the headphones off Dustin's head, so he could listen to what was being said through Lily's microphone.

"Mr. Flynn?" she inquired, looking up into the same blue eyes she saw when he was just a boy, those same blue eyes, which were now deeply encased in wrinkles.

"That's right," the old man answered in his gravelly Irish accent.

"My name is Lily."

"And to what do I owe this extreme pleasure?" he barked, sarcastically. "Are they finally going to tear down this rotting cesspool? Historical landmark, bullshit! It should have been destroyed years ago!"

"We're sorry to have called you out here like this."

"Yeah, me too! You mind tellin' me what the hell this is all about?"

"Well, it may sound strange," she hesitated. "But your mother …"

"My mother is dead!"

"Yes sir, I know. But your mother is still … she needs you. She needs your help."

"What is this? What do you think you're pulling, Missy? You think this is a joke? Is this how you get your Goddamn kicks? My family was …" he stuttered with anger, his hands shaking. "…. slaughtered! Do you find that amusing?"

"No sir, I …"

"I've had enough of this … horse shit!" He yelled, storming back to his car.

"She needs you …"

"*Go to hell!*"

"BEAN!"

He *stopped*, then sharply turned back to look at her.

"What did you say? What did you call me?"

"Bean … that's you, isn't it? They called you, Bean?"

The old man stared at Lily for a few moments; then tears welled up in his eyes.

"String bean Dean, that's what my mama called me," the old man whispered, thoughts of his mother, and *that night*, flooding his mind. He remembered standing in the exact same spot out in front of the house, like he had when he was a boy. Just letting the pouring rain pound down on him, as he heard his loved ones being brutally killed at the hands of a madman; a madman, he called, *father*.

"Coward, I can still hear that vile devil call me," Dean started to cry openly. "That was the last time I ever saw my family. He took them from me; he took my life, my future. I never had a chance to say goodbye. I should have died up there with them, but I ran."

"You did the right thing."

"No, don't you see? My father was right, I was a coward!"

"You were just a little boy."

"I have had to live with that decision, every day of my wretched, miserable, life."

"Will you come with me?" Lily said, taking his weathered hand, walking with him. Darby and the others followed, filming them as they walked up to the house.

Entering the house, Dean paused, a bit overwhelmed. They continued up the front stairs to the second floor, stopping in front of the attic door. Lily opened the door and ushered the old man in, before turning to Darby and the others.

"This is private, okay?" Lily said quietly, entering the attic and closing the door, shutting everyone out. Darby again grabbed Dustin's headphones and kneeled down, leaning back against the attic door. He stared down at the floor, concentrating, trying to hear what was happening through Lily's microphone.

After a few minutes of silence, he saw a soft luminous *light* and felt a cool *breeze*, coming from the crack under the door. He could hear the old man openly weep and the sound of Lily's voice.

"Olivia, this is your son, Dean. He is *alive*. He ran … he got away; he is an old man now. Time has passed you by." After a pause, she added a prayer. "God, please allow these angels to tiptoe back into heaven where they belong."

A few moments later, the light faded from under the door. Darby jumped up, feeling the door open, and Lily walked out of the attic, practically holding Dean up, as he sobbed. They all walked outside and stood in front of the house. Dean gave Lily an emotional embrace, having a hard time letting go of the girl, who apparently, had just changed his life significantly.

Darby watched Lily *whisper* something in the old mans ear, something that made him grin. The embrace finally released and he took Lily's hand and kissed it graciously.

"God bless you, dear girl. God bless you! You will be in my thoughts and prayers, always!" Dean smiled at her through his tears, holding her hand until the last moment, before walking away. Everyone watched, as he took one last glimpse of the house, then got back into his truck and drove off into the night.

"I'm hungry," Lily stated. "Y'all hungry?"

"I'm totally hungry," Dustin added.

"Me too," Chloe chirped.

"Starving," Dave said, as they started back to the bus. Darby and Nigel just stood looking at each other.

"Do you have any idea, what just happened here?" Darby asked Nigel.

"Not a clue, not one single clue," Nigel shook his head and tailed off after the others, leaving Darby standing alone in front of the shadowy house.

"What just happened?"

The bus drove back down fraternity row toward town. Everyone was in high spirits, everyone except for Darby, who sat in the kitchenette booth, staring out into the darkness at the passing street lights.

"You're very quiet, sittin' back here all by your lonesome," Lily said, sitting down across from him. "You alright?"

"I'm just trying to take it all in. It's a bit mystifying."

"It's all just energy; it's what makes our spirits, our souls. It's a very strong thing … energy. Did you ever walk into a room and immediately get an uneasy feeling, like you weren't alone? There's a very good reason for that feeling, it's all energy."

"I just want to understand what I saw, but I … really didn't see anything."

"Just because you can't see something, doesn't mean it isn't there. I mean, you did feel something … yes?"

"Yes … I guess, I mean, I'm not sure."

"Darby, you've been in love right?"

"Yes, I have."

"How did you know?"

"I don't know … I just knew."

"You felt something, some sort of change inside you. It's not something tangible that you can grasp or hold onto, it's more a feeling. Do you believe in God?"

"Yes."

"Have you ever seen God?"

"Well, no."

"Hmmm, well how can you believe in something you can't see? You may not be able to see God, but you can see God's beauty, God's wrath, God's power. You can *feel* God. That's called *faith*. You have to have faith to believe in something you can't see, right?"

Darby thought about what she said, but he was still skeptical of her supposed "powers". *I just need proof,* he thought. *"I need to see something with my own eyes.*

"Oh, don't worry, you will," Lily said, looking deeply in his eyes. "You just need to keep an open mind."

"Did you just read my mind?" Darby asked, taken aback.

"Will it freak you out if I said I did?" she raised a curious eyebrow and then smiled. Darby smiled back and thought she was charming, even if she was nuts.

"So is that old house free of spirits now?" Darby asked.

"No, not yet, but I have a feeling it will be very soon. The problem is you never know what is going to be built on the same piece of property in ten or twenty years time. Come on, this is a great restaurant, let's eat!"

"Regular or sweet?"

"Sweet please," Lily answered, and the waitress refilled her glass of iced tea and took away some empty plates of food. Finishing a late dinner, everyone sat around a table in the exposed brick building, that housed a bohemian restaurant known as, "The Grit".

"Oh tell them about the sapphire ring," Chloe urged Lily. "That's a good one."

"The sapphire ring, ahhh a classic," Lily Laughed. "Yep, that was one of the first times I can recall something about me was … a bit odd. My grandmother used to have these amazing elaborate parties at the house. When it got late, my parents would put my brother and me to sleep in one of the many bedrooms, and they would go back down to the party. Of course, we would sneak down and sit on the stairs and watch the party. They would have these huge champagne fountains and everyone was dressed so beautifully. Everyone had cocktails and ate fancy hor d'ourves; it was all so glamorous. Well, we would sit up there on our little perch in our pajamas, watching the festivities. This one night, I remember, we were caught by this couple; a young woman and a much older man, who didn't look like they belonged together at all."

"Was he robbing the cradle?" Nigel asked.

"Pretty much, she was so young and pretty and he was so much older; at first we thought he was her grandfather. The man pointed up at us. We were about to run and he called out, "Come down here, spies". We thought for sure he was going to tell our mother on us if we didn't come down, so we wandered down to the bottom of the stairs. We told them that we just wanted to watch the party and begged them not to tell on us. They just laughed and said they would keep our "spying" a secret. I remember being just amazed at this sparkling sapphire ring on the woman's hand; it must have been at least five-carats."

"Nice," Nigel added.

"So I asked her if it was real. She called me "adorable", and took the gigantic rock off her finger and placed it on mine. I looked at this huge ring on my little finger. It was incredible, just gleaming in the light. But right away, I felt strange. A few other wealthy couples came over, seeing this little girl in her pajamas, wearing this enormous ring. The pretty woman asked me if I liked her ring. I told her yes, very much, but ... it's *not* your ring. "What do you mean," she asked, looking at me with this funny smile. I told her it wasn't hers; it belonged to another lady. She said, "No sweetheart, you must be mistaken. My husband bought me this ring on our first anniversary". And I told her this other lady said it belonged to her. And she asked, "What other lady?" I told her a German lady calling herself "Sylvia" said it was *her* ring. I saw the husband turn pale, white as a sheet. I knew right away I shouldn't have said anything, but it was too late. I told her Sylvia was very unhappy that she was wearing *her* sapphire, and added, Sylvia said, "you're a ... ""

"You're a what?" Nigel implored with great interest.

"I knew better than to say a bad word, but she insisted, so I told her ... Sylvia said, "You're a dirty, gold-digging whore!" The crowd of people that had gathered around me, gasped in unison. Apparently, she knew her husbands' deceased wife's name was "Sylvia". The young woman asked her husband if the ring was "*her* sapphire?" The poor guy didn't know what to say, he was so stunned. So he didn't say a thing and she then knew he had given her his dead wife's' ring. The young woman was pissed; she *slapped* him so hard that it left a red hand print on his cheek."

"That's hysterical!" Nigel laughed, along with the others. Everyone stopped talking momentarily, hearing blaring sirens. They looked up and saw two fire trucks speed past the restaurants large front windows.

"Looking back, it was kind of funny," Lily said. "Then my mother saw the crowd and came over to see what was going on. And there we were ... the center of attention. It wasn't bad enough that we were caught out of bed, but she thought we were putting on a show for the guests just to embarrass her. She grabbed us and pulled us back upstairs and gave us this *look*, like she was going to kill us."

Lily stopped talking, obviously reliving what had happened to her and her brother. Without looking up, she quietly muttered, "I hope ... she rots!"

Lily abruptly stood up from her chair, spilling her tea across the table.

"Whoa!" Dustin cried, quickly grabbing the glass and some napkins.

"I'm sssorry, sorry," Lily said, walking toward the door. "Excuse me."

"Lily?" Chloe called after her sister. "Lily!"

Darby and the others watched Lily walk out the door into the dark night.

"It's really late, let's head over to the hotel and get some sleep," Dave suggested, standing up, tossing a wad of cash on the table. "We have to be on the road pretty early."

As they were heading out of the restaurant, a young hippy-kid rushed in past them and called out to some of his friends chatting at a table.

"Did you hear?" he cried with excitement. "That shitty old house at the end of fraternity row, D Phi U; it got torched tonight ... burned right to the ground."

CHAPTER 10

▼

SPARK

Everything was white … pristine, perfect, white. The tiles, the towels, even the heap of bubbles glowed white from the single spot-light, shining down upon the porcelain tub.

Lily sat with her knees tucked up close to her chest, staring at the water falling hypnotically from the spout by her feet. She was enveloped in the warm soapy water in the Jacuzzi tub of her hotel suite, trying to soothe her sore muscles, and calm her already delicate state of mind. But no matter how hard she tried to be cheery and put her past demons to bed, they always managed to seep out time and time again.

There was one memory, one image, which she so desperately tried to bury; her *mothers' eyes*. She could not shake her mothers' eyes, staring into the back seat from the rearview mirror on that beautiful snowy morning, as she ever so calmly told her children she was just "waiting for the car to heat up". Her mothers beautiful green eyes always haunted her. Lily would never be able to get away from those eyes, she saw those eyes every single day of her life, and would see them until the day she died … for Lily had her mothers' eyes.

Lily tried desperately to stifle the emotions building up inside her, but they could no longer be contained. Silently, she cried out. Her mouth wide, but no noise escaped. She made a fist and slammed it hard against the side of the tub, trembling with sadness and covering her face with her hands, as she sobbed.

Up in his hotel room, Darby sat in the blue glow of his laptop, watching the digital film he had taken earlier that day at the old frat house. Through headphones, he listened carefully to every sound made, while watching the footage shot in the foyer of the old frat house.

"Jesus!" Darby heard his own voice exclaim on the shaky footage.

"She must like you," Lily whispered, looking down at his side. "She's holding your hand. You can feel her, can't you?" The memory was very fresh in his mind. He still could not explain how his hand suddenly became so cold. Darby did feel *something*, some sort of presence did wrap around his hand; but he still had serious doubts about Lily, even with all he had experienced back in London.

He continued watching the footage, hearing what sounded to him like the *laughter* of small children. It gave him instant chills. He quickly reversed the footage and listened again, hearing the same high-pitched giggles.

"Unfuckingbelieveable," he said with a wry smile.

He continued watching the footage. Everyone was now in the candle-lit living room. Darby had focused the camera specifically on Lily, when the *presence* entered the room and she asked it questions out loud.

"What is your name?" Lily asked on the footage, looking at the doorway.

After a pause, Darby thought he heard a very faint breathy *voice* whisper, "Olivia". He immediately reversed the footage and played it again, turning up the sound.

"What is your name?" Lily asked.

Again, a soft female voice whispered the name, "Olivia".

"Hello, Olivia. My name is Lily."

Darby heard the voice whisper, "*people*".

"These are some of my friends," Lily stated.

"*You can hear me?*" the voice asked.

"I can hear you, Olivia. Why are you still here? Was this your house? Why do you stay in this house?"

Darby hears the word "*Bean*" whispered.

"Bean?" Lily asked. "What is Bean?"

"Bean?" Deek, the massive football player, who appeared to be crying, repeated.

Darby turned the volume up all the way, hearing the panicked voice cry out, over and over, "*Beeeaaan, help! Help me find, help … help!*"

"What is Bean?" Lily asked again. "Olivia, it's okay. Please we want to help you! We are here to help you, Olivia. Please calm down. She's just panicking, saying help over and over."

"Help," Deek wept.

"Who are you afraid of?" Lily pleaded. "We want to help you!"

"*Help me! Help, help, help!*" the voice begged.

"Help me," Deek whispered.

"What the fuck?" Darby exclaimed. He quickly jumped up, ran out of his room and down the hotel hall to Nigel's room. He banged on his door. "Nigel! Wake up!"

"Darby?" Nigel sleepily opened his door, wearing nothing but satin boxers. Darby grabbed his arm and practically dragged him down the hall into his room.

"You have to hear this mate!"

"What the bloody hell is it?" Nigel asked drowsily. Darby put the headphones on Nigel's head and hit play. Nigel leaned in close to the monitor and listened silently for a few moments. "Did she say her name? She did, she said, Olivia!"

"Ha-ha, I'm not mad, you heard it too?"

"Shhh, shush, wait a tick, let us listen," Nigel said, rewinding the footage to watch it again, now wide awake. "Help ... it was female, a female voice. Did you hear that? I don't bloody well believe it, but its right there, clear as day."

Lily squeezed the water out of a hand towel and laid it over her sore eyes, before turning on the Jacuzzi jets in the tub. She put small earphones in her ears and pressed play on her iPod. A melodic and calming song flowed into her consciousness, instantly transporting her far away. Finally she was able to lay back and relax in the sumptuous bath, as water pulsed all over her body, putting her in a wonderful relaxed state.

With her eyes covered and tranquil music filling her head, she was unaware that the soft light above the tub had *flickered off*, and the bathroom heat lamp had turned itself on, creating a soft hum, while bathing the bathroom in a harsh red light. The vapor from the hot water swirled around the bathroom, creating an extraordinary thick haze. The knobs in the shower stall, and double sinks on the vanity, slowly turned themselves on and hot water ran freely, adding more steam to the room, thick and wet.

Lily sensed the heat, but was completely oblivious to the strange activity going on around her. She did not hear the distant *laughter* that echoed through the room, demented and sinister, followed by frightening giggles.

In the far corner of the room, a *spark* burst out of nothingness, producing a small smoldering ember of fire. In an instant, the ember began to expand and grow into something resembling a crumpled piece of paper. The burning paper continued to float flimsily in the air, moving slowly toward Lily, a trail of smoke following.

By this time the room was getting very hot. Beads of sweat trickled down Lily's face, as she rolled her head from side to side. The smoldering ember was hovering just above her head. It suddenly began to rapidly contort, growing in size and dimension, throwing off small sparks of fire, as it shook and rolled. It was much larger now, looking like a wrinkled old coat that had been tossed into flames. It seemed to move with a purpose, like it had a life of its own.

As the shiny, cloth-like, bundle elongated and stretched, a flash of untamed red hair shot up wildly from the top of a head, rising out of the mass. Then a face started to become visible through the steam. There were eyes, jet black eyes, sheathed with the glow of fire in the pupils. A bulbous nose was melted onto the face painted up with dark, soot tarnished, white grease-paint. Chunks of missing skin exposed bone and muscle. The mouth was encased in a bright red whimsical smear. The lips had been partially melted away, revealing jagged broken teeth, which looked unnaturally large and gave the face a huge sadistic grin.

Then the sole of a large black shoe stretched out from the smoke, then another shoe. Both shoes were much longer than regular shoes; these had a funny, cartoon-esque, shape. The shoes seemed to be stepping out from the smoldering mass onto the bathroom floor, rising larger and larger, standing up into a human form wearing a shiny multi-colored jumpsuit.

Lily sensed she was not alone. But before she could pull the towel off her face, a long boney hand, barely covered by tattered gloves, reached out and viciously slammed a rotted palm over her mouth. As the towel was ripped off her eyes, the music abruptly ceased. Lily immediately tried to stand up, but her wet body was roughly *pushed back down*. The laughter became louder and more crazed, as Lily's head was continually forced back under the hot water. She struggled and kicked, before finally being able to make it to the surface, gasping for breath.

"Surprise!" a voice very familiar to Lily, spoke angrily with a thick Bulgarian accent. Holding her tightly in his angry grasp was Lily's childhood nightmare, Varton Muntz. The clown smiled psychotically, exposing his rotted jagged teeth, while he caressed her hair with his skeletal hands, lovingly. He then harshly *shoved her* back under the ravaging water.

She tried frantically to grasp onto something, but her hands just slid off the wet porcelain. Varton pulled her back up to the surface and lovingly wrapped his smoldering satin arms tightly around her neck. "You have been … very bad, little Lillian."

Lily's eyes widened with shock, as Varton tightened his hand and lifted her naked body from the tub by her face, and pushed her cruelly up against the bathroom door, leaving her feet fluttering in the air. The thud in the bathroom slightly roused the sleeping Chloe, laying on one of the double beds out in the darkened attached suite.

"Don't want to wake sister, now do we?" Varton sneered, covering Lily's mouth. Lily shook her head "no", staring into the face of the gruesome burned madman, holding her tightly in his grasp. His ravaged clown costume and sash were singed and charred; a billowy satin collar framed his misshapen head. "We have business, you and I. It was rather unkind of you to try and distance yourself from me in the manner you chose. You thought you could just banish me into the darkness forever, but I am far too smart for any of your childish tricks. No more games! Do we understand each other?"

Lily nodded, "yes". Varton lifted one charred finger at a time from her mouth and she was able to take a deep breath.

"In the name of God," Lily prayed quietly.

"In the name of God …" Varton repeated dramatically, then snickered.

"I bind all powers and all forces that are not from God," Lily quickly whispered her protection prayer. "In the air, the sky, the ground, the underground, the waters and the netherworlds."

"Ohhh, the nether … worlds," Varton laughed, mocking her.

"Please, pppleeease, forbid any kind of demonic interaction or communication, in Gods name, amen."

"Aaaaah-men," Varton spoke like backwater preacher, full of fire and brimstone. The big top nightmare harshly pulled Lily close to his hideous disfigured face. She tried to move her face away from his, smelling his horrid rancid breath, pouring across her face, as he released an evil chuckle. "I have told you, Lillian, I will never leave you. I am the only one who ever loved you. You will always be my daughter, you know that."

"Yes, I know."

"No matter what you do, no matter where you go," Varton mused, caressing his blistered hand across the side of her face. "I will always, always, find you!"

"Lily? Are you okay?"

Lily heard Chloe call through the door from the other room. Varton put one of his mangled digits up to his horrible mouth and released a slither, *Shhhhh!* Chloe saw the hazy red light and steam billowing out from under the door. She quickly jumped out of bed and tried to open the door, it was *locked*. She began to bang on the door, which she could feel was very hot.

"Lily, open the door!" Chloe exclaimed, but there was no response. Chloe began to panic. She ran out of the room and down the hallway to Dave's room, where she pounded on his door. "Dave, Dave, come quick, there's something wrong!"

In the room next to Lily's, Darby and Nigel were still looking at the footage of the frat house on the computer, when Darby hit the pause button and raised his hand.

"Listen," he whispered. They both looked up from the screen, hearing what sounded like Lily arguing with another person, a person whose deep voice they did not recognize. Then they heard Chloe's screams and quickly rushed into Lily's room, where they saw Dave, already pounding his shoulder repeatedly into the bathroom door.

"Help me!" Dave barked, and all three men slammed their bodies into the door, which splintered and buckled, but would not give.

"Lily! Lily! Are you okay?" Chloe cried out. "Please, open the door!"

The men backed away from the door, hearing the lock click and the door handle twist and unlatch, slowly opening on its own. Lily emerged through a thick puff of red steam. She was soaking wet with a towel wrapped around her trembling body.

"Lily!" Chloe exclaimed, throwing her arms around her sister.

"I'm okay," Lily smiled, obviously shaken, trying to cover her fear.

"What happened?" Darby asked.

"I guess I was just totally relaxed and didn't realize how overheated I was getting," Lily said casually. "When I tried to stand up, I must have fallen. I'm such a klutz. You guys are really nice to check on me, but I'm fine now, really."

While the others tended to Lily, Nigel looked into the bathroom. He flicked on the regular lights and slid, as he stepped into the drenched soapy tile floor. Tossing down several thick towels to sop up the water, he carefully tiptoed over to the Jacuzzi tub and turned off the water jets. But he still heard water, and saw it pouring out from the shower stall and sinks. He turned them off and shivered, inhaling a horrific stench that was still permeating the air. Just as he was about to exit the bathroom, he looked up. To his surprise, he saw a word written in the steam on the mirror above the sink, which he recognized as the Russian word for "WHORE".

Back in the room, Darby noticed Lily giving Dave a horrified look as she mouthed, "*Varton.*"

"She's fine," Dave announced, immediately taking over the situation, becoming a pit-bull, fiercely protective of Lily. He quickly ushered Darby and Nigel out the door into the hallway. "She's fine, just go back to your rooms. I'll handle it from here!"

"Lily, was there anyone else with you?" Nigel asked. "I thought I heard a voice."

Lily looked as though she was going to speak.

"No!" Dave interrupted. "Do you see anyone else?"

"No, I was alone," Lily said quietly. "Thank you both for your help. Please, go get some sleep."

"Nighty-night" Dave said, rudely slamming the door in their faces.

CHAPTER 11

▼

SPIDER WEBS

"Alllll Aaaaabbbboarrrdd-hhahaha!" Dave screamed, laughing maniacally along with the Ozzy Osbourne song, *Crazy Train*, being played at a high decibel over the bus speakers.

It was the morning after Lily's bathroom incident and everyone was acting completely normal. It was as though nothing bizarre had happened the previous evening. They had breakfast, loaded up the bus and hit the road. Darby watched Lily sitting alone, listening to the music on her headphones. She did seem a bit more quiet than usual, her face a bit more serious.

"Storm ahead," Dustin informed the group from his co-pilot seat in the front of the bus, next to Dave. Rather ominous dark clouds filled the sky up ahead. Drops of rain sprinkled down on the wide front windshield. Within a matter of seconds, the soft rain quickly turned into a downpour, making it difficult for Dave to see the road.

Later that night, after many hours driving through the pounding rain, the big black beast had finally reached the next destination. The bus pulled up in front of the middle-class home of the Barrett family of Kingsport, Tennessee. Chloe stayed on the bus to watch the final tribal counsel of her favorite television program, *Survivor*.

Darby and crew filmed, Mark and Tina Barrett, as they excitedly told of the recent "goings on" in their house. They explained how their thirteen year-old son, Dylan, had been plagued for the past few months, by an unfriendly spirit whom they called, "Haverghast". Apparently, Haverghast was very in tune with young Dylan and had been making his life a living hell. Even a videotape, made by the family, showed how Haverghast would not even let poor Dylan do his homework. The spirit would either pull the chair out from the kitchen table or move the table away from where the boy was trying to work. Another video showed Dylan being tossed out of bed, over and over, as he was trying to get to sleep. Haverghast's other target seemed to be the father, Mark, who lifted his shirt to prove to everyone that, deep red marks, had been clawed across his back by *unseen hands*.

As the couple showed everyone around their small cluttered house, the lights kept flickering off and on. Both parents stated they were sure it was a poltergeist that was invading their house and were very afraid for their son. They had pretty much told anyone who would listen, their frightening ghostly tales. The family had been inundated by the local media, and had gained quite a bit of notoriety in the small town, as well as quite a bit of money to share their story. They seemed thrilled that Darby and his film crew were there to witness the events.

"Cream and sugar?" Tina asked Lily.

"Please," Lily answered politely, sitting at the table in the small kitschy kitchen, covered with vintage signs and collectables. Tina handed Lily a cup of coffee, then proceeded to sit down on the other side of the table, between her husband Mark and son Dylan. Dylan was playing a handheld videogame and seemed annoyed by the intruders.

"Mmmm, it's good, thank you," Lily said, after taking a sip and placing the cup on the table. "You say a lot of the activity seems to center around Dylan?"

"That's right," Tina admitted with a sigh, overwhelmed. "It's been an almost nightly occurrence, Dylan is very upset. He doesn't want to sleep alone in his room."

As Darby and crew filmed the discussion, Lily's cup of coffee leisurely *slid* across the table. Lily quickly caught the cup, before it could plunge to the linoleum floor. Suddenly, the lights in the kitchen flickered off, and then turned back on. Darby watched Dustin's eyes grow wide.

"See what I mean? Everyone has been talking about it, positively everyone in town," Tina stated, emphatically. "People have even stopped by and taken pictures of us, and the house. The television program, *The Dark Side*, recently did a story on us that is going to be shown worldwide. We're thinking about writing a book, ya know, about our experiences … like Amityville."

Darby saw Dave scanning the area discreetly. He quietly left the room for a few moments, then popped back in without anyone noticing.

"Dylan has Haverghast ever hurt you?" Lily asked the boy.

"Yeah," Dylan responded, never looking up from his Game Boy. "I guess".

"You don't know?" Dave inquired.

"It must be really scary for you, huh?" Lily added.

Dylan just shrugged his shoulders and mumbled something incoherent.

"Dylan is excruciatingly shy, as you can see," Mark offered. "Dylan, tell them about how the ghost pushes you out of bed. Tell them how afraid you are."

"It pushes me out of bed," Dylan stated flatly. "I don't want to sleep in my room."

Darby felt young Dylan was more aloof and rude, rather than a shy frightened kid.

"Dylan, is it possible you might be fibbing about your little ghostie? I mean, no offense, but you're not really very convincing," Dave asked Dylan, taking the videogame from his hands and continuing to play, obviously trying to get a rise out of the teenager. Dylan just glared at him. "Maybe you could get old Haverghast to, I don't know, move this table."

The thunder rumbled outside, the falling rain tapped on the kitchen windows.

"Haverghast, move the table, show the doubter," Dylan requested of his ghost. After a pause, the table suddenly *jerked* a few inches across the kitchen floor.

"The spirit gets very angry to those who aren't nice to Dylan," Mark stated. "That is when we notice *things* happen."

"You should never be mean to me," Dylan warned Dave, looking up at him under his long dark bangs. "Bad things happen to people who are mean to me."

"Well, I'll take my chances," Dave whispered into Dylan's ear, then gave Lily a curious glance; a glance that Darby also caught. "Let's see if we can talk to old Haverghast, shall we? Lily is going to go into a deep trance; she can talk to the dead."

"Yes, I will now contact the tortured soul of Haverghast," Lily announced, as she closed her eyes and threw her head back dramatically. "In the name of God, I bind all powers and all forces that are not from God, in the air, the sky, the ground, the underground, the waters and the netherworlds. Please protect all who enter here from any evil forces. Please forbid any kind of demonic interaction or communication, in Gods name, amen."

All of a sudden every light in the house went out, leaving them in the dark. Only the flicker of lightning from the thunderstorm outside lit the kitchen occasionally. Dave grabbed a small flashlight and pointed it at Lily, who spoke in a disturbing monotone voice. To Darby, it almost seemed as if she were mimicking the spirit medium, Gaia. Lily gave quite a performance, truly over the top; her eyes wild, her movements theatrical.

"Sweet spirit, Haverghast, will you speak ... please speak to us. Send us word from the other side that you can hear us. The time is now, sweet spirit. Send us a sign from beyond the grave!"

A few loud *knocks* seemed to emanate from one of the kitchen walls. Darby noticed that none of the family members seemed at all surprised when the kitchen table suddenly moved. And when the lights went out, they didn't even flinch. But when the *knocking* started, they all jumped, their faces panicked. From the freaked-out look on Dustin's face, Darby thought he may pull his "chicken shit card" before this was over, but the rookie stayed and held the microphone in his trembling hands. As for Darby, he watched the scene playing out in front of him with more curiosity than fear.

"We hear you, sweet spirit, Haverghast. Please keep communicating with us. One knock for no, two knocks for yes. You seem very disturbed and angry, Haverghast. Is someone in this house disturbing your eternal slumber? Is there someone you want to confront?"

KNOCK, KNOCK.

"Is it young innocent Dylan?"

KNOCK.

Dylan looked extremely relieved.

"Who is it that you do not want in this house anymore spirit? Is it the father?"

KNOCK.

"Is it the mother, sweet spirit? Is it Tina whom you want to confront?"

There is a long pause, then a succession of continuous loud angry *BANGS*, which did not cease.

"I didn't do anything! Please, make it go away! We just wanted, we wanted," Tina stood up from the table, looking absolutely petrified, begging Lily to make the spirit leave her alone. "We just wanted ..."

The knocking stopped at the same moment Dave's flashlight went out, leaving the room, once again, in complete darkness.

"The batteries in the flashlight just completely drained from all the energy in the room," Dave called out in a frightened voice. "Prepare yourselves, something is coming!"

"Sweet spirit, Haverghast. I feel you coming to us, coming to Tina! Show yourself to us!" Lily's voice rose, as the intensity grew. "There, look, it's Haverghast!"

Everyone watched a dark shadowy *figure* slowly walking through the living room, wearing what appeared to be a hooded cloak. Darby saw the Barretts' terrified faces in the flashes of lightning, as they watched the figure coming closer and closer.

"No! No! Send it away!" Tina cried out. "I'm a good person! We didn't mean to cause any harm, we just wanted some free publicity!"

The figure stopped in the kitchen door, raised its arm up and pointed at Tina.

"The spirit has come for you Tina," Lily announced. "It has come for you."

"Dear Jesus, Mary and Joseph, please help me," Tina begged. "We made the whole thing up! We lied! We lied! Please God, help me!"

"Mickey! Turn the lights on!" Mark stood up and screamed out, stomping his feet on the kitchen floor. "Mickey, turn on the damn lights!"

Every light in the house came on at once, revealing Chloe standing in the kitchen doorway, wearing a bright yellow rain slicker, with a big happy smiley face on the front.

"Boo!" Chloe playfully giggled. "Nah ... ha ha, gotcha!"

Dave lifted the side of the kitchen table and pulled up a long steel rod attached to one of the legs, which came down through a tiny cut made in the kitchen floor. He then let the table drop, sending it crashing back down.

"Awouchhh, dammit!" a muffled cry could be heard from the basement below.

"Hey Haverghast, why don't you come on up and say hello," Dave called out, loudly stomping his boot on the floor. "We'd love to meet ya!"

"I don't get it," Dustin whispered to Nigel, perplexed. "Where's Haverghast?"

A pudgy man sporting a thick, salt and pepper beard, came out of the basement door looking rather timid and embarrassed. It turned out Haverghast was Tina's older brother, Mickey, who was in on the whole preposterous ghost scheme.

"Dustin, meet Haverghast," Nigel laughed.

"Really, I mean is that the best you could come up with?" Dave sarcastically asked the family, as he systematically ripped long pieces of clear fishing line from hidden spots around the kitchen. He pointed out how a magnet under the kitchen table had made the cup of coffee slide across the table. "Cheap parlor tricks."

"Liar, liar, pants on fire," Lily scolded the guilt-ridden Tina and her family. "Shame on you ... shame on all of you!"

"After all that foolishness last night, I want to hear a *real* ghost story," Darby stated, looking at Lily across the fire, through the lens of his hand-held camera. "Lily, do you remember the first time you actually saw a ghost?"

After the disastrous previous night with the "Fake ghost family" and a long day spent on the road traveling to the next destination, Lily thought it would be fun for everyone to spend the night at a campground in the mountains. The group was sitting on wood logs, huddled around a roaring campfire to keep warm. They were feeling no pain, as they passed a bottle of rum, and toasted marshmallows for s'mores.

"The first time I actually remember seeing a ghost?" Lily reminisced, popping a puffy marshmallow into her mouth. "I was about six. My family was driving back home from the Georgia State Fair. I remember my brother and me sitting in the back seat of the car, singing along to the radio. It was that Springsteen song, you know, "Got a wife and kids in Baltimore Jack, I went out for a ride and I never came back."

"Hungry Hearts," Dave clarified with a belch.

"Yeah, that was it! Anyway, it was night and we were driving down a very busy boulevard. It had rained earlier and the streets were especially slick. I remember my father suddenly turned the radio off and started driving really slow, he said, "there's been an accident." There were all these flashing lights up in front of us and a parade of headlights from looky-loos. As we got closer, my brother and I saw all the flares, brightly burning on the black pavement around the area where a car had been rear-ended by a dump truck. The front of the dump truck had literally smashed in the entire back of the car. It was really bad; the policemen were directing the cars around the wreck. When my father saw us peering out the side window, he told us not to look. He told us to close our eyes and put our hands up over them, until he said to open them again. The closer we came to the accident, the harder it was for me to keep my eyes closed. I could hear my mother gasp in the front seat. I knew I shouldn't, but I just had to see what was so awful. As we pulled up alongside the crumpled wreck, I peeked. Opening my eyes just enough to see the absolute most gruesome thing I had ever seen in my young life. It was a little girl, about my age, she had been thrown, head first, from the passenger seat into the windshield."

"Damn," Dustin sighed.

"The top half of her body … up to her upper arms, was sticking out through the glass; the rest of her body was still in the car," Lily continued. "Her face was framed in the golden halo of light from the fire. It had been cut by tiny chards of cracked glass, which made a spider web pattern of blood on her face. It was truly

… horrible. It seemed so strange to me, all this frenzied activity going on around her, police and ambulance workers frantically running around, the flashing lights. She looked completely frozen. Her eyes were wide open, like she was still alive, but I knew she was dead. She had the most unbelievably horrified look, literally cemented on her face. I wanted to look away, but I just couldn't. I looked right into her dead eyes, staring blankly out at nothing. Then I felt a *cold hand* on my leg. I remember saying, "Stop it, Tyler" as I pushed the hand away, but it came back. And then, as I turned to sock my brother, I saw the girl with the bloody spider web imprint on her face, sitting in the back seat between the two of us. Tyler was still covering his eyes, completely oblivious to everything. I remember the girl turned her head and looked right at me. I screamed bloody murder, I was so freaked out. My father swerved the car. It just missed sliding off the road and came to a screeching halt. When he turned around to see what was wrong, of course, she was gone. I don't think I have ever been the same since. So to answer your question, that was the first time I remember seeing a ghost. It still freaks me out to think about it."

"Why do you think you can see them and other people cannot?" Nigel asked.

"I think most people can do what I do, and see what I see, to some degree or another. Just for some reason, I am really in tune to it. I don't know why. Most people don't want to think about death, or I should say, choose not to think about it. It makes them uncomfortable. But when you're confronted by it at an early age, like I was, you have no choice but to deal with it. I think we are better off thinking about the inevitable and not spending so much time and energy on wasteful things. There is no expiration date tattooed on our bottoms, no one knows when it's coming, none of us. You could say every prayer … to every god in the world. You could have tons of money, but that isn't going to stop it, so you might as well face it. Life is a ride, you really don't have much control over it; so you might as well just fasten your seatbelt and go along with the ride. Any other questions?"

"Yeah, pass the booze!" the very drunk Dave, requested.

"I think you've had enough, David," Lily informed him.

"Yes, but I want more than enough, Lillian! I am the captain of this ship," Dave announced stumbling over to the side of the bus and patting it lovingly. "If I want another drink, by glory and God, I believe I am entitled!"

"I would like to make a toast to the captain of our ship," Nigel announced, holding up the bottle of rum. "To Captain Dave! Here, here!"

"Here, here!" The group toasted Dave.

"Thank you, George Michael, you're too kind," Dave held up his drink to Nigel, swaying as he attempted to bow to the group. "I would also like to thank the Academy, my beautiful mother, Janice. Mrs. Kinkle, my first grade teacher, whom I also liked to call, Mrs. Tinkle. I would also like to thank all of you, the little people."

"Alright, ya wanker, enough!" Nigel and the others laughed. Dustin started playing his guitar, trying to show off his mediocre vocal stylings to Chloe, who seemed to be quite enthralled with his serenade.

"Damn dude, you are so off-key," Dave said to Dustin, covering his ears.

"I know … and I don't care," Dustin continued to sing blissfully.

"And, with that, I bid you all adieu, as I must take a serious piss," Dave announced, stumbling up to the bus. "Then I am going to pass out!"

"I too have officially had enough to drink. I'm off to bed," Lily announced, as she stood up. "Thank you all for a fun night. Oh, and Dustin, be careful."

"Why?" Dustin asked, just as a flaming spark popped out of the fire and landed on his jeans. Panicked, he jumped up and poured beer on his leg to put out the flame.

"Night," Lily said, as she disappeared onto the bus.

Darby could only smile.

The next morning, Darby abruptly woke in his small sleeping compartment on the bus, breathing heavily. The nightmare he had just experienced was so intense and seemed so real, he momentarily questioned whether it truly happened or not.

The dream began with him walking into an oddly shaped, moving room, enclosed with windows that let in only sporadic flashes of light. There was some kind of wild celebration was going on. The room was packed with eccentric people, dressed in peculiar party outfits and strange hats. Darby could remember seeing an enormous hairy baby and pudgy strippers. He watched other bizarre creatures with twisted "out of proportion" features, dancing and singing with abandon in a strange blurred motion. But for some reason he could hear no noise, just eerie classical music. Through the gyrating bodies, Darby saw a set of dark "dead-eyes" staring at him with an unwarranted hatred.

Then, before he could figure out where he was or what was going on, a huge bright light exploded in the moving room … which is when he abruptly woke up.

CHAPTER 12

▼

THE PASSENGER

It was dusk when they walked under the gigantic illuminated sign—*CRYSTAL BEACH*. Screams and laughter could be heard coming from the captives of the various thrill rides inside the park.

Surrounded by towering, hundred-year-old trees, Crystal Beach Amusement Park had been operating since the early 1900's. The park was extremely well maintained, with beautiful flowering picnic areas, spouting fountains and park benches. A boardwalk and beach looked out upon the sparkling water. It was truly one of the last "family-themed" amusement parks left in the world. It had kept its vintage rides, as well as adding newer, more updated ones. There was no denying the charm of the historic park, which boasted "thrills and rides for everyone from tykes to tycoons", not to mention the sugar waffles and Hall's famous suckers, everyone craved.

"We have to meet Mr. Travers at midnight in front of the Comet. That gives us a few hours to screw around and hit some rides," Dave informed the group, as they walked down the neon-lit midway, under twinkling white lights strung in the trees. Lively barkers beckoned, trying to coax them into playing various games of "chance and skill".

Darby continually won several giant stuffed animals playing, "Whack-A-Mole". He gave Lily and Chloe the toy of their choosing, then proceeded to give all the kids who gathered around to cheer him on a stuffed toy. In fact, Darby won so many toys that the guy who ran the booth politely asked him to leave, stating he was "running out of prizes". They continued down the midway where they came upon Dustin, who was looking extremely agitated.

"Is that all you got there, Sally?" A hefty carny teased, wearing bright orange overalls and a top hat. He was sitting in a cage on a plank perched over a large container of water, tormenting Dustin through a loudspeaker. "Hey Sally, how many is that you missed? Come on, whiff one of those powder puffs over here, I think my face is shiny!"

As the others looked on, Dustin threw one ball after another at the red bull's-eye sticking out from the side of the cage, missing *every* time.

"Come on, it's that BIG red dot, its right there Sal!" he cackled. "You can't miss it! Oh yeah, wait a minute, *YOU* can!"

"You are so over, dude!" Dustin threatened, throwing another ball way off target.

"Are you kiddin' me?" the carny snickered. "My grandma was here five minutes ago and I paid her twenty bucks NOT to hit it!"

"This is the ONE!" Dustin pledged, his face burning red with anger. His eyes focused like a Dodge City gunslinger, as he took his shot.

"Oh, come onnnnn! You're embarrassing *me!*" the fat carny grimaced with glee. "Here, toss me a ball, I think I can hit it before you and I'm on the inside of the cage!"

Chloe, sensing Dustin's eminent doom, joined him and faced the carny.

"Ohhh yes, yer gonna let your girlfriend try now!" the carny laughed. "Damn, she's really cute. What's she doin' with you?

Chloe snatched the ball from Dustin and weighed it in her hand. Then, without blinking, she hurled it like a closer in the World Series. The sound of the ball whizzing through the air on the way to its target was deafening. It was a direct hit. As the wise-ass carny in the orange overalls fell toward the depths of the chilly pool of water below, all he could see was the look of total joy and vindication beaming across Dustin's smug face. Everyone cheered, as Dustin "high-fived" Chloe.

"I'm so in love with you," Dustin pledged his undying devotion to Chloe. "Where'd you learn how to do that?"

"Junior varsity softball, division Seven champs," Chloe boasted. "Boo-ya!"

For the next few hours, the group happily smashed into each other in bumper boats, spun into oblivion on the *Monster*, and dined on a feast of classic park fare—funnel cakes, deep fried Twinkies, Loganberry soda and french fries.

As they neared the back of the park, they heard the sounds of an old Wurlitzer pipe organ, wafting through the breezy night air from the grand, "Crystal Ball-room". When the ballroom was built back in the early 1900's it had cost an astro-nomical "quarter of a million dollars". It was truly dazzling. Everyone from Glenn Miller to Frank Sinatra had played in the stunning, art-deco, building. The entire roofline was covered with shimmering glass windows, which could be opened on hot summer nights to let the breezes off the lake "cool the dancers' heels".

They entered the gigantic open space and watched a group of older ballroom dancers', sweep across the dance floor, under luminous colored spotlights and a sparkling mirror ball overhead. The women were gussied up in long flowing gowns, and the men were dressed in sharp black tuxedos. Darby was filming Lily with his hand-held camera, leaning on a wooden railing, mesmerized by the graceful couples.

Suddenly, Darby heard his mobile phone ring; he quickly rushed out of the ballroom to answer it.

"Hello," Darby said, watching a colorful neon Ferris wheel spin.

"Darby McGregor, well, well, well, long time no hear!" Ian Sharpe, Darby's ultra-pushy money man, was calling from London. "Is this broad on the level or what? She the real deal or is she wasting your time and my money?"

"You know Ian … you can be a real prick."

"Yeah, I know, I pride myself on it. So what's the deal … she a looney-toon?"

"Honestly, I think we're really onto something here!"

"When can I see some footage?"

"Well, technically, I don't have much yet."

"Darby, you're fuckin' kiddin' me right? I have distributors already lined up. You'd better not be yankin' my chain, McGregor. I got a lotta fuckin' money invested!"

"Ian, I promise … soon. I have to go we're about to start shooting."

"Call me, Darby!"

"Absolutely, I'll call!" Darby tried to appease him. He closed his phone and joined the others, as they came out of the ballroom and headed back up the mid-way.

It was getting close to closing time. Sleepy children with balloons tied to their wrists, were being carried out of the park by their equally exhausted parents. While Dave and Nigel went back to the parking lot to retrieve the bus and drive it onto the amusement park property for the night's surveillance, the others tried to go on as many rides as they could before the park officially closed for the night.

"Look a fun house!" Dustin called out, pointing to a funky red building decorated with glowing paper lanterns. The large neon sign above the entrance was written in crazy Chinese lettering—"*LAFF IN THE DARK*".

They walked up the steps to the old fashioned, ride-through, funhouse and paired up, getting into rickshaw carts. Dustin and Chloe jumped in the first cart. They laughed out loud, as the ride operator pushed a button and their rickshaw quickly took off. Lily looked a bit apprehensive, but Darby grabbed her hand and together they hopped into the next cart. Lily let out a little squeal, as the rickshaw smashed through a set of doors and disappeared into the entrance of the funhouse.

The spook house was totally dark. Crazed frenzied music played at high velocity. The rickshaw would speed up and then slow down abruptly, spinning and dropping unexpectedly, as loud sound effects blared. Bright flashes of light illuminated frightening "nightmarish visions" as sudden jets of air blew in their faces. Lily and Darby giggled and screamed like little kids, as they sped through the creepy tunnels.

A glowing green sign read—*Circus of Horrors … Dead Ahead!* The rickshaw then slowed down considerably, as it turned into a long spinning tunnel. Psychotic flashing strobe lights and painted swirling designs, gave them a dizzy feeling.

Lily's playful attitude changed drastically when she spotted a giant mechanical clown at the end of the tunnel. She could see his deranged eyes; his arms were flailing, raised high above his head, like he was reaching out to capture his next victim. The frightening clown's demented laughter echoed through the tunnel. Darby continued to laugh and enjoy the ride, until he felt Lily grab tightly onto his arm and bury her head in his shoulder. At first, Darby thought Lily was just having fun, that is, until he felt her entire body trembling.

"Lily … you okay?"

A strong current of cold air steadily blew on them, as they came closer and closer to the enormous clown. The clown seemed to rise up, towering over them with a vicious prickly smile, writhing violently back and forth. The rickshaw broke through a set of black doors, back out into the bright lights of loading platform. Lily still had her head buried in Darby's shoulder.

"Lily it's over, the ride is over," Darby whispered. "It's okay."

Lily slowly raised her head. Dustin and Chloe stood waiting for them. Chloe had a worried look on her face, knowing the clown would have frightened Lily.

The people waiting in line were snickering at Lily for being so afraid of the silly "spook house". Darby helped her out of the cart, she still seemed shaken.

They decided to slow things down a bit, and boarded the "*Gondola Sky Ride*", so Lily could get some air. Darby and Lily got into the two-person chairlift, and an attendant closed a metal safety bar in front of them. Dustin and Chloe followed in the next chair. They all gradually lifted up into the night sky, their legs dangled down, as the chairs swung slightly in the breeze. The gondolas moved on the thick overhead cables, out over the calm lapping waters of the lake at the far end of the park. It was much quieter being up so high, but they could still hear the joyful sounds of the park and the wonderful Wurlitzer in the distance.

"This is much better, thank you Darby. It's just breathtaking, isn't it? The moon shining off the water and the stars, it's so tranquil and beautiful," Lily said with a smile. "You could almost imagine yourself being back in the forties, when the park was in its heyday."

"The whole place is rather romantic," Darby added.

"I'm really glad you're here," Lily whispered. "I'm really glad I met you."

"I'm glad I met you, too. Can I ask you a question, Lily?"

"Sure."

"Who is Varton Muntz?"

Lily's face dropped, she looked at Darby in disbelief.

"Well, I guess you did do your homework," she sat for a long moment, debating whether she should elaborate. "Varton Muntz ... and I first became acquainted when I was a little girl. It was just after I fell asleep one night; I woke hearing funny noises coming from my closet. It was really dark in my room, well, other than a small nightlight. I sat up in bed and watched curiously, as the door opened and a red balloon floated out. I remember hearing this funny little song, like old-fashioned carousel music."

"The music was coming from inside your closet?"

"Uh huh, but I wasn't scared, actually, I was intrigued. A second balloon appeared, followed by more, they all just floated around my room. The door opened wider and a white face appeared. It was watching me, peering out of the dark closet. Then suddenly, this extraordinary cartoon-like clown sprang out. Like I said, it was dark, but I could make out a huge red smile on his white face. His eyes were encased in black with high arched brows. His hair was this shock of wild red tufts, sticking out from the top of his head, matching this bulbous red nose. He wore a shiny striped satin costume with a wide collar that wrapped in sharp pleats around his neck. He was wonderful, jovial, dancing around in the shadows of my room, doing his strange little jig. I had never been to the circus, so it felt like the circus was coming to me. The clown put on a great show; it was as if he was making the balloons dance around by themselves. He would go back into the closet and peek out."

"Making sure you were still watching?"

Exactly, he knew how to seduce a child and the truth was … I couldn't take my eyes off of him. I thought he was just the most fabulous thing I had ever seen. I remember when he popped back out … he took an oversized stick of dynamite and lit the long fuse. It sizzled and burned up before exploding, shooting colorful confetti at me. I squealed and applauded all his antics. Then he waved goodbye, and disappeared back into the closet. I was bummed. I even went so far as to look into the closet, but he was gone. So the next night I waited with anticipation for my new friend to come back and put on another show. And he didn't disappoint. I heard the peculiar carousel music and a red balloon floated out from the darkness of the closet. Once again, the clown danced out.

"Ah, he returned."

Yep, but this time I was ready for him, I had a flashlight hidden under my pillow. As he danced around the room, I lit him in a bright spotlight, and boy did I get a shock. I gasped, just horrified by the ghastly monster, dancing merrily around my room. He just kept dancing, unaware of the bright light illuminating his ghastly body. He was badly burned, the absolute most frightening vision …"

"… from every child's worst nightmare."

Yeah. The red ball nose was half melted onto his grotesque face, and there were bullet holes in his tattered costume. When he noticed the light shining on him, he stopped dancing and looked straight at me. He was angry, really livid; rage seething from his fiery eyes. I quickly turned off the flashlight and hid under the covers, praying he would just go away, disappear … *die*."

"But he didn't?"

"No, he didn't," Lily admitted, then sat in silence. The memory obviously pained her. "The covers were sharply pulled off and I found myself face to face with him. His eyes were dark and large; they had this amazing glow, like sparkling rubies reflecting fire. He smelled of putrid simmering smoke; he was just the most foul, horrible fiend. Some years ago, Dave and I, we … well, let's just say we sent him on a rather long dark vacation."

"You know, I don't like clowns either, never have," Darby admitted. "There is something very fake about them. I know most people love clowns, not me. They are simply bullies. If they sense that you are afraid, they'll zero in on you. Like dogs, they can sniff out fear. They love to know they are making you squirm. There's just something so sinister about them, always laughing and acting so happy with their fake painted-on smiles and freakish oversized shoes. You never know who's under that makeup."

"Exactly, clowns obviously hide a deeper evil," she admitted. "They are supposed to be fun and make people laugh. But what they really do is seek out victims to ridicule, trying to make up for their own … I don't know, lack of soul."

The gondola turned around at the end of an old pier, before it headed over the dark water, back toward the park.

"Darby, I know all this madness sounds absolutely absurd; the ghosts, demented clowns and all the rest," Lily commented quietly. "I understand … I mean … I know it all sounds crazy and you don't quite believe it. But I want you to know that I trust you. Please don't make me a joke."

"Lily, I promise, I would never do that. I think you are truly one of the most amazing human beings I have ever met."

The ride came to an end back at the loading platform. Darby helped Lily out of the gondola and they waited for Chloe and Dustin, who were caught making out, as their gondola headed into the platform.

"Well, hello," Darby said, clearing his throat to get their attention. They quickly pulled apart, looking a bit embarrassed, yet acting giddy. Darby checked his watch; it was just after midnight. The park had almost completely emptied out. They quickly made their way over to the roller coaster that had a sign out front, "CLOSED FOR REPAIRS".

"Killer!" Dustin mused, as they walked under the bright flaming letters of the tremendous illuminated "COMET" sign. The massive *Comet* roller coaster was a structural masterpiece, standing majestically at the far end of the park. The entire 4,800 feet of coaster was completely covered in glittering chasing lights, which reflected brightly off the tranquil dark water sitting beside it.

Built back in 1948, this art-deco treasure could give any slick modern roller coaster a serious run for its money; it was the pride of the park. The size and magnitude of the coaster was truly a sight to behold. It has been billed as one of the "Top Ten Roller Coasters in the World". And although the ride only lasted a few minutes, for most, it is the most thrilling minutes of their lives.

Darby, Lily, Dustin and Chloe, excitedly ran over to the bus which had been parked at the front entrance to the Comet. They grabbed some warmer clothes, then quickly headed up the steps and through the empty turnstiles of the station platform, where Dave and Nigel had been busy setting up the cameras and equipment. The park had set up a comfortable area on the coaster loading platform with a heat lamp, chairs, snacks and a machine that made coffee and hot cocoa.

"Hey, you're here," Nigel said, walking over to the others.

"Finally," Dave added. "Nice of y'all to join us."

"Oh, just ignore him, we finished a while ago," Nigel informed them, as Dave slyly smiled. "This is Mr. Travers, the owner of the park; he set up this great spread."

"Good evening all," Harry Travers, a small stocky man with a thick handlebar moustache, beamed cheerfully as he walked over.

"Wow, thank you so much," Lily said, extending her hand to him.

"Really, it's no problem at all. We want to make you as comfy as possible while visiting us," Mr. Travers stated. "I have already gone over a little of what has been happening with your associates, so let me explain a little more to you."

"Great," Lily said, hopping up on one of the turnstiles.

"This park has had an impeccable safety record. And except for a few rare instances, minor cuts and bruises, sun exposure and the occasional heart attack, we have been incredibly fortunate. Now, there was one incident which took place back in 1978. It was the one and only fatality to ever take place in the park. It is the reason you are here … because it happened on the Comet."

"Did someone fall out?" Darby inquired.

"No, but I'm afraid a girl who worked on the ride did die … Tim!" Mr. Travers waved to a lanky man in his early fifties, standing at the far end of the platform, wearing a dark blue mechanics jumpsuit, his arms covered in colorful tattoos. "Come on over here, meet our friends. Maybe you can tell them a little about what happened in '78."

Tim Stock, the Comet's mechanical engineer, jumped onto an empty car as it pulled into the station, and rode it up to Mr. Travers' side, where he hopped off. Tim reminded Darby of an old hippy with his cool laidback attitude, white ponytail and beard.

"Hello!" Tim said, wiping some grease off his hands on a bandanna in his back pocket. "Back in 1978, ahhh man. Let's see, Arden, what can I say about Arden? Arden Miller was one of the best-natured, sweetest young ladies, I have ever been fortunate enough to meet. Arden was just as beautiful on the inside, as she was on the outside. She wasn't a great beauty, but she was so cute. With her long dark hair and perfectly manicured nails, she was always upbeat and happy, always smiling. We were all friends, all the kids that worked on the Comet back then. We always had such a blast; it felt more like we were just hanging out, than working. Arden was one of the ride attendants; the young people who assist the riders getting in and out of the cars. I knew she had been seeing one of the other ride attendants that summer, a boy named, Chris Milligan. None of us were really friendly with Chris. He thought he was better than everyone else and treated us all like crap. But Arden thought he was the end all be all.

"You didn't care for him, huh?" Lily asked.

"I always thought Chris was nothing more than a good-looking "rich punk". The day it happened, I was in the control booth. It was late afternoon at the tail end of the balmy summer season. I remember seeing this really stunning girl come onto the platform and start kissing Chris. I remember the redhead was wearing a KISS army t-shirt, two sizes too small, and skintight hip hugger jeans. She undeniably fine, but you could tell she was trashy. They went down on the exit ramp, which riders took after getting off the coaster. It was out of sight from the people standing in line. But from where I was in the control booth, I could see them perfectly. They were just goin' at it, right there.

"Where was Arden when this was happening?" Lily inquired.

"Arden had the day off, so I was very surprised when I saw her walk up onto the platform. She was wearing this pretty white summer dress. I can't explain it, but she looked just *radiant,* standing there in the rosy late afternoon sunlight. She came up and gave me a big hug. I can still see her standing there; she just looked so happy. She told me she had "big news" and asked where Chris was. I tried to distract her so she wouldn't be crushed, but she happened to look down on the ramp and saw them kissing. I think, at first, Arden was humiliated; she had no idea Chris had a girlfriend. It was just one of many things he had "conveniently" forgotten to mention to her. Arden didn't have a mean bone in her body, so I was really surprised when I saw her walk over to them and confront Chris. I could see them fighting. He was such a jackhole; I think he thought it was cool that two chicks were fighting over him."

"Typical," Lily commented.

"I saw the girl *slap* Arden really hard across the cheek, so hard she fell to the ground. She stayed down for a minute, and then you could just see the rage building up inside her. In the blink of an eye, Arden flew from the ground and lashed out at the girl, *scratching* the side of her face with her nails. Just as the girls were about to really go at it, Chris pulled them apart, trying to calm them down. I saw him take Arden by the arm and pull her down to the shady covered alcove at the end of the platform, where the train first pulls into the station after it has finished the course.

"What was said?" Lily asked curiously.

"I couldn't hear what was being said, but I could tell they were arguing. Arden was just sobbing. According to what Chris told the police, he informed Arden he was breaking up with her. Arden really liked this creep, but now she knew she was nothing more to him than a warm body while his girlfriend was in Europe for the summer. Chris said that Arden became really upset and started yelling at him, saying, "she didn't want to live without him" and threatened to kill herself. He thought she was just bluffing, playing those, girl games, as he called it. He said as he turned to walk away from her, he heard a loud *thud*, just as one of the carts sped past him into the platform. When he turned back to look back at her, she was *gone*."

"Oh my, "Lily gasped.

"He said he couldn't understand how she could have disappeared so quickly. Then he heard the *screams*. Chris felt Arden was so distraught about losing him, that she threw herself in front of the speeding cart. Her body was crushed and dragged up to the platform, where dozens of people were waiting in line. Her body was badly mangled; there was blood everywhere. I lost somebody I really cared about, a good friend. I had no idea she was so sad, so troubled."

"Where did it happen?" Dave inquired.

"It happened at the other end of the platform, where the cars come into the station, just out of eyeshot for the people waiting in line. So unfortunately, no one saw exactly what happened until after it happened. Chris was the only witness and Arden wasn't talkin'. The investigating officer considered the incident a probable suicide. The park did its best to keep the tragedy out of the papers, but word spread like wildfire."

"Now we come to the strange part, which is where you come in," Mr. Traver added. "Recently we refurbished the ride and have been getting reports of a girl with long hair and bright green *glowing* eyes, standing at the top of coaster. She is reportedly wearing a shredded, bloody, dress. She is only seen at night, just staring out into the sky. And there have been reports of people, mainly young women with red hair, getting scratched."

"Scratched?" Nigel queried.

"Yes. Last week, a young woman who was in an odd numbered party of friends was riding alone in one of the seats. The girl told us that after she had gone down the first steep hill she looked over and saw a, "mangled girl with long hair and long broken fingernails", suddenly sitting in the seat next to her. She said, the girl just lifted her hand and slashed her face with her jagged nails. It was so bad the girl needed stitches and now her family is trying to sue the park."

"Another thing to mention," Tim added. "Since she was first spotted, we have been having some mechanical problems. At night, the coaster's lights will turn off and on. The carts will ride the track with no passengers. The air gates open and close by themselves, and the carts will just stop at the top of the hill for no apparent reason. The huge fans above the platform, used to keep the riders cool while waiting in line during the hot months, will turn on by themselves and spin out of control. It's sheer madness."

"Have all the electrical systems been thoroughly checked," Dave inquired.

"Son, I know every inch of this old coaster," Tim explained. "It is in perfect working condition, except when *she* is present. But to me, the absolute creepiest thing is the music. Music will start playing on the speakers all over the coaster. And if that wasn't eerie enough, it plays only music from the seventies, when Arden died. I assure you, I do not play any seventies music. The young people today want to hear modern rock songs, which I think are mostly crap, aside from a very few exceptions. I don't even have any seventies tracks here. You can look. I cannot explain where the music is coming from. It turns itself on and turns itself off. I've seen her myself, standing up there at the top of the coaster summit. It's her, it's Arden! I don't know how or why she's there, but it *is* Arden and she *is* pissed."

"In regards to this magnificent old coaster, they literally don't make 'em like they used to. And they never will make another like this old girl," Mr. Travers stated. "I don't want the legacy of this park to be damaged or to have people think this wonderful old coaster is cursed. Like I said, this is a very safe park, but stories are starting to surface. Our attendance has already dropped from the competition of newer amusement parks. And if this continues, I am afraid I will have no choice but to close down. Okay, so Tim will be staying the night, operating the coaster for you. If you need anything at all, let him know. I'll return in the morning. Try to keep warm and please, be very careful."

"We will, thank you sir," Lily said, shaking his hand.

"Have a good night," Mr. Travers replied, as he walked off the platform, got into a golf cart and drove off.

"The cars consist of four carts coupled together, each cart holds four people. Dave and I set up cameras on the cars, both front and back seats," Nigel explained, as he walked Darby over to the black and white television monitors he had set up. "There are six cameras set up on the coaster itself, one at the summit of each of the two main hills. A camera is also positioned at each turn-around. There are two cameras set up in the station; one where the riders get in the carts and one where the carts come into the station after the ride. I'd say we have it pretty well covered."

"Brilliant," Darby said. "I'll stay here the first few rides and watch the monitors to make sure the cameras are working properly."

"I have a question Tim," Dustin asked, excitedly. "When can we ride?"

"Hop in my friend!" Tim said, walking over to his control panel.

"Hoo-hah, let's go!" Dustin yelled as he put a fleece, "court jester" type hat with dangling horns, over his mop of blonde hair, then hopped into the front seat. "I'm ready!"

Everyone got into their own separate seat, except Nigel, who jumped into the seat next to Dave, just to annoy him.

"There are how many empty seats and you have to sit here, Elton John?" Dave asked, annoyed.

"I'm nervous," Nigel sighed, feigning anxiety. "Just let me sit with you for the first ride, and then I'll be okay to ride alone."

"Dave, you insensitive brute," Lily teased. "Can't you see he's scared?"

"Just one ride, you big puss," Dave relented, "that's it!"

"Just one," Nigel beamed. "Perhaps two …"

Dustin noticed Chloe still standing on the platform, nervously biting her lower lip.

"Chloe, come on, get in," Dustin called, motioning to the empty seat next to him.

"I want to so badly, but I'll be sitting this ride out," Chloe informed them, making herself a hot cocoa and sitting down in one of chairs next to Darby.

"Chloe you love rides, especially coasters," Dave pointed out. "What's up?"

"She's a young girl, red hair, just what Arden seems to target," Lily reminded them. "Chloe, you don't have to do anything you don't want to do."

"Trust me. It's not that I don't want to; I would looove to go on this amazing roller coaster. I'm totally bummed, but I'm nervous about … *her*."

"You just stay here and chill out with me," Darby said, trying to put her at ease.

"How 'bout some music?" Tim asked, over the loudspeaker and they all cheered.

"Absolutely," Lily laughed. "Anything but seventies music."

"You got it!" Tim pressed play on the stereo system and the *Gorillaz*, "Feel Good Inc." played loudly over the entire roller coaster. "Okay cats, everybody ready?"

Tim checked every seat, making sure that all the safety bars were secured, before hitting a button on his control panel. Everyone cheered and clapped their hands, as a bell noisily rang out. A red signal light above the track turned green, and the air gates opened with a breathy *gasp*.

"Good luck!" Chloe called out, as the carts headed away from the bright lights of the station platform and into the darkness of the track. Darby and Chloe watched them on the monitors, being filmed by the cameras set up all over the ride. Dustin, Dave and Nigel, clapped their hands above their heads, as the cart climbed the extremely steep first hill with a noisy, *CLACK—CLACK-CLACK*.

Darby particularly watched Lily, who was sitting in the very last seat. With her eyes closed, she was grasping onto the padded handrail in front of her, it looked like she was quietly reciting her protection prayer. She then stared up at the top of the hill, where a trio of flags attached to the summit of the coaster, blew in the cold breeze.

"Here we gooooo!" Dustin yelled out, as the cart stopped for a split second at the summit, before letting go. The captives of the coaster screamed at the top of their lungs, as the cart plunged at top velocity down the seemingly vertical hill. They laughed and screamed with happily terrified faces, racing up another smaller hill and dropping once again. Nigel screamed like a little girl, Dave couldn't help but laugh. They looked so small on the enormous white coaster with its wild chasing lights, holding on tightly as the cart sped up the next big hill and suddenly banked around the curving white framework.

Then, almost as quickly as it started, the thrill ended. The air brakes closed and caught the cart, bringing it to an abrupt halt at the far opening of the coaster platform. After a moment, the air break released again, and the cart slowly rolled forward back into the bright lights of the platform.

"That was so, AWESOME!" Dustin gushed, laying back in his seat in ecstasy.

Nigel had one hand over his mouth, the other hand up in the air; the universal sign for "I'm going to puke".

"Kidding, I'm kidding," Nigel snickered, looking over at Dave's horrified face.

"Lily!" Darby called out in a panicked voice. Lily was sitting in the back seat, her eyes closed tightly, her body shaking, situated in a semi-fetal position. "Are you alright?"

"Nnnooo," Lily said, through her chattering teeth. "I'm frrreakin' freezing. Chloe, pppplease get my bbblue jacket."

Nigel hopped out and headed to where Darby was seated at the monitors.

"Darby, your turn, that was a little too intense for my liking," Nigel admitted.

"It was AWESOME!" Dustin repeated.

"Oh God, I want to go," Chloe whined, handing Lily her jacket.

"Ahhh, bbbless you," Lily smiled and immediately put the jacket on over her long sleeved white thermal top. She then took a white woolen cap from the pocket of the jacket and placed it low on her head.

"Let's go again!" Dustin called out.

"You may want to pace yourself, young man," Tim warned. "We have all night."

"I will ride this rollercoaster, all night long," Dustin sang. "Please, please, please, *again*, I can take it!"

"Suit yourself," Tim added.

Lily saw Darby start to get into one of the empty seats in the cart.

"Sssit with me, Darby. You can help kkkkeep me warm," Lily shivered with a sweet smile.

"Alright! Let's do this!" Darby shouted, as he eagerly hopped into the seat next to Lily, a handheld digital camera in his hand. Tim rang the bell and the air gates, once again, opened. Off they went; back out into the dark night, under a sign that read, "*Warning—Anyone standing up while the ride is in motion will be removed from the park!*" As the cart rounded the first corner, heading toward the first hill, Darby turned to Lily.

"Warmer?"

"Much warmer, toasty in fact, thanks."

"Did you see anything up there?"

"Not a thing," Lily sighed. "This may take some time, I'm afraid."

Dave looked back at Darby and Lily talking, he felt a touch of jealousy. He turned back around and joined Dustin in his cheers.

"Whoooo hooo!" Dave cried out, Darby and Lily joined in. The wind had picked up significantly since the first ride. The massive chain lift system engaged the cart with a loud metallic bang and jerk, as the massive gears turned. The chain made a loud, *CLACK-CLACK-CLACK*, as it slowly pulled them up the hill, higher and higher.

Darby was excited; he was really hoping to see, something, anything. The closer the cart came to the summit, the more his excitement peaked. The view of the park and lake from that vantage point was simply breathtaking. The white chasing lights reflected off the water, making it appear like two regal coasters were sitting side by side.

The cart finally made it to the top and paused for a few seconds. There was nothing there; Darby's heart sank with disappointment. That was, until the cart released, dropping straight down into the breathtaking thunderous abyss. He could not wipe the smile off his face, as the cart soared around the massive rollercoaster. It was such a wonderful free feeling, flying through space. The twinkling lights made it seem as though they were going even faster than they were.

The chilly night air blew warm against his face. Down another hill they soared, momentarily coming up out of their seats, over and over again, on the smaller hills that slalomed together. The cart turned once again, cornering sharply, but with a smooth motion. They were flying through the darkness alongside the moonlit water, the thrilling feeling of the G-forces pressing against their bodies, made them scream even louder. They finally landed, abruptly coming to a stop at the far end of the platform, and then slowly pulled back into the brightly lit station, applauding the magnificent coaster.

Hours passed, everyone took turns riding the rollercoaster, except for Dustin who had yet to get off. Chloe sat envious, watching each time the carts came into the station with excited passengers. She wanted so badly to take a spin and be able to sit in the cart with Dustin.

At two in the morning, they decided to take a break and have something to eat. Dustin still sat in the front cart, wanting to continue riding. He looked over at Chloe and mouthed, "Come on Chloe, just one ride?"

She thought about it for a moment. Then a big smile beamed across her face, as she ran over to Dustin and jumped into the front seat next to him.

"I'm ready," Chloe called out.

"Chloe, you sure?" Darby asked. "Don't let Mr. peer pressure, pressure you."

"No, he's not," she giggled. "I am so ready!"

"Is it okay?" Tim the mechanic looked to Lily.

"Chloe, just be careful," Lily warned. "I mean it!"

"It'll be fine, nothing is going to happen," Chloe assured her.

"Just because you can't see something …"

"Doesn't mean it isn't there," Chloe finished her thought. "I know, I know."

Lily kneeled down next to Chloe and took her hand.

"You're all I have left," Lily said thoughtfully. "If anything ever happened …"

"Lily, I know, you have my word," Chloe said, holding up two fingers in a Girl Scout pledge. "I totally promise … I'll be extra careful."

Lily stood back up and nodded to Tim.

"Yessss!" Chloe squealed, as Dustin joined in clapping and howling. Lily looked very worried, as Tim rang the bell and released the air break, sending the cart off into the dark night. Everyone gathered at the monitors and watched as they started up the first hill, paused and plunged, dropping the screaming twosome straight down. They laughed and held onto each other, as the cart burned around the track at top speed, finally coming back into the station, windblown and cheering.

"Oh, my God!" Chloe gushed. "That was incredible! The best roller coaster I have ever, ever, been on! Can we go again Tim? Please, please?"

"Please, please," Dustin joined in with Chloe's begging.

The hypnotic song, "More Human than Human" by *White Zombie*, blared over the sound system speakers, as the cart pulled back out onto the dark track. Over the next half hour, while the others relaxed and ate, Dustin and Chloe continuously rode the massive coaster. They seemed to enjoy it more each time they pulled back into the station. Lily sat under the heat lamp to keep warm, sipping cocoa from a Styrofoam cup, while chatting with the others, but never taking her eyes off the monitors.

"I have to hit the loo," Darby said. "Can I get anyone anything from the bus?"

"Grab my leather gloves," Nigel requested. "They're in my black bag."

"Anything else?" Darby asked. "Speak now or forever hold your peace."

"No thanks, we're good Darby," Lily murmured.

"Alright, I'll be back," Darby said, as he casually walked off the platform, hopped over the turn styles and made his way down the steps. He took his time, strolling out under the illuminated COMET sign. Dustin and Chloe's laughter echoed through the sky, as they left the platform on yet another ride. Darby walked over to the bus, opened the door and pulled himself up the steps.

He yawned, as he wandered back to the bathroom and closed the door. After a few moments, he emerged. A digital clock on the wall just changed to 2:45 am. He walked over to one of the couches, where he spotted Nigel's black equipment bag.

A new song began. Darby bobbed his head along to the opening drumbeat of a familiar tune, which could be heard faintly from outside the bus. As he sat on the couch rummaging through Nigel's bag, he quietly sang along.

"You got me runnin', goin' out of my mind. You got me thinkin' that I'm wastin' my time. Don't bring me down. No, no, no, no, no … ew-weeh-whoo!"

Darby abruptly stopped singing and his brows furled, as he suddenly realized the song he was singing was "vintage seventies"—*ELO's*, "Don't bring me down", pounded from the sound system.

Darby cried out, "Oh, shit!"

Knocking everything out of the bag, he bolted off the couch and dashed out the bus door. Running back up under the Comet sign, he abruptly stopped, noticing the sign was *flickering* with an unsettling loud electrical *buzz* emanating from it. Darby looked up and saw that the entire rollercoaster was flickering uncontrollably, like a defective toy whose batteries that were going dead. The music was slowing and speeding up erratically; a cart was just about to reach the summit of the first hill.

"*CHLOE!*" Darby shouted, just as the cart was released and plummeted down. He ran through turnstiles to the station platform, where the enormous fans above were blowing wildly.

"Make it stop!" Lily screamed, begging Tim. "Make it stop … please!"

"I can't, I'm sorry," Tim explained. "Once it lets go, it's in motion, I can't do anything! My God, I remember, this was one of her favorite songs."

"What the bloody hell is happening?" Darby yelled, running over, scanning the bank of monitors, everyone was frantically huddled around.

"Darby!" Lily cried out. "There's no way to stop the cart!"

"Look!" Dave pointed to one of the black and white screens. It clearly showed Dustin and Chloe, who seemed to be having a blast, laughing and screaming with enormous smiles on their faces, as the cart sped rapidly along the track. "They're okay."

"What's wrong with the camera on the back seat?" Lily asked. "The screen is completely dark."

Just as Darby looked at the shadowy monitor, he noticed it beginning to *lighten*, seeing what appeared to be the back of a person with long hair. He looked at another monitor that had been mounted on the front of the cart. It looked as though a person was standing up in the very last seat.

"It's her," Lily gasped. Looking away from the monitors, she gazed helplessly up at the actual cart flying around the track. Even through the erratic flashes of light and distance, Lily knew it was her; shredded, mangled, horrible … *Arden*.

Lily followed the cart with her eyes. She could see Arden climbing over the back seat, slowly but with ease, her long frayed dress flapping violently in the harsh wind. Like a spider, she reached her long thin arms out, moving from one seat, forward to the next, coming closer and closer to the front seat. As the cart violently shook and banked harshly around turns, Arden was barely affected, she just seemed to be one with the coaster; as though gravity did not apply to her.

"Mother-fucker, she's climbing over the seats, up to the front … closer to them!" Dave cried out, intensely watching the monitors, holding himself back from just running out onto the track, but he knew better. Frustrated, he grabbed Tim's arm. "Come on man, there's got to be something you can do!"

"I've already tried the emergency shut down, it's been overridden," Tim told him. "I'm totally powerless!"

"That's fitting," Nigel commented, as the music crackled and changed to another seventies favorite, "Rollercoaster" by *The Ohio Players*. "Why don't they notice the music and the lights?"

"I don't think they're quite into that decade's tunes," Tim added. "And the lights, they're going so fast, they may not even be aware of it."

Without warning the bell signaling the start of the ride rang out, startling them.

"What now?" Nigel asked, as he saw the light above the track turned from red to green, the air gates opened under their own volition, releasing another cart which had been sitting in a holding area off the main track. They could do nothing more then watch the empty cart race off onto the track under its own power.

"Madness," Darby mused, unable to believe what he was actually seeing. He looked back at the monitors, Dustin and Chloe were still laughing, completely oblivious to the horror, now sitting in the middle of the seat, directly behind them. Darby could see only glimpses of Arden's destroyed face, peering out from under strands of long stringy hair. She sat motionless, staring directly at the back of Chloe's head, her body barely moving, as the coaster rocked harshly.

"Chloe, turn around," Lily whispered, praying somehow her little sister could hear her. "Turn around, she's right there."

Chloe laid her head on Dustin's shoulder in playful flirtation. When she lifted her head back up, Dustin smiled at her. Something behind him caught his eye. As he turned his head to look back, a long white arm with bone exposed through its shredded skin, reached out for Chloe.

"What the ..." Dustin yelled, grabbing the arm just as it was about to take a chunk of skin from the side of Chloe's face. But instead of getting Chloe, the long jagged nails sliced deeply into Dustin's neck. Almost immediately blood began to flow from the open gashes. Chloe screamed, seeing the ghosts' *glowing* green eyes, burning through the darkness.

Arden viciously ripped her arm from Dustin's grasp and pushed him hard, causing his head to slam down against the side of the metal cart; instantly knocking him out. He slumped down in the seat, his right arm dangled dangerously out of the cart, barely missing the coasters wooden beams blazing by. Chloe quickly reached over, pulling his arm back into the cart, just as it cornered a sharp turn. She held onto the unconscious Dustin, making sure he didn't fall out, his limp body moved erratically with each turn.

There was no where to go, Chloe knew they were trapped. The look of sheer terror was frozen on her pretty face. Arden stood up in her seat, gaunt and elongated, towering over them. The lights surrounding the coaster flickered, turning off and back on in a confused strobing frenzy.

Arden stared at Chloe, her eyes never blinking in the ruthless wind. Chloe could barely look at her gruesome face, which looked like she had been through a shredder. Muscle and bone were showing through the areas on her body missing skin. Her hair, some pieces of frayed fabric and peeling skin, moved sharply, flapping in the wind.

"Leave us alone!" Chloe cried, as Arden balled her hands into tight angry fists at her side. She opened her half missing mouth in the guise of a scream. Nothing came out … at first. Then, a *blast* radiated out of the dead girls' throat, shrill and deafening; a detonation so intense it *shook* the frame of the massive old coaster and was heard clearly by the others down on the platform. The deep inhuman howl lingered, emanating out of Arden's mouth from somewhere deep inside the bowels of hell. Chloe closed her eyes tightly, cringing, as Arden held her angry arpeggio, echoing and piercing through the night sky for what seemed like an eternity.

"Please God, make it stop! Please God, make it stop!" Chloe repeated, over and over, as the white globe lights that ran the length of the rollercoaster, popped and exploded, from the distorted scream, as the cart passed.

Chloe watched Arden spread her hands out like the claws of a vicious animal about to attack. Just as Arden raised her boney arms to seize Chloe, the cart dipped suddenly, as it flew back toward the stations' covered platform.

As the cart entered the edge of the brightly lit platform, Arden's form rapidly *disintegrated*. The bright lights on the platform were so intense they incinerated the apparition into a million burning embers, which burst back into the darkness away from the cart. As the air brakes caught the cart, it came to a screeching halt. Everyone ran to the cart, afraid it may start up again and quickly pulled Chloe out. She was stunned

"Lily," Chloe sobbed, as she grabbed onto her sister for dear life.

"Chloe, my God you're bleeding!" Lily cried, seeing blood on Chloe's sweater.

"No, its Dustin, he's hurt, help him!" Chloe screamed. "She cut him!"

The men were carefully pulling Dustin out of the cart, laying him down on the platform floor. Darby grabbed a towel and applied pressure to his neck, as Tim stuck smelling salts under his nose. Dustin quickly shot up and opened his eyes, regaining consciousness. Chloe stood behind the group, nervously biting her fingers, as the others were tending to Dustin.

Suddenly, the bell *rang out* and the air brake opened on its own, releasing the cart back out onto the track.

"Dustin, can you hear me?" Darby asked, holding Dustin's head. "You alright?"

"I'm cool, I'm good," Dustin said weakly. "Did ya get that guys' license, Chief?"

"He's okay, Chloe. Come on, why you don't come over here and be with Dustin," Darby said, holding his hand out to her. Chloe calmed and smiled at Darby.

Just as she raised her hand up to take his, her body suddenly jerked and she harshly *fell* backwards, falling down onto the coaster tracks. Stunned, she turned her head just in time to see the second cart come speeding back into the station. She closed her eyes, bracing for the impact, when the air brakes caught and stopped the car mere *inches* from her face.

Dave and Darby jumped onto the track and lifted Chloe's shaking body up to Nigel. Lily ran over and grabbed onto her tightly, taking her warm jacket off and wrapping it around her shocked little sister.

"She pushed you?" Lily asked urgently, holding Chloe's face tightly in her hands. "She pushed you, didn't she?"

Chloe couldn't answer she was so shaken. She just nodded, *"yes"*.

"This ends now, get them to the bus!" Lily instructed. Dave put Dustin's arm around his neck and helped him walk off the platform, as Darby and Nigel escorted the traumatized Chloe down the steps. They had just walked out from under the illuminated COMET sign, when they heard the opening chorus of *Abba's,* "Dancing Queen" start to play over the speakers and Tim calling out from the platform.

"Hey, hey, where are you goin'? You can't go up there, it's too dangerous!"

"Oh no, Lily!" Darby murmured. He quickly spun around to see that Lily was *not* walking to the bus behind them; she was already halfway up the first steep hill with a determined angry look in her eyes. Darby ran back up the steps, Tim was on the phone to park security, when he saw Darby rush back onto the platform; he looked grateful.

"She can't go up there!" Tim frantically told Darby. "She's gonna get killed!"

Standing on the platform, Darby looked up through a tangle of snarling steel girders, to the highest point at the top of the gigantic rollercoaster. He could see a distinctly *female figure* in flowing garments, standing at the peak in all her gruesome glory, silhouetted in the soft glow of the moon. Without a second thought, Darby started up the extremely narrow wooden slats, which made up the catwalk steps beside the rollercoaster tracks. One false move and Darby knew he was toast.

"YOU CAN'T GO UP THERE!" Tim called after him, but he kept going.

Lily was nervous and shivering, but also livid. She tried not to look down, as she climbed higher and higher, trying to stay focused, until she finally made it up to the top. She crouched down and held tightly to one of the numerous metal beams, holding up the strings of chasing lights, just a few feet from the top of the massive hill.

Lily could see Arden, standing just above her on the summit. She looked up at Arden's shadowy profile, studying her mutilated body. Her severe luminous face seemed utterly void of life; her body was as rigid and stiff as a cadaver. Her right ear and most of the right side of her face was gone. Her long frayed nails were dark blue in color and her long white dress was stained, saturated with dark dried blood. It fluttered out in long tattered shreds, exposing far too much of the damage her body endured when it was dragged under the grinding metal wheels of the heavy cart.

If Arden knew Lily was a few feet behind her, she surely made no notice of it.

"*You can dance, you can jive, having the time of your life,*" Arden quietly sang along to the chorus. "*Owooh, see that girl, watch that scene, diggin' the dancing queen.*"

"They would like you to leave, Arden," Lily called out over the music and cold wind. Arden did not move. "You do not belong here."

Darby had just started his hike up the first hill, when all of sudden an *empty cart* flew up from behind, passing him. He tried to move out of the way in time, but the cart hit the back of his leg and he fell off the side of the track, down to the gravel pit on the ground below. Darby immediately looked up to Lily, as the cart headed in her direction.

"LILY!" he yelled. "LOOK OUT!" Lily quickly turned and saw the cart, just as it was about to hit her. She swung her body out of the way, just in a nick of time, and clung tightly onto the rail. In her precarious position, she couldn't help looking down at the ground so far below. She saw Darby looking up at her; it was then she truly realized just how far up she was. Lily's heart raced, as she turned her attention back to Arden.

"You don't belong here, Arden!" Lily said, raising her voice. "They would like you to leave." The old wooden coaster creaked and moaned with each gust of wind, the lights flickered madly to the music. Arden's long hair blew in cold night air, as she vacantly stared out at the dark water from high atop her glimmering perch; she did not move ... she did not blink. "They would like you to leave Arden, you're frightening people. You need to make peace with yourself."

"The air is burning," the words seethed out of Arden's disfigured mouth.

"You died many years ago."

Arden did not move.

"Do you remember?"

Arden did not answer.

"Do you remember?" Lily asked. "You, killed yourself,"

"Pushhhed!"

"What?"

"Pushhhhed!"

"You were pushed?"

Although her body never moved, Arden's head sharply *twisted* and *popped* unnaturally, as she turned and stared down at Lily with her glowing eyes. For a split second, Arden and Lily's *eyes locked*, and Lily was immediately transported back to the warm summer evening in 1978.

Standing on the station platform in the midst of a heated confrontation, Lily could see through Arden's eyes. A handsome young man stood before her, holding her arms tightly at her sides, talking to her in an angry hushed tone.

"I'm going off to college in a few weeks and if you think I'm going to let you, fuck up my life, you're delusional! You're not going to ruin my future because you got knocked up!"

"Chris, how can you say that," Arden pleaded. "Why are you being so mean?"

"Grow up Arden, welcome to reality. You knew how things were. I bet you got pregnant just to try and keep me here. It's probably not even mine. I won't let you do that; I won't let you do that to me!"

Lily watched Chris turn away from Arden, then suddenly turn back and sharply *push* her by the shoulders. She could feel her body helplessly *falling* backwards, and then everything went *black*. Lily broke her gaze with Arden, finding herself back on the top of the rollercoaster.

"Pushhhed," Arden repeated.

"He pushed you?"

"Pushhhed, pushhhed, pushhhed!"

Darby got back up onto the tracks and continued heading up the hill. Another empty cart had pulled out of the platform. He quickly jumped into one of the seats in the middle of the cart and rode it around the turn that lead up to the first hill. Looking up at the top of the hill, he could see Lily crouched down under Arden's lean body. The wind had picked up considerably, pushing Lily off balance. Arden held her gaze, repeating her mantra, her voice becoming intense, angry, irate.

"Pushhhed, pushhhed!"

"Arden!"

"Pushhhed, pushhhed, pushhhed, pushhhed!"

Darby could only watch helplessly from the cart, as it inched closer to the summit. He climbed clumsily over the seats, trying to get closer to the front. The wind continued to gust, the flags above blew harshly, ripping and shredding.

Arden opened her mouth and a painful *scream* escaped, so loud and violent, it shook the old rollercoaster. Lily grabbed onto the thin railing for dear life, but the vibration was too strong, she was quickly losing her grip. As Lily tried to regain her position, she lost her footing and slid, clinging desperately to the track, dangling by her hands, until a pair of hands grasped them.

"I've got you!" Lily looked up to see Darby, leaning out of one of the carts as it reached the top. He pulled her into the seat beside him, just as Arden was reached out to attack. Darby stood up and leaned back, trying to shield Lily.

For a split second, he found himself face to face with Arden; awestruck by her horrifying visage, he could only stare into her face, paralyzed with a bizarre mixture of fear and fascination. She was not completely transparent, she seemed solid like a normal girl, but there was something very unnatural about how she stood so rigid.

"PUUUSHHHED," Arden cried, leaning so close to Darby, he could smell the decayed aroma emanating from her. He could feel an electric sensation, a strong energy in the air all around her. She reached out with her vile frayed nails and viciously scraped through the skin by his left eye, an inch closer and she would have taken his eye out. Darby screamed in pain, just as the cart released and plummeted down the hill.

Lily held tightly onto Darby's waist, but he lost his footing when the cart burned around a sharp corner of the track. Luckily his foot got caught on the safety bar and with Lily's help he was able to get back into the cart.

Lily turned and looked over her shoulder, seeing Arden gliding effortlessly through the air, keeping perfect pace with the speeding cart. She grasped onto the back of the last seat and began quickly climbing over the seats, until she was right behind them. The ghost stood up in the cart, her body moved effortlessly, as it flew up and down the hills and around the sharp corners.

"Darby! Just hold on, we're almost to the platform!" Lily yelled over the roar of the metal tracks. Arden let out another ear shattering, *shriek*. They shielded themselves from flying glass, as the lights surrounding the track *popped* and *exploded*, as the cart soared by.

"ARDEN, STOP THIS!"

"PUUUSHHHED," Arden continued her unrelenting chant. Lily watched in horror, as Arden laid her disfigured hands upon her own belly and ripped open the already shredded fabric, exposing her wretched scraped skin and dug her hands deep into her belly, pulling the skin apart, revealing a tiny *fetus*.

"My God," Lily cried. Arden let out one last tortured banshee *scream*, as the cart headed into the bright lights of the station and she was incinerated, burning up into fiery ash embers that blew off into the darkness.

The cart came to a stop under the covered platform. Immediately, two park security guards ran over and pulled them out of the cart before it, once again, started up and sped back out onto the track and back into the dark night.

"That's it, we're done, pack everything up," Lily exclaimed, as she quickly walked down the platform towards the stairs. "Where's my sister?" Where's Dustin?"

"They're on the bus," Dave responded.

"What happened?" Tim asked, quickly following Lily.

"She was pushed, she was pregnant … she is *not* leaving."

"I knew it, I knew she was pushed," Tim cursed angrily. "That son of a bitch!"

"Please tell Mr. Traver, there's nothing I can do. I'm very sorry, but it's not safe."

"Lily!" Darby called after her. "Lily, we can't just leave."

Lily turned to Darby and touched his bloodied face.

"We're leaving Darby, there's nothing that can be done!" Lily admitted. "The living … will always come before the dead!"

The cut on Darby's eye was superficial and only needed to be treated with antibiotics and bandaged. Dustin's cuts required several stitches. It was rather obvious the emergency room staff didn't buy the "Bear Attack" scenario, Dustin was giving them.

After getting patched up, Lily insisted Dave drive directly to the nearest airport, where she promptly bought Chloe a ticket home. Chloe looked dejected, as she said goodbye to her sister and her new crush, Dustin. The two took a few private moments, and tearfully kissed before parting ways. Chloe continued to weep, as she headed down to the gate and took one last look at Dustin, who blew her a sweet farewell kiss.

Darby was very surprised when Dustin declined his offer to buy him a ticket back to California, he wanted to stay and continue on to the next job.

CHAPTER 13

▼

SAWDUST IN THE BLOOD

It was an overcast afternoon when they pulled up to the hotel entrance. Being thoroughly exhausted, they grabbed their bags and headed into the ritzy lobby to check in. Darby and Nigel stood at the front desk, where they were told they would have to share a room, as space was limited. They didn't care; they just wanted some sleep after the previous bizarre night.

Darby turned and noticed that Lily had stopped at the elegant brass doors. She looked to be talking to *someone* that was not there, then she nodded graciously to the air.

"Here are the keys to your rooms," the man behind the desk smiled, handing Darby keycards. "Enjoy your stay."

"Thank so much," Darby said, as he and Nigel walked over to meet Lily in the center of the posh lobby, and together they walked to the elevators. "You alright?"

"Oh, you mean," Lily was amused, figuring Darby had seen her peculiar, "one-sided", conversation. "That was Arturo Martinez I was chatting with. He was the bell hop in this hotel for fifty years. He hopes we have a nice stay and if we need anything, we should not hesitate to ask him."

"Ah, how nice," Nigel mused, as they entered the elevator. "Service from both the living and the dead."

After sleeping the day away, Darby and Nigel had dinner in the swanky hotel restaurant. They discussed the amusement park and what they had experienced, trying to soak it all in. Following dinner, they headed to a packed sports bar, across the street from the hotel, for a few beers and to catch a game on one of the many big screen televisions.

Darby opened his laptop and began surfing the internet, looking for any information he could dig up on Lily's childhood nemesis, Varton Muntz. He found several websites dedicated to the former actor, who apparently had a bit of a twisted following; a macabre "fan club" of sorts. Darby clicked into one of websites called, *"Memoirs of a Dark Circus"*.

An old black and white image popped up on his computer screen. It was a picture of a rather dashing man with dark slicked back hair and a thin moustache, wearing a stylish black tuxedo. There was a definite air of sophistication to his face.

The website told the story of Varton Muntz, a well-known and respected actor, raised in the Bulgarian city of Plovdiv, also known as "The Valley of Roses". The idyllic storybook city built in tiers up the side of a mountain with cobblestone streets and beautiful stone houses with thatched roofs. The valley below the city was covered in a carpet of every color of rose imaginable, framed by the majestic trees of the Black Forest.

As a young man, Varton grew increasingly bored with small town life, fearing that he was destined to follow in his fathers footsteps, and be stuck in the family blacksmithing business. At the age of seventeen, Varton escaped to the capital city of Sophia, where he worked various odd jobs, until he was accepted into a prestigious theatre company. Within a few years time, he had become one of the most famous theatrical actors in Eastern Europe. For years, he relished in his lavish life of wealth and fame, and indulged whenever possible in liquor and young women; the indulgences that initially led to his downfall.

In the 1940's, he began a torrid affair with the sixteen year-old daughter of one of the countries highest ranking officials. When the affair was discovered, there was a hefty bounty placed upon his head. He escaped to Varna, a tourist city on the shores of the Dead Sea, where he worked incognito as a longshoreman, until he could secure passage on a ship to Spain. Within a year, he decided to head to America; a place he heard was the "land of opportunity". He arrived looking for great success on the stage, but finding nothing but disappointment. Due to his strong accent and limited English, the only job he could get as a performer was in a traveling circus.

Varton was humiliated to be put in the position of having to take a job as a clown, a joker, doing absurd slap stick and pratfalls, throwing buckets of confetti while wearing a ridiculous satin costume. Back in Bulgaria he had been a serious dramatic actor, now he was a performing buffoon with a serious drinking problem. Varton had only been with the circus a few weeks, but had such anger and venom towards everyone around him, he was constantly getting into scraps and fist fights with the other performers.

In September of 1944, the circus train arrived too late to perform the first of a three day engagement. In the circus business, missing a show is considered extremely bad luck, but there was no way they would have set everything up in time.

The next afternoon, Varton was seen wandering around the midway; an area outside the main entrance of the big top, lined with concessionaires, rides and sideshow attractions. Nursing a bottle of cognac, hidden in the puffy sleeve of his clown costume, he would pickpocket circus patrons in order to maintain his liquor habit and stay perpetually drunk.

That evening, Varton had been caught peeping by some of the young female performers, getting into their sequined costumes in a small tent backstage. He was not at all embarrassed; he simply cackled and sauntered away.

The opening of the circus was always a big production number involving an "over the top" introduction by the ringmaster, followed by a parade of animals and performers, who traipsed around the hippodrome track. The show included amazing performances by jugglers, acrobats, aerialists, trained wild animals and of course, *clowns*. The owner of the circus noticed Varton stumbling around the arena. He was unwilling or unable to keep up with the other clowns, who taunted and tormented him, knowing his drunken state. The crowd just laughed, assuming it was part of the act.

When Varton finally made his way back into the backstage area, he was fired on the spot for insubordination and performing while intoxicated. Witnesses' say he became enraged, admonishing the owner of the circus in his thick Bulgarian accent.

The clown was last seen out behind the big top tent, laying in some bales of hay by one of the performers, a young woman named Darla, who had been harassed by Varton a few days earlier. Standing in the back of the tent in her shimmering gold costume, she watched Varton take a swig from his bottle of cognac and spit it onto the back of the tent.

"I salute you, you who are about to die," he toasted to the curse he placed on the world which had shunned him. Then without pause, he tossed his lit cigar onto the side canvas of the massive enclosure, and watched with a pleased sneer on his face, as the flames grew and danced up the oiled cloth. Varton rocked and swayed, as if he were the conductor this psychotic symphony of fire. Darla screamed for help, as smoke started to fill the arena.

Hundreds of audience members, mainly children, were seated watching the "Flying Fitzpatrick's", swinging high in the dome of the structure. With the house lights down and all eyes looking up, no one noticed the flames, until it was too late. Most would not make it out in time.

The tent had been waterproofed with a mixture of kerosene and paraffin, a highly flammable combination, but a common waterproofing method of the time. Amazement turned to horror, as the tent exploded into flames, quickly speeding along the canvas. Hindering the escape of many were the steel railings placed along the front of the bleachers. Hundreds swarmed exits in a panic, but they were blocked by iron cage chutes, filled with snarling lions and clawing tigers, awaiting their turn in the center ring.

Panic-stricken people began a desperate stampede to escape the flames that flowed like a *breeze* across the tent top, a square mile of canvas. Seconds later, the fire reached the roof and at the top of the center pole, it split in three different directions. The ring master begged the audience not to panic and leave in an orderly fashion. But his efforts were in vain, no one could hear over the scream-ing and chaos. Many people were badly burned by the melting paraffin, which rained down from the roof like napalm. Engulfed by a tsunami of flames, the big top collapsed with a deafening roar, dooming those still alive inside and trapping hundreds of spectators beneath it.

People feverishly threw buckets of water on the fire, but it was hopeless. One minute the audience was laughing and cheering, having a wonderful magical night, listening to the happy circus music played by the brass band. The next moment, they were running for their lives in a hellish inferno. It all happened in less than ten minutes.

Previous mysterious fires at the circus had been put out without incident. No one ever connected them to Varton, the culprit. But when it was found that Varton had purposely started the fire … a manhunt was on. Varton was discov-ered passed out in a corral with some elephants. He was taken away by an angry mob, who hung him from a giant sycamore tree. But he did not die right away; he struggled, swinging from the noose, as a horde of onlookers cheered. A fellow clown doused Varton with his own bottle of liquor and set him ablaze.

In the darkness, he lit up the tree, as he twisted and kicked in the wind like a fiery piñata. Two men with guns stepped through the crowd and shot Varton repeatedly as he burned. Apparently, he wasn't dying quick enough.

Darby hit another highlighted box that read—VARTON MUNTZ 1944. The picture was a group shot of the entire circus company; performers, stage hands, trainers, and animals. They were standing in front of the massive red and white striped tent. At the side of the picture was a group of giddy clowns, making silly faces and poses. One clown in particular stood out. He was neither smiling nor jovial; his stare was cold and dark, void of conscience or feeling.

Darby zeroed in on the clown, staring directly into the camera with fierce intensity. It was Varton; part devil, part serial-killer, dressed in typical clown garb; baggy multi-colored costume and whitened face, with a grotesque smile painted over his smirking mouth. He remembered, Lily's words, "clowns so obviously hide a deeper evil."

Darby clicked on one last highlighted bar that read—"VARTON MUNTZ IN DEATH." Darby actually sat back in his chair, taken aback by the picture that appeared on the screen before him. He truly *was* … the absolute most frightening vision of every child's worst nightmare. The picture had been taken after Varton had been burned alive by the lynch mob; it was truly startling.

He had been laid out on some sort of slab, still wearing his satin clown costume, a wide white collar wrapped in sharp pleats around his neck. He was quite obviously dead, but his glazed eyes, sheathed in black, remained open. His mouth, encased in whimsical red greasepaint, had been crudely sewn shut; yet he still appeared to be smiling. The painted white skin had been darkened with soot; the skin had melted away in places. He wore a quirky bald cap with bright red tufts of fake hair coming out on either side of his badly singed head. His red ball nose appeared to have melted onto his face.

Darby took out a picture from his file. It was a picture Lily had drawn with crayons of her clown when she was small. It was almost identical to the picture of the dead clown staring out from his computer screen. He now understood Lily's fright in the fun house.

"Hey Darby, isn't that the freakish Spanish psychic, Gaia, on the tele?" Nigel asked, pointing to one of the numerous televisions surrounding the bar. "It looks like she's in the house with that family, the ones with the bullshit phony ghost, *"Haverghast."*

Darby and Nigel walked over to the television and watched Gaia contact the bogus spirit. The family pulled all the same amateurish parlor tricks, but instead of calling them out, Gaia went along with them, fueling the fire and giving them credibility.

"I can't believe that bloated codfish is perpetuating such a blatant lie," Darby mused. "Unbelievable."

"Well, at least they are getting what they wanted, free publicity."

Knowing they had to be on the road early the next morning, Darby and Nigel decided to call it an early evening and headed back across the street to their hotel.

"Speaking of bloated codfish," Nigel said, with a heavy disdain, seeing the "larger than life" mystic, Gaia, sitting in the lobby of their luxury hotel, being interviewed by a local news crew.

"I have an idea. Nigel, give me the microphone and film this at a distance," Darby said, handing Nigel his digital camera.

"You got it."

Darby hid the microphone under his shirt and took Angela's ring off the leather cord around his neck. He walked over to where Gaia was being interviewed and waited until the camera crew finished.

"Excuse me, Gaia," Darby approached the ever perspiring woman sitting on an oversized gold couch, flanked by her many keepers, while fanning herself with a vibrant Chinese fan. A giant diamond encrusted cross hung down into her ample cleavage. Heavily made-up with brightly painted red lips and a terrific jet black bouffant hairdo, she reminded Darby of an overstuffed, Snow White. "I just wanted to say, I'm a great admirer of your work."

"Aren't you a darling," Gaia gushed in her thick Spanish accent, not noticing Nigel filming her. "What would you like me to sign?"

Darby fumbled for a piece of paper and a marker, and then handed them to her. Gaia signed her name with huge cursive letters and gave the items back to Darby.

"Thank you very much, I'll treasure it always," Darby lied. "I was wondering if it might be possible to get you to perhaps … read this *ring*?"

Darby held up Angela's platinum wedding band on his pinky. He noticed Gaia quickly glance at his hands, looking for a wedding band on his ring finger.

"I'm afraid Gaia really has to be going," Kenny, one of her uppity handlers cut in. "She has a seminar in an hour with over a thousand paying guests."

"No, Kenny, it is okay, I read ring for this handsome young man. What did you say your name was darling?"

"Darby."

"Alright Darby, give me the ring." Darby handed Gaia the ring. She held it tightly in her hand, closed her eyes, and summoned her spirit guide. "Asreal, could you please find the owner of this ring for me. Yes, yes, thank you, sweet spirit. The ring belonged to a woman, yes?"

"Yes, it did," Darby admitted, looking over at Nigel, who put a finger to his mouth motioning for Darby not to say too much.

"Thank you, sweet spirit. My spirit guide Asreal tells me this was a wedding band. Is that correct?"

"Yes, ma'am, it was."

"What was that Asreal, yes, yes, thank you. Asreal tells me the woman this ring belonged to has passed over fairly recently. Is this correct?"

"Yes, it is," Darby answered, rather surprised.

"I see, yes, it was your mothers' wedding band. She's coming through to me."

"Really?"

"Yes, I can see her. She was quite beautiful."

"She sure is."

"She tells me, she misses you a great deal and she is always around you, watching over you. She says, she does not want you to be sad any longer, she wants you to go on with your life."

"Wow, she said all that from beyond the grave? Can you hold on for just a sec?" Darby asked Gaia, politely. He took out his cell phone, dialed a long number and held on as it rang. "Hello Dad, it's me. I'm fine, how are you? Hey, I know it's early, but is mum anywhere close?"

Gaia grimaced, she knew something was up.

"Okay, great, I'll hold," Darby smiled at Gaia, as he waited. "Mum, hello, how are you? No, just wanted to say hi and make sure you were doing well. Yes, I'm still in America, should be home by Christmas. Right, me too, I have to go, talk to you soon."

"That's quite enough!" Gaia's face reddened, overtaken with pure, unadulterated, anger. She attempted to get off the couch, but her large bottom pulled her back down. Her assistant quickly pulled her to her feet. "I will not be made a fool of by the likes of you!"

Gaia stormed out of the lobby, her assistants in tow. Darby looked over at Nigel.

"Please tell me you got all that?" Nigel nodded with a grin. The friends shared a hearty laugh at Gaia's expense, as they headed into the elevator.

Up in their hotel suite, Darby decided to test the sound activated EVP recorder he had borrowed from Dave, earlier that afternoon. He set the small device on the table between the two beds and turned it on before turning off the light.

"Wake up mate," Nigel said sleepily, as he awoke to the sounds of Darby flailing about in his bed. Nigel nudged Darby on the shoulder, trying not to startle him. Darby woke with a sharp gasp. He had experienced the same persistent nightmare of the "Dead-eyed" being, leering at him, across the wild party in the moving room. "You okay?"

"Yeah, just a nightmare, I've had the same bloody nightmare so many times in the last few weeks, I've forgotten what a regular dream is like."

Darby noticed the EVP recorder sitting on the table next to him. He quickly sat up in bed and listened to what the machine may have caught over night; disappointed to hear nothing more than a distant train and Nigel snoring.

CHAPTER 14

▼

SYMPATHY FOR THE DEVIL

On the first day of school, Trent Leek put on his flashy new red parachute pants, a white button-down shirt and skinny black tie. He was even so bold, during this decade where clothes looked more like costumes, to line his eyes with black eyeliner and gel his hair.

Trent thought he had changed so drastically, that the other kids wouldn't even recognize him. They might even think he was a new student. He was elated, a whole new life was about to begin. He took a deep breath and walked down the crowded main hallway with an air of confidence. For the first time in his young life, all eyes were on him and he felt cool. Then it started … quietly from behind, the *snickers*, were they real?

Please God no, he thought. But the vicious finger-pointing and mockery were all too real. Then he heard the familiar laughter, which within in a few moments had turned to full-on mocking fits of hysteria, which echoed through the massive hall. He could feel his face redden and get hot. Trent wanted to curl up and die right there. He walked faster and faster, his head lowered in shame, as the hysterics continued.

"Look, he's wearing eyeliner!" he heard a girl yell.

"INNN COMING!" A football player yelled, as a can of grape soda was thrown over the mob and scored a direct hit, drenching Trent's white shirt in sticky purple sap. Nothing had changed, to them, he was still the same loser he always was, and always would be. A long leg stuck out of the sea of laughing faces and Trent took a nose dive on to the rough tile floor, which caused the laughter to crescendo to a fevered pitch.

After an entire summer of preparation, it had only taken ten minutes before *they*, once again, ganged up and crushed him. He picked himself up and ran out the back doors.

A few weeks earlier, Trent turned sixteen and was about to begin his junior year at Walker High School in Black River Falls, Wisconsin. Over the summer he had formed a plan to finally be one of the "Accepted".

Working in the sweltering kitchen of the local greasy spoon flipping burgers, he had saved up enough money to buy a slick new wardrobe. After years of being called "Pizza Face", his terrible skin condition had finally cleared up. All he ever wanted was to be *cool*. But no matter what he said or did, he always seemed to end up the butt of the joke, the object of ridicule, the outsider to be tortured. The awkward phase had set in when he was born, and it didn't look like it was leaving any time soon.

It was the same horrible kids, year after year, ever since elementary school, who would not let him forget he was their "whipping boy". If he sat down at a crowded table in the cafeteria, the other kids would move. He didn't have one friend to his name; he didn't belong to any group. He wasn't a jock or a mod or a punk or even a band geek. Trent was alone, invisible, anonymous.

The kids simply called him "the rat", because he always looked grungy, like he hadn't had a bath in weeks. He wore the same ripped-up blue jeans and extremely faded AC/DC t-shirt, almost every day. He was gawky and painfully shy, wearing his shoulder length black hair down over his eyes, as a sort of protection, a way to hide. He wasn't from a good neighborhood and his family was not rich. He was simply an outcast who spent every free moment playing video games in the local arcade.

But things were going to change, and 1985 was going to be the year Trent's life changed forever. Regrettably, it was not to change for the better. Trent Leek had finally had enough. Since the humiliation on the first day of school, a plan in his head had been formed. It was a plan that took weeks to prepare, but when it was finally set in motion that Friday afternoon, *nothing* was going to stop him.

Trent sat in biology class with a sly smile upon his face. He watched, as the other students quietly worked at their lab stations, and then looked up at the clock above the blackboard. It was just before three pm when he raised his hand.

"Yes, Mr. Leek," the balding teacher asked in an annoyed tone.

"I need to go to the bathroom."

"There are ten minutes left in class, Mr. Leek," the teacher said. "You can wait."

"But I really have to go."

"Leek must have to take a shit," a voice yelled and the kids all snickered.

"Fine," the teacher said, holding up a hall pass. Trent walked over and took the pass. As he headed for the door, a *baby pig*, taken from a jar of formaldehyde was thrown from the back of the room. As the slimy pig smacked Trent in the back of the head, the kids roared with laughter.

"That's enough," the teacher said. "Hey, cool it!"

Trent just kept his head down and continued to grin, as he headed out into the hallway. Tossing the hall pass to the ground, he bound down the staircase leading into the main hallway atrium. He then put his headphones on and pressed the *play* on his walkman.

"Please allow me to introduce myself, I'm a man of wealth and taste," he sang slightly off-key to *The Stones*, "Sympathy for the Devil" with a fevered jovial intensity. Casually, he walked up the cavernous empty hallway, humming and moving along with the song. He was is great spirits, as he opened his locker and took out a navy duffle bag. Spinning on his heels, he slammed his locker closed, and continued down the hallway toward the boys' bathroom. "Pleased to meet you, won't you guess my name?"

A bell loudly *rang* out and teenagers quickly flooded the hallway from their classrooms. The last class of the day had been cancelled, so the school could celebrate with a Friday afternoon pep rally. The entire school crammed into the gymnasium, both students and faculty. That night the "Red Devils" were to play their arch rivals in the biggest game of the year. The energy was infectious. Everyone sang along and stomped their feet, as the marching band played, *Queen's*, "We Will Rock You".

The football players broke through a large banner, bursting onto the gym floor to the frenzied applause of the revelers. The cheerleaders jumped around, excitedly shaking their pom poms. As Coach Matthews got up to give "the big speech" about how they were going to crush the competition, a mysterious, *dark being*, walked through the gym doors wearing a long hooded cloak. One of the football players, standing off to the side of the gym, immediately took notice.

"What are you, some kind of a joker?" the bulky, spiky-haired jock asked the mysterious creature, trying to show off in front of the other players.

"Tick, tick, bang! If you think I am a joke, well you just might be wrong," the being spoke in a strange deep voice. "You should have a little, sympathy for the devil."

After the coach finished his speech, the hooded being leisurely walked into the center of the gymnasium floor and bowed graciously. Crossing his arms in front of him, he stood completely frozen. The crowd became quiet and watched curiously, as the being pulled his black hood down, revealing a grinning red façade with a pencil-thin moustache, high cheekbones and pointy black horns. The crowd went crazy, seeing what they believed to be their new school mascot; a fiendish, hedonistic, *Devil.*

The devil moved with very animated, elegant gestures, and overly-exaggerated body movements, as he danced around the gymnasium floor, raising his arms, egging the crowd on, wanting them to cheer for him. He was in complete control of the entire school. They screamed their applause, raising and lowering with excitement each time the devil motioned his arms up and down. The devil never spoke, he placed his hands on his belly and laughed while pointing at them; playfully mocking them. They lapped it up. Suddenly, he stopped his antics and once again stood completely still.

Gazing around at the faces of the adoring energized masses; the devil nodded his head approvingly and then pulled a nine millimeter black Berretta pistol from a shoulder holster under his cape. The crowd became quiet. They watched, as the devil turned, pulled back the barrel, and pointed it directly at the obnoxious spiky-haired football player. Then, he pulled the trigger and the devil finally had his due.

"Trent Leek took fifty-two young lives, as well as the lives of six teachers on that fateful day. He had absolutely no remorse or regrets," Deirdre Lange, a petite and energetic young woman, explained to Lily, Dave and Darby, as she escorted them through the hallways of the school.

"That's so terrible," Lily said.

"Honestly, he was an odd boy. After he shot his classmates, he walked to the school cafeteria, went into the walk-in freezer and shut the door. It was hours before the police had completely secured the school and searched it. When one of the policemen opened the freezer door, he found the devil, frozen solid. It was reported he looked back at his fellow officers and told them that, "Hell froze over".

"Literally," Dave mused.

"Some people thought Trent went into the freezer to dump the costume and run out of the school, like he had nothing to do with it. Nobody knew it was him; he could have most likely gotten away with it. But the freezer door automatically locked and trapped him inside. If it wasn't by mistake, it really was such a bizarre way of offing yourself; the whole thing was really so heartbreaking. The school sat empty for the past twenty years. You can't blame kids for not wanting to go to school where something so gruesome happened. Then last year it was turned into what it is now, an Adult Learning Annex. We have night classes for anyone and everyone, anything you can imagine from performing arts to cooking lessons to car mechanics."

"What are some of the occurrences you have been experiencing?" Dave asked.

"Well," Deirdre started to speak, but was cut off by the school bell, *ringing* loudly through the hallway. "Hold on!"

"Are classes over already?" Darby asked Deirdre loudly.

"Nope, hang on; it'll stop in a minute."

The bell continued to ring out for a few more moments, then suddenly stopped.

"The school bell, which we don't use, rings all by itself at all different times," Deirdre continued. "Strange unrecognizable sounds and voices can be heard over the loudspeakers, while classes are in session. Sometimes the lights will turn themselves off and on. Doors to the classrooms will open really slowly and then suddenly slam shut. At night, the custodial staff says they hear gunshots. By the way, this is the fourth cleaning crew we have gone through in the past six months. Basically everyone thinks the school is haunted, because of what happened back in the eighties. Most people are kind of fascinated with it. I think it's so exciting ... ya know, having ghosts here."

"So you're not scared?" Darby asked.

"I'll admit, I'm not easily spooked, but as soon as school is over for the evening I am outta here. I tend to freak myself out when I'm in the school alone. We had a flashlight "ghost walk" through the school this past Halloween. During the evening, we did hear what sounded like gunshots and two women saw something so scary, they just ran out in the middle of the night and never returned."

The doors in the long hallway began to open, as people filed out of the classrooms. Once the school was empty, they walked with Deirdre to the front entrance.

"Here are the keys to all the doors," Deirdre said, handing a large key ring to Dave. "Feel free to wander around, but please keep the exterior doors locked. As requested, the cleaning crew was given the night off. You have my cell phone number in case you need anything. I'll be back first thing in the morning. I'm so excited; I just can't wait to hear if you see anything. Have fun!"

"Okay, see you in the morning," Lily called out, as Dave locked the doors.

Moonlight shined down from the lofty skylight running the length of the long hallway ceiling. They laid five cushy sleeping bags out in front of a bank of lockers in the middle of the atrium, and sat down to feast upon two, extra-large, pepperoni pizzas that had been delivered, courtesy of Deirdre.

"Friend of yours?" Lily casually asked Darby, seeing Gaia's large, very distinct, signature in his paperwork.

"Not quite," he smiled. "I had and interesting conversation with her last evening. She's quite the character."

"Yes, she is. Miss Gaia doesn't particularly care for me. I'm sort of a thorn in her paw. And she is everything I *never* want to be; a fake, money-hungry, unsympathetic, fraud."

After feasting on the warm pies, they got down to work setting up the motion-sensitive, night-vision, cameras in the cavernous main hallway, cafeteria and gymnasium.

Once they "went dark", shutting off all the lights in the school, the only light remaining came from the moonlight and the brightly glowing green exit signs, mounted above the doorways.

Nigel sat in front of the television monitors in the hallway, sipping coffee. He watched, as the others paired off with handheld cameras to explore the school. Lily and Dustin went up to the second floor, while Dave and Darby wandered into the gymnasium.

"Up for a game?" Dave asked, tossing a basketball through the darkened gym to Darby, catching him off guard. "Little, one-on-one?"

"Alright," Darby responded. "I'll give it a go."

Darby began to dribble the ball down the shiny wooden court, under the dim glowing lights of the exit signs. Dave quickly ran upon Darby and snatched the ball, tossing it up toward the basket.

"Swish," Dave exclaimed, watching the ball sink into the basket. "Three points!"

"Pure luck, nothing more."

"Thank you, thank you, I know … sheer greatness!" Dave threw up his arms and cheered for himself, as though a massive crowd were watching up in the bleachers.

"So you want to dance?" Darby asked as a challenge, grabbing the ball with vigor and immediately driving it toward the hoop. "Have at it!"

The two alpha males waged war on the basketball court, each getting more and more aggressive. Dave charged in hard, trying to push Darby out of scoring range. But he charged roughly past Dave, pounding the ball into the basket.

"How do you like that, greatness?" Darby chided, tossing the ball back to Dave.

"Oh, did you want this?" Dave teased, standing in place, bouncing the orange ball from one hand to the other. "Why don't ya come get it?

Darby lunged at him and in one swift move, grabbed the ball from a stunned Dave. He faked right, and then spun left, banking the ball into the basket, once again.

"Oh, the humanity!" Darby cried.

"Okay, okay, that's how you want to play, huh?" Dave grunted, taking off after Darby. The two men battled, neither one willing to back down. They were getting exhausted, breathing heavily, but neither would give up. The game was turning into more of a fight for dominance, than a casual friendly game.

Suddenly, the school bell loudly rang out, interrupting the war, and startling them. The sound was much louder than a normal school bell. They covered their ears with their hands, but the earsplitting noise did not cease. They tossed the ball away and quickly headed back to the atrium hallway.

"God, that's so freakin' annoying," Dave barked loudly, as he and Darby walked up the hallway toward the others. The bell continued its torturous, unrelenting, ringing. Nigel was eyeing the monitors. Lily and Dustin had returned from their exploration and were sitting on the sleeping bags, also holding their ears. Then, just as suddenly as it had begun, the bell ceased ringing. Dave threw up his hands and cried out. "Thank you!"

"What have y'all been up to? You're all, sweaty," Nigel commented. "Is there something you want to share with us about your … relationship?"

"Simmer down, sista, this ain't no disco," Dave jabbed at Nigel, sitting down in a chair by the monitors.

"Anybody want something to drink?" Lily asked. "Dave, coffee?"

"Hold on a tick, come look at this," Nigel mused, leaning in closely to the video monitor, as the others stood behind him, studying the screen. "See that, I know it's slow, but it looks like they're opening."

From a camera shooting down the main hallway, they watched as each of the doors on either side of the hallway slowly *opened* in unison. Then, after a moment of silence, the heavy doors all began to *slam shut*. Starting at the far end of the hallway, one by one they slammed, faster and faster, as they worked their way down the hall toward where the group was standing. Darby glanced up the hallway, watching as the doors closest to them, slammed harshly. He continued watching the doors close, all the way from one end of the hall to the other. After running out of doors, the commotion suddenly ceased. Everyone stood in stunned silence, their ears still ringing. Dustin's body began to shake nervously.

"It's okay, they're just letting us know they're here," Lily smiled, rubbing Dustin's arm reassuringly. "Let's try to help them."

It was well past one am when they decided to take shifts watching the monitors. Lily, Dave and Nigel went to sleep in a spot of moonlight flooding in through the atrium skylight, high above their sleeping bags. Darby sat watching the monitors, playfully nudging Dustin, who leaned sleepily on his arm and kept nodding off.

"Dustin, you asleep?"

"No, I'm awake Chief, I'm awake," Dustin whispered sleepily, eyes half closed.

"Dustin, why do you call me Chief?"

"Cause you're the chief, the leader of the tribe, the head honcho, the big Kahuna, John Wayne. It's a term of respect."

"Hmmm, I see. Well, we have another half hour. Do you think you can make it another half hour or should I wake Nigel?"

"No, Chief, I'm good. I can make it."

"All right, I have to take a pisser. You aren't going to fall asleep while I'm gone?"

"No Chief, I've got this."

Darby took an ice cube from his drink, and slid it down the back of Dustin's shirt. Dustin quickly jerked awake and noiselessly screamed, trying to not wake the others, as he located the frozen cube of ice.

"Damn, that's cold, man!" Dustin squealed.

"Be back in a flash. And hey, big Chief say … stay awake," Darby called out, as he walked down the long hallway into the darkness. Dustin went back to staring at the monitors, laid his head back down on his arm, and in less than a minute, he was off to dreamland.

Lily was also slumbering in her warm sleeping cocoon. Her cheek twitched, feeling something wet drop on her face. Another drop fell and her eyes fluttered open. Looking down upon her in the darkness was a *lucid girl*, naked and dripping wet. Lily could feel her heart begin to pound in her chest. The apparition was semi-transparent and took on a green glow from the lighted exit sign, that shown through her body. The girl looked dreadfully sad; her large dark eyes never blinked, as she gazed down upon Lily.

"Hello," Lily whispered to her.

The girl tilted her head slightly; surprised that Lily could see her. Lily looked at the girl's youthful face and healthy young body, dripping with water. It was then she noticed a small dark hole in the middle of her chest. When the girl turned and began to walk down the long hallway, Lily gasped, seeing a *gaping wound* in her back, exposing part of her spine.

The girl glanced over her shoulder, making sure the stranger was following her, leaving wet footprints on the shiny tile floor. The motion-activated camera in the hallway turned itself on and followed Lily, as she got up out of her sleeping bag. Lily followed a few paces behind the girl. All was quiet except for the soft mechanical drone, emanating from the cameras set up throughout the hallways, as they focused in and followed Lily. From the corner of her eye, she could see people; dozens of young people staring at her, watching her with their serious translucent faces, as she passed. They stood completely silent and still on either side of the hallway in front of the lockers, dressed in distinctive eighties fashions.

Lily was nervous. She only slightly glanced up at the apparitions, afraid of making contact with too many spirits at once, which had proven to be a very bad idea in the past. She could see their heads slowly turn and their eyes followed her down the hallway, behind the naked girl; a parade of one. They whispered in eerie breathy voices.

"*We're watching, watch, watching you. We've been waiting, wait, waiting for youuuuu. Staaaay with ussss, stay, stay, staaay with ussss.*"

The naked girl walked through a set of open doors and rounded a corner, before continuing down another hall, which led into the gymnasium. Cameras set up at either end of the gymnasium turned themselves on. They followed Lily, as she continued walking behind the naked girl, across the large basketball court. Lily looked around the shadowy echoing space. She could see the ghostly faces of more teenagers sitting up on the bleachers. Quickly hurrying along, she followed the ghostly girl into a door marked—GIRLS' LOCKER ROOM.

As soon as Lily entered the dark room, she could hear numerous shower nozzles turning themselves on, spraying out hard streams of water in the open shower room. The girl turned back one last time, making sure Lily was still following, before disappearing into a dense vapor of steam. Lily hesitated, not sure what might be in that cloud of steam.

"Show me," Lily whispered, closed her eyes, and walked into the haze. When she opened her eyes again, she had entered another time.

The sudden harsh fluorescent lights in the locker room made her instantly squint. Lily saw three nude young girls, their voices echoing, as they giggled and chatted excitedly about a boy. Each stood under their own stream of water in the blue and white tiled shower room. One of the girls was the ghost Lily had been following through the halls, but she was now a real flesh-and-blood girl, smiling and laughing with the others.

Lily heard a series of *popping* sounds that could barely be heard over the noisy spraying water. Suddenly, the girl turned and looked directly at Lily, then released an ear-shattering *scream*.

A loud *BLAST* echoed with deafening intensity. Lily watched in horror, as the young girl's chest seemed to *explode*, and she immediately fell to the tile floor, her bright red blood swirling with the water and rushing down the drain. Startled after seeing what happened to their friend, the other girls looked up, just as another angry *BLAST* rang out. The girls screamed, trying to run out of the shower. One made it … the other didn't; she fell onto the locker room floor in an ever-expanding pool of her own blood.

There was another, *BLAST*. Lily spun around to see a grinning devil wearing some sort of a long shroud, standing directly behind her, aiming a gleaming black gun in her direction.

"Trent!" Lily gasped. The devil laughed, *possessed*, his eyes gleaming through the small eye holes cut in his mask. Trent lowered the gun and looked at the naked female forms, lying motionless and glassy-eyed, on the floor. With the adrenaline pumping through his veins, the devil ejected the spent magazine and slapped in a new one. He then jacked a fresh round into the chamber, before running out of the locker room.

Screams could be heard in the direction he ran. Lily took off after him, running back out into the sun-drenched gymnasium. She stopped abruptly, putting her hand over her mouth, as she looked at the wrath of horror all around.

The air was thick with smoke and the smell of gunpowder. Dead bodies were strewn over the bleachers and around the floors. A few were still moving, struggling unsuccessfully, to crawl to safety. Lily heard some more gunshots echoing through the air. She quickly followed the sounds, catching up to Trent in the main hallway. He opened his cape, took another clip of bullets from his shoulder rig, ejected the spent clip and popped a new one into the bottom of the gun. Lily tailed closely behind, as the devil ran down a bright sunny hallway, merrily hopping over a few of his classmates' bodies.

"Nowhere to run, nowhere to go," Trent cackled, as he raised the gun and started firing. The gunshots ricocheted off the lockers, the empty shells falling on the floor.

"LOOK OUT!" Lily yelled to some kids, knowing all too well that no one could hear her. Lily watched, as a boy dropped his books, clutched his abdomen and slumped to the ground. Everywhere she looked, people were running in pan-icked chaos. Unfazed, Trent just continued to shoot at anything that moved; a spark of crazed enthusiasm glimmered in his eyes.

"A GUN, HE HAS A GUN!" A male teacher screamed, as a bullet ripped through his right shoulder and he flew back into a bank of lockers. Lily continued to follow Trent into one of the classrooms. He looked out the windows, where he could see kids running out of the school and across the campus. Several police cars had just pulled up in front of the school. Trent leaned out of a broken win-dow and took a few pot shots at them, before casually making his way into the cafeteria kitchen. He grabbed a slice of pizza from a glass heating enclosure, and then opened the door to a tremendous stainless steel freezer. Lily quickly fol-lowed him in before the door closed.

Inside the freezer, Trent sat down on a large plastic container of blue cheese and pulled the devil mask off. Lily sat down next to him and watched as he low-ered his sweaty head and quietly *snickered* at his own private joke.

"God, that was fucking amazing! Those assholes never saw it coming," he cried out. "How do you like me now, huh? You *never* wanted to know me, now you'll *never, ever* forget me! Years, you tortured me, but now who has the last laugh, huh?"

Trent took the gun and held it up to his chin.

"Thank you, my friend," he whispered. With tears welling up in his eyes, he pulled the trigger and *nothing* happened. He quickly stood up and opened his long black cloak, looking for another clip of ammunition in his pockets.

"Where are the damn bullets?" he cried out, feeling all over his body for more bullets; but there were none. His easy exit out of this world was gone. He quickly became agitated, kicking at boxes and knocking over a giant metal shelf of frozen hamburger patties. Throwing the gun, he cried out in misery. "What have I done? My God, what have I just done?"

He immediately tried to open the thick steel door, but it was locked. His body dropped to the floor. Lily watched the boy pull his legs up close, wrapping his arms around them in a fetal ball. He clenched his fists and pushed them hard into his tear soaked eyes, and moaned like a wounded animal.

As horrified as Lily was about what this young man had just done, in some twisted way, she understood his pain. She wanted to comfort him, tell him, she knew how he felt. She had been there herself, once upon a time, and knew how horrific it was. Lily could still see the faces of her own tormenters, as unwelcome as they were. The peculiar little "Goth" girl was still trapped inside her and always would be.

It was always the same; the laughter, the cruel comments, vicious shoves into lockers. Every day a new torture, a new agony, she knew what this boy went through, but it didn't in any way excuse him. Trent felt he was stuck, that it would always be the same, but that was where the similarities between the two ended. Lily braved through it and survived, making something positive out of something negative. Trent simply gave up and took the coward's way out.

The freezer was getting colder by the minute. Lily was completely unaffected, but she could see the vapor of breath from Trent's mouth, as his breathing became more and more shallow. The tears from his eyes began to harden on his cheeks, as he stared up at the door, wanting to leave the frozen room. But even if he did live, his life was over, his future was gone. It was a choice he made for himself. With his finger shaking, he managed to scratch "forgiv ..." in the frost on the silver aluminum wall next to him.

"Please God, pleeease help me," Trent whispered, his teeth chattering. The more time that passed, the more his muscles began to tighten; hypothermia was setting in. With his last bit of energy, he put the devil mask back on and sat back against the wall. Lily's eyes welled up with tears, as she literally watched the young man's *spirit* illuminate and ascend up and out of his body. The bright sphere of light hovered for a moment, before disappearing from the frozen room.

Lily took a deep breath, closing her eyes tightly. When she opened them again, she found herself in a dark empty freezer, which had its door completely removed. She stood up and walked out of the freezer, wiping her teary eyes.

"Fancy meeting you here."

Lily smiled, seeing Darby's sitting in the dark on the cafeteria steps.

"Likewise," she responded. "How did you know I was ..."

"I had just come out of the restroom, and saw you running through the dark hall with a rather horrified look on your face. I knew better than to call out to you, so I quietly followed you down the steps into the cafeteria."

Darby put his arm around her shoulder, as they walked up the cafeteria steps.

"So, was it Trent?" Darby asked. "Is he still here in the school?"

"He's been gone for a while. But there's another matter we need to take care of."

Lily stood in the middle of the dark gymnasium, bathed in the green glow from the exit lights brightly gleaming off the shiny wood floor. She was obviously deep in thought, staring up at the large clock enclosed in a protective metal cage, mounted up on the wall by the girls' locker room.

Darby quickly moved up into the bleachers to oversee the filming from a birds-eye view. Cameras had been set up on the bleachers and in the four corners of the gym. Nigel roamed the area, panning his hand-held camera; a nervous Dustin followed close behind, more for his own security than good sound quality. Dave sat on the floor about ten feet in front of lily, preparing for whatever was about to happen.

"Y'all ready?" Lily called out.

"Nigel, you ready?"

Nigel heard Darby's voice coming over his earphones.

"I hope so," Nigel spoke softly into his headset microphone, back to Darby.

"Ready whenever you are," Darby's voice echoed down from the top of the shadowy bleachers. He looked around the vast gymnasium through a night-vision camera and swallowed hard; excited, but unsure what was about to happen.

"In the name of God, I bind all powers and all forces that are not from God, in the air, the sky, the ground, the underground, the waters and the netherworlds" Lily spoke softly, staring at the clock, watching the second hand, as it ticked around the numbers. The clock began to move faster and faster, sharply passing the numbers, until it was spinning furiously. "Please protect all who enter here from any evil forces and forbid any kind of demonic interaction or communication, in Gods name, amen."

Darby could hear frenzied *voices* coming through the earpiece on his headset. He was unable to make any sense of the panicked words and jumbled conversations, flooding his head and sending chills up his spine.

"Nigel, can you still hear me?" Darby asked through his microphone.

"Just barely," Nigel responded, also hearing the voices. "Who the hell are they?"

"I don't know, but I have a funny feeling ... we're about to meet them."

Suddenly, the school intercom *crackled* with thunderous static, which amplified, echoing through the immense shadowy room. Darby looked down, noticing an extreme drop in the temperature. He could see his breath hanging in the air as it left his lips.

With a sharp spark, the scoreboards at both ends of the court came to life; lights flashing, numbers flipping out of control on the digital counters. The buzzers began to sound, as the school bell rang out, erratically reverberating off the walls, unnerving everyone except for Lily. She simply tilted her head back and held her arms out with fingers spread wide.

"Don't be scared!" Lily called out. "This is your time!"

Suddenly, everything ceased, the room became very *quiet*; there was no noise, no movement. Then Darby saw small, *balls of light*, softly glowing all around him. They seemed to appear from out of thin air in different locations all around the room. The orbs of energy, which intensified and brightened, seemed to each have an individual aura. Darby looked around; the gymnasium resembled a planetarium of sparkling stars.

"I don't believe what I'm seeing," Nigel gasped in his headphone.

"What is it?" Darby asked.

"Look … through … your … thermal!"

The temperature in the room dropped forty degrees in a matter of seconds. Darby quickly picked up his thermal camera and squinted, peering through the lens. His head shook in disbelief, seeing the familiar shadowy outlines of *people,* sitting up in the bleachers all around him.

When Darby sat down at the top of the bleachers five minutes ago, he was completely alone. Yet in the blink of an eye, he was suddenly in a crowd. He could easily make out the silhouetted, translucent bodies, scattered around the gymnasium with quite a few more coming in through the gym doors.

Darby quickly turned his camera, catching the spirit of a girl, wearing a long billowy top, standing up right next to him. She seemed to effortlessly float down the bleacher steps. When he looked up from the camera and could only see the *balls of light* moving all around the gymnasium, like giant fireflies, all gliding down toward Lily. The light and energy given off by the orbs lit Lily in a strange pulsating spotlight, as they encircled her. Lily seemed to dance in a hypnotic state; so beautiful, so graceful, so powerful, a guiding light for the apparitions. Darby's eyes slightly teared up at the sight.

"Don't be scared," Lily called out to the sparkling spheres of light, just as she had with the victims of the airplane crash, when she was just a girl. "There is a better world awaiting you!"

Darby looked back through the thermal camera lens and focused in on Lily. An incredible amount of brilliant "otherworldly" energy seemed to be coming out of her in a strong violet aura. It was beautiful; the room had taken on a peaceful warm feeling.

Then in an all-encompassing whirl of vibrant light, Lily threw her arms up and the orbs quickly swirled through the air high above, then disappeared up through the rafters in the gymnasium ceiling. The strong surge of intense energy *blew* the glass out of the old lighting fixtures. Lily shielded her face, as tiny shards of glass shattered and fell, raining down all over the wood floor. As the last sphere of light disappeared, the room fell back into darkness.

"That it?" Dave asked looking up at Lily.

"I believe so," Lily said happily to Dave.

"Did ya get that?" Lily called up to Darby.

Darby sat in bewildered silence, after witnessing this "life changing" experience.

"Yes, it was brilliant," Darby whispered. "You were, brilliant."

"Darby, you okay up there?" Darby heard Nigel in his earpiece.

"I'm a bit blown away at the moment," Darby said into his microphone. He could see Nigel waving up at him from the other side of the gym, and Dustin literally sitting on the floor in a puddle of himself. "Nigel, how's our boy doing down there?"

"He's fine, but I think we may have to mop him up."

"Please, for fuck's sake mate, tell me you got all that?" Darby begged Nigel.

"Oh, I got it! I still don't bloody believe it, but I got it."

A light snow was falling from the hazy morning clouds. Dustin was already on his cell phone talking with Chloe, telling her the excitement of the previous night. Nigel was busy rolling up one last long cable, and Dave and Darby were in the midst of loading the last of the equipment into the bus.

Lily sat on the steps leading up to the front of the school, sipping coffee from a mug, when Deirdre pulled up in her yellow Volkswagen Bug.

"Mornin'," Lily greeted Deirdre.

"Good morning, I brought donuts," the small woman cheerfully sang out, as she bounded over carrying a box of fresh donuts. "How did it go? Do you see anything? I'm dying to know, did you see any ghosts?"

"Um, why don't you come onto the bus? There're some things you may be interested to see," Lily said, as she opened the bus door and gestured for Deirdre to head up the steps.

"This is so exciting," Deirdre chirped, hardly able to contain her anticipation as she hopped up the steps. Dave grabbed Lily's arm as she started up the bus steps.

"Lily, you know she is going to freak out," Dave said flatly, loading the last of the monitors into the storage compartment. "Are you sure you want to show her?"

"She invited us here; she wants to know the truth. Now, whether she can handle the truth is another thing altogether."

Everyone assembled inside the bus, where a laptop computer was set up on the table in the kitchenette. Lily turned to look at Deirdre, who was sitting on the couch next to her, munching on a donut.

"Sometimes something so terrible happens, so suddenly or violently, that the spirit doesn't know that they have died and they just kind of end up wandering, looking for someone to show them a way out."

"Wow," Deirdre exclaimed.

"What you're going to see may be a little *unsettling*, keep that in mind. Ready?"

"I'm totally, ready," Deirdre beamed with excitement.

"Dave," Lily looked over at Dave, who walked over to the table and hit a button on the computer. On the computer screen, the main atrium hallway could easily be recognized. There was movement on the screen, as Lily was seen getting up from her sleeping bag, following a faint *glowing figure*, which could be seen through the darkness moving down the hallway.

"Oh," Deirdre gasped, sitting forward on the couch, moving closer to examine the screen. "It's a naked girl?"

The cameras switched, as Lily headed toward the end of the hallway. Another camera turned on and although the figure was hazy, it clearly showed a naked female form, moving swiftly toward the camera. A thick, *greenish haze,* occupied either side of the hallway. Upon closer inspection, Deirdre could see the faces of dozens of *teenagers* standing in front of lockers, peering out of the darkness, watching Lily pass.

"Those are *kids*," Deirdre spoke quietly, tears filling her surprised wide eyes. "Look at all of them, they look so sad."

"Listen carefully," Lily instructed.

Very faintly, a series of frightening, overlapping voices, male and female, could be heard whispering, echoing, begging to be heard. *"We're watching, watching, watching you. We've been waiting, waiting, waiting for youuuuu. Staaaay with usssss, stay, stay, staaay with ussss."*

"They were taken from life, before their time," Lily explained, as they continued to watch the spirits on the monitor. "Fragments of these spirits can exist, continually reliving whatever drama or trauma they went through right before they died. They are trapped on this mortal plane, lost. A lot of them are just that, lost souls. They have no comprehension of time. Years are like seconds, decades fly by in a matter of hours."

Deirdre was then shown the footage taken later in the evening, as Lily stood in the middle of the gymnasium and numerous spheres of light came into her and then shot up and out of this dimension.

"There are … so many of them," Deirdre sniffed back tears. The sadness was devastating her, yet she was unable to take her eyes off the screen. "They were never truly real to me until this very moment. They were just something fun, they weren't really real; they were figments of our imaginations. But they were *real*, real people, all around us. Thank you for helping them, thank you!"

"When I went to high school, the worst possible thing you had to worry about was being humiliated by a hideous blemish on your skin or something fuckin' stupid like that," Dave scoffed, looking over at Darby, as he drove down a busy freeway. You never said, "Hey, I wonder if I'm gonna to be blown away in math class today?"

"I could be wrong here, but it seemed like Lily had a great deal of empathy for the boy who caused so much pain for so many people," Darby stated, sitting in the co-pilot seat with his feet up on the dashboard. "She told me she understood how he felt, that she had been in the exact same position when she was young."

"She was! I met Lily in high school," Dave reminisced. "She was not the person you see today. She was a weirdo, the goth chick with pale skin, always dressed in black."

"Was she picked on by the other kids?"

"Constantly, she was constantly picked on by the other kids. It had got around that she was in a loony bin when she was a kid. I remember the cheerleaders would shove her into a locker, slam the door and leave her there. And she didn't have any friends; she just lived in her own little world, listening to all those dark "doom and gloom" bands like, *The Cure* and *Siouxsie and the Banshees*", and she was obsessed with *Bauhaus*. She always walked with her head down and wore headphones; like she was trying to tune the world out. To be honest, I was one of her worst tormenters, just a total jerk really."

"No, not you?"

"I know it's hard to believe, but I was a typical jock asshole. She sat in front of me in literature class. I used to love to put my feet under her chair and lift her entire body, raising it up and down, over and over; she *never* said a word. Then one day I think I must have pushed her too far. After a round of chair-lifting, she turned and looked me dead in the eye and said, "Your grandfather would like you to stop picking on me." I was floored … my grandfather, how weird a comment was that? I said, "Oh really, what would my grandfather's name be?" And she replied … his name is Donald Cooper, you were named after him. He also told me that you have been taught better manners and if you do not leave me alone, he is going to "*take you apart.*"

"Take you apart, huh?"

"Man, I cannot tell you how freaked out I was. No one knew he had recently passed away. My grandfather was my absolute hero. He and my grandmother had practically raised me. I loved the man. But when I misbehaved, he would give me this stern look and say, "I'm gonna take you apart!" When I was small, I actually believed this "taking apart" threat, but as I got older, I would just kind of laugh. Then he would laugh; it was a funny little joke between us … and only us."

"There was no way she would have known about it?"

"No way in hell. After that, I started watching her, following her around. I just became infatuated with her. We were total opposites; she was a loner, dark and odd and I was the king of the school. Not to brag, but I pretty much had a smorgasbord of girls to choose from. I always thought Lily, as peculiar as she was … I thought she was undeniably cute. It's funny, with her blonde hair; she looked just like a punk rock version of Marilyn Monroe. I would make every excuse in the book, just to be able to talk to her. I went from being her nemesis to her fiercest protector. We dated for a few years, even talked about marriage. But things got a bit … complicated."

"I see," Darby said, feeling that Dave was possibly referring to Varton Muntz.

"We went through a lot of shit together, good and bad. I'm not gonna lie, I was in love with her. I would have done anything for her. But for whatever reason, she pushed me away, like she was trying to drive me away. It literally ripped my heart out, but I respected her wishes and backed off. I have regretted …" Dave stopped speaking, his head full of memories. "I stay around because … I don't want anything to happen to her … ever"

CHAPTER 15

▼

SOMEONE TO DIE FOR

It was simply known as the *Wedding Cake* Mansion, and it was even more stunning than he had imagined; graceful, detailed and elegant. Darby stood out in front of the massive house and took a few exterior pictures of the grand old antebellum mansion, which did indeed look like an enormous, three-tiered, wedding cake. No detail had been overlooked, no expense spared, on the opulent plaster moldings and fancy cornice icing; it was simply grandiose in every imaginable way.

The fabulous, twenty-room, dwelling had been renovated back in the early nineties and was turned into a five-star hotel, as famous for its "Immaculate Lodgings", as its "Resident Ghosts". This was to be Darby's last adventure with Lily before heading back home to London and he wanted to absorb everything.

"I'll go check in," Nigel called out to the mesmerized Darby, as he walked up the front steps to the porch, and into the lobby. "Ground control to Darby, come in, Darby!"

"Okay, meet you in a second," Darby mumbled, as he continued to snap pictures. Dustin wandered up the steps, chatting on his cell phone, having another marathon phone call with Chloe.

"Dustin, will you help Dave with the bags please," Darby requested. "If you can pry that phone from your ear for a few seconds."

"Right, chief ... gotta go, babykins," Dustin said, then turned slightly and whispered into the phone. "Call ya in five minutes.

The radiant late afternoon sunlight streamed in through the tall windows of the magnificent open lobby. As Darby entered the massive etched-glass doors, a piano echoed an elegant melody through the pink marble foyer. Stately columns held up the second floor landing. But the most stunning feature was the dramatic horseshoe staircase, with its ornate black iron railing; it was the centerpiece of the entrance hall.

The hotel staff was busy putting the finishing touches on a dramatic Christmas tree in the lobby. Guests milled about, taking pictures and setting up dinner reservations. Pretty girls wearing beautiful long, *turn of the century* dresses, were giving tours of the house and grounds.

A soft tinkling of glass caught Darby's attention, as he walked under the stunning five-tiered crystal chandelier, hanging majestically in the center of the lofty entrance hall. Looking up, he noticed it was *moving* ever so slightly. He held up his camera and focused in on the dazzling crystals glimmering in the early evening light. The movement was subtle, barely evident; no one else in the crowded lobby seemed to take notice. Darby was the sole witness to the dancing chandelier, slowing swinging back and forth. He watched the spectacle curiously, before noticing that the front doors had been opened by a bellhop, causing a slight breeze to drift through the lobby.

Darby sat down on an antique couch by the staircase, figuring the breeze from the door must have caused the chandelier to sway. He laughed to himself and sat back on the comfortable couch and studied the detailed crown moldings.

Across the room, he could see Dave and Dustin bringing in the bags, and joining Nigel at the front desk. Then Lily walked in and looked around the fabulous lobby. A short man with a fancy moustache, immediately rushed over, and shook her hand; as two young bellhops, fell over themselves to carry her bags. After a few moments, Darby heard the chandelier *tinkling,* once again. He immediately looked up and saw it was indeed moving. He quickly looked back at the front door; this time it was closed. He picked up his camera and took a few pictures of the chandelier and lobby.

Out of the corner of his eye, he noticed one of the tour guides, a beautiful girl with thick chestnut hair piled high upon her head, sashay through the lobby wearing a stunning blue dress. She was looking around at the people milling about, but no one seemed to notice her. It seemed as though she was searching for someone or something.

Then she suddenly stopped when she spotted Darby; she smiled at him. He politely, smiled back. The young woman quickly headed across the lobby, a veil of sunlight silhouetting her in a pinkish hue. Her long dress whooshed gracefully, as she made her way over to Darby. She stopped and stood directly in front of him, clasping her hands very delicately and properly in front of her. He breathed in deeply, smelling a wonderful sweet lilac fragrance.

"Good evening, sir," she said in a charming southern drawl.

"Good evening," Darby responded, with a pleasant smile.

"My piano is to go in the ballroom," she stated in a breathy voice. "Please tell them."

"Your piano?" Darby questioned.

"Yes, it belongs in the ballroom. It sounds much better in the ballroom. They have moved it and it must be put back in its proper place, immediately."

"Okay."

"And I do not favor gladiolas."

"Gladiolas, flowers?"

"I have told Hildie many times, but they keep putting gladiolas in my room."

"Okay, I'll let them know," Darby played along, a confused look on his face.

"Thank you ever so," the young lady smiled graciously, bowing her head. She then lifted up the front of her skirt, turned and headed back through the foyer. Darby watched, as she made her way back through the crowded lobby, walking right through a plump woman who made a strange face, like she felt something "unusual".

Darby quickly picked up his camera and snapped one last shot, before the girl promptly disappeared, walking straight into a wall. As soon as she disappeared, the chandelier ceased moving.

Darby sat with a flabbergasted look on his face.

"Darby! There you are," Lily called out, as she and the others approached. "You alright? You look kind of funny."

"I just saw a ghost," Darby managed to whisper. "A girl, I saw her! She was just beautiful and she spoke to me."

"What did she say?" Lily asked, her face lighting up.

"She said she wants her piano put back in the ballroom. She said, it sounded better in there," Darby said with a silly, bewildered, grin. "And she doesn't want gladiolas in her room anymore; she doesn't like them. Then she just sort of walked into that wall over there."

"There used to be a door there," explained Max Flores, the flamboyant manager of the hotel, standing next to Lily. "That used to be the entrance to the dining room. It was closed off during the renovation. I believe you just met, Miss Julia."

"Darby?" Lily laughed. "You look a bit like a deer caught in headlights."

"Yeah, I'm sorry. I just … oh, I almost forgot my camera!" Darby excitedly remembered that he had taken a few pictures of the lobby just before the girl appeared. He quickly scanned through the digital pictures in the small screen on the back of the camera. The first few pictures showed people in the lobby obliviously going about their business. Others were pictures of the chandelier. Then he stopped on one particular frame which very clearly showed the hazy pinkish outline of a female in a long full dress with a bustle in the back as she walked away from him. "There … there she is!"

Darby held the camera out for the others to see.

"It's amazing," Nigel gasped. "Truly amazing."

Lily never looked at the picture; she just smiled and shared a private wink.

"I know wat I see … I'm not crazy person. Miss Julia just likes to scare me! She don bother any of de other staff like she does me," the head maid, Hildie, an older Haitian woman dressed in a crisp, black and white, tailored uniform, continued to make up one of the rooms, as she spoke to Lily. Darby and his crew were close by, filming the obviously stressed woman. "I turn 'round for a second and when I turn back … she is standin' dare watchin' me!"

Lily asked, "Can you actually see her?"

"Sometimes, but I always know when she in da room with me. I can feel her, I can see her and it gets very cold … and there is always this smell, a sweet smell, like flowers. She calls me by me name. She say, *"Hildie, I want dis, Hildie, I want dat!"* I know she don't like gladiolas, but it's not up to me wat flowers go in wat rooms. I will have jus made a bed up, and if Miss Julia don't like how it was done, she will pull the sheets right back down. I just shield me eyes and run out da room. I don't want ta look at her, she is so scary. She is not of this world. She's a haint, a spook, a ghost, and I don want anyting to do wit her. I also see da man, da man in the military uniform. He don really bother me, he jus' wanders around da house. But not Miss Julia, she won't leave me be!"

"This was Julia's room. It has become known as the "Brides Room", mainly because the brides who get married at the mansion use this room to dress in. In fact, this beautiful mansion was built specifically for Julia's wedding; it was built to resemble a tiered wedding cake," explained Max, as he showed Lily and the others around the luxurious suite. "Like I said, we have done our best to squelch these rumors, but word is getting out and truly about seventy-five percent of our clientele are here for weddings."

"Young beautiful brides, having their grand weddings in her wedding cake, house," Lily mused. "Ouch! That's gotta smart."

"Exactly, brides say they feel like someone is walking down the stairs behind them when they make their grand entrance down the staircase. A few have been pushed. One bride had these tiny ivory buttons going down the back of her gown suddenly all pop open. I saw it myself; it was as if an invisible finger just went down her back in one swift motion and popped them all apart. Miss Julia has also been spotted dancing alone in the shadows of the ballroom. But the second you turn on a light, she's gone. And I can't even tell you how many damn' flower arraignments she has rearranged or destroyed, tossing the flowers everywhere; the decorators are furious. There she is."

Max pointed out a large painting of a beautiful dark-haired young woman, sitting above the marble fireplace lit by a bright spotlight. The nameplate read—Julia Anderson.

"That's her," Darby confirmed happily, looking at the painting of the delicate beauty he met in the lobby, decades after her demise. For Darby, it was the icing on the supernatural cake. "She's lovely."

"This was *her* mirror," Lily stated, matter of factly, looking at a reflection, no one else could see; the reflection of a beautiful, dark-haired, girl in the full-length antique mirror in the corner of the room.

"Yes, it was. It's funny, only women have said they have seen Miss Julia staring back out at them from this mirror," Max continued. "Pictures of brides taken looking into the mirror have shown the face of a female looking back out at them. There have been sightings of her for years, ever since we renovated. It seems like she is trying to sabotage other brides on their wedding day."

"Because her own wedding day …" Darby murmured. "… was so horrible."

"Perhaps," Max admitted.

"What exactly happened," Dave asked. "How did she die?"

"It was truly a Greek tragedy played out in the Louisiana bayou. Captain James Anderson had the house built on his sixty-two acre plantation, as a wedding gift to his beloved only child, his pride and joy, Miss Julia. The gazebo out on the side of the house under the old oak, that was where she was to be married. They were very wealthy, the upper echelon, and Miss Julia got pretty much whatever she wanted, spoiled until rotten. So the stage was set and all the upper crust of New Orleans society was there to see the wedding of the decade, but apparently the groom … never showed."

As Max continued talking, Darby watched Lily, who continued to stare into the mirror and was whispering quietly to herself. Lily seemed to be watching something in the mirror. As the others followed Max around the room, Darby focused his camera on Lily. He watched as she quietly closed her eyes and whispered, "Show me."

When she opened her eyes again, she was in another time, yet the same exact room. It was early evening and she found herself standing in front of the same mirror, but it was not her reflection in the mirror, it was most definitely, Julia's.

"We'll have our first dance together as husband and wife. He is such a glorious dancer," Julia bragged to two servants helping her dress. Lily was standing behind Julia watching, as the beautiful young woman finished dressing.

Julia was simply stunning, a vision of loveliness in her white wedding dress. Her long chestnut hair was done up in a dramatic upsweep, fringed with delicate white tea roses. Her cheeks and perfect pouty lips were the same pinkish hue. She stared happily at her reflection. Pleased with her appearance; she smiled. It was her wedding day and she was deeply in love. "We have decided to have two children, a boy and a girl."

Lily noticed the newly renovated, air-conditioned, room she had been standing in only moments before, was now warm with the open windows letting in the humid summer air.

"He's a *dead man*!" Lily heard a male voice roar from the floor below. Both she and Sophia turned in the direction of the door. Then Lily followed Julia out of her room and onto the wide hallway overlooking the entrance hall.

"I'll kill him myself … if I ever get a hold of him!" Captain Anderson, Julia's rather imposing father, shouted furiously, impatiently pacing the enormous foyer in his finest military uniform. The Captain clenched his fist and slammed it down hard on the receiving table, knocking off a few of the beautifully wrapped wedding gifts. "If that son of a bitch thinks he can do this to me!"

"Shhh, Papa please, keep your voice down, the guests will hear," Caroline, his adoring mouse of a wife, rushed over and picked up the fallen presents. "I'm sure there is a very good reason he's late. He loves Julia, he wouldn't …"

"Wouldn't what? Make a fool of me? I always knew there was something about that boy I didn't like!"

It was starting to get dark; the sun was setting. The servants were quietly lighting the numerous candelabras all around the house. Candles had been lit on the stunning chandelier, which was being hoisted back up to its place of prominence in the center of the lofty entrance hall.

Crouching up at the top of the dramatic horseshoe staircase, peering through the ornate black railing, was Julia. Her big brown eyes filled with tears, as she listened to her parents in the foyer below. She could see the guests through the tremendous open front doors, walking around in front of the stately home. A beautiful white gazebo, covered with blooming flowers, had been built under an enormous oak especially for the occasion. The entire house had been built in honor of this day and everyone knew it. The guests were some of New Orleans' wealthiest and most prominent citizens who had all come out for the wedding of the year. But as more time passed, it was quickly becoming the scandal of the year.

"I won't let him do this to me," Captain Anderson barked. "… or my baby girl!"

"Captain please, we don't want everyone to hear," Caroline said, quickly shutting the front doors. She leaned her back up against the doors and covered her mouth with her hand in silent shame. "What are we to tell everyone? What will *they* think?"

The whispering had already begun, as the wedding that should have taken place hours ago, had yet to produce a bride or groom. Julia knew what *they* were saying.

"William Banks, why would you do this to me?" Julia whispered, then quickly whirled around in her gown and ran to her bedroom.

"GET OUT! GET OUT OF HERE!" she yelled.

Two female servants, who had been attending to Julia, quickly escaped from the room before the bride slammed the door and locked it. She cried out, throwing an expensive Chinese vase filled with fresh flowers, careening into the full-length mirror that held her image. Breathing heavily, she looked up at her cracked reflection, before putting her face in her hands and sobbing. She slowly backed into the wall behind her and slid down to the floor.

"Why, why? I love him so much!" she cried. "And he said he loved me."

"The boy probably came to his senses. He realized the money he would inherit was not worth the trouble he was getting into with such a spoiled little horror."

Hearing the snickering voices of two women standing below her open bedroom window, Julia crawled over and peered down, listening to the women discussing her.

"He comes from money you know," An elegant older woman gossiped. "He most likely fled, the poor silly lad."

"How mortifying for her family," said the other snooty woman.

"Looks like another … old maid."

Julia was crushed, but she knew what the women were saying was true. She had acted like a spoiled diva in the past, but since she had met her fiancé William, she had changed; his love had made her a better person. She watched as the callous women mingled back in with the other guests, some of whom were beginning to leave in their fancy carriages, tired from so many hours of waiting.

The wedding that never was would be the talk of New Orleans society. The embarrassment, the shame on her family; she would indeed be an old maid. Julia watched as her mother toiled around the guests, making improbable excuses. Her heart sank when she spotted her father, pacing like a caged animal, alone under the flower-draped gazebo; obviously cursing her betroths name and swearing revenge.

She clung onto the thick draperies, her head flooded with fears. Her whole body quietly shook, as she sobbed. Overcome with sadness, she watched the scandal of her life being played out before her eyes. There was a *knock* on the door.

"Miss Julia, Miss Julia," the voice of one of the servant girls called through the door. "Your Mama is worried about you, Miss Julia."

Lily watched as Julia's eyes seemed to glaze over and she just stared into space.

Another hour had passed with no sign of the groom. Mrs. Anderson was overflowing with apologizes, as she bade farewell to the last few lingering guests. Captain Anderson was sitting on the front porch in furious silence, puffing on his cigar angrily, while nursing his fifth glass of whiskey.

Everyone watched as Captain Anderson stood from his chair, eyeing the dark figure, slowly walking up the long oak-lined drive. He stared with fuming eyes at the shadow of a man riding a horse with a distinct limp. As the shadow came fully into view, everyone saw it was Julia's' fiancée; William Banks.

"Mr. Banks, you are a dead man!" the Captain bellowed, flying into a rage. He threw down his cigar and lunged at William, dragging him off the horse. "DEAD MAN!"

Two men grabbed the Captain and pulled him away from the exhausted young man in the tattered military uniform, who was simply too tired to fight back. William just stayed on the ground trying to catch his breath.

"Captain Anderson," William panted. "Please sir, I understand your anger with me, but there was an accident. The front wheel on my carriage was destroyed by a large rock, sending … sending it into flight; it flipped over just outside Shreveport. One of my horses was killed; the other has a distinct limp. I give you and Mrs. Anderson my most sincere apology for my being so inexcusably late. But I assure you, nothing, nothing in this world could keep me from my bride. I just want to take her in my arms and dance her around the ballroom. I couldn't miss my wedding day to my beloved Julia."

After a pause, Captain Anderson held out his hand to the fatigued soldier. The young man took the older man's large hand and was pulled to his feet.

"You look like hell, boy, but your apology is sincere and accepted," Captain Anderson said, patting William's back, causing him to cough. "Sorry to hear of your harsh journey; you are indeed the man I thought you to be. But keep in mind I get a dance with the bride too."

"Yes sir, of course."

"William, why don't you go to Julia, she will be so happy to see you," Caroline cried happily, putting her arms around the young man. "She was so upset; she locked herself in her bedroom."

"Yes, I'll go to her and explain everything," William exclaimed. "I don't ever want her to have even one day of sadness."

"And get yourself a drink," Captain Anderson called after him. "A good stiff shot!"

"Yes sir," the young man grinned, as he entered the front doors.

"That's what he really needs," the Captain added with a hearty chuckle.

William entered the foyer, closing the doors behind him. The foyer was dark, lit only by soft candlelight. He had begun to walk through the entrance hall, when he stopped, hearing the tinkling of glass. He thought the sound was strange; he looked around trying to place where the unusual sound was emanating from, and then looked up.

There he saw Julia, hanging from the chandelier in her exquisite wedding gown, the braided gold tieback from her drapes forming a noose around her neck. Long tufts of her dark hair hung down loosely in her face. Her skin was already bluish in color; he knew instantly ... she was dead. Tears filled his eyes as he watched the love of his life, swaying ever so slightly, back and forth in the air above him.

"We will reschedule the wedding for a later date," Captain Anderson announced in good spirits, holding court on the front porch. "We'll just explain to everyone the unfortunate incident that made Mr. Banks late."

"Oh, I'm so very pleased papa," Caroline gushed. "I was so worried that ..."

A single *gunshot* rang out from inside the house, followed by a piercing scream that startled everyone.

"What the devil is going on?" Captain Anderson bellowed.

"CAPTAIN ANDERSON! CAPTAIN ANDERSON!" one of the servant girls cried, as she came running out the front doors, continuing to gasp over and over. "They dead, they dead! Miss Julia hung herself up on the chandelier and Mr. Banks ..."

Captain Anderson pushed past the hysterical girl. Mrs. Anderson and the other remaining guests quickly followed him into the foyer, where they came upon a horrific scene. The bride hanging lifeless from the chandelier and the groom lying on the marble floor beneath her in an expanding pool of blood; a smoking pistol still clutched in his hand. The men gasped in shock; the woman screamed, quickly hiding their eyes. Mrs. Anderson passed out cold.

"Get the chandelier down, NOW!" Captain Anderson ordered and the servants quickly untied the cord, lowering the enormous chandelier. Julia's lifeless body moved limp like a rag doll, as it was laid out on the marble floor next to Williams. "God no, please."

Lily sat on the landing at the top of the dramatic horseshoe staircase, peering through the ornate black railing, watching the terrible scene play out just as it had so many years ago. She closed her eyes and rested her head against the cold iron railing.

"Are they doing some sort of historical reenactment, honey?"

Lily heard a female voice ask. When she opened her eyes again, she noticed a small audience of hotel guests and tourists, standing in the foyer below. They were watching curiously, some were even taking pictures of her, as she looked down at them from the landing, being filmed by Darby and crew.

"Hello everyone, hello … sorry for the disturbance. Nothing to see here," Max, the flustered hotel manager, quickly tried to do some damage control with the curious guests. "Complimentary hor d'ourves and cocktails are being served in the Oak Room. Please feel free to enjoy the mansion and grounds.

"Ya back with us?" Dave whispered, leaning down to help Lily to her feet.

"Yep, I think so."

"She wants the piano back in the ballroom, right?" Darby asked, curiously.

"If that's what she told you, then that should be done. But I think she's really looking for someone, waiting for someone. I believe they just need to be brought together. It's cool, I know what to do, I just need to figure out how to do it," Lily informed the others. "But first, cocktails are being served in the Oak Room!"

Dinner had been a wonderful event. Lily dramatically told everyone the tale of the young bride and groom, and their untimely demise. But before dinner had even finished, she excused herself and never returned. The others ended up retiring to their rooms early. But not Darby; he had other things on his mind.

"Beautiful evening, isn't it?" Darby politely stated to a well dressed couple, making their way through the virtually empty lobby. The couple smiled and bid him a good evening. Darby was sitting on the same oversized antique couch from earlier in the day. He decided to sit in the lobby and wait with his digital camera, hoping against hope, he might catch another glimpse of Miss Julia. This time, he assured himself, he would be less *spooked*.

So he sat watching people, coming and going. At one point, he heard the soft tinkling of crystal from the fabulous chandelier high above the foyer. But it was just the bellman opening the door, letting the chilly night air briefly blow through the lobby.

Being at this stunning, wedding cake house, Darby couldn't help thinking about Angela and his own tragic wedding. Looking down at his watch, he realized it was almost midnight and as much as he wished for another brief glimpse of the ghost, he decided she would not be making a return engagement.

"Waitin' for someone?" A familiar voice above Darby asked. He looked up to find Dave with one of the pretty tour guides on his arm.

"Just soaking in the atmosphere," Darby replied.

"This is Rosalie," Dave announced blatantly. "She's giving me a *private* tour."

"Hi," Rosalie curtsied in her full dress.

"Brilliant. Well, I hope you all have a lovely tour. If you will excuse me, I am heading to the bar for a warm snifter of brandy and then retire to my room where, hopefully, I will promptly pass out. Goodnight."

"Adios," Dave called after Darby, who was already making his way down a hallway toward the bar. Halfway down the hall, Darby stopped dead in his tracks, hearing music coming from the ballroom; a sign in front of the door read—PRIVATE PARTY.

Curious, he opened the door slightly and peered into the empty room. The only light in the massive space came from the tall spots of moonlight cascading in through the windows on either side of the room. Darby could see the shadow of someone sitting at a majestic grand piano. As he quietly made his way closer, he could tell from the contours and curves that the person sitting at the piano was *female*.

"Lily," Darby spoke quietly; the piano abruptly stopped. "Oh, please, don't stop, that was amazing."

"Ah, I've been discovered," Lily said.

"I heard the music. Is this the infamous piano of Julia's'?"

Darby leaned his folded arms on the top of the piano and looked down at Lily. He noticed that she seemed strangely distracted, looking past him at something moving around the empty ballroom.

"Yes, it's hers. They moved it from the dining room back into the ballroom at Miss Julia's request, through you, of course. She was right. It does actually sound much better in here, doesn't it?"

"Absolutely, it does! We looked for you after dinner, you disappeared."

"I had a little something to take care of. Something I had to do alone."

A soft smile overtook Lily's face. Darby watched her eyes; they seemed to be following something across the dance floor.

"God, how I wish I could see what you see."

"You can, you did, I mean just not to the degree I can."

Lily continued to watch the dance floor with great pleasure.

"What is it you see that has you so giddy?"

"Let's just say Julia is happier now. She found her dance partner."

"How about playing another song," Darby asked.

"Oh I don't play."

"Was it Julia, was she playing the piano?"

"No," Lily laughed, flicking a switch next to the keys, causing the piano to play a lovely concerto by itself. Lily smiled and raised her eyebrows teasingly. "It's magic!"

"May I have this dance?" Darby asked, holding his arm out very formally to Lily.

"Why I do declare Mr. Darby, I would be delighted. Do you know how to waltz?"

"But, of course," Darby said coyly. "Actually my mum forced me and my brother to take ballroom dance classes when we were boys."

Lily took Darby's arm and together they spun across the dance floor with a casual ease, laughing and whirling. Darby thought it was just the two of them dancing on the vast empty dance floor, but Lily smiled, knowing they weren't alone.

"You look cold. Here, put my jacket on, warm yourself up," Darby insisted, wrapping his jacket around Lily's shoulders. They were strolling on a path lit with old fashioned fire burning lanterns, through the lush gardens behind the mansion.

"Your mum should be proud, you are quite a gentleman. She did a good job."

"Why, thank you, I'll tell her you think so the next time we chat."

"Let's go sit in the greenhouse. I have something I want to do for you," Lily said, taking Darby by the hand and leading him into the dark, glass-encased, building filled with empty tables and chairs. A few members of the mansion staff were rushing about in the background, readying the otherwise empty greenhouse, for the next day. "They have afternoon tea in here, I believe. Oh look, there's a fireplace!"

"That'll warm us up," Darby said as they sat down upon the stone hearth of the enormous fireplace, which silhouetted them in the golden glow of the fire.

"Did you bring what I told you to?" Lily asked Darby. "Her ring?"

"Angela's ring? Yes, I have it right here," Darby stammered, caught completely off-guard. He took the diamond encased ring from the leather cord around his neck and held it out to Lily. But she didn't take it. "Oh, I'm sorry. I thought …"

"Let me explain what is going to happen. I'll be able to see what she saw and feel what she felt. I just need a second to prepare myself. I don't really like doing this and have only done it for a few people. But I think you may really need this and I truly owe ya one for saving my ass from that crazy bitch on that roller-coaster," Lily smiled. "Just do me a favor."

"Anything."

"If need be … catch me."

"Of course."

"Okay then," Lily said. Taking a deep breath, she closed her eyes and opened her right hand. "I'm ready."

Darby placed the shiny ring in the palm of her hand. She closed it tightly and shut her eyes, as Darby curiously looked on. After a long moment, she spoke.

"It was on top of the hot fudge sundae in the whip cream," Lily smiled, never opening her eyes, able to watch the past through Angela's eyes. "Clever."

Darby's heart immediately sank and his eyes welled up with tears; there was no way Lily could have known Angela's ring was placed in her dessert.

"She loved red roses, but not lilies, no lilies," Lily continued, pausing occasionally. "I can see you kissing her surrounded by flowers in some sort of big refrigerator. She watched you sleep, and she didn't want you to see her on your wedding day, before the wedding. I can see your hand on a glass window. You kissed her though a window; I can feel the warmth of your lips. She had a gorgeous wedding dress; I can see looking at her reflection in a mirror. Oh, she was so lovely Darby."

Darby was very happy Lily's eyes were closed, as he wiped the flood of tears rolling down his cheeks with his sleeve.

"She is standing in front of an old car, like a …"

"Rolls Royce."

"Yeah, and there's a big fountain. She's having her picture taken in front of a fancy hotel. Awh, there's a crowd of people watching her and telling her how beautiful she looks and giving their congratulations to her. She kissed her family on both cheeks, and then she got into the back of the car alone. It looks like a chauffeur wearing a fancy uniform shut her door. The car drove off and she was waving out the back window to everyone. She was absolutely overwhelmed with happiness," Lily's face contorted strangely, as sudden graphic flashes poured into her head. Darby knew what was coming, and could only watch helplessly, as Lily cringed and squirmed, letting out a gasp, before collapsing forward into his arms. After a pause, her eyes fluttered open and she looked up at him.

"You okay?" Darby whispered.

"Yes."

"Please, tell me what you saw. I have to know."

"There was this huge double-decker bus. It cut them off," Lily stopped speaking and gave Darby a concerned look. "Darby, are you sure you want to hear this?"

"Please … continue."

"It happened very fast, before she ever really knew what was happening. The bus slammed into the front right side of the car; it was going really fast. All she saw was the advertisement on the side of the bus right before it hit. Her head hit the side window. It shattered and partially crushed the door."

"Was she dead at that point?"

"No, she was still alive when the car went over a cement median in the middle of the road and became airborne. When it crashed back down on the pavement, she was thrown to the other side of the backseat. Then everything went into slow motion, like in the movies. The car spun around in circles; she grabbed onto a leather strap hanging down in the back seat, trying to brace herself. Everything outside the car was a blur. The scenery swirled around and she could see the car was heading for the metal barricade surrounding the entrance to an underground rail station. She raised her arms up to shield her face from the impending impact, but there was nothing she could do; the car smashed into the metal barrier. The impact was fierce; she could see the glass windshield shatter and fly into the car at her. When the car finally came to a stop, she was trapped in the backseat. I feel like her neck was broken, but she was still hanging onto life. She could see people all around the car, trying desperately to get her out, but the door was crushed. Everything started to become hollow, the faces of the people talking to her, their words, everything sounded distant. She looked down and could see the blood on her white gown. After a moment, everything went dark. I'm sorry; I didn't see anything more after that."

Darby sat completely motionless, literally unable to speak. Lily took his hand and placed Angela's ring in it, then closed his hand around it.

"This ring meant a lot to her," Lily said quietly.

"Was she in a lot of pain? I need to know?"

"What you need to know is that … *you* were her last thought," Lily wiped tears off Darby's face with her hand and forced him to look her in the eyes. "It was your face, your sweet smiling face, she thought of before she died. I don't think she had any idea of how bad the accident had been. She seemed more concerned that she was going to be late for her wedding"

"She was always late," Darby smiled, through his tears. "A few years ago I renovated an old church that Angela and I lived in. After she … died, I had a rather disturbing encounter with a *bride*."

"Angela?"

"At first, I thought it was Angela, but it changed into something, something perhaps … inhuman. It was that particular incident that brought me to you. I think, maybe, Angela might be stuck or lost …"

"If you're asking me if I think the bride is Angela … no, I do not. I believe she is somewhere … better.

"But …"

"Darby there is no way to predict what will happen in this life. We human beings are so fragile, we break rather easily. What we have to learn to do is live every single day like it's our last. And be happy for the time we have with people we love, no matter how long or short, because there is no telling when any of us will be taken from this world. Celebrate who she was and your love and just keep living. She wouldn't want you to be sad, would she? If you were the one who had died, you wouldn't want her to spend the rest of her life being miserable. I know you wouldn't, neither would she."

After reading Angela's ring, both Lily and Darby decided it would be a good idea to get a brandy at the hotel bar to calm their nerves. At last call, Darby graciously walked Lily back up to her room.

"Thanks for the drink," Lily said, handing Darby his jacket.

"Thank you, for … well, thank you. What you did, it meant a lot to me."

"Um Darby, I don't want you to think I'm being too forward here. But I was wondering if you would mind coming in and staying with me until I fall asleep. I know it's a strange request, but I'd really appreciate it."

"It would be my pleasure."

Lily opened the door to her room with her pass card and entered. Immediately, the door next to Lily's opened and Dave stepped out holding an empty ice bucket. He looked over and saw the back of Lily and Darby as they entered the room.

"Davie, get me some candy from the vending machine?" A female voice called from inside his room. It was obvious that even though he had company, he had been waiting up; making sure Lily made it back to her room safely. Dave stood in the empty hallway staring at Lily's door ... floored.

"Davie?"

"Yeah," he snapped. "I hear you."

The bluish glow from the television lit Darby's face. He was watching an old movie in the darkened room, still fully dressed, sitting above the sheets. Looking down on the bed next to him, he saw Lily sound asleep with her head resting on his shoulder. She had literally fallen asleep the moment she laid her head down. Darby studied her face and body. She was wearing a long football jersey, her hair was tousled, and one of her long creamy legs was slightly bent above the covers.

Darby was getting very tired himself, but he wanted to make sure Lily fell asleep first. He glanced at the digital clock on the nightstand; it was two am. Picking up the remote, he turned the television off and blinked, seeing what looked like electric sparks running faintly across the ceiling above the bed. He watched the sparks dance across the ceiling for a few moments, then shook his head, closing his eyes tightly. When he opened them again, the sparks had disappeared. A trick of tired eyes, he supposed.

He carefully moved Lily's head off his shoulder and placed it down on the pillow, trying not to wake her. She made a soft moan, as she turned over into a new position on her side with her back to him.

"Where are you going?" Lily asked softly, never moving.

"I just have to use the loo, I'll be right back," Darby whispered, softly caressing her cheek with the back of his hand. "Go back to sleep."

Walking into the bathroom, he closed the door, leaving the room in darkness. Lily fell right back to sleep. After a few moments, she woke slightly, feeling Darby get in the bed; this time he got in under the sheets. Lily felt him pull her close and run his hands up her back, massaging her, touching her body with loving caresses. Lips softly placed a kiss on the nape of her neck, sending wonderful chills up her spine. She moaned in pleasure, as his hands found their way under her nightshirt; one hand went up to her breasts, the other down between her legs.

"Oh Darby," she moaned, finally giving in to the passion.

"Dis' is how ... a whore likes to be touched!" a deep, gravely, voice spoke. Though Lily could not see anything, she instantly knew who was touching her— Varton Muntz had returned. She quickly tried to escape, but the demented clown held her tightly in his wicked grasp. When she tried to scream out, a bony hand harshly covered her mouth. "You don't want your laddy to know what a whore you are, do you?"

Lily shook her head, *no*. The clown removed his hand from her mouth, cuddling in close, caressing her hair and inhaling her scent, which was intoxicating to him.

"Ahhh, I've missed you my precious child, it has been much too long. I want you to do something for me, Lillian. I want you to get rid of the filthy Englishman.

"He is none of your concern."

Under the sheets, Varton jumped on top of Lily, pinning her arms up above her head by her wrists.

"Dis boy is going to get himself hurt, if he doesn't stay away from my child."

"Don't you dare go near him!"

"I see, you are falling under his spell. But you know the truth; I am the only one who loves you. I am the only one who could love such a strange little girl."

"I'm not afraid anymore. You can't hurt me, I won't let you!"

"You threaten me, Lillian? You treat your father dis way?"

"I'm no longer your property! And you're *not* my father!"

"No longer you're father, I see. Your disobedience is intriguing."

Lily closed her eyes tightly, preparing for Varton's cold hands to assault her like they had so many times in the past, but he did not.

"I see you have made your choice, Lillian. Perhaps you are right. Perhaps ... I need to find ... *new* daughter. I will leave you now ... and forever."

Darby flicked off the bathroom light, opened the door, and walked back into the dark room. He instantly smelled a horrible odor and when he glanced over at the bed, it looked as though someone was under the sheets with Lily. Darby quickly rushed over. As he ripped the sheets off the bed, a powerful, unseen force, literally knocked him across the room. He slammed into the wall, momentarily stunned, then immediately got right up and ran back to the bed.

"Darby!" Lily screamed, grabbing onto him for dear life.

"What, in the name of all that's holy ... just happened?" he asked, turning on the light over the bed.

"I was having a horrible nightmare. When I felt the sheets move, I woke, still thinking I was dreaming. I'm so sorry, did I hurt you?"

"No, but you are much stronger than I thought you were. That must have been one hell of a nightmare!"

"It was," Lily lied, as Darby sat back down on the bed and held her in his arms.

"You know, I have sympathy. I know how it feels, not knowing if the things you are feeling and seeing are real," Darby explained, lightly stroking her hair, trying to calm her. "I've been having the same mad dream for a while now. It's always the same; I'm in the middle of this crazy party in this moving room, surrounded by windows that let in no light. There are all these people and creatures with twisted "out of proportion" features. There's an enormous hairy baby and pudgy strippers."

"A hairy baby and pudgy strippers, huh?" Lily giggled. "Sounds intriguing."

"Its' rather freakish, frightening actually. And it always ends the same way, with these eyes; these dark, hate filled, dead-eyes, which just stare at me through this insane crowd of creatures. I can't make out any other features, just the eyes. And just before I can make out the features of the person, there is a shock of bright light and a massive bright light, like an explosion. That's when I always wake up. It's totally unnerving; I can't make any sense of it."

"You should always heed your dreams, Darby. They're more powerful than you might think."

"I know, it's crazy, but I just can't seem to shake it. Damn, my watch!" Darby exclaimed, looking down at the face of his watch. "The bloody glass cracked."

"I'm so sorry Darby, it's my fault. I'll make it up to you."

"Lily, don't even worry about it. I shouldn't have left you alone and I did. I'm here now and I won't let anything happen to you."

Darby kept his word; he snuggled in close, and didn't leave Lily's side the rest of the night.

"Let's go, let's *gooooo!*" Dave yelled impatiently out the open door of the bus, as he began to pull down the long drive, away from the wedding cake mansion. Darby, who was the last passenger not yet aboard, was running to catch up. The closer he got, the faster Dave would go, laughing as he watched Darby run next to the speeding bus.

"Good morning to you, Dave," Darby said with cheerful sarcasm, finally grabbing onto a metal bar on the door and hopping on the bus. "Thanks so much for waiting."

"It's not a good morning, it's a fantastic morning!" Dave beamed. "We're off to the airport, and you and Queen Nigel are going to be heading back across the puddle. Home sweet home for you both! Have a crumpet on me and cheerio!"

"Actually, only Nigel is going back today. Lily invited me to spend Christmas with her and I accepted. Dustin is also staying, with Chloe."

Dave's joyful attitude quickly slid away.

"Well, how lovely for you," Dave added with icy sarcasm. As Darby walked further back into the bus, Dave gunned the engine, throwing him forward. "Oops, so sorry."

"Stodgy sod," Darby said, under his breath.

Standing outside the International Terminal, under a large—*VIRGIN ATLANTIC AIRLINES* sign, Nigel said his goodbyes to everyone; then turned to his best friend.

"Ya gonna be alright without me, Darby?" Nigel asked with a wily nudge.

"I think I'll survive," Darby laughed, handing the last of the large metal film containers to the sky caddie, who was busily loading them onto a baggage push-cart. "I cannot wait to see what we got on film!"

"I'll get right to work as soon as I get back to London. Take care, mate!"

Darby and Nigel hugged warmly, then parted ways. As Nigel began to walk down toward the terminal entrance, he stopped, turned back to Darby, and flashed him a peace sign.

"It wasn't perfect," Nigel called back. "But it sure was a lot of fun!"

CHAPTER 16

▼

SEASON OF THE HOLLOW SOUL

"It's beginning to look a lot like Christmas," Lily sang, as the bus pulled up in front of her beautiful mansion, which was abuzz with activity. There were catering vans and workers were busy rushing about, putting up decorations and lights.

"LILY!" Chloe screamed with glee, as she and Mama Nadine came out on the front porch, as the bus pulled up. Chloe ran over and gave Lily a tight squeeze, as she stepped off the bus. "I missed ya!"

"Hello, miss thing," Lily cried.

Dustin hopped off the bus and looked lovingly at Chloe, who quickly ran over and jumped into his arms; he happily spun her through the air. They bounded into the house, hand in hand, as Darby helped Dave unload the bus. A mob of small furry creatures ran out the open front doors to Lily, except for one; Lily's little black dog, Bozzy, who ran right past her to Darby.

"Look out Darby!" Lily warned. 'She's comin' for ya!"

Darby looked over just in time to see the petite dog, take a flying leap up into his arms, tail wagging, tongue licking, welcoming him back.

"Well, hello!" Darby laughed, as he fell back onto a large duffle bag.

"Are y'all hungry?" Mama Nadine asked.

"Starving," Lily admitted, as they hugged.

"Well, come on in, rest your tired bones," Mama Nadine said, rubbing Lily's shoulders, steering her toward the house. "Oh, Mr. Darby, a package arrived for you this morning. It's on the entrance table, dear."

Darby picked up the FedEx envelope, and strolled down the cobblestone paths into the vast backyard. He sat down upon a large wooden swing overlooking the river and opened the envelope, which contained some important information he was waiting for.

Savannah Police Department—Incident Report—January 17th 1976

At approximately, 9:45 am, Mrs. Karla Dufrene, age thirty-two, awakened and dressed her two twin children; Tyler Andrew Dufrene, age seven, and Lillian Rose Dufrene, also age seven. Mrs. Dufrene had written a note and taped it to the front door of the house before taking the children to the garage and loading them into the back seat of the family car at street address, 5828 Colfax Avenue.

Mrs. Dufrene informed the children they were going to spend the day at the home of their grandmother, who lived a few miles away. Mrs. Dufrene had the children put on their seatbelts. Then she put the key in the ignition and started the car, but failed to open the garage door. She turned the radio on to distract the children and when asked by Tyler why they "weren't moving", Mrs. Dufrene stated the "the car needed to warm up because it had snowed the previous night and the engine was cold."

At approximately 10:30 am, the neighborhood postman, Mr. Frank Sherman, age forty-six, was delivering the mail to the residence mail box by the front door, when he noticed the note taped to the front door by Mrs. Dufrene.

"CALL THE POLICE—
THE DOOR IS UNLOCKED.
EVERYONE INSIDE IS DEAD."

The postman, then stated, he heard the sound of an engine running inside the closed garage, and could smell exhaust fumes. He immediately lifted the garage door and was hit with the powerful poisonous vapors from the cars exhaust. He called out for help to a neighbor who was walking his dog nearby, and the two men pulled the unconscious mother from the car and placed her out on the front lawn.

At this point, other neighbors had come over to see what was happening. Police and fire rescue were called. A few moments later, Mr. Sherman stated, he saw a pink jacket through the back window. He ran back into the garage and saw the two children sitting in the back seat with their seatbelts still on. The children were holding hands. He grabbed Lillian Dufrene's unconscious body and then went back to retrieve Tyler. The unconscious children were placed on the front lawn next to their mother.

Mrs. Dufrene, who was eight months pregnant, began to cough and gasp for breath. She was rushed to Savannah Regional Hospital, as was Lillian. Tyler Dufrene was pronounced dead at the scene. He was taken to the county morgue, where his remains were identified by his grandmother. The child was buried in the family plot at the Bonaventure Cemetery. Karla Dufrene was acquitted in the attempted murder of her two children by reason of insanity. She currently resides at Whitemarsh Hospital outside of Savannah. Lillian Dufrene was placed in a wing of an undisclosed psychiatric hospital in Atlanta. She is believed to be suffering from a rare form of childhood schizophrenia. The child believes she can speak with the dead, and is currently under observation.

Officer Gary Bailey.

"Any good?"

Darby was startled hearing Lily's voice. He quickly turned and saw her standing behind him, holding a tray of goodies in her hands, her little dog Bozzy stood at her side.

"Hello," Darby greeted her.

"I brought you a sandwich and tea. I know how you English like your tea."

"Thank you so much."

"So, is it any good?"

"Any good?"

"What you're reading?" Lily smiled, handing the cup of tea to Darby, then sat down on the swing next to him.

"Uh, no just some background information that's all."

"Can I see?"

"Uh, yeah … sure," Darby stammered, not wanting to hand the file to her.

Lily opened the front cover and began to read the details of the private nightmare she had lived through as a child. Tears fell from her eyes, as she read through the pages, reading one line aloud, "The children were holding hands."

Lily handed the report back to Darby and stared out at the sparkling river.

"I'm sorry," Darby whispered. "I'm sorry all that happened to you."

"When they put me in that hospital, I tried to tell them what was happening to me. I foolishly thought they would help. But the more I told people, the more they doped me up. I was in what they called a children's psychiatric intensive care unit of this huge hospital. Just try to imagine all the people who were so tortured by their own minds that they killed themselves in that hospital, and they all wanted to have a chat with me. I was what you would call a captive audience. The problem was … I didn't know they were dead. I just thought all these people were allowed to come into my room, a constant barrage of insistent angry people and voices. I think that is why I loved "Alice in Wonderland" so much. It was always my favorite book. I literally carried a copy with me for years; it was kind of like my bible."

"You were kind of like Alice in a lot if ways," Darby stated. "You were trapped in a strange and surreal world with all these extraordinary creatures surrounding you."

"Yep, but there was no happy ending for me; I could never find my way out of wonderland. So one day, I just decided to stop talking. I didn't say one damn thing. I never stopped seeing the spirits, I just knew better than to tell anyone. I was done, I had had enough and I wanted out of my cage. Then one day my prayers were answered; someone had left one of the unit doors slightly open, and I ran. I could hear a "Doctor Strong" being called through the entire hospital. I only got a few hundred yards when I tripped and a security guard carried me back. They set me up in the BCR."

"BCR?"

"The Behavior Control Room, it was just what you would imagine, a padded room, padded walls, floor and ceiling. I was given a sedative and told I had just set my progress back and would be kept longer. What they didn't know is that I had another plan. When I fell to the dirt outside, I had grabbed a little piece of glass from a broken beer bottle, which I hid in my sock. I was thoroughly checked when they brought me back into the unit, but they didn't find the glass. The second they left me alone, I took the glass and cut through my wrist. The spirit of a boy named Dax, who had killed himself in my room just before I arrived, showed me how to do it. I felt so hopeless, like that was the only way out. It would be calm and quiet and dark; no more problems, no more sadness, pain, no more … anything. When you are young, you think the world is at your feet and you can do anything … that you are invincible. Then something happens, something so profound, that it shakes your whole being. And you realize the ground you stand on is not always solid, it can crumble away in the blink of an eye. I don't remember anything after I passed out. I was told one of the nurses looked in the little window to check on me and saw the blood. When I woke up in the hospital, I woke up to the most beautiful face I have ever seen, my grandmother's. My grandmother was a very powerful person, and she knew a lot of powerful people. She sprung me from the hospital and took me away, she understood me."

"That's how you came to live here in this house?"

"Yes. I have lived in this house ever since, and plan to live here until the day I die. I am so grateful to my grandmother, she was the coolest person. She and I were ... let's just say we were very much *alike*. Still it was hard, I spent most of my teenage years trying to figure out if I was asleep or awake. I lived through other peoples nightmares every day, and I let them control my entire life. That's what it was ... one big nightmare, that no matter how hard I tried; I could not wake up from. I didn't sleep for most of my childhood, which took its toll as you can imagine.

"Have you talked to your mother since?"

"I don't have a mother" Lily stated flatly, her face turning sour with disgust. "Do you know what the first thing my lovely mother said after murdering my brother? She said that she was "disappointed I was still breathing". I remember that morning, I remember everything about it. It had snowed the night before; Tyler and I were so excited because she said she was going to take us over to Grandma's house to make a snowman. She got us all dressed up in our warmest jackets and we got into the back seat of the car. I remember the song on the radio was "Don't Go Breaking My Heart". I don't know why I remember that, but I do. She started the car but never opened the garage. She told us the car had to warm up and it would warm up quicker if the garage door was closed. We were little kids, we had no idea. The most haunting thing I can still see to this very day was her *eyes*. I could see her looking back at me in the rear-view mirror. She didn't have tears in her eyes, she wasn't sad or remorseful, she knew exactly what she was doing. The last thing I remember was being very hot and getting very sleepy. Tyler took my hand in his and smiled at me, he was always my little protector. My mother completely damaged me. I am still damaged to this day, I know that. Perhaps, I always will be in some way. But if I let her get to me, she will have won. She tried to snuff out my little life, but couldn't, I'm stronger than she thought."

"That's for sure."

"I am living proof that surviving and succeeding is the best possible revenge. I live every single day as though there will not be another. I have fun, I have parties and I spend money. You can't take it with you, ya know. I love and hug everyone around me, every chance I get. Every single day we have choices, choices that can either change our lives for the better or for the worse. But whatever choices we make, good or bad, they are our choices and we have to live with the consequences of them. I'm big now and I am not going to let anyone else rule my destiny or make me so sad that I ..." Lily stopped speaking, overcome with emotion. "Darby, do you know what my mother called me ... she called me *evil*. She told a little kid ... who was totally afraid of her own shadow, that she was evil. Lily stood up and screamed out loud. "Damn you to hell, Karla! You sad crazy bitch! You possess the evil … not me! Not me."

The scream echoed over the river. Darby was surprised, he had never heard Lily raise her voice, let alone release such a barrage of obscenities; but he understood. Lily turned and looked directly at him, shaking with rage.

"And you can tell her for me. Tell her … I hope it hurts, every single day! I hope her memories burn and cut and cause her insurmountable pain, every day of her pathetic existence. Tell her, I hope she rots in hell!" Lily cried out. A great surge of energy sizzled through the air, blowing out two of the lights on the nearby dock. Lily quieted down. "Please, tell her that for me."

Lily and her little black dog headed back to the house, leaving Darby sitting alone on the swing. It was true; Darby was planning to meet the illustrious, Karla Dufrene. How Lily knew about his impending visit with her mad mother, simply escaped him.

"Do not speak to any of the patients, cause they are crazy. Do not give anything to any of the patients, no matter what they say. And most important, don't touch any of them … they tend to freak and it ain't pretty!" the hefty male attendant informed Darby, as he turned the key, and escorted him into the locked unit.

The stench of urine drenched the air in the unit totally lit with stale fluorescent lights, which gave it an ugly greenish hue. Darby followed the attendant through the ward. A scraggily-haired man jumped up and eagerly begged Darby to help break him out, stating his "space ship" was waiting to take him back to his planet. Then a woman wearing a pink tutu and holding a wand, tried to get him to open his mouth, stating she was the tooth fairy. Darby just smiled politely and kept walking.

Once through the main ward, Darby was taken out onto a non-descript screened porch, overlooking a murky pond of water. The attendant pointed to a woman sitting alone in a plastic chair, chain-smoking one cigarette after another, before he disappeared.

Darby was admittedly curious to meet Karla, having absolutely no expectations of what she would be like. But there was one thing he already knew before he ever met her; he hated her guts. How could a seemingly, well educated, normal woman, snap and do such an unspeakable thing to her own children? He had questions that needed answers; he would be civil.

"Mrs. Dufrene?"

The woman did not respond, just took another long pull on her cigarette.

"Hello, Mrs. Dufrene. My name is Darby McGregor," he introduced himself politely, moving closer, pulling a chair up next to her. "Mind if I have a seat?"

Again, no response, Karla stared straight ahead and released the toxic cloud from her lungs. Darby sat down and got his first real look at Lily's mother. Her face was haggard and looked much older than her years, but still, she and her daughter looked eerily alike. Her hands shook like that of an elderly person. Her wavy hair was mostly grey, and she looked as though she hadn't eaten or bathed in days. Dark circles hung under her eyes from years of being sedated with the antipsychotic drug, Chlorpromazine.

"I was wondering if I could ask you a couple of questions?"

No response, no movement.

"You know, it's getting rather cold out here. Would you like me to get you something warm to wear, a sweater?"

Karla paid no attention to Darby. She leaned down and snuffed out her cigarette in a large metal coffee can, full of snuffed out butts, before taking a pack of cigarettes from the pocket of her housecoat. Her face cringed; it was empty.

"Here," Darby said, remembering he had one last cigarette left in the pack of cigarettes, he had not touched since his arrival in the States. He quickly took the pack from his jacket and popped the single cigarette halfway out, offering it to her. She looked into his eyes, leery of him, but she wanted another cigarette. As she went to pull the cigarette from the pack, Darby pulled it away.

"I would like to ask you a few questions?" Darby repeated. Karla gave him a dirty look, and then proceeded to pull the cigarette out. He offered fire from his lighter, which she also took. "Karla, why did you want to hurt your children?"

After a long drag on the cigarette and a period of silence, she finally answered in a slow, deliberate, rasp of a voice.

"I didn't want to hurt them. I wanted to send them back to God."

"Why?"

"They were … *damaged*. It was the only way."

"Could you tell me, how they were damaged?"

"They were born that way; it wasn't their fault. They were so small and help-less. My little Tyler, I was so in love with him. I named him after my great grand-father; he was the most beautiful baby in the world, sweet and happy."

"What about Lillian?"

"Lillian, she was named for my husbands' mother, the witch! Lily was strange. I knew from the moment I looked at her, there was something wrong with her. She never cried, never. It was odd for a tiny baby like that to be so content. I couldn't understand. And as she got older, the only time she ever wanted love or a hug, she always went to Sutton, her father, never me. I was afraid …"

"You were afraid of your daughter? Why was that?"

"I wasn't afraid of Lily, I was terrified," Karla snapped, coughing bitterly, and gasping for air. After a moment, she relaxed and took another long drag. "It wasn't just Lily; it was whatever was around Lily … and Tyler for that matter. The fires, the crying and screaming at night. And that damned clown, she was not normal."

"Not normal, in what way?"

"I woke up one night, it was very late. I thought I heard something coming from the nursery. I got up from bed and walked down the hall to check on the babies. As I got closer, I could hear this little lullaby, like a sweet voice singing. I thought the song was maybe coming from a music box or a toy. I gently opened the door and saw the rocking chair between the cribs moving back and forth on its own. I watched it move for a few seconds and then this *light* caught my eye. It was a dull blue glow that had a form, a shape. I stepped in closer and saw an older woman in a long, turn of the century dress, which buttoned up the back. Her dark hair was wrapped in a tight bun on her head; she was humming the soft melody, watching over the children. I can still hear the melody now; it was so beautiful, haunting."

Darby watched as Karla closed her eyes and hummed the strange, eerie, tune.

"I must have made a sound, because the woman quickly stood up from the rocking chair; her face was so stern. It was then I realized I could see right through her. She was translucent, see-through! I was so afraid, I just froze. In a split second, she flew across the room and was standing right in front of me, staring at me directly in the eyes. I know I gasped out loud, and this *thing*, put a finger up to her mouth and hissed; *shhhhhh*. It then quickly sank into the floor and was gone."

"It was a ghost?"

"Whatever it was, it was not of this world. From that night on, I made Sutton, their father, check on the children; I refused. I know that after Sutton died, I changed. I was alone with those children. I began drinking heavily and sleeping most of the day. I carried around a 7-UP bottle that I would fill with vodka every morning. That way, I could stay intoxicated through the day and no one would realize. I did not consider myself an alcoholic; I just needed to be "anesthetized".

"What happened? What made you want to kill them?"

"It was a winter afternoon and I had admittedly drunk myself into a stupor and fell asleep on the couch in the living room. I was awoken, hearing Lily pulling the cord on her favorite toy … that god-damn little cartoon dog …"

"Snoopy."

"Yeah, it was a *Snoopy*; her father gave it to her just before he died. She took it everywhere with her. She would continually pull the cord on the back of the thing, over and over, playing that annoying theme music. I called out, telling her to "stop the noise", but that little shit just kept pulling the cord. The more she pulled the cord, the angrier I became. I stumbled off the couch and made a mad dash to the front porch, where she and Tyler were playing. I grabbed the toy and dragged Lily back into the house. Tyler followed … grabbing frantically at my robe, begging me to stop. "You see this?" I yelled, shaking the toy in her face. "Say goodbye!" I tossed it into the fireplace and went back to the couch and laid down. I could see Lily's eyes well up with tears, watching her beloved toy contort and burn slowly into nothingness. I knew how much the toy meant to her, but at the time, I just didn't care. It must have been around two in the morning, when I woke again. The house was dark except for a pile of burning embers in the fireplace. I got up and walked to the picture window in the front of the house, it was snowing. It rarely ever snows in Savannah. I walked upstairs and down the hall toward my bedroom. What I heard next, I will never forget."

"What was it?"

"It was that annoying theme song from Lily's Snoopy. I couldn't believe it, I burned that thing. I turned back and unlocked Lily's bedroom door. It was dark in the room, but I could see her soundly asleep in her bed. I swallowed hard; there it was, that God-damned, Snoopy! It was badly burned, but still intact, tucked snugly under her arm. It was smiling up at me, as though it had won some secret war and was taking pleasure in my defeat. I was shaking my head in disbelief, when a sudden icy blast of freezing cold air blew right at me. The blast was so powerful it threw me back out the bedroom door and slammed me up against the wall in the hallway. I fell to the floor a crumpled mess. It was as if whatever was in Lily's room had been waiting to release its anger upon me. I watched as the door slammed itself shut, like it didn't want to be bothered by anyone … *living*. I crawled to the small bathroom across from Lily's room, bent over the toilet and threw up. And then, I just laid down on the cold tile floor for hours, staring at the falling snow outside the bathroom window. That was *it*."

"It?"

"That was it, the final drama. I knew I couldn't fight anymore," Karla made a bizarre quiet laugh, her eyes feral. "I knew that either I had gone completely mad or all these things really were happening, and I had to do something about them. I had to do something about my children. You see, Mr. McGregor; people say I'm the crazy one, that I'm plagued by hallucinations and delusions. But I'm not crazy. My children were *evil* and needed to be taken from this world."

"Mrs. Dufrene, I must be honest with you; I have never in my life felt such a complete feeling of loathing, repulsion and disgust for another human being, until today. You are one sick bitch, Mrs. Dufrene," Darby growled, grabbing Karla's chair and pulling her close to him. He took the cigarette from her lips and snuffed it out before its time. His eyes narrowed with rage, as he got right in her face. "You … are … evil, and the only person that should have died in that car … should have been *you!*"

Karla did not flinch, she just smiled, as Darby stood up and headed for the door.

"You should cease asking difficult questions, if you do not wish to hear the truth."

"Karla, I have a message from your daughter, who is very much alive and very much loved. She hopes it hurts, every single day. She hopes the memories of what you did to your children, burn and cut, and cause you insurmountable pain, every day of your pathetic existence. And she hopes you rot in hell! But as I can plainly see, you already are. Oh yeah, Merry Christmas!"

Karla let out a frenzied little giggle, as Darby walked away.

It was just an ordinary house in an ordinary middle-class American neighborhood, nothing too extravagant; small and white with blue trim. A Christmas tree with multi-colored lights brightened the front bay window. Darby never got out of the car; he just rolled down the window and studied the house, paying close attention to the garage before driving away.

After leaving Lily's childhood home, Darby drove out to the Bonaventure Cemetery. A few people were putting flowers on loved ones graves on this chilly Christmas Eve, as Darby drove the SUV through the sprawling graveyard, closely following the map; he received at the security office. He slowly made his way around the maze of narrow roads, but quickly became hopelessly lost.

The sun was setting and Darby was getting frustrated, looking for the Dufrene family plot, when suddenly … his engine stalled, sputtered and died.

"Brilliant, now what?"

Looking out the driver side window, he saw the name DUFRENE carved into a large marble tomb with smaller gravestones in front. Darby smiled, finally having found what he was looking for. Taking one of the two large bouquets of white calla lilies, he had bought from an old man standing at the front entrance of the cemetery; he got out of the car and closed the door. Looking more closely, he read the names on the stones of the Dufrene family plot.

"Happy Christmas," Darby greeted the dead respectfully. He spotted a gravestone with the name, Sutton C. Dufrene, next to a smaller gravestone that read, Tyler Andrew Dufrene. "Happy Christmas, brother."

Darby took the flowers from their cellophane wrapping, and placed one on top of each of the gravestones, then stood for a moment watching the sun set.

A flock of cawing black crows flew overhead. It was a surreal moment; he knew if things had happened differently, Lily may have been in the ground below his feet. Knowing the gates would be closing soon; he crumpled up the cellophane, tossed it in the back seat of the car and drove off.

CHAPTER 17

▼

POSSIBILITIES

It was dark by the time Darby drove up the long drive leading up to the mansion, which was lined with dozens of parked cars, just as it was on Halloween. The house was decked out in dazzling white lights; a Christmas party was well under way. Darby parked, grabbed the bouquet of calla lilies he bought at the cemetery, and walked up the drive.

"Oh no, she didn't," Darby laughed, seeing a spotlight upon a set of dangling red legs sticking out of the top of one of the largest chimneys, making it look as though Santa Claus had gotten stuck. Two snow machines were set up, blowing flurries high into the night sky, creating a winter wonderland in front of the mansion.

The wonderful aromas of Christmas permeated the house. Girls dressed as sugar plum fairies, passed out mugs of cocoa and eggnog. A group of carolers, who looked as though they had been plucked directly from a Dickens novel, were strolling through the house singing Christmas standards. Darby noticed Dave standing by the bar with an armful of pretty sugar plum fairies, who were hanging on his every word. Dave nodded to Darby as he passed. Darby nodded back. It was a small show of respect between them.

A little boy narrowly missed running Darby down with his brand new Big Wheel. Darby just laughed, watching the boy race down the mansion hallways, draped with lush boughs of fresh greenery and holly.

Darby continued walking through the crowd, until he stood in the arched doorway of the Palm Court. The statue of Poseidon usually sitting in the middle of the fountain, had been replaced with an enormous sparkling Christmas tree, decorated with colored lights and whimsical ornaments. Sitting in an ornate gold chair at the base of the tree was Dustin, dressed in a Santa Claus costume, complete with a pillow stuffed red suit and white beard. Relishing his part, he loudly chuffed with a hearty, *"Ho Ho Ho"*.

On either side of Santa stood his helpers, Chloe and Lily, wearing cute red "mini-dress" versions of the Santa costume with fluffy white trim. The girls handed Santa beautifully wrapped gifts to give to a line of extremely excited children.

Darby's heart warmed seeing Lily standing in front of the tree, smiling happily. It was at that very moment, he realized how strongly he felt about this woman, never thinking he could feel such love again. There were so many beautiful things about her. She was incredibly honest; not many people would ever be willing to go so deep and be so honest. She was witty, eccentric and giving. This thoughtful poetic woman was so full of both pleasure and pain. She truly was a young woman with an old soul.

Darby was pulled from his gaze by the ringing of his cell phone.

"Hello?" Darby said into the receiver.

"Happy Christmas, Darby!"

"Nigel, happy Christmas to you!"

"I just wanted to call and let you know how amazing the footage is ... wicked amazing! That wank, Ian Sharpe, mooched his way over here yesterday; I thought he was going to come unglued when he saw the footage from the school. This guy's already trying to make deals. He's talking big money deals, Darby."

"He knows that nothing gets released without Lily's permission."

"I reminded him of that. He wasn't pleased."

"Oh well, that's how it is. He knew the arrangement before we began filming."

"Absolutely. Well, I just wanted to call and say hello and see how you're doing."

"Honestly mate, I have never been better," Darby mused, looking at Lily. "I can't explain it. I know it may sound corny as hell, but I think I'm totally ..."

"In love."

"What makes you say that?" Darby questioned, unable to take his eyes off Lily.

"Oh, come on Darby, I'm not blind. I saw how the two of you looked at each other … everyone did. We were all just wondering when the two of you would admit it. Darby, its fantastic and about time."

Lily suddenly looked up and saw Darby standing across the room looking at her. A huge Cheshire cat smile brightened her face, reminding Darby of when they met on Halloween. Once again, it was as if she knew he was there. Lily waved and pointed him out to Chloe and Dustin, who also waved. She hopped down from the fountain and quickly made her way through the crowd toward him.

"I have to go, Nigel. Please give my love to your family."

"Cheers mate. I wish you all the luck in the world and will talk to you soon."

"Keep in touch," Darby said, quickly closing his phone. Lily ran up to him and gave him a big hug.

"Darby, I'm so happy you're here," she beamed. "I'm sorry if I was rude earlier, I didn't mean …"

"You weren't at all," Darby said, handing her the exquisite flowers. "For you."

"Lilies, my favorite, no pun intended. They're beautiful, thank you. Oh, I have something for you too," Lily smiled mischievously, taking a beautifully wrapped box with a shiny red satin bow, from a pocket in her skirt. "Go on, open it!"

"Lily, you didn't need to get me anything," Darby said with surprise, pulling the bow off and ripping open the paper. A shocked look overtook his face as he opened the box; it was a brand new Rolex watch. "Lily!"

"You like?"

"It's amazing, but you shouldn't have."

"Merry Christmas, Darby," Lily whispered, putting a finger on his lips to hush him. She excitedly took the expensive silver watch out of the box and flipped it over, showing him the inscription on the back.

"I knew when we met, an adventure was to begin. All my love, Lily,' Darby read aloud and laughed. "Winnie the Pooh! I don't know what to say!"

"Say … thank you."

"Thank you."

"So, when are you going to kiss me?"

Darby stood in surprised silence. Lily looked up at the top of the doorway, and then back to Darby, who looked up and saw a small bush of green *mistletoe* hanging directly above them.

"I'm afraid if you don't kiss me soon," she smiled. "I may burst."

Darby looked into her eyes and softly kissed her lips; their gaze never broke. Something changed in both of them from the moment their lips touched. It just felt right, like puzzle pieces fitting perfectly together.

Darby took Lily's face in his hands and looked deeply into her eyes.

"Your face," he mused.

"What's wrong with my ..."

"Not a thing. It's perfect."

Darby put his hand behind her neck and pulled her close, kissing her more passionately. Even with all the people surrounding them, they were alone in their own private world. The kiss lingered for a wonderful eternity and when they finally parted, Darby saw that Lily was shaking.

"You're trembling," he whispered.

Lily took Darby by the hand, leading him through the crowd to the brass elevator in the foyer and pressing a button that immediately lit up. The door opened and they entered. Lily took off her Santa hat and closed the door behind them. The elevator began to rise. They stood patiently, just looking at each other in polite silence. Yet, the anticipation in the air between them, sparked with electricity. The door opened and Lily stepped out ahead of Darby. She looked back at him occasionally, making sure he was following. Down at the end of the lengthy hallway, she stopped at a dead end with no windows and no doors.

Watching curiously, Darby saw Lily push against a wood panel on the wall and a secret door opened. She stepped through the door and began to walk up a spiral staircase, while looking back at Darby, her face mysterious, beckoning him to follow as she disappeared into the darkness.

At the top of the stairs, Darby found himself in a large shadowy space; he did not see Lily anywhere. Looking around, he noticed the flame from a single match lighting through the darkness. It was followed a moment later by a great swelling of fire, which erupted in the open growling mouth of a tremendous Dragon head fireplace, which was carved completely of stone.

In the glowing light, Darby could finally make out his surroundings. He was standing in Lily's magnificent bedroom suite in the fourth floor tower of the mansion. The room was an eclectic mixture of a luxury suite at the Ritz-Carlton and a room straight out of a medieval castle; with a towering twenty-foot ceiling, exposed brick walls and arched windows covered with lush burgundy drapes. A custom-made bed with an exquisite dragonfly headboard, sat upon a round, under-lit, platform in the middle of the room, laden with lavish bedding and enormous cushy pillows. A wrought-iron chandelier hung down from the dramatic mahogany ceiling.

Lily stood in front of the dragon's mouth in a halo of flickering golden light. Up until that point she had been in control, but once in the bedroom, it was Darby who took charge. He walked over and traced her mouth lovingly with his finger, before grasping her hair in his hand and pulling her head back, as he took her in his arms and kissed her passionately. Pulling the zipper down in the back of her dress, he ran his hands lightly over her soft skin.

A quiet moan escaped her lips, as she felt his hands moving over her body, causing chills throughout. He pulled her red *Santa* dress over her head, exposing her bare breasts and satin panties. Darby could feel the warmth of the fire on her bare back, as he traced over an elegant dragonfly tattoo on the small of her back.

"You are so beautiful, you take my breath away," Darby whispered, softly kissing down her neck to her breasts and belly, breathing in her intoxicating scent. "I have thought about this moment since the day we met. I have wanted to touch you so badly."

Darby took off his jacket, then unbuttoned his shirt and jeans, peeling them off and tossing them to the ground, yet he never stopped touching and kissing her. Slowly moving backward toward the bed, they unwittingly hit the platform the bed sat upon and promptly fell onto the mattress, giggling in a fit of laughter. They looked deeply into each others eyes and kissed again, before making love in the shadows of fire.

"You know, I've waited a long time for my Prince Charming, had to kiss a few frogs along the way," Lily laughed, lying in Darby's arms on the sumptuous bed. Darby looked at Lily in the soft shadowy glow of the dwindling fire, as she gazed in a far-off daze at the smoldering embers.

"I can actually hear those gears clicking in your head. What are you thinking?"

Lily sat in silence, never looking at Darby.

"You," she finally responded.

"Well, that's a good thing," Darby said happily. "Right?"

"Yes … it is," Lily half-smiled at him.

"Then, what's wrong?"

"I find myself in a situation that I never thought I would be in again."

"What kind of situation?"

"I met this amazing person that, I do believe I have fallen head over teacup for. Mind you, I did try and fight it. But alas, I could not."

"Well, he must be a pretty wonderful fella."

"I think so. Do you think, perhaps, this rather wonderful fella, might feel the same way as I do?"

"He just might."

"Well, do you think this … very wonderful fella, might consider staying in my …"

"… little shack on the river …"

"Yes, my little shack on the river? What do you think? Would it be worth my while to ask this spectacular person to stay here with me in my little shack on the river?"

"I think to find out you have to ask the person. I don't feel comfortable answering for such a brilliant person, who I bet would give you an amazing and ingenious answer."

"Darby McGregor, would you be interested in perhaps staying here with me in my little shack on the river?"

Darby twisted his mouth up, raising one eyebrow, looking for just the right words.

"Yes," he smiled.

Darby kissed Lily's head, as she laughed.

"Are you quite sure? Seriously, I am who I am and don't make any bones about it. I have no false front. I'm strong willed and I don't make any excuses. It would take a very strong person to be with me; I really think in you I have found a soul mate. I'm so in love with you. I can't believe it; once again, I dove into the deep end without testing the water."

"Lily, I feel the exact same way about you. I have spent the past few weeks try-ing desperately to figure out how to say to you, everything you just said to me. Sometimes you just have to just take a deep breath and jump in. If that tidal wave is comin' for us, at least we'll be together."

"It's not that easy, Darby. I have some pretty serious baggage."

"Lily, I … don't … care! Everyone has some sort of baggage; you can't let that stop you from living. I never I thought I would feel this way about anyone again either. I am here … I am not leaving. I will protect you no matter what! I want to see your beautiful face every single day … until the day I die! I love you, Lillian Dufrene, you and your big bag of bullshit!"

Lily couldn't help but grin, as she moved closer, coming face-to-face with Darby. She kissed Darby's lips, then down to his neck and on down his body.

"Merrrry Christmaaas!" Mama Nadine's cheery voice resonated from the intercom. Darby opened his sleepy eyes, shielding them from the sunlight streaming across the bed, flooding in from the tall windows surrounding the cir-cular room.

"Good morning," Darby said aloud, stretching his arms above his head, realizing he had a very peaceful night with no hint of his crazy "recurrent" dream.

"Mr. Darby, is that you? Well, I'll be dipped! I didn't expect to hear your voice. Good mornin'! I wanted to let Miss Lily know that Christmas brunch will be served in the Palm Court in a half hour."

Darby looked at the other side of the bed; it was empty. He instantly sat up and searched for Lily, who was nowhere to be found. He noticed some sheer drapes, softly blowing through a set of open French doors, on the other side of the suite.

"I'll let her know. Thank you, Nadine," Darby got up, pulled his jeans on and walked over to the doors leading out to the balcony. Looking out onto the lofty porch, which overlooked the glorious gardens and river behind the mansion, he saw Lily leaning upon the stone balustrade, wearing a white terry cloth robe. She was looking down at a stunning indigo dragonfly sitting on her hand.

Darby quietly walked up behind her, wrapped his arms around her waist and kissed her sweetly on the back of her neck.

"Mmmm, good morning," Lily cooed. "I must have been a very good girl this year. Santa brought me the best present in the world."

"How beautiful," Darby mused.

"Isn't it, I just love dragonflies. And it's rare to see one in the winter."

"I wasn't talking about the dragonfly," Darby laughed, then looked over at the small insect. "I don't think I've ever seen one of these beautiful creatures in person. What's with all the dragonflies around you?"

"I just love them. They're so colorful and free. If there is such a thing as reincarnation, when I die I want to come back as a dragonfly."

"Then I should like to come back as a dragonfly also. That way we can fly around together. Let me tell you something, I woke up this morning and you weren't next to me. I don't ever want to wake up without you next to me again. I love you, Lillian Rose Dufrene."

"I love you too, Darby … what's your middle name?"

"Lawrence," he smiled.

"I love you, Darby Lawrence McGregor!"

Christmas morning was spent devouring a delicious eggs benedict breakfast, followed by the opening gifts under the great tree. Later that afternoon, Lily took Darby to her garage. He stood astounded, watching the monstrous elephant doors open, revealing a prized collection of automobiles, all lined-up perfectly in the cavernous room.

"Good … Lord!" Darby gasped.

"These cars were my grandfather's pride and joy. You can drive any car you wish," Lily stated. "Go on, choose."

"You're serious?" Darby said elated, looking around at the fabulous selection of vintage and modern cars. "It really is Christmas."

"Here we have the '57 Thunderbird convertible, powder blue with white leather," Lily showcased some of the cars like a game show hostess. "Nah, you don't look like a powder blue kind of guy. We have a "little red corvette", a '78 Corvette, very sleek. There's the silver Astin Martin DB5, James Bond preferred, or the Mercedes' SL 500, rather roomy."

"I want …" Darby excitedly pointed to the very last car. "… that one!"

"A black, 996 twin turbo Porsche, stage 2 upgrades, 550 horsepower, silver with black interior, good choice," Lily approved, dropping a set of Porsche keys into Darby's hand. "A personal favorite of mine."

"How did you know I'd choose the Porsche?"

"Lucky guess," she said, as she got into the passenger seat. "Let's go!"

Darby drove the powerful black sports car carefully out of the garage and slowly down the lengthy drive from the mansion to the road. He stopped and cautiously signaled at the main gate, before gently pulling onto the road. Lily looked over at him, curiously.

"What is it?" Darby questioned Lily's look.

"Um, is that all ya got?"

Darby looked at her perplexed.

"It's the vertical pedal on the right," Lily instructed. "You push it down and the car goes, like, really fast!"

"Alright, you asked for it!" Darby grinned slyly at Lily. "I never get to drive in London." Lily squealed excitedly, bracing herself in anticipation, as he down-shifted and floored it. The turbos roared … shooting the sleek silver Porsche, like a bullet, flying down the long winding roads. They drove over the vast bridges connecting the inter-coastal waterway into Savannah; the water sparkling in the brilliant sunlight.

"It's Christmas night," Darby said, as he drove the Porsche through the quiet streets. "Do you think any restaurants will be open?"

"I have a little something cooked up for us," Lily smiled. "Let's park over there."

Darby parked the car on the side of the street and they got out. Lily giggled, pulling Darby with her into one of Savannah's beautiful, fountain-laden squares, where a horse and buggy was waiting under a glowing street light.

"Merry Christmas, Mr. Hennessey!" Lily called out to the older black gentleman wearing a top hat and tails. "I'm sorry we're a little late."

"No Worries," Mr. Hennessey called down cheerfully from his perch high atop an old fashioned carriage, gussied up with strands of garland and holly. Even his horse was wearing a top hat with two holes cut through for his ears to stick out.

"This is Darby," Lily said.

"Nice to meet you, sir," Darby said, extending his hand.

"Well, it's very nice to meet you Darby," said the elegant man with the charming smile, as he reached down and firmly shook Darby's hand. "I've taken the liberty of orderin' a tasty dinna of fried chicken and the cheesiest macaroni and cheese in Savannah. For dessert, I ordered a scrumptious strawberry cheesecake, all courtesy of "The Lady and Sons" restaurant. So come on up, crawl under that there warm blanket; there's hot cocoa in the thermos to keep ya' warm and toasty. It is gonna be a bit chilly this fine evening, but the view will be just glorious. Are y'all ready for your dinner cruise around our beautiful city?"

"Absolutely," Darby said, helping Lily into the back of the open carriage. They sat snuggled under the blanket, sipping cocoa. Lily laid her head on Darby's shoulder, while viewing the exquisite Victorian homes decked out in twinkling lights. Through the window of one of the houses, she saw a large family; children, parents and grandparents, all sitting around the table in their dining room, toasting their happiness and good fortune. Lily closed her eyes and smiled lovingly, snuggling so close to Darby she could hear his heart beat. For the first time in her life, she knew for sure, this was the man she would spend the rest of her life with.

"I love you," he said, looking down at her.

"I love you … more," she whispered.

Darby quietly smiled.

Over the next few days, Darby and Lily stayed secluded from the world in a private suite at the Jekyll Island Club. One evening after dinner, Lily talked Darby into skating at a local ice rink.

"I haven't done this since I was a lad," Darby laughed. "And I wasn't very good at it then."

"Be brave," Lily egged him on, as she grabbed her ringing cell phone. She looked down at the small screen on her cell phone and saw that Dave was trying to call her. In fact, Dave had been trying to call her for the past few days, but she did not return any of his calls, she just wanted to be left alone.

"Who's that?" Darby asked.

"Nobody," Lily replied, turning off the phone.

Old-fashioned organ music accompanied the skaters making their way around the enormous ice rink, surrounded by strings of white globe lights. Standing up on a pair of "well-worn" rental skates, Darby's legs wobbled. He helped Lily to her feet, but it soon became very evident that he was the one in need of support. As they stepped onto the crowded ice, Darby instantly lunged back and forth, trying unsuccessfully to secure his footing.

"Come on, handsome, I'll help you," Lily said, taking Darby's hand. "I used to be pretty good back in the day."

"So much for my trying to impress you, let me see your fancy moves. Go on, it's not like I'm going anywhere fast."

Darby watched Lily skate off into the crowd; he applauded, as she did some fancy jumps and spins. After a few minutes, he finally seemed to get the hang of it and ventured around the rink, picking up some speed as other skaters whizzed by.

An adorable little girl with big pink pom-poms on her skates, glided over to him.

"Hi," she smiled up at him, rather smitten.

"Hello, I like your skates."

"Thanks."

"I'm afraid I don't remember how to stop," Darby admitted.

"Use the sides of your skates, like this," she said, demonstrating her skills.

"Ah, I see, you're very good. Are you training for the Olympics?"

"No, but I've been skating since I was little. Do you have a girlfriend?"

"A girlfriend?" Darby smiled, caught a bit off guard. He looked up and saw Lily skating over to them. "Lily, this is my new skating coach."

"My name is Maddy," the little girl introduced herself.

"How do you do, Maddy?" Lily nodded to her.

"Fine, thanks."

"Thank you for your help," Darby said, kissing Maddy's mitten covered hand formally. The girl was love-struck, unable to take her eyes off Darby, as she made her way back into the crowd. Lily and Darby shared a laugh. "I never knew I was so desirable to the younger set."

"Perhaps she likes older men," Lily teased, taking Darby's hands. She skated backward, facing him, while pulling him around the rink. "Darby, I've been thinking."

"You don't want to skate, you want to go back to our room and make love until we both pass out from sheer pure … ecstasy."

"No," she laughed. "I've made a decision that I have been thinking about for quite some time. It's a rather important decision."

"You have my undivided attention, because if you let go, I will fall."

After a momentary pause, she spoke.

"I want to retire from my current profession."

"What?" Darby exclaimed with shock, his legs promptly going out from under him. He fell to the cold ice, inadvertently pulling Lily down with him.

"God that really sounds funny doesn't it?" Lily admitted. "Retiring, like I'm sixty-five. Here's your gold watch, thanks for your contribution to the company, now sail off into the sunset."

"Are you serious about this?"

"I'm tired Darby. I'm tired of living through other peoples nightmares. I mean, I know I can't turn it off, I can't stop the spirits from seeking me out, but I most certainly don't have to put myself into such bad situations. I want to be a little selfish for once in my life. I want to do something for me. I want to have a normal life … with you. What do you think?"

"Truthfully, I couldn't be happier. I'm stunned, but couldn't be happier. Let's be honest, it's very dangerous what you do. I don't know how you have done it as long as you have and come out alive … not to mention sane."

"Well, that went much better than I thought," Lily let out a relieved sigh, as she helped Darby to his feet. They moved into the center of the rink, so they wouldn't get hit by skaters passing by. "I don't know if I was nervous telling you or just nervous to actually hear the words come out of my mouth."

"Lily, I want you to do whatever makes *you* happy," Darby said, thoughtfully. "I feel so lucky to have met you, so grateful to whatever twist of fate brought us together. And no matter what happens in this mad world, I will always be by your side."

"Well, that's really good to hear, because I've made another decision."

"Okay, lay it on me!"

"First, let me say, I really had every intention of going through with it. I mean, I don't want you to be angry with me. But the more I think about it …"

"Lily, what is it?"

"I don't want the footage you shot made public … ever," Lily admitted, full of apprehension. Darby put his head down. "Oh Darby, please say you don't hate me."

"I'm afraid," Darby said, looking up at Lily with a stern look in his eyes. "That's going to cost you, Miss Dufrene."

"Cost me?" Lily was shocked. She couldn't believe Darby would turn on her so quickly. "Cost me what?"

"A kiss," he grinned.

"A kiss?" Lily quickly exhaled with relief. She took the ends of the red wool scarf around Darby's neck and pulled him close, kissing him passionately.

"I don't give a damn about the documentary, it was bullshit. I used the film simply as an excuse to meet you. I really had no idea what I was getting into. I mean, the footage is incredible and in truth it would ..."

"Destroy my life."

"You have my word," Darby looked at her adoringly. "The footage will never see the light of day."

"Thank you, Darby. I trust you. Hey, have you ever been to Vegas?"

"Las Vegas? No, I don't believe so. Let's go to Vegas to celebrate your new life."

"*Our* new life," Lily added.

"*Our* new life. It's only eight o'clock. If we left as soon as possible, we could be there by tomorrow night, New Year's Eve!"

"Wonderful things are coming Darby, I can feel it!"

The couple checked out of the hotel and drove back to Lily's, pulling up in front of the mansion in great spirits. Bounding into the foyer, the plan was to grab a few items, let Nadine know where they were headed, and drive to the airport to catch a late flight.

"Five minutes," Lily squealed with anticipation.

"Okay, meet you back here in five minutes ... ready ... steady ... go!" Darby stated, looking at his watch, as though he were going to time her. As Lily started to rush off, he quickly grabbed her by the arm and pulled her close.

"Thank you, I enjoyed our first official date," he grinned, kissing Lily lovingly, before stepping into the elevator. He shut the brass cage door and called out, as it headed up. "Five minutes."

"Five minutes," Lily called back with a silly laugh. She quickly rushed into the kitchen where she could hear soft Christmas music playing on a radio. Mama Nadine was sitting on a barstool at the center island, humming along to the music, flipping through an antiquing book.

"Nadine," Lily breathlessly hugged her.

"Miss Lily, did you have a nice time?" Nadine asked.

"We really did. It was nothing but peaceful bliss. So, Darby and I are gonna fly to Vegas tonight," Lily beamed. "He's never been and I want to show him around. We're not going to be here for New Year's."

"You're leaving tonight?

"Yes, isn't it exciting, he's so amazing."

"Sounds like someone is a bit smitten," Nadine commented. "Speaking of smitten, Miss Chloe and Mr. Dustin drove off to Miami this afternoon with some friends to celebrate New Years."

"No kidding, good for them. I'm telling you, wonderful things are happening. Since no one is going to be here, why don't you and your girlfriends go off on your antiquing trip to England … on me?"

"Lily?" Nadine exclaimed. "Are you sure?"

"Of course, don't worry, Dave will take care of everything around here."

"We would love that sweetheart, thank you," Nadine gushed, giving Lily a hug. "Oh, did Dave get a hold of you? He's been asking for you, he said, he's been trying to call you."

"What does he want?"

"I don't know, he just said it was important. He's in the billiard room."

Lily made her way down the hallway to the Billiard room, where she could smell the sweet smoky aroma of a fine Cuban cigar. As she came closer, she heard the melodic blues guitar of *Led Zeppelin's*, "All My Love", a known Dave favorite, playing on the jukebox. Entering the darkened room, she looked around; a fire burned in the fireplace, but there was no sign of Dave. Then, just as she turned to leave, she heard Dave's voice.

"Where ya been?"

Lily turned back and walked deeper into the room, seeing a perfectly formed smoke-ring rise up above a leather chair facing the fireplace. She walked up beside the chair, where Dave sat looking into the fire, puffing casually on his cigar. It was obvious he was slightly annoyed, having obviously been waiting for her.

"We went to the Ocean Club, then ice skating in …"

"How romantic," Dave cut her off with quiet scorn. "Been trying to call you."

"I'm sorry, I didn't take my phone."

"I need to talk to you."

"I need to talk to you, too," Lily admitted. "I've made a pretty big decision."

"Let me guess, you and Shakespeare have fallen in love, and you're flying off to Vegas to get married."

"Look, I know you don't really care for Darby, but I …"

"Want a beer?" Dave asked, as he got up and walked over to the bar, not really listening to her.

"No, thanks."

"So is that what you wanted to tell me?"

"No," Lily paused. "I've decided to quit."

"You sure you don't want something, milkshake, martini ... absinth?" Dave asked, puffing on his cigar, ignoring her comment.

"I'm going to stop, retire."

Dave did not respond. He sat back down in the chair by the fireplace.

Did you hear what I said?" Lily asked.

"Yes."

"Well?"

"Oh, am I allowed to retort now?"

"Please do."

"That's all fine and dandy that you want to quit; great, fantastic, I think you should. But before you do, I suggest you hear what I have to say. I think you may be interested."

"Go ahead."

"There's a little girl that lives in a penthouse apartment with her "ultra-rich" parents in New York City. It seems a few days ago, she was down in the swimming pool of her building and almost drowned. Thing is, this girl is a really good swimmer. The nanny was sitting right there, reading a magazine, when the girl went under. She told her parents that she felt a hand grab her leg. She tried to scream out, but was rapidly pulled under the water. The nanny looked up and saw the little girl go under, but thought she was just playing a game, seeing how long she could hold her breath. When the nanny looked up again; she was still under the water. The girl was pulled out of the pool, paramedics were called and she was revived, but has never been the same since. When asked what happened, she said, she was pulled under the water by a ... *burned clown*."

Lily's eyes instantly welled with tears. After a moment, she gathered herself, took a deep breath and looked over at Dave.

"He told me ... he was going to find a *new* daughter and he did."

"Still gonna quit?" he asked, already knowing her answer.

"Charter a plane to New York ... as soon as possible."

"There you are," Darby exhaled, as he breezed into the billiard room all smiles. "What happened to five minutes?

"We've had a little change in plans," Lily said, rushing past him.

CHAPTER 18

▼

PRECIOUS THINGS

"Good evening Ladies and Gentlemen, this is the Captain," a deep voice spoke over the dull hum of the engines. "As you may have noticed, we are heading through a bit of a storm system. We'll do our best to get through it quickly. We ask that you remain seated with your seatbelts fastened. We should be arriving at LaGuardia in approximately two hours. So just sit back, relax and enjoy the remainder of your flight."

The next evening they chartered a private plane to New York City, and got caught in a nasty bit of weather along the way. Dave was oblivious of the storm, sitting in a row by himself, encompassed in the blue glow of his laptop.

Darby sat next to Lily, who was clutching the armrests in the back of the plane. A brilliant *flash* of lightening made her shield her eyes. She took a deep breath and sunk deeper into the darkness of her seat, trying desperately to conceal the absolute terror inside her. All she could do was stare out into the inky blackness of night, watching the lightning brighten the angry billowing storm clouds outside her window every few seconds. Darby pulled down the shade and kissed her cheek reassuringly.

After passing through the storm, the rest of the flight went relatively smooth. Upon arrival, they took a cab from the airport into Manhattan. The car inched its way through the massive crowds of New Year's Eve revelers, causing traffic to back up all over the city. After checking into their hotel, Dave, Darby and Lily, immediately made their way over to the little girl's building.

Dramatic spotlights lit the front of 1930's art deco structure, standing majestically on ritzy Fifth Avenue, overlooking Central Park. The building was a New York City landmark, where the rich and famous lived and played in extravagance and luxury.

Lily stood on the terrace of one of the fabulous penthouse apartments, gazing at the shimmering city lights. She breathed in the chilly night air, watching delicate swirling snowflakes blanket the city; finally feeling some calm from the bumpy flight.

An elegant man came out onto the snowy terrace of the penthouse next door. Dressed for a night of New Year's merriment, the gentleman wore a debonair tuxedo with tails and a crisp white bat-wing collar. He stood with one hand behind his back; the other held a fancy Meerschaum pipe, which he puffed on.

"Good evening," the man greeted Lily, tipping his shiny top hat.

"Good evening," she responded with a polite smile.

The distinguished man looked out upon the immense metropolis before him with a regal air, as though it all belonged to him.

"I do not wish to live in Mr. Roosevelt's world any longer," the man informed her, as he stepped up on one of the large metal light fixtures on the terrace ledge. He looked over at Lily, then back out at his city. In one quick movement, he casually *stepped off* the terrace; his hat blew off as he glided down through the air toward the street … thirty-stories below.

"Noooo!" Lily cried out, leaning far over the ledge, watching the man *disappear* into thin air, just before he was to be impaled on a tall street light. Lily stepped back and closed her eyes. Suddenly, the terrace door opened and Darby stepped out, startling her.

"Feel any better?" he asked, putting his arms around her.

"Much," Lily lied. "I just needed a minute to chill out. I'm ready now."

"Come in, chilling is good, but it's freezing out here," Darby said, rubbing Lily's shoulders, ushering her into the luxury penthouse apartment of Alexander and Helena Laurent. Alexander was a prominent Manhattan real estate developer, his wife, a Swedish ex-model turned socialite. They were parents of Elizabeth Laurent, an extremely bright, seven year-old girl, who had been plagued by hallucinations and mysterious fires.

"We are extremely concerned for her safety," Alexander Laurent explained with true concern on his face. Wearing a crisp black tuxedo, Alexander stood next to his gorgeous blonde wife, who was sitting in an elegant chair in a dazzling red-sequined gown. "This is just not like her; she is such a wonderful smart child."

"When did you first notice things happening?" Dave asked the parents.

"After the *incident* in the swimming pool," the father stated. "Ever since then, Elizabeth will not go near that pool. She wakes every night screaming, talking about a clown coming out of her closet, and she's suddenly fascinated with fire. Her nanny, who had been with us for many years, quit, she said she was starting to be fearful for her own safety after putting out three small fires in Elizabeth's bedroom. Now we can't find another nanny willing to watch her. My lovely little daughter even smells of smoke; her clothes, her skin, her hair. I'm fearful she is going to burn down the entire building."

"Alexander, when will you see that she just wants attention," Helena interrupted, speaking in a thick Swedish accent. "I mean a clown, please. I love to see clowns; the entire world loves a clown. Clowns are happy; they are to make you laugh. They're fun, not frightening. She has always had imaginary friends that she talked to … ever since she was very small. But this *clown* business, it is absurd! She is living in a fantasy world she has made up to get attention. And her lies have worked; Alexander just bought her a puppy. What are people going to say? I think she needs a shrink!"

Dave and Darby looked over at Lily; they could see she was fuming inside.

"I'm curious. Where did you get your doctorate?" Lily asked abruptly.

"Lily, please," Dave said softly, trying to calm her.

"Well, it's obvious you know an awful lot about absolutely *nothing*."

"Excuse me," Helena responded, not used to being spoken to in such a manner.

"No, ya know what, you're not excused!" Lily stated angrily, moving toward the mother. "Its people like you that screw up their kids."

"Who do you think you're talking to?" Helena snapped back.

"You don't know what's happening to her; you have no clue," Lily continued her rant. "You don't know what she's thinking, what she's feeling, and worst of all, you really don't care! And, I mean, what kind of a psycho likes clowns?"

"Why don't we all settle down a bit," Dave stepped in and pulled Lily back. "Everyone is a little stressed out."

"I'm ready to leave now, Alexander," Helena fumed, grabbing her Chanel bag.

"Yes, we should go. We're hosting the annual New Year's gala in the ballroom. We do need to leave; it is already nine o'clock," Alexander stated, extending a hand to his wife, escorting her formally to the front door. As Helena briskly walked out, she darted Lily a sharp glance. "Elizabeth is in her bedroom with the sitter. Our cell number is by the phone. There is a fire extinguisher in every room. We can be reached right away. Please, don't hesitate to call for any reason. Thanks so much for your help."

Darby was busy helping Dave set up night vision cameras in the corners of Elizabeth's perfect pink room; one camera facing her closet, the other facing her bed. Television monitors were set up on the dining room table, where Dave could watch the activity in the little girls' room.

"Hello Elizabeth, my name's Lily," Lily said, smiling down at the shy girl with the very serious face, sitting quietly on her bed in her nightgown. Elizabeth was cradling a tiny fluff-ball of a puppy, curiously watching all the activity going on around her. "If it's okay, I'd like to hang out here with you tonight. Would that be alright?"

"Yes," Elizabeth answered instantly.

"What exactly is a vortex? Should I be looking for something in particular?" Darby asked Dave, as they stood in the ritzy brass elevator.

"Oh trust me, if you see it, you'll know," Dave warned, as a bell *dinged* and the elevator doors opened, revealing a shadowy black room. Dave felt across the wall through the darkness for some light switches. "A vortex is like, like a passage-way or doorway leading from one dimension to another. Usually some pretty nasty spirits use vortexes from what I'm told."

"Nasty, meaning evil or something?"

"Exactly, they use it as a quick escape from doing rather naughty things. Also, just to put out the fire with gasoline, tonight is what is known as a "Dark Moon". Which, if you believe in astrological divination, makes tonight … one of the rare nights of the year that the veil between life and death is very thin, and spirits can pass easily from one dimension to another. I'm not really into astrology or any of that crap, but I do believe very strongly in the "Dark Moon". Ha, there you are!"

Dave flicked on the light switches which illuminated the massive room.

"It's remarkable," Darby mused, captivated by its sheer grandeur.

"It's fuckin' creepy."

"It's brilliant," Darby laughed, his voice echoing off the marble walls and floors. "It's like stepping back in time."

Massive columns held up the open, second floor observation gallery, where a bank of three ornate elevators stood overlooking the perfectly preserved center-piece of the room; a stunning art-deco pool. Dave instantly got a strange feeling in the room, but Darby loved everything about it.

The entire pool room was tiled in a striking smoky-green marble bordered with black trim. The floors were the same green marble but with geometric black patterns which linked the entire area. The pool itself was covered with darker tiles, making the water glow a deep jade green. The cavernous domed ceiling was inlaid with glimmering mother-of-pearl tiles. A double set of stairs, lined with a streamlined black metal railing, led down from either side of the second floor observation gallery, meeting in the middle on a small landing. A dramatic backlit glass panel etched with images of plump koi fish, sat prominently in the middle of the wall, where the stairs split, once again, in opposite directions as they descended down to the pool.

On the other side of the room was a wall of chunky glass tiles with an open doorway in the center, which divided the area between the pool and the ladies' lounge. There were no windows, but the curved walls featured impressive, up-lit, art nouveau wall sconces, which surrounded the entire room. Even with the many light fixtures, the room was surprisingly dim.

Dave and Darby walked down the stairs carrying the cameras and equipment. Darby immediately took off his coat and walked around the area, exploring his new surroundings, and taking pictures with his digital camera. Dave got right to work setting up the cameras in various spots around the pool. He then set up the monitors on a table facing the pool and pulled up two striped lounge chairs.

"It's just incredible, isn't it," Darby's mesmerized voice resonated across the pool. He ventured through the open doorway that led to the women's lounge. Art deco globe lights lined a trio of mirrors sitting above black pedestal sinks with shiny chrome fixtures. Passing a few bathroom stalls, Darby walked down a narrow corridor with small individual dressing boxes on either side covered by sheer white curtains.

Dave finished setting up all of the equipment by the pool and sat back in his chair.

"You have to see how incredible the women's toilets are!" Darby said excitedly, walking back out into the pool area and sitting down in a chair next to Dave.

"Oh boy … can't wait," Dave sarcastically mocked. "I do have to take a piss."

"Everything ready to go then?" Darby asked.

"Yeah, you sure you'll be okay down here alone?"

"I believe so," Darby exhaled.

"Well, I figure if you can survive six months of genocide and being chased by militant forces in Darfur with that family, you can make it through a night alone in a creepy old pool."

"Dave, you saw my film?" Darby looked at him with surprise. "I'm stunned!"

"Well, don't be; it was good, really good. In fact, it was amazing," Dave stood up. "Now, I really gotta take a piss. Where are these fabulous toilets?"

"Through that door across the room."

Dave walked across the pool area and disappeared through the doorway in the block glass wall. Darby drank coffee from a silver thermos, hoping to caffeinate himself conscious through the entire night.

Suddenly, he sat straight up in his chair, hearing soft *footsteps* echoing off the marble walls from the shadowy observation deck above. He had a very strong feeling, he was not alone. Scanning the second floor landing, he saw two, *human figures*, standing in the shadows, the chrome sconces backlighting them. Darby could not help thinking they were spirits from another time. They stood very still and seemed to be discussing him, apparently as curious about him, as he was of them.

The bang echoed off the marble walls in the ladies lounge, as Dave let the stall door behind him slam shut. He walked over to one of the pedestal sinks and splashed cool water on his face. As he looked up at his reflection in the mirror, he saw *something* pass behind him; swiftly moving from one dressing box across the passageway into another.

"Hey," he called out, quickly turning around. There was no answer. He shut off the water and dried his hands, all the while staring down the narrow passage. The figure moved again, this time quicker, moving further into the back of the dark passage, lurking in the shadows.

"Darby, that you?" Dave asked, as he flicked the switch turning on the lights above the corridor, causing the old lighting fixture to buzz and strobe erratically. Bursts of crackling light broke through the darkness, allowing him to catch occasional glimpses of the black mass. The figure seemed to look over at him, as it once again moved from one dressing box to another. "Hey, whoever you are, I know you're fuckin' back there!"

The passageway was eerily silent and the temperature dropped drastically. Dave choked back his queasiness, smelling the foul stench of rotting flesh that permeated the stale air. Suddenly the mass appeared, it intensified, growing larger, hovering at the end of the passage. Dave could not make out any discernable features, though he felt it seemed to be sizing him up; he knew he was in over his head.

In the blink of an eye, the mass exploded down the passage toward him, sucking the curtains up into the air, blowing them wildly, as the lights above exploded, one by one, like roman candles.

Dave felt his throat suddenly constricting, like he was being choked by unseen hands. He gasped for air, feeling all the energy drain from his body, as he was slammed up against the side wall, literally pinned, unable to move or breathe. Then, the black mass released him. He inhaled a deep breath, watching it rapidly disappear from the room. Dave slowly collapsed to the floor, as he tried to catch his breath. He then pulled himself to his feet and made his way back out to the pool area.

"Did you see it?" Dave breathlessly called out to Darby, who he found huddled under the table where the monitors sat, taking pictures with his digital camera. "Tell me you saw it?"

"Yeah, I got pictures," Darby whispered in a panicked voice. Grabbing Dave's arm, he pulled him down to his level. "Look ... up there on the observation deck. Do you see them?"

"Them? There's more than one?" Dave asked, looking up; seeing an older man and woman, standing among the shadows. He looked at the monitors and saw that the cameras were also picking up the figures. "It's an old couple."

"Hello?" a voice echoed from above.

"Did you hear that?" Darby asked excitedly. "They're trying to communicate?"

"Yeah, I heard it. What about it?" Dave stood, looking up at the figures standing above them, moving closer. He shined his flashlight up at the couple, dressed in their finest evening clothes. He examined them for a moment before looking back at Darby with a questioning glance. "The people standing up there, is that what you're talking about?"

"Right, you can see them too."

"That's definitely *not* ... what I saw," Dave said with disappointment, scanning the pool for any sign of the black mass. "What I saw ... didn't have a face."

"What do you mean?" Darby asked confused.

"Hello there," Dave called out to the couple. "How are y'all this lovely evening?"

"We're just fine. I hope we didn't scare you," the man said. "We're the Sampsons, my wife and I are attending the New Year's party in the ballroom."

"Hello, boys," Mrs. Sampson called down with a wave. "What are you doing down there?"

"We're making a film about, uh, pool safety, apparently. That young man there with the camera is a very well known, award-winning, director," Dave announced with importance, pointing to the incredibly embarrassed Darby, still crouched behind the monitor. "Why don't you stand up, Herr Direktor, take a bow."

"Evening," Darby mumbled, standing up from behind the table.

"He's a little sketchy," Dave announced loudly. "He's English, you know."

"I'm English also," Mrs. Sampson stated, excitedly. "I was born in Brixton."

"My family is from Kent," Darby said. "I live in London now, Shepherds Bush."

"I have a cousin in Shepherds Bush. Maybe you know her, Margie Kling?"

"Sorry, doesn't ring a bell."

"I was taking my wife on a little tour," Mr. Sampson explained. "I grew up in this building."

"Really, you lived here?" Darby asked. "So you swam in this pool?"

"Back in the day, when I was a young boy."

"How long did you live in the building?"

"Oh, 'bout ten years."

"Do you know if anything, *strange*, ever happened in here?" Dave inquired.

"Strange?" the mature man repeated, his face dropped, as he looked at his wife knowingly; then back at the pool. "I can tell you this pool should be condemned. Bad things have happened here, things no one could ever explain. You should be very careful. It was nice meeting you both. Happy New Year, gentleman."

The couple walked away, leaving Dave and Darby standing alone by the pool.

"Well, that was weirdly amusing," Dave stated, looking around the pool area. "Darby, are you sure you didn't see anything come out of the ladies lounge?"

"No, not a thing. What happened?"

"I saw something moving around the passageway by the changing boxes. It was this mass, a dark mass. It came at me, full force. I felt freezing cold hands around my neck, but I couldn't see a thing. I couldn't breathe; I got really weak, literally drained of every ounce of energy in my body. There is no way anybody could have gotten out of here without at least one of us seeing."

"Maybe it was just your mind playing tricks on you. It is really stuffy in there, lot of chlorine in the air. It's a very old building and there's not a lot of ventilation."

"My friend, stale air doesn't slam you up against a wall and try to choke you."

"True."

"Alright, I have to go back up to the penthouse and watch over Lily and the girl. This is your last chance to use your "chicken shit" card. I'd totally understand if you didn't want to stay down here by yourself."

"I'll be fine," Darby assured him. "Really."

"Darby, seriously, you need to be very careful," Dave warned again. "Don't go into the ladies changing rooms. Take this walkie-talkie; if you need anything, call me. I'll get down here as soon as I can."

"Thanks mate," Darby said thoughtfully, hooking the walkie-talkie to his belt. He extended his hand to Dave, who took it and shook it.

"Honestly, I didn't picture you as the type to make the long haul, but you have. For that, I give you credit. Promise me you won't take any foolish chances; if you feel uncomfortable, leave!"

"Promise."

Dave took the long ride on the elevator up to the thirtieth floor. He immediately checked in with Lily, then went out to the dining room table and put his headphones on. He sat down behind the bank of monitors in the palatial penthouse living room. He was listening in on the quiet conversation between Lily and Elizabeth, while watching them from the camera set up in the little girl's bedroom just a few feet away.

Lily had turned off all the lights except for one, a small round lamp used as a nightlight, which spun around projecting a parade of circus animals on the walls.

"Elizabeth, you know, these things you can see are really special. Only a very small number of people in this whole entire world can see the things that you can," Lily explained, kneeling in front of Elizabeth's bed, petting the sleeping puppy in her lap. "I'm one of those people too."

"You are?"

"Yep, I can see what you see. I don't always want to. You know why?"

"Yes."

"Why?"

"'Cause, it's scary?"

"Yep, it can be really scary. I know exactly how it feels. What you have to understand is that some of these people, the people that try to chat with you, some of them have been here for many years, before you were even born, before I was even born. And there will be people here long after you and I are gone. Try to put yourself in their shoes. Some are just confused and sometimes you can help them. The clown though, you must never ever give the clown ... any part of you. Do you understand?"

"My mother thinks I'm making everything up. She says, I just want attention, but I swear, I'm not lying," Elizabeth said, tearfully. "I just want him to leave me alone."

"I know, sweetheart."

"You believe me, don't you?"

"Absolutely, I used to have your same serious face for a very long time. You see, I had lost my smile too. But I decided to face my fears and put them in their place. Once I did that, my smile returned. You know what? I think your puppy ... what's his name?"

"Moose."

"I think Moose is holding onto your smile, keeping it until you're ready for it again"

Elizabeth smiled.

"A-ha, I see you're almost ready!"

"Are you still going to stay with me tonight, all night, when *he* comes?"

"I am ... I need to have a little chat with him."

"Thank you," Elizabeth whispered, wrapping her arms lovingly around Lily.

Inhaling the chlorine saturated air, Darby yawned, gazing at the eerie glow rising up through the pool from the underwater spotlight. He tapped his hands along with the big band swing music, heard faintly coming through the walls from the ballroom next door. He yawned again, momentarily putting his head down on the table in front of him.

A sudden *splash* of water echoed off the marble walls. Startled, Darby immediately jumped to his feet and ran over to the pool. A perplexed look overtook his face; the water was completely still, dead calm.

"What the bloody hell?"

Up in the penthouse, Dave took off his headphones, hearing obnoxious laughter. He looked over at Elizabeth's chubby teenage babysitter, who was casually lounging on the nearby couch feasting on a carton of ice cream, cheering along with the New Year's celebration in Times Square playing on the big screen television.

"Do you think you could turn that down a bit?" Dave asked her.

"Turn what down?"

"The television ... and yourself ... turn 'em both down."

The girl rolled her eyes, and reluctantly turned the volume down.

"Thaaanks," Dave sarcastically mouthed, before going back to monitoring Elizabeth's bedroom. He saw Lily pulling a blanket up to cover Elizabeth. She then sat back on the bed, holding the sleeping child in her arms, watching the cute cartoon circus animals on her lamp, spinning across the wall in the darkened room. Lily closed her eyes momentarily, fighting her own sleepiness, while waiting patiently for the confrontation she knew was coming.

"Surely if anyone had jumped into the pool, Houdini or not, they would have absolutely drowned by this time," Darby said quietly. Several minutes passed as he stood at the edge of the pool peering into the dim glowing water. He turned and walked back to the table where the monitors sat and plopped back down in his chair, figuring the chlorine was finally beginning to take its toll. As he continued to glance at the pool, he unscrewed the cap from his thermos and took a swig of coffee; his eyes unconsciously following a small trail of *bubbles* moving from the far end of the pool toward him.

Unexpectedly, a *woman* broke up through the calm surface of the water and swam across the pool with long, eloquent strokes. She seemed oblivious to the fact that she was being watched by the astonished eyes belonging to Darby, who choked down the warm coffee in his throat.

"I'm sorry Miss, I didn't hear you come in," Darby called out to her politely. "The pool has been closed for the evening." The woman swam over to the edge of the pool where Darby stood. She never looked at him and never spoke, as she climbed a stainless steel ladder out of the swimming pool, wearing a vintage forties, halter-top, bathing suit and swim cap. Walking over to an empty towel rack, she picked up an invisible towel and dried her face and body, before taking off her bathing cap and shaking out her dark bobbed hair.

Darby noticed the young woman was bathed in an extraordinary greenish radiance, yet she appeared rather solid. It quickly dawned on him that she was not of this world. Surprisingly, he was in no way afraid of the spectral woman, as she was not scary or threatening in any way and did not seem to be aware of his existence.

Bravely moving closer, Darby was able to really look at her. She was quite beautiful with delicate features: high cheekbones and arched brows. He could actually see the beads of water running down parts of her body, and standing just a few feet from her now, he studied her every detail while she gazed into the pool. The apparition then abruptly turned and walked *through* Darby. He could feel the cool vaporous mist, which emanated from her, softly lay upon his skin. He watched, as she walked barefoot into the ladies changing room.

"My torch," Darby whispered aloud, rushing over to the table and grabbing his flashlight. He pulled the walkie-talkie off his belt trying to call up to Dave, as he rushed across the pool area.

"Dave, Dave, can you hear me?" he said quietly; but nothing came through except for static. Darby abruptly stopped walking, standing right next to the pool, noticing a *mist* hovering above the water. Though he took note of the strange mist, his mind was totally focused on the ghostly woman, so he continued following her wet footprints into the ladies changing room.

Looking around the room with disappointment, Darby noticed that the woman was gone; she seemingly *vanished* into thin air. The room was quiet other than a soft repetitious drip of water. The lights that had not blown out were still flickering, just as they had been when Dave had his run in with the black mass. Something didn't feel right; the air felt electrically charged. Out of the corner of his eye, Darby saw a sudden quick movement at the end of the narrow hall containing the changing boxes. He instantly became uneasy, standing alone in the middle of the darkened room.

Darby stood completely still, concentrating, straining to make sense of the recognizable sound he could not believe he was hearing. A very faint resonance could be heard coming from the end of the passageway. He could see the sheer curtain on the very last changing box in the back of the corridor, moving back and forth in a sensual rhythm. Darby lit his flashlight to get a better look, but as soon as he turned it on, it quickly drained and died.

"Brilliant," he nervously whispered, continuing to move closer, more curious of what he would find than fearful. The further he ventured down the shadowy corridor, the more recognizable the sound became. It was unmistakable, full of lush intensity; the sound of a woman repeatedly *moaning* in the throws of passion.

Darby was almost to the end of the corridor when he stopped abruptly. He saw the back of a massive bald man wearing dark blue coveralls; one of his long legs stuck out from under the sheer curtain attached to the top of the changing box. Grunting gruffly, the man thrust his entire body forward and back. With each mounting thrust, the woman's moans would increase in crescendo, louder and louder, echoing off the marble walls, over and over again. The sound was chilling … unnerving. It seemed to go on for a long period of time, then the moans … abruptly ceased.

The man stood motionless, breathing heavily, his enormous body throbbing. Suddenly, his face emerged from the shadows and he glanced out into the passageway, looking past Darby, obviously unaware of his presence. He was covered in blood, an ice pick grasped tightly in his right hand, his face was vicious, flush with anger, his shoulders rising and falling with each deep breath he took. Then, without warning, he ran full throttle directly at Darby, who didn't have a chance to move before the mad man ran right through him.

"Noooo!" Darby yelled, putting his hands in front of his face, trying to shield himself from the impending collision. Time seemed to slow drastically, as the man infiltrated Darby. He could feel electric chills sparking over his entire body, as though he had touched a live wire. It was not the pleasant feeling, like he felt from the woman. This was horrible, frightening, painful. In that split second, he could see the crazed thoughts rushing through the deranged man's mind in rapid flashes, as he recounted brutally hurling the ice pick through the air, over and over again, puncturing something writhing around in the darkness beneath him.

Once the man passed through Darby, he continued running down the corridor and disappeared into the darkness. Darby collected himself and slowly approached the last changing box. Pulling back the curtain, he took a step back, covering his mouth in horror.

Lily's eyes fluttered shut for a moment, before they opened wide, hearing soft growling. Sitting on the end of the bed, she spotted Moose, who was beside himself, snarling at something in the dark corner of the room. The puppy jumped to the floor and quickly scampered under the bed cowering in fear. Lily smelled a familiar smoldering aroma wafting through the ever-increasing warm room.

"Varton," Lily whispered, glimpsing the sinister outline of wild crimson hair and white facade of greasepaint, glowing faintly through the darkness.

"I see you have met my new daughter." the mangled clown spoke; his eyes were flickering flames, dimly illuminating his grotesque melted face in a crimson glow. He was holding something in his arms, cradling it like a baby. "She is quite beautiful, yes?"

It was then Lily noticed Elizabeth was no longer slumbering in her lap. Varton looked down upon the child sleeping peacefully unaware in the puffy sleeves of his scorched satin costume.

"She is not yours to have, Varton," Lily whispered, trying not to wake the sleeping girl in his arms. "You're not going to ruin another child … like you ruined me!"

"Lillian, do you really think you can bend my will?" Varton laughed with his ghastly painted-on smile. "You are really such a foolish girl. You think you are powerful enough to tell me what to do?"

"I'm stronger than you think I am."

"You defy me again? I was the only one who has ever loved you. I gave you choice," the disfigured clown's voice was chilling; his glassy stare narrowed, glaring angrily through black-encased eyes. "Now I have, new daughter, one that will listen to me, one that will obey my every command. And best of all, one that no one believes. Sound familiar?"

Darby looked down upon the lifeless body of the delicate young woman from the pool, splayed out on the small seat in the blood-drenched changing box; her body covered with puncture wounds, her glazed eyes staring blankly up at him. Just as Darby reached down to touch her, she *disintegrated* into nothingness.

"Darby, can you hear me?" Dave's voice finally came through the static on the walkie-talkie.

"Yes, yes, I can hear you!" Darby called back. "There are some absolutely bizarre things happening down here!"

"What happened?" Dave asked.

"I think I just witnessed a residual haunting? I saw a man in the changing boxes! He was a maintenance man or something," Darby reported, excitedly walking out of the ladies lounge, heading back to the pool area. "He killed a woman with an ice pick."

Darby was stopped in the doorway, hit by a wall of sweltering *hot air*; his lungs stung from the steamy heat, his face rapidly warmed as though sunburned. In the few minutes he had been away, the room had become an enormous sauna. The pool was simmering like a pot of water just turned down from a rapid boil. Long black marks were seared into the marble floor, leading from the edge of the pool to the middle elevator, where they vanished. "Dave, I do believe something has happened."

"Darby, what is it?"

"Hold on a tick!" An idea popped into Darby's head. He quickly made his way through the steam over to the monitors. Wiping the condensation off the main monitor with his sleeve, he hit rewind, and then sat dumbfounded, watching the black and white footage filmed after he went into the ladies changing rooms.

First, a thick *steam* shot up at the far end of the pool, like a hot springs geyser. Then, within mere moments, the water began to bubble and gurgle, quickly turning the entire pool into a giant vat of boiling water.

Then, a frightening form emerged up through the steam. Darby again wiped the condensation off the monitor, revealing a tall lanky *clown* in a flowing striped satin jumpsuit, rising up through the water, yet not at all wet. He was hideously charred and smoldering, looking more like he had just stepped out of a blazing furnace, instead of a pool of water.

The mangled circus freak was moving fast. Each sharp step he took across the top of the water produced a shot of steam. He released a sinister laugh for no apparent reason with a peculiar delighted grin on his face. His teeth looked unnaturally large and jagged; part of his lips had been melted away. His fingers were unnaturally long and boney. A shimmering heat radiated from his body in waves like a desert mirage. As he stepped out of the pool onto the marble floor, he left scorched footprints in the shape of his oversized freakish shoes.

"It's Varton Muntz; he's here!" Darby shouted into the walkie-talkie, but there was no response, only more static. "Dave, Dave can you hear me? Its Varton, he's already here in the building!"

"Don't be sad Lillian," Varton said with warped sentiment. "Out of all my children, over these many many years, you will always be one of my absolute favorites. But, unfortunately, I have no use for you now."

"Leave here, Varton. You can't have this one," Lily warned, showing no fear, holding her own against the frightening clown standing before her. "I'll make sure of it!"

"Well, it is not your choice to make Lillian, it is mine," the demented clown seethed, stretching out his boney emaciated arm out towards Lily. "You had your chance to make peace with me and you foolishly chose that foul English filth!"

A small fire suddenly erupted in the palm of his hand. He blew on it lightly, sending a stream of flame across the room, barely missing Lily's head, but catching a teddy bear on fire. Lily quickly reacted, grabbing a glass of water from the bedside table and spilling it on the fire, as Varton chuckled. "Oh no, dis little girl, she must have started another fire. We shall have to lock her up in a hospital for the naughty children who like to play with fire."

"Let her go, Varton!" Lily warned.

"As you wish," Varton obeyed. With one quick movement, he effortlessly threw the little girl across the room. Elizabeth woke abruptly, landing on the bed, looking up with sheer terror at the real-life nightmare towering in the corner of her room. She began to panic and cry. Lily quickly pushed the girl behind her, trying to protect her. "My darling child, after all I have done for you, did you ever take into consideration that it was your disrespect that has caused me to seek out this little girl?"

"I meant no disrespect; I just wanted to live a normal life."

"Lillian, did you ever stop to think that dis little girl was the bait to catch, how do you say, the bigger fish?"

"What are you talking about?"

Although he could not see Varton standing in the corner of Elizabeth's room, Dave did witness the ball of fire shoot across his monitor and ran to the bedroom door.

"Excuse me a moment," Varton said politely, as he stepped over to the bedroom door and casually touched a single boney finger on the brass handle. The handle heated up immensely, making the metal bright red, as it began to melt.

"Awhhh, mother … fucker!" Lily heard Dave release a pained cry from outside the bedroom door. His hand was burned when he grabbed the doorknob; he then angrily began trying to kick the door in.

"Lillian, as you well know, there is *someone* between us. I will not stand for this."

"Leave Elizabeth alone and I promise I will do anything you wish."

"Anything? Get rid of the Englishman!"

Lily just stared at him, unable to make that promise.

"You have fallen in love with him, I see. You have made your decision. It is time for my exit," Varton smiled, exposing his razor-sharp jagged teeth. "I'm going to go for a little swim."

"Leave him alone, you side-show psycho!"

"Parting is such sweet sorrow," Varton announced, holding out his arms, bowing dramatically like the great actor he once was. He then opened both his palms and blew a ball of fire at the bedroom door, causing it to burst open; knocking Dave to the ground and out of his way. Varton walked out of the room, leaving a halo of fire burning around the doorframe.

"He's going for Darby!" Lily screamed frantically to Dave.

"Darby?" Dave repeated, confused.

"Where's the pool?" Lily cried out. "Where's the damn pool?"

"Oh my God, what's going on?" The babysitter bawled seeing the fire.

"Call 911! Then, call the parents! DO IT NOW!" Dave yelled spraying the fire with an extinguisher. Take the elevator to the second floor. The entrance to the pool is next to the ballroom! Go help Darby, I'll be right there!"

Lily ran out of the penthouse into the hallway, where she saw that Varton had left a trail of large flaming footprints all the way to the elevator door.

"Dave, can you hear me? I am officially pulling out my "chicken shit card" here." Darby kept trying to get his walkie-talkie to work, but still nothing but static came through. He had finally had enough, he quickly made his way through the dissipating, steam-filled air, toward the staircase leading up to the bank of elevators.

"10 ... 9 ... 8 ..."

Darby looked at his watch, it was just hitting midnight. He heard the partygoers in the ballroom next door, excitedly counting down to the New Year.

"7 ... 6 ... 5 ... 4 ..."

Darby's face dropped when he turned and peered back at the pool, watching as the water seemed to take on a life of its own. It began to splash and swirl around, creating a fast-swelling miniature whirlpool. He could feel the warm air leaving the room; the temperature dropped, every second it became colder and colder. Something was certainly happening, something was coming. Just as he grabbed the stair railing, the light above the middle elevator ... *dinged.*

"3 ... 2 ... 1!"

The elevator door opened.

"HAPPY NEW YEAR!"

From out of the elevator came a sudden blast of freezing air, accompanied by an intense beam of brilliant blue light, which flooded the entire pool area. The cold air mixed with the warm air in the room, creating a thick eerie fog. Darby was petrified, his ears filled with the sound of a thousand terrifying voices, all echoing off the marble walls with incoherent words, deep moaning, and sadistic maniacal laughter. A sharp ear-shattering scream cut through the confusing noise and rotten stench.

The water in the pool was swirling higher, forming into an enormous spinning funnel. The tornado-like mass of air, water and energy, spun rapidly, creating a great vacuum. Warning bells went off in Darby's head, as he slowly backed up, sensing a powerful presence about to make its way down the staircase through the dense fog.

Losing his footing, Darby awkwardly slid on the sweaty floor tiles, then quickly scurried to his feet. His heart raced as he continued to back away from the menacing light, horrified, yet unable to look away.

Emerging from the elevator were illuminated human forms, backlit by the supernatural haze. An inconceivable amount of ghosts slowly glided out from the elevator, their bodies' radiant, glowing. Darby could make out forms of men, women and even children. It was a horrific social event, a twisted inter-mingling of souls, a ghastly gathering of the damned and the banished, those caught in a bizarre otherworldly limbo. It was the coming together of the dredges of the underworld; all from different decades and social classes, all meeting up in the pool. Grand Central Station for the dead.

None of them seemed to take note of Darby, as the ghostly masquerade party passed on either side of his shaking body. The wind from the swirling vortex sounded like a runaway freight train. The freezing air instantly turned the room from a sultry steam bath into a massive refrigerator.

Another one of the elevators *dinged* … its door opening with a second blast of freezing air and shock of light. More spirits followed, slowly appearing, coming out of the fog. Darby could make out a few features on some of the ghosts, but there were so many it truly overwhelmed him.

He could see a long knife sticking out the back of a bug-eyed waitress from the 1950's. Then a burly man in a blood-soaked apron, carrying a large duffle bag dripping with a foul fluid, pushed his way through the crowd. Darby also saw the bathing beauty, who was so mercilessly butchered in the ladies changing room. She glanced up at him as she passed. Quite a few of the ghosts were dressed in their fine funeral attire, their skin significantly rotted and decomposed; one woman carried a bouquet of dead flowers.

The phantom crowd continued entering the pool area, coming down the staircases in droves from the above observation deck. One by one, they stepped into the pool and were pulled into the powerful vortex. The image was unnerving and chaotic for Darby, who was doing his best to keep his wits together.

The last elevator opened, releasing one last blast of cold air and harsh light. The tremendous illumination pouring out of the elevators, cast off the marble walls and floors, bathing the entire pool area in an effervescent indigo radiance. The more spirits that entered, the colder the room became.

Darby watched additional ghosts exit the elevator. There was a young woman with a bouffant hairdo, wearing in a frilly pageant dress, with a pair of handprints bruised onto her pale neck. There was an old weathered priest drinking from a whiskey bottle, a pretty cheerleader with her wrists slashed, and a sailor wearing a crisp white uniform, his back riddled with bullet holes. Shivering and petrified, Darby watched the parade of specters making their way past him, before casually vanishing into the powerful vortex swirling around the center of the pool. It was as if they all knew this was the one night the temporary portal to the other side was open to the otherworldly public.

"DARBY!" A voice called out over the chaos. Darby saw Lily across the pool, standing at the opening of the ladies lounge, waving her arms to get his attention. She quickly rushed over to him, making her way through the oncoming spectral crowd. Lily hugged him tightly. "Thank God, you're alright … I was so worried my darling!"

"Lily, we have to get out!" Darby called out. "We have to get out of here!"

"The only way out is the pool!" Lily exclaimed. "We have to go through the vortex!"

"What, are you mad?"

"It's the only way! You must trust me, my darling!"

"We'll be killed!"

"I love you, Darby. I would never do anything to hurt you," Lily said, looking deeply into his eyes and kissing him passionately. Darby quickly felt his lips get very warm from the intense heat of her lips. He pulled away, holding Lily firmly by her arms, closely studying her face. There was something strange about her eyes; they had a slight reddish glow.

"Lily?"

"The portal is going to close soon. We must go into the pool! It's the only way!"

The last few spirits were swirling up into the vortex. Lily walked over to the edge of the pool and held her hand out to Darby.

"Take my hand, my darling. I know how to make it through!" As Darby took hold of Lily's hand, he remembered Dave telling him that a demon "*will appear as something or someone desirable, to make you believe it, to make you trust it*". "We'll be protected, I promise."

"You're a liar!" Darby said flatly. "You're … *not* Lily!"

"DARRRBY!"

Darby heard Lily's voice call out from the top of the staircase behind him. He quickly turned and saw, *another* Lily, standing on the staircase landing.

Darby felt his hand suddenly becoming extremely hot. Turning back, he watched in astonishment, as Lily's *twin* began to spark and morph, like a fourth-of-July sparkler, and she rapidly changed into her wretched mother, Karla.

"What the hell are you?" Darby demanded.

"You should cease asking difficult questions, if you do not wish to hear the truth, Englishman," Karla responded in a gravely voice, as she blew a cloud of putrid smoke at him.

Karla's hate-filled face sparked and changed, this time into Darby's deceased fiancée, Angela.

"Angela," Darby gasped, so shocked, he was unable to function.

"I'm scared, Darby," she whispered, tears running down her pale beautiful face. "It's so dark." Suddenly, her tears turned to blood, her cries turned to deep psychotic laughter, and her skin rapidly dehydrated and decomposed. Sparks popped from Angela's body, as she twitched, morphing into the frightening "corpse bride".

"Don't you love me anymore, Darby?" the bloody bride asked, sarcastically. She laughed with venom, her voice shrill. Then her eyes sharply rolled back into her head, as she began to elongate and sparks began pouring off her.

In a split second, Darby found himself face to face with … Varton Muntz, who was looming over him with a prickly grin covering his mangled face; larger than life … and death.

"You flaming freak!" Darby angrily berated the clown. Varton just grinned, releasing his wickedness with an obscene *cackle*, as he harshly grabbed Darby.

"This is the one you love, Lillian?" the clown laughed, holding Darby up in front of his mangled face, inspecting him with a crazed look in his fiery eyes. In one swift movement, Varton nonchalantly tossed Darby up into the air like a rag doll and caught him by the neck with his boney fingers, holding him up in the air with his feet dangling. Darby struggled, grabbing onto Varton's hands, desperately gasping for breath. "He is weak, so fragile; still he will make a lovely addition to my collection."

"Please … please," Lily begged. "I'll do anything you ask, just let him go!"

"We both know as long as dis person breathes, you will never completely be mine," Varton seethed, shaking Darby's semi-conscious body angrily at her. "I will not stand for it!"

"I promise you, Varton," Lily pleaded, rushing down the staircase.

"Unfortunately, you are not to be trusted ever again, Lillian," As Varton spoke, his fury grew, his skin began to fester and boil, radiating with heat. "As I recall, the last time you made a promise to me, you tried to banish me into oblivion! But your little diversion back-fired … too bad!"

The clown glanced back at the raging vortex. It was starting to diminish in size; he knew he had limited time to enter before his exit to the netherworld closed for good.

"Now, I bid you, adieu," the clown blew Lily a farewell kiss, then tossed Darby into the swirling funnel of air and water.

"Varton noooo!" Lily screamed.

Varton casually followed Darby's body into the pool, stepping into the vortex and disappearing. What he did not realize was that Darby was not lightweight.

He was not easily sucked into the vortex like the spirits had been; his heavy "living" body was taken by the current and viciously spun around the base of the diminishing whirlpool.

Suddenly, Dave came running out of the shadows and slid across the wet tile floor on his chest.

"GRAB MY LEGS," he shouted to Lily, as he leaned forward from the side of the pool, reaching out, trying in vain to grab Darby's body as it repeatedly passed in the powerful circular current.

"He's coming around again," Lily yelled, holding onto Dave.

"I need to get closer!" Dave said, stretching out as far as his body could. On the next pass, Dave finally grabbed hold of Darby's shirt and held on firmly, as the strong current continued to pummel his limp body. "I've almost … GOT HIM!"

The vortex was slowing considerably. Darby raised his head up and opened his eyes. He looked up at Dave's panicked face, wondering how he got into the pool. He grasped onto Dave's arm, hanging on for dear life, as the unforgiving water kept pulling him under.

Dave reeled Darby in and he was momentarily able to catch his breath, when an emaciated satin arm bubbled up from the center of the vortex. The arm reached out and grabbed onto Darby's pant leg, trying ruthlessly to yank him back into the vortex. Darby was already weak from the tremendous current, which was taking a toll on his body; he was having a hard time continuing to fight. He could see Varton under the bubbling pool water, doing his best to drown him.

"Hang on Darby, just a little longer," Dave called out, realizing there was only a matter of seconds before the vortex closed for good. But Darby's shirt started to rip and ended up being pulled off over his head. Dave tried desperately to maintain his grasp on Darby's wet arm, but his hands were quickly slipping. Varton viciously pulled Darby back under the water; his overpowering strength was beginning to overwhelm him. Dave knew he had to do something fast.

"Get rid of your pants! Take them off!" Dave shouted to Darby, who reached down under the water and unbuttoned his jeans with one hand. Instantly, he felt the pants slide down his legs and disappear into the vortex, still in Varton's ferocious grasp.

"IT'S CLOSING! HURRY!" Lily cried out. One last angry blast of steam shot up from the center of the water. It then subsided and mellowed; repeatedly sloshing against the sides of the pool, until it finally came to a halt. Darby's underwear-clad body was lifted out of the pool by Dave and Lily, and laid down on the cold wet tile.

"And then … that happened," Darby smiled up at them, worn out, but very happy to be alive. Lily grabbed Darby's wet body, holding him tightly in her arms.

"Lily, I'm okay," he sighed, exhausted.

"You were almost toast, my friend," Dave said, extending his hand to Darby, helping him to his feet. The two men hugged warmly.

"Thank you, Dave. I most surely wouldn't have made it without you."

"Let's get you something to wear, Aqua Man," Dave suggested, walking over to the table where the monitors were set up. He grabbed his duffle bag from under the table and took out a pair of navy sweats, a long-sleeved grey thermal shirt, and a pair of sneakers. He threw the clothes to the shivering Darby, who was drying himself with a towel. "Sorry man, I don't wear underwear, so you're stuck with your own skivvies."

"You know, after everything that just happened, the pool is surprisingly undamaged," Darby mused, putting the dry clothes Dave gave him on. "And Varton Muntz is no longer! Isn't that right Lily? Lily?"

Darby looked around the pool area; Lily was nowhere to be found.

"Lily?" he called louder, becoming concerned.

"Lily?" Dave called out. "Lily!"

"He's gone, for now," Lily's voice quietly echoed through the pool area. Darby and Dave looked up to see her standing at the top of the staircase, pressing the button to summon the elevators.

"Maybe this time he won't be able to find his way back?" Darby said.

"Varton Muntz will be back. He always manages to find his way back!" Lily looked drained; her normal cheery attitude was gone. "A vortex is just a doorway, an entryway or exit to other dimensions. All he has to do is find another vortex; it's just a matter of time. Then what? He'll be unbelievably pissed and looking for revenge. I can't deal with the consequences my life brings … I'm sorry, I just can't do it anymore."

The elevator *dinged*, the middle door opened and Lily stepped inside.

"Lily, where are you going?" Darby called out, moving toward the stairs.

"There are things I have to deal with," she said, pressing a button. "I need …"

"Wait … Lily!" Darby pleaded.

"I need to do that alone," Lily murmured, as the elevator door closed. Darby immediately grabbed his coat and he and Dave ran up the massive staircase.

Wealthy party-goers mingling in the lobby just outside the ballroom watched the completely disheveled Lily emerge from the elevator.

"Another, god-damn fire!" Helena Laurent yelled, as she came storming out of the ballroom. She saw lily and rushed over. "Do you know how much my Indian tapestries are worth? They are priceless and now they are ruined! You will be paying for the damage to all my things!"

"Yeah, that's right," Lily said. "Don't worry about your daughter, just your crap!"

"How dare you to speak to me in this manner!" Helena fumed, angry that Lily never looked at her, as she calmly headed through the lobby to the front doors of the building. "I demand that you … *listen to me*!"

As Darby and Dave came out of another elevator, Darby saw Lily walking through the revolving brass door leading outside. Helena quickly rushed over to Darby. Darby simply raised his hand up, blocking her, as he pulled his leather coat on and ran out after Lily, which infuriated her even more.

"My things are ruined!" Helena bellowed. "You'll be hearing from my lawyers!"

Dave snagged two glasses of champagne off the tray of an oblivious waiter, put his arm around Helena, and strolled with her through the lobby.

"Mrs. Laurent, let me try to explain," Dave spoke calmly, using his charismatic smile, he instantly charmed her. "Wow, you know, you look really stunning this evening."

CHAPTER 19

▼

BY MY SIDE

Fifth Avenue was packed with cars and people, making their way home from the New Year's festivities in Times Square. Darby darted in and out of the mob, trying to catch up to Lily, who was standing at a crowded street corner waiting for the light to change.

"STOP!" Lily screamed in absolute terror; seeing a *little boy*, no older than five, about to be hit by a fast moving cab on the other side of the road. The taxi immediately slammed on its brakes. Lily dashed through the traffic, accompanied by furious honking. When she made it to the front of the cab, she got down on her hands and knees, searching for the child; but he was nowhere to be found.

"Jesus, what did I hit?" the cabbie cried, jumping out of his car. Lily stood up and looked around, spotting the boy across the street at an entrance to Central Park. He was smiling, seemingly unfazed by the chilly weather; wearing nothing more than a pair of shorts and a yellow t-shirt. He giggled playfully, wanting her to chase him into the park.

"I'm sorry," Lily apologized to the cabbie and quickly ran after the child.

"What is your damage girlie?" the cabbie screamed after her, punching the top of his cab, blowing his fuse. Darby watched Lily run into the park. He darted through the traffic, briefly knocking into the cabbie. "Whatsamatta with you freakin' people!"

Central Park after dark was a dream-like experience. Darby felt a strange mixture of fear, exhilaration, and calm, which was hard to describe. Low dark clouds were releasing a blizzard of snow flurries. The ornate iron streetlamps illuminated the snow-covered footpaths and towering trees with a beautiful sparkling luster. The lights from the distant shimmering buildings loomed over the trees, the size of the park seemed limitless, the whole mood … surreal.

In a matter of moments, Darby went from being crowded by a multitude of people, to being completely alone in a peculiar alien landscape. There was no one around; he felt like he was the last person on earth. All was quiet and serene, except for the snow crunching under his feet. Darby stopped momentarily in front of a snowy statue depicting *Alice*, and her cohorts from *Wonderland*, sitting upon an oversized mushroom.

Darby looked around; Lily was nowhere to be found.

But she *was* in the park, just slightly ahead of him, running to catch up to the little boy, who was standing up on a stone bridge waiting for her. Once she spotted him, she stopped running and tried to catch her breath.

"Hey, little guy," Lily called out to him, breathlessly. Wanting the game to continue, the boy giggled and ran down the other side of the bridge. "WAIT!"

When Darby finally made it up onto the bridge, he could see Lily in the distance, running across a wide open section of the park. Unexpectedly, she awkwardly fell and slid a good distance on her belly, before finally coming to a gradual stop.

Quickly raising her head, she searched the landscape in a panic, unable to find the child anywhere. The ground beneath the snow was incredibly hard. Lily looked down and realized she was lying on an ice-covered lake. Tears flooded her eyes when she noticed a shock of *yellow* under the immaculate white snow. She got up to her knees and wiped snow from the frozen water; a small face peered out, perfectly preserved under the ice.

Darby walked up behind Lily and kneeled down. Though he never saw the small ghost boy, he did see the deceased child under the ice. He wrapped his arms around her body, holding her, as she rocked back and forth, weeping.

"I'm here for you," Darby whispered, trying to comfort Lily as she quietly sobbed. "We'll deal with it, I'll help you."

"No, I won't put you through that," Lily said, as she turned to look at him. "I want you to leave."

"Lily we've already been through all this, I'll never …"

"Don't you see … it's never going to stop. They will always find me!"

Darby stood up and helped Lily to her feet.

"Lily, I'm not afraid!" he said, passionately. "What more I can do to prove my loyalty? You are my world! Please, I just found you; I can't lose you like this."

"Darby, you're not listening! My life is never going to change!" Lily shouted, pushing away from him. "It doesn't matter that I want it to, it will always be this way!"

"Lily, stop this, I know what you're doing! It won't work, I love you!"

"Fuck Love! Don't you get it? I can never have a normal existence. I can never have a normal life! *They* will always be there and there's nothing I can do to stop it!"

"I don't give a damn … I want to be with you! I'll deal with it, all of it!"

"If you love me like you say you do, you'll leave … you'll leave right now."

"This is madness."

"Please …" Lily whispered, unable to even look at Darby. "… leave."

Darby stood in silence looking at Lily.

"I respect your wishes," Darby mumbled. There was nothing more to say; he shook his head in disbelief, before turning away. Lily watched him walk through the darkness, intermittently lit by the soft glow of the light posts. He stopped and turned around, taking one last glance at Lily, standing alone in the falling snow. Looking away, he continued walking.

"I will always love you, now and forever," Lily whispered, tears running down her face, as she watched him walk down the snowy path and disappear into the crowded streets. Once again, her insane life and existence have forced her to be alone. But she felt she was doing the right thing for Darby. She was giving him a chance at a normal life; she knew he would be much better off without her. "I wish you would turn around and come back to me, but I don't blame you. If I could leave myself, I most likely would."

Walking aimlessly through the bustling throng of jubilant New Yorkers, Darby really wasn't sure where he was going, he was just walking. Every cab he tried to hail was in use. He saw an entrance to an underground subway station, and decided to head to the airport to catch the first flight back to London. Just as he took his cell phone from his jacket pocket to make the airline reservation, it *rang*. He quickly answered it.

"Lily?"

"Darby," a familiar voice spoke on the other end of the line.

"Nigel?" Darby said, slightly disappointed. "How are you, mate?"

"I hate to bother you, I'm sure you're out partying it up."

"Actually no, I'm about to get on a subway carriage in New York City. I'm heading to the airport, coming home."

"Where's Lily? Did something happen between the two of you?"

"I'll explain it all when I get back," Darby said softly. "All I can say is that it's been madness here. Also, I've got some bad news about the film."

"Not as bad as the news I have."

"Why, what's going on?"

"Last night, some of the footage was *stolen*."

"WHAT?"

"Someone broke into my loft and took some of the film right out of the editing bay. By someone, I mean Ian Sharpe; he was the only one who knew what we had."

"Please Nigel ... please, tell me you're kidding!"

"Wish I could."

"Fuck, fuck, fuck, fuck me!" Darby cursed aloud. People walking by made space for the mad man. "Nigel, I can't believe this! Why, why is this happening?"

"I am so sorry, Darby. You know how anal I am about locking everything up. All the locks were broken; all the footage from the school and the amusement park was nicked. Everything else was locked up in the film vault. He couldn't get in there, only because the bastard didn't know the combination. I overheard the bastard already making deals, big money deals. He wasn't very pleased when I reminded him that nothing could be released without Lily's permission."

"Alright, I'm on my way back, I'm heading into the subway queue right now. I'll ring you the second I touch down and we'll figure this whole fucking mess out."

Darby closed his phone and walked down the steep steps into a subway station. He pushed through the turnstile, just as a subway car sped into the station and screeched to a halt. He wasn't in the mood to battle the onrush of people that packed into the train like sardines, so he waited. As the train sped off, he leaned up against the cold tile wall and laid his head back.

A few minutes later, another train pulled up to the platform bringing with it a slight breeze. Darby stepped into the subway car, along with a dozen other people. The doors slammed, and the car took off, swiftly moving along the tracks.

Darby sat down at the far end of the car and pulled his hands through his cold damp hair. He felt great sadness, looking around at all the New Years revelers in high spirits, wearing funny masks and party hats, blowing noisemakers, while singing and dancing with abandon. He put the headphones from his iPod on and listened to Mozart's dark "Requiem" symphony, while watching the wild party going on in front of him. He saw two chubby girls doing a tipsy dance on one of the steel poles in the middle of the car to the laughter of onlookers. An exhausted man held onto his girlfriend, who had passed out cold on his shoulder.

A few people, who had obviously come from a masquerade party, wore bizarre costumes and masks with strange "out of proportion" features; long noses and huge ears, some sprouting vibrant colorful feathers. Across from him sat a hairy fat man wearing diapers, with a sash across his chest that read, "*Baby New Year*". The man seemed to have more hair on his body, then on his head. At the other end of the car, Darby watched a group of alcohol saturated, twenty-something's, with their arms draped around each other, joyfully singing a rendition of "Auld Lang Sygne" with a great deal of enthusiasm.

He put his head down, trying to tune the world out. Once again, his heart was crushed, his happiness had turned disastrous. And now, a whole new set of problems showed their ugly face. The New Year was not getting off to the most promising start and the gravity of the situation was starting to weigh heavily on him. He could not stop seeing Lily standing alone in the snow covered Central Park. Things truly could not get worse.

At that moment, Darby felt the hair on the back of his neck stand on end; he could sense someone staring at him. He looked up through the crowd of revelers and his eyes locked with a set of dark "*dead eyes*", staring at him from across the moving car. He was immediately smacked with a very strong sense of deja-vu … realizing that these were the same "dead eyes" that had been plaguing his dreams. Suddenly his nightmare seemed to make sense as it came to life before his eyes.

The strange creatures having a party in the moving room with windows that let in no light … were the New Year's revelers in the subway car. The dark angry eyes belonged to a young Middle Eastern man with jet black hair, standing on the opposite side of the car holding onto a steel post. He was trying desperately to act inconspicuous, but failing miserably, shaking and sweating profusely. None of the other people on the train paid any attention to the clean-cut young man, except for Darby, who watched him with fierce intensity, noticing a blue backpack resting on his shoulder.

The young man stared at Darby with his dark brown eyes, obviously angered this stranger was taking such an interest in him. Darby kept flashing back to his recurrent nightmare, which he remembered, always ended with a horrifying *blast*.

Darby knew he had to act; he knew something was about to happen and quickly stood up. As he started to make his way through the animated crowd, he abruptly stopped, seeing the young man take hold of his backpack, and grab onto a small cord sticking out from the side.

"PRAISE ALLAHHHH!" the "dead-eyed" man screamed.

With the haunting Mozart requiem still playing in his head, Darby felt the world fall into slow motion, as an overwhelming *pressure* hit his body. A severe blinding light accompanied by the thunderous sound of ripping metal and shattering glass, sent flames shooting down the side of the subway tunnel. The cars were blown off the track and sent flying in every direction, smashing into each other and the tunnel walls.

A soft gust of wind whistled eerily down the gloomy fire-engulfed subway tunnel. Darby knew he was still alive; he could smell smoke and the salty metallic taste of blood saturated his mouth. Then, he felt his heartbeat go from speeding wildly, to slowing, to a *complete stop*.

The bomb blast had been so strong; it literally blew the life right out of him. He felt weightless, as he moved effortlessly up and away from his body.

All was peaceful and calm in the murky haze; there was no pain, no hurt, just a sense of light and tranquility. Time and space did not exist anymore. Darby felt dimly associated with the damaged young man that so resembled him, lying in the wreckage of the tragic scene below. He felt like he was up on a lofty balcony looking down upon his own body, which was lying in a peculiar bent position, among the other bodies in the mangled steel. His spirit was free of physical limitations; having been released from its earthly host, it was able to soar.

A wonderful sense of serenity flowed from the warm breeze blowing gently from above, like thousands of doves all flapping their wings at the same time. It looked as if the ceiling had been lifted off the subway tunnel and streams of beautiful effervescent light were shining down upon the mortals below, like sunlight sparkling through clear water, welcoming them up into paradise.

Darby watched as the translucent souls, lit with soft pastel illuminations, left their damaged shells and flew up, disappearing into the shimmering lights above. Death was not the final ending; it was just the beginning of a new journey. It was an amazing transformation from one plane of existence to another. Darby was also intent on moving closer to the immaculate light. He could hear the loving voices of those that had already passed inviting him to join them.

He saw flashes from his life—when he was a baby being tossed into the air by his father, as he giggled with delight. Then, as a toddler playing with his brother, both naked, chasing squirrels in the backyard of the family home. He saw his mothers young face in the darkness, kissing him goodnight and blowing him a kiss before closing his bedroom door. He saw the neighborhood pub on the night his father proudly bought his two boys their first pint of beer. He could also see the faces of his family, as he proudly received his first award for filmmaking. He saw Angela standing up on the catwalk landing, flashing her bare bottom at him, and felt the warmth of her lips through the glass of his bedroom door, as they kissed on the morning she died.

This was no dream; the realization that he was truly dead was gradually sinking in. And although Darby was overwhelmed with a feeling of peace, he was wholly heartbroken that he never got to say goodbye to those he loved.

Thoughts of his brother filled Darby's mind. All he had to do was think of his brother, and in an instant his spirit was transported to his brother's home in England. He was now a ghost, a spirit, able to soar at will to anywhere he wished. Darby moved about his brother's kitchen with ease, unseen and unheard, feeling weightless, like he was gliding underwater. Andrew was sitting at the kitchen table with his two small boys, who were playfully wetting their fingers and putting them in the other's ear, giving each other "wet willies".

"Boys, settle yourselves please," Andrew's pretty wife, Paula, scolded the boys. She was standing at the stove cooking up some steak and eggs for New Year's Day breakfast. "I won't say it again."

"Yes, mummy," the boys responded, politely.

"Love, turn up the volume, I think something has happened," Andrew stated, and Paula quickly turned up the volume on the small television on the kitchen counter.

"The six coordinated explosions hit the New York City subway system at approximately one am, just as thousands of people were returning from the annual New Years celebration held in Times Square," the BBC reporter stated somberly, as footage from the tragedy was shown. "Information is still coming in regarding this obvious terrorist attack, but it has been reported that a few hundred people may have perished or may still be trapped in the wreckage. Some of the passengers who did survive the blast, emerged from the subway covered with blood and soot, stating they saw body parts scattered around the station. Emergency workers have set up medical command posts in nearby hotels. Rescue workers, police and ordinary citizens, have streamed into blood-splattered streets to help, as buses ferried the wounded to nearby hospitals. It is still not clear how many will be effected by this terrible act of cowardice. On this New Year's Day an eerie quiet has taken hold of the world. Our thoughts and prayers go out to those touched by the tragedy."

"How terrible," Paula gasped. "Andy, is Darby still in the states?"

"Yes, but he's down south," Andrew answered. "Georgia, I believe."

Darby's next thought was his best friend, Nigel. Just the mere thought of Nigel and Darby was immediately with him. He found Nigel alone in his loft, standing in front of his television, crying openly, as he watched the horrible images from the New York subway flash across the screen. Nigel was continually dialing Darby's cell phone, praying he would answer; but he *never* did.

"Please don't be down there, mate," Nigel whispered. "Please, answer."

Nigel knew that Darby had gone into the subway about the same time the bombs went off. He had a terrible feeling that his best friend may be gone. Unable to reach Darby, Nigel hung up the phone and then dialed another number. He took a deep breath and waited as it rang. "Andrew, hello, it's Nigel. Uh, I have something I need to tell you. It's about Darby."

Darby felt overwhelming sorrow, realizing this was how his family and friends would hear of his demise. He wanted to tell them how much he loved them. He wanted to have just a few more moments with them, but it was not to be.

Then Darby thought of his beloved haunted Lily and his mind quickly took over. Memories came flooding into his subconscious and in an instant, he was by her side.

Lily paid no attention to the chaos and sirens blaring up from the street outside the hotel. She was lying on a large bed, desperately clutching onto a pillow crying. Darby wanted so badly to kiss her, to hold her in his arms and tell her everything would be alright. As he slowly moved around the bed, he noticed that she had abruptly stopped crying and lifted her head from the pillow. She stood up and looked around. And although she could not seem to see him, it was obvious she was sensing him.

"Darby?" she whispered, smiling through her tears.

There was a *knock* on the hotel room door.

"Lily, it's Dave! Open up! There's been a massive bombing in the subway!"

Darby watched Lily's face contort, as she slowly began to disintegrate, realizing the only way she could be feeling Darby's presence was if he was … *dead*. As Lily collapsed to the floor in heavy sorrow-filled sobs; Darby felt a fierce sharp pain quickly shoot through his body.

"Lily, are you alright, open the door!" Dave called. "Lily?"

A thunderous pounding echoed harshly in Darby's ears, as another sudden twinge of pain hit him like a Mac truck. He felt like he was being pulled away from Lily, pulled away from the room and falling down into a long dark tunnel. Everything was growing distant; Lily's cries echoed loudly and the air quickly became stale. The pounding in his ears continued getting louder, as confusing voices yelled out over the shrill of screams.

Darby felt a heavy force push down on him, over and over, until once again he felt his heart beating in his chest and his spirit was harshly thrust back into his body.

"Welcome back," said a gruff voice. Darby opened his eyes and faintly saw the fuzzy outlines of two paramedics, leaning over him, performing CPR. He coughed and right away tried to sit up. "Take it easy, take it easy."

Darby awoke in a fiery pit of hell. The horrible sounds of crying and moaning were only overtaken by the sound of heavy generators and machinery. Firefighters were trying to contain the various infernos, burning in different areas all around him. Police and rescue workers, wearing coats with reflective linings, were running through the frenzied darkness. Sparks shot through the air from heavy industrial saws slicing through the twisted metal, urgently trying to cut survivors out of the massive wreckage. Debris was scattered everywhere. The train was a crumpled mass of steel that was simply unrecognizable.

Darby pulled an oxygen mask off his face and inhaled a deep breath of smoky air; then coughed putrid grit and blood from his mouth. He saw the shocked and exhausted faces of even the most seasoned professionals, who were noticeably overwhelmed by the carnage. The paramedics rushed off to help other victims before Darby could thank them.

Although he felt lightheaded, Darby stumbled to his feet, carefully stepping over the bodies of the obvious deceased, joining in with other bewildered strangers, slowly making their way out of the smoke-filled subway tunnel.

With their bloodied bodies and tattered clothes, they looked like they stepped out of a scene from "Night of the Living Dead". Darby took hold of a badly burned woman and helped her down the long dark tunnel away from the fiery nightmare; a journey that seemed to go on forever.

A bright ray of light shined through the darkness at the end of the tunnel. They stepped out onto the street, which was covered with rescue vehicles and crowds of onlookers. Darby passed the injured woman off to some paramedics, who immediately took her into a make-shift triage. He continued walking out into the glorious morning sunlight, taking a deep breath of fresh air.

Numerous TV crews pressed against police tape at the scene, trying to get pictures and video of the victims exiting the subway station. As Darby approached, the sea of onlookers parted way, letting the damaged man walk through. Reporters rushed up, sticking microphones in his face, asking intrusive questions, and snapping photos of him. He just ignored them and continued walking down the snow-covered sidewalk with one thing on his mind—getting to Lily as quickly as possible.

Gardening at Night

The girl stood on the vine infested terrace watching the last remnants of sunlight glimmer on the river, before being replaced by a breathtaking harvest moon. A smile appeared on her face, as she basked in the brilliant orange radiance, proud to have finally completed her long journey. She was not disappointed, for even through the years of damage and neglect, she could see the ornate beauty of the majestic mansion still remained.

The girl was slightly startled, feeling something lightly touch her hand. Looking down, she saw a vibrant indigo dragonfly with large dark eyes and outstretched wings.

"Hey pretty," she whispered to the creature, as tears of happiness welled up in her eyes. For whatever the reason, the dragonfly had a very special meaning to her. In fact, the whole place had special meaning for her. It was a part of who she was, there was no denying it and she didn't want to. Marveling at the beautiful creature sitting calmly on her hand, the girl heard a *loud voice* cut through the calm.

"Come on out! I know you're up there!"

The dragonfly suddenly flew off and she quickly hurried back into the darkened master suite. She saw a beam of sharp light moving up through the darkness, coming up the steps into the tower.

"The fireplace," she whispered, immediately deciding to hide, not knowing who or what was coming. She dashed up the steps into the tower, and quickly crouched down in the mouth of the enormous dragon head fireplace. All she could see was a tall shadow.

"Come on, I know your in here," the deep voice called. "Come on out!"

She did not move, she did not breathe.

"I tell you what ... I'll give you to the count of three, ready? One ..."

Hearing a rustling behind her, the girl sensed she was not alone in the fireplace.

"… Two …"

Slowly, she turned, seeing two bright yellow *eyes* peering at her. She let out a shriek, as a large brown owl started flapping his wings, stirring up a cloud of soot. They both flew out of the fireplace at the same time; the owl continuing out one of the broken terrace windows, the girl stumbling, falling right into the arms of the stranger.

"… Three! Well, I have to say this is a first, no one has ever actually come out when I counted to three."

The girl looked up at the ruggedly handsome face smiling down at her in the darkness. The young man wore a faded denim shirt, under a long black coat, and a dark fisherman's cap, turned backwards over his light brown hair. He had a cool casual air about him, which instantly put her at ease. "Here, take my hand."

"Thank you," the girl spoke in a crisp British accent.

"Well, I think you sufficiently spooked that owl."

"I spooked him?" she giggled, wiping her soot smudged face and shaking out her wavy blonde hair. "I think it's the other way around."

"I don't know, you had him pretty petrified," he teased. "Let me guess, from your muddy boots, I'd say you took the long way … you got in through the tunnel?"

"Right."

"I'm Michael," he said, lighting his face with his flashlight, then shining the light down on the girls face. "And … you are?"

"I'm …"

"Good Lord," Michael whispered, cutting her off, staring at the features of her familiar face with a hint of awe. "It's incredible."

"It is?" she replied, squinting from the bright light in her eyes.

"I'm sorry," he said, lowering the flashlight. "It's just … you look so much like, never mind. So let me guess, the house, you just had to see it for yourself, right?"

"Right again. May I ask … how did you know I was in here?"

"Everyone hides in the fireplace."

"No, I mean, how did you know I was in the house?"

"I saw *her*, I mean you, standing out on the balcony," Michael laughed at the notion. "You, I thought you were … let's just say, I thought I saw a ghost!"

"So, do you remember how the house used to be?"

"Oh sure, I know every room, every tunnel, every secret passage. My friends and I have been chased by practically every cop in Savannah. I actually got to go to one of the infamous Halloween parties when I was seven. It was amazing."

"I'm jealous," the girl admitted.

"You should be, not to boast or anything, but I have never seen anything like it, and most likely, never will. Ever since the first time I saw it, this house has become a little obsession of mine."

"Mine too. Did you ever get to meet *her*?"

"Yes I did, I can totally remember her. Trust me; she wasn't a person who could easily be forgotten. I didn't know anything about her at the time, I just knew her as the nice lady with the really big house. I have to admit, I had a bit of a crush on her, then again, everybody did. I thought she was so pretty and warm; everything you would hope she would be. I was just a little kid, but she never treated me like a little kid, you know? When you talked to her she looked you right in the eye, like you were the only person in the world. I really think she liked kids more than adults, kids and animals. I don't think she ever trusted adults, it was like she was a kid herself, she related better to them."

"She was really into holidays from what I heard."

"My grandmother Nadine used to work for Lily, when I was a kid. My family was always invited to every celebration, every holiday. I used to see the Easter bunny here and go on egg hunts on the grounds. Fourth of July there was fireworks, and Christmas was just amazing, all the lights and food, it was beyond description. I remember one year, Lily gave me a Big Wheel and let me ride it all through the mansion. After she died, the house was shut down. It was like without her, it couldn't survive, she gave it life. When I returned from college, I was really shocked to see what had happened to this amazing place. To this day, I still can't believe it."

"It's far worse than I had anticipated also, except for this room, it's pretty well preserved."

"The only people who even know this room exists are the people like you and me, that make their ... I'm not sure what you call it, pilgrimages? They just want to be close to her, close to the one place she truly loved, it really was her, *sanctuary*. She wasn't bothered here and you had to be trusted to be invited into her world. There is no denying her energy is still here. All the vandalism in the rest of the mansion was caused by punk kids, who don't give a damn. I consider myself to be just another gargoyle watching over the house."

"Is that what you were doing up here?"

"It's Halloween night, the teenagers will come out here like they do every year, just like my friends and I did years ago, and try to scare the crap out of each other. Last year, the kids started a fire in the kitchen. I don't want to see that happen, I don't want to see this place destroyed, it can still be saved. To be honest, I have tried numerous times to buy the property, but it's tied up in legal bullshit. It may sound crazy, but ever since I was a kid I have wanted to buy this house and fix it up. Return it to its former glory, you know, "*resurrect the dead.*"

"I truly envy you. I would have loved to have seen this place in all its glory. I would have loved to have really known her."

"You know, after the film came out, there was so many terrible lies written about Lily and Darby McGregor. But if you really wanted to know who she was, you just had to come to this house. This house was Lily Dufrene. With all its wonderful eccentricities; it was a lot like her, she put so much thought into every little detail. I'm an architect by trade, but I wrote a book about the architecture and history of the house a few years ago."

"Really, what's it called?"

"*Spook Palace*, that's what we kids all called it, the fabulous Spook palace."

The girl rifled through her bag and pulled out a book.

"How bout an autograph then, Michael," she glanced at the cover. "Dunn."

"Incredible, you have my book," he beamed. The girl handed him the book and a pen. He opened it and spoke out loud as he signed it, "To my new friend, what did you say your name was?"

"Lily."

"To my new friend, Lily."

"My real name is Tigerlily, my mother named me after the Indian girl...."

"... in Peter Pan," Michael finished her thought, stopped writing, and looked at the girl with a curious smile.

"That's right. Tigerlily ... Rose ... Dufrene. My parents had a grand sense of humor, I suppose."

"What did you say?"

"My name is Tigerlily Rose Dufrene ... McGregor."

"Dufrene?" Michael mused, looking as though he had just been hit in the head with a sledgehammer. "McGregor?"

"I'm sorry; I didn't mean to catch you off guard. That wasn't my intention."

After a few moments of silence, Michael suddenly snapped out of his daze.

"You know, it's getting late. Come on, I'll show you the way out," Michael said abruptly, as he quickly handed the book back to the girl and started down the stairs leading from the master suite. Halfway down the stairs, he stopped, realizing the girl was not following him. He walked back up the steps; the girl was gone. He noticed a soft glow lighting the darkness from the tower bedroom, getting brighter and brighter.

Michael slowly walked up the steps that lead up into the tower. He saw the back of the girl kneeling on the floor, lighting the many wicks on the numerous candles in the dragon fireplace. "Let's go, come on now, it's time to leave."

"I'm not leaving," she announced without turning around.

"Listen, if you think this place is confusing in the daytime ..."

"I'm not leaving."

"You know you are trespassing."

"This is *my* house ... and I'm never leaving it again," the girl replied, looking up at him with a smile. "And so technically, that means, you are the one trespassing."

"Who are you?" he asked with a hint of anger. "What are you trying to pull?"

After she finished lighting the candles, she turned and looked at him, her face framed in the soft glow of candlelight. She stood, picked up his book, and while walking over to him, leafed through the pages, stopping on a section of pictures, before handing it to him.

"Me," the girl said, taking Michaels flashlight and pointing it on a picture of a family, obviously taken by paparazzi. The picture showed a pretty blonde woman, smiling happily, leaning lovingly back against the chest of a pensive young man with mysterious good looks. They both wore sunglasses, looking more like rock stars, then parents. In the woman's lap sat an adorable three year-old girl, dressed in a miniature, blue satin, Cinderella costume with a matching ribbon in her blonde curls.

Michael obviously knew the people in the photo well.

The caption read—"*In happier days; the proud parents take Tigerlily on her first "trick or treat" outing in London. Lily Dufrene, Darby McGregor, and their precious daughter, Tigerlily.*"

"Are you trying to say ... you're Lily's baby?"

"How about this," she offered. Rifling through her bag, she pulled out her passport, opening it and laying it on top of the book. There was a current picture of the girl standing before him with the name, "*Tigerlily Rose Dufrene McGregor*". Then she took out a drivers' license and a few credit cards, all with the same name. There was no mistaking it; she was the little girl in the picture. "Hang on ... I think I have a library card here somewhere."

Michael put a hand on her arm, stopping her search, looking deeply into her eyes.

"I don't believe it," he said quietly. "You're Tiger?"

"I just go by Lily now. She was my mother, Michael. Lily was my mother and Darby was my father."

"Ah ha-ha, I knew it! I knew it was her, I mean you!" he excitedly grabbed her, lifting her off her feet, then putting her safely back down. "You look so much like her. I thought I was crazy, I thought I was seeing things! But I felt something the second I saw you and heard your accent! I tried to find you when I was writing the book. I always wondered what had happened to you; we all wondered what happened to you. I can't believe you're actually here."

"Trust me, neither can I."

"It was just so terrible, I mean after everything that happened. My God, I can't even imagine going through all you went through at such a young age," Michael stopped speaking, seeing tears well up in Lily's eyes. He quickly took her in his arms and hugged her warmly. "I'm so sorry. I'm so sorry, Lily."

"I try my hardest to not think about it, but being here …"

"I understand."

"No you really don't, no one does," she spoke softly. "Think about it, you knew my mother better than I did. Do you know how strange that is? I feel so alone sometimes."

"You are not alone, just look around … this whole room is in dedication to you. You are a part of your mother, a little piece of her that still exists in this world. All these people wondered what happened to you, all these people … *love you.*"

Lily walked around the room, looking at the dedications of love, noticing the different shades of lipstick that had adoringly kissed the walls. She smiled; she too could feel the love.

"Michael, I have a proposition for you," she said, looking out a broken window, spotting an intricately spun spider web lit with moonlight, containing a little black spider patiently awaiting his next meal.

"What might that be?"

"How would you like to help me … *resurrect the dead?*"

Acknowledgments

To the coolest guy in the universe, my beloved husband, Douglas! Without your encouragement & love, this book would not exist. Thank you for making every-day Halloween! And to my beautiful little pumpkin, my son, Logan, I thank God for you every day. Love to my furry children—Marley, Jetty, Buster, Quiche & Kiki.

Special thanks to artist, Kerry Kate of October Effigies, for her wonderfully eerie cover art, "Skull and Corset Bones". Please visit—www.kerrykate.com.

Writing this book has been a huge labor of love & would not have been possible without the wonderful support of my brilliant Daddio, Lawrence Dunn, for all your help and supporting all my crazy dreams … I love ya! To my favorite ghost-hunting partner, my sister, Deirdre—there is still much we must explore. To my beautiful mother, Patricia & stepfather Bill—your love means the world to me. To the best in-laws a girl could ask for—Gary & Liz Bailey! Thank you both for being so very wonderful! Extra special thanks to Douglas, Claudia & Hillary Eason, my second family, for your never-ending encouragement! Thanks to Mr. Disney and my grandparents for that first "awe-inspiring" trip to the most magical of kingdoms & the greatest spook palace in the world. Thanks to Edward & Eva Stotesbury for building, Whitemarsh Hall.

To all my friends! The members of Troop 854—Jennifer & Adrianna, I love y'all! To the nicest boy in the world, Art Martinez, Erika, Shawna, Lindy (the blessed), Louis (the corpse boy), Rosalie Bender, Lori Way, Robb Baade & Joe Mercado, Donna Moore, Donny Kuhn, Tao Nguyen, Kurt Langenhahn & Dustin Bodony. To "Dark Delicacies" and everyone at 5828 Colfax Ave., N. Hollywood. To my friends at Paramount and ICON. The Grit Restaurant and the inspiring spirits in the fabulous old house on Prince Avenue in Athens, GA!

I'd like to thank the following artists for their inspirations—Dead Can Dance, Trent Reznor, Poe, PJ Harvey, Gorillaz, Blur, Billie Holiday, Tori Amos, Marilyn Manson, Radiohead, Olivia Newton-John, Nirvana, Mozart, The Shins, REM, David Bowie, The Cure, The Stones, Jane's Addiction, U2, Vic Chestnut, Michael Hutchence, INXS, Duran Duran, Rob Zombie, Nick Cave, Madonna, Bauhaus, Led Zeppelin, Midnight Circus, Courtney Love, Iggy Pop, No Doubt, Bush, The Beatles, Korn, Lazy Lane, The Killers, Coldplay, Sublime, Ana Black, Vast, Sinisstar, Garbage, and Midnight Syndicate, truly the soundtrack to this story!

And thank you, dear reader, for taking the time to come into my spooky little world!

Hauntingly Yours,
Sidney Fox

For further information please visit—spookpalace.com

Made in the USA
Lexington, KY
18 December 2009